WAR IN PIECES 2

The Holly Wood Years of Ivan the Terrible

WAR IN PIECES 2

The Holly Wood Years of Ivan the Terrible

Sean Dennis Cashman

First published in the United Kingdom in 2017
by Sixth Avenue Books

ISBN 978-0-9571281-2-5

Produced by
The Choir Press, Gloucester

For Alison Baerman
and to the memory of Basha Baerman,
dear friends whose unstinting support over many
years enabled me to write this and other books.

Contents

Early 1990s

THE TSAR'S BRIDE

Groznyy had got away with murder.

Not just any murder but the murder of his legitimate son, Modest, whom, supposedly, he loved to death. But for how long could he escape justice? He was not afraid that his second murder of a family member would come to light. No one had realized that that had also been murder—as yet.

President Cesare Groznyy of Babel City University in New England had already survived much. He had masterminded the scheme whereby struggling BCU had incorporated the poor Norse Hoven University into a larger university. Yet there had been a serious upset in his campaign to become president when the college movers and shakers had found themselves being blackmailed over his secret love child.

But it was going to be hard to savor his triumph in surmounting all problems and becoming president of the new conjoined university, for, when he got there, the cupboard was bare. He went into the office of the departed president of Norse Hoven University. He sat down behind the imposing desk and pulled open the top drawer. In it he found a scrawled note from retired NHU president Casper Corelli: "Dear Nemo, there's no money. It's all gone: spent."

It seemed Cesare had risen for no reason. At the insistence of his mentor, he had changed his name from Nemo to Cesare Groznyy, gone through hell and high water in political troubles as provost of BCU, and now it had all been for nothing.

By his side at NHU his faithful secretary, Bee Flute, read his mind. She explained that many and varied were the stories told of the last days of the previous president of NHU

1

and of his energetic sex life, which was why his residence was known as Corelli's bordelli. Rather than tell Groznyy everything by herself, Bee called in Lorraine Boe, head of human resources at BCU, who brought with her a young accountant, Parthy Burnable, to tell Groznyy how theft had been rife at NHU.

Parthy, an ambitious twenty-five-year-old Italian American from Rhode Island, was adept at all sorts of accounting, and fearless even before someone who made others tremble. Tossing aside her cascading hair, she said, "What Bee and Lo are saying is true. Sub-treasurers took away cash in twenty, fifty, even hundred-dollar bills, in shopping bags."

The ruined economy at NHU was now Groznyy's most pressing problem. He joked to intimates that he was trying to find where his predecessor had hidden the money. Was it under the mattress? It certainly was not in the bank. NHU's debts were now the responsibility of the larger BCU, itself a faltering institution.

Behind the scenes, Groznyy cursed not only Casper Corelli for hiding the scale of NHU's debts but also his old mentor, Franklin Miller, the last president of BCU, for not standing up for him when he was in dire straits as provost. And Miller had probably misapplied BCU funds to entertain his political friends to advance his own preferred career as a US ambassador. US ambassador? Yes, there was the onion because BCU more than ever needed the kudos of having fielded Miller as the new ambassador to some God-forsaken part of East Asia. But what on earth was Groznyy to do so that little BCU and tiny NHU could survive? How could he pay his employees at the end of the month?

Looking over Parthy Burnable, Groznyy wondered if this wan, small-town girl with the mighty ideas was the answer to his problems.

"This is where Parthy comes in," said Lorraine. "She's

crunched the numbers. There's light at the end of the tunnel. Tell him, Parthy."

"There's $4.5 million in uncollected tuition fees that we can go after. As things stand, students in arrears of fees at NHU are allowed to go on taking new classes. The professors sometimes teach students who aren't even registered and some who haven't paid."

"So everything's in disarray?"

"Yes, but we have untapped assets. We have cash in non-interest-bearing accounts. They could be moved into accounts that give interest."

Groznyy was almost struck dumb by the accounting skill of this waif beauty with such steely grasp of financial essentials. He would move her from accounting at NHU to treasurer at BCU, promoting her to keep himself afloat. Thus, with new treasurer Parthy in tow, Groznyy tried to show local banks across Norse Hoven County that the two of them represented business as usual for BCU and NHU—prudent investment for local banks.

By taking the better ledgers for those departments where BCU and NHU were financially viable and transferring these funds to insolvent areas, and then by presenting select blocs of departments as economically viable, president and treasurer secured a bridge loan from one bank for six months. Then they presented the same figures for another bloc of university departments before another local bank. Hence Cesare bought NHU twelve months' reprieve. He got some release from financial pressure while concealing the two universities' dire straits from the very employees who needed his services but disparaged him.

Where charm and bluster counted, Groznyy was master. But inwardly Groznyy was shaking for what might lie in store should the police resolve the mystery of his son Modest's death.

At nights Groznyy had a recurrent nightmare. As a

troubled child back in his family dacha in Russia, he kicked the secret family Bible in a temper tantrum. Out of the Book of Numbers sprang a cascade of figures—whole, prime, and fractions. A sheepdog that looked like his consigliere, Larry Dawdler, appeared to herd numbers up like sheep through a farmyard gate. To test Cesare's, the former Nemo's, ability to save BCU and add up NHU's non-existent funds correctly, Parthy Burnable in all her steely beauty demanded particular answers from him. These were not ordinary exercises about apples and oranges but statistical problems about mentally ill, retarded, and physically disabled people.

The numbers appeared in the dream looking like the professors Groznyy despised. He detested Lucy Kaye, the pompous new provost known as the Commodore, and Ace Ferrari, the acerbic dean of psychology. Most particularly, Groznyy loathed historian Mordred Stickleman, who had been his rival when they were students and was now his ardent political foe since he had become a president.

In this horrible dream the professors' yelling was like an unending scream.

The nightmare always came to the same end—with Groznyy collapsing on the floor, listless with exhaustion. Then he would awake expecting to see Modest, the son he had killed, bloodied and accusing.

Funds were not Groznyy's only problem. There was the quandary posed by Caesar's new wife.

For, after a decent interval following the expected death of his second wife, Anna Stasinova Groznyy, in her losing battle with recurrent pneumonia worsened by her uncontrollable grief over their son's death, Groznyy had taken a new trophy wife. That was not, in itself, a surprise. It was Groznyy's duty. It was in the tradition of New England worthies from Colonial days onwards. It was his choice of wife that caused comment: a white devil in a little black dress.

There they were: tsar and star. University gossips heard

how Cesare Groznyy had lusted after singer Holly Wood from the start—supposedly after a casual meeting in the Golden Cockerel, the restaurant in Midtown Manhattan he used as a hidey-hole for secret deals. Groznyy had wooed Holly with surprising intensity. Gossips said she thought he was passion personified.

"Yes, I'm near sixty, and you are in the fresh flush of youth, still blossoming. But you can be June to my December. My Scheherazade of song."

People assumed Holly Wood accepted him because he represented security and social betterment. After all, her artistic career was as a show-tune singer in shabby Manhattan taverns. Her day job had been as a secretary in Dr. Chicago's eye clinic in the hospital. But no one really knew.

When Groznyy took Holly on the little tour of the campus that she had taken not so many months before with Modest, his son whom she had been dating, she understood that he wanted to impress her with his power as the new president. First came the source of that power: the Treasurer's Office with its fake gold seal on the door and ochre carpet inside, where she met the young treasurer. The two women looked at one another with polite indifference. Next came the benefits of that power. There were the blue-green presidential gardens with lavender and hibiscus and a vista of the better buildings of Babel City University, Groznyy's domain in its splendor—all immaculately manicured.

At BCU and NHU Holly had the same sense of blood on everything that Groznyy touched as had Anna, his late wife. But, then, Holly was already convinced the blood of Modest, her late fiancé, was on Groznyy's hands.

Holly wondered if any of this—Groznyy's proposal and her marriage to him—was the revenge of Princess Glinskaya. Princess Nadezhda Arachnova Glinskaya was Groznyy's supposed great-aunt, living in hiding in the Golden

Cockerel, the restaurant in Midtown Manhattan. Was the princess so manipulative that she would encourage Holly to put her head into the noose of this sterile marriage on the pretense of revenge but in reality to torture her for her affair with Modest?

As Holly watched Groznyy play his night-time game of chess at a table with a swivel top, she wondered if Anna, his second wife, had hated this ritual as much as she did— Groznyy's sucking of the rounded mitres of the bishops like nipples on the breasts of his supposed conquests—and that must have been a long time ago.

Holly was not going to get anywhere in the princess's scheme to expose Groznyy as the real murderer of his son. She knew that. She felt crushed by defeat, ashamed that she could not help Modest. Yet her inner depression made her singing more exalted. Her voice expressed her loneliness and the pain of love. As she sang beautiful music, the combination of the songs and her interpretative powers held her listeners spellbound. Word of mouth about Holly was such that her every gig in New York and New England became an event for music lovers.

News of the Groznyy wedding flew to the Golden Cockerel. This was the pretentious restaurant in midtown Manhattan run by portly restaurateur Benny Vincenzo. He had taken over the restaurant after the mysterious disappearance of its elderly Russian owner. In the dining room upstairs from the main salon, Hermione Eterna, Benny's assistant, was fit to be tied when she heard about Groznyy's new marriage.

"She has betrayed us! This damned bitch. She has betrayed Modest! This is worse than just sleeping with the enemy."

"Calm yourself," said Benny. "It's part of the princess's plan. Our plan to bring Modest's murderer to justice."

"How could it be part of the plan? Holly's role was to get a gig at BCU, to ask questions—not to go over to the other side."

Far from having drowned in the East River as Groznyy had speciously confirmed, the princess was still alive and living secretly in the next building. She sidled into Benny and Hermione's conversation and took over. "Hermione, consider that tired old cliché of politics: 'keep your friends close but your enemies closer.'"

"But don't marry them so you can't testify against them."

"Hermione, listen to reason—that other cliché—that revenge is a dish best served cold."

Hermione's temper had worn her out. She let the princess continue.

"Yes, Plan A was for Miss Holly Wood to ingratiate herself at BCU and by her presence there be a latent threat to Groznyy—to get him to expose himself, so to speak. That was Plan A. Agreed?"

Hermione nodded.

"But there was also Plan B, already in place."

"Plan B?"

"Yes. You must know Shakespeare's *Macbeth*. What happens?"

Hermione was in no mood for mind games. "Really, these two—they're each as bad as one another," she thought about Benny and the princess. But what she said was, "Macbeth is a victorious general. He's stirred by the prophecy of three witches that he will become king of Scotland. His wife plays on her intimate knowledge of his strengths and weaknesses to make sure Macbeth kills the rightful king and seizes the throne—with disastrous consequences for the kingdom and for the Macbeths themselves as they discover one murder leads to others."

"That sums it up," said Benny. "Supposedly, *Macbeth* is an unlucky play—all sorts of things can go wrong in production. Many actors fail."

"And your point is?"

"Well, a famous actress once said, 'You have to be married to play the Macbeths,'" purred the princess. "So, now Holly is married to Groznyy, not only will she get to know him psychologically inside out—"

"But she will also come to hate him even more than she does now," said Hermione, continuing the princess's thought.

"It would be impossible not to loathe him if you had to live with him twenty-four-seven," said the princess. "And she will learn his every trick."

"Plan B is actually better than Plan A—it makes it more likely that the truth behind Modest's murder will come out," said Benny.

"Think about Miss Holly Wood—marrying the man who killed her boyfriend. Think of the living hell she has put herself in to get at the truth."

Hermione was silenced—less by Plan B, but more by the princess's brazen manipulation of Holly, putting her in danger without scruple or remorse. Hermione sensed that underneath the princess's passionate account of what Holly was to do lay some never-to-be-broken link between Groznyy and herself.

Benny and Princess Glinskaya had told Holly she must look step by step for clues about Modest's death by such simple means as asking to see everything—all the documents relating to Groznyy's academic tasks. Each time she was to give him her overwhelming love as the reason. Yet Holly knew Groznyy would resist her knowing his darkest secret—that that dark door would remain shut.

To launch a fund-raising campaign for the renovation of the university theater which an anonymous donor had started with a generous gift, Holly organized a jazz concert followed by a champagne supper. Now a seasoned pro, for her set she followed a sure-fire showbiz formula of alternating fast and slow numbers. Holly chose three songs from *Showboat*: "Can't Help Lovin' Dat Man," "Life Upon the Wicked Stage," and "Bill."

The rapt audience of Babel City University focused on her rose-reddened lips. They smiled as she finished a lovely turn of phrase. They detected that, somehow, singing liberated Holly Wood. Then she sang a solo version of Stephen Sondheim's duet to unhappy marriages: "Every Day a Little Death."

Her encore took the audience by surprise. Instead of a popular standard, it was a reworking of an aria from Mozart's *Cosi fan tutte*.

"Despina, the maid, tells her mistresses, two lovelorn sisters whose fiancés are away, that there is no harm in a little flirtation: '*Una donna a quindici anni*.' Don't you agree, ladies?" Holly asked. "A girl who knows the arts of attracting men can have them at her mercy."

Holly had the audience eating out of her hands.

Whereas Groznyy was profligate in acquiring art masterpieces and in wining and dining at expensive restaurants, he was a Scrooge when it came to housekeeping. Holly was expected to run the house, keep the fridge fully stocked, prepare gourmet dinners at a moment's notice for crude professors, dress to look like a million bucks, and employ help for $400 a month.

The only additional expense Groznyy allowed her was beautification of the garden. He wanted a protective hedge around the president's new house overlooking the Sound that was still being built. He expected Holly to create something special both as a project to satisfy her artistically and to distract her from her independent singing career. Here, no expense was to be spared. She could even have a gazebo aside a wasted pear tree.

In his flights of silly rhetoric, Cesare murmured with that indeterminate European accent Holly found increasingly irritating, "This beautiful garden, surrounded by high hedges, will be our own private Garden of Eden. And in the gazebo we can do things we cannot do in bed."

This was a surprise to Holly, who had never had any sexual experience with Cesare Groznyy since their marriage beyond a peck on the cheek. For, although Groznyy might have fancied himself a virile man about town with a dangerous rattle, in their private life it was she who would stoop to conquer. Holly quickly learned she could get no sexual pleasure from Groznyy, that he was now a barren rock. She tried all her alluring wiles to arouse him but he could not manage even so much as a half-erection. In herself, she was relieved, but she had learnt from her friend Carmine that, if only for a divorce settlement later, she had to ensure that they consummated the marriage at least once.

"Why are you so cold? Hold me in your arms. Tighter. Tighter still."

She tried caresses, moving around the house semi-naked under her bathrobe in an attempt to titillate him. She tried fellatio when he was dozing. She pondered his innermost sexual preferences. Then she understood that Groznyy was interested only in wielding political power and spending other people's money.

So she decided she would turn the sexual desert of her marriage to her advantage by becoming a sexual predator. It was to be a twist of her plan with her offstage allies. Her Garden of Eden would bring down upon this tawdry king the marital ridicule he deserved.

His repeated nightmare about financial problems made Groznyy consider the professors of Babel City and Norse Hoven Universities anew. The professors who hated him but whose jobs he was saving now seemed no better than the worn-out anarchists and revolutionaries of a novel he had

10

read in college: Joseph Conrad's *The Secret Agent*. To Groznyy the malcontent professors were like the extinct volcanoes of armchair communism in Conrad's story. They clung to trifles of bourgeois comfort. They mouthed threadbare ideologies about socialist utopias but did nothing. Groznyy was determined to bring that to an end.

"These ingrate professors, whose bacon I have saved, would complain at the Feeding of the Five Thousand that Jesus had not brought any tartar sauce for the fish or butter for the bread."

Groznyy's way of running things as president was just as it had been when he was provost, the highest academic officer—via a kitchen cabinet, described maliciously by his enemies as the Chosen Council. This was no fashion-plate assembly of beautiful people. Principal was the mighty new treasurer, Parthy Burnable. In second place was Provost Lucy Kaye, known as the Commodore.

As to other appointments in the Chosen Council, Groznyy chose from his old pals. First was Larry Dawdler, the man who had finessed his campaign for the presidency and who had managed to get him over the scandal of his old affair and love child with one Esther Vashti. Groznyy had already made Dawdler the university's attorney general. He expected Dawdler to conduct a concerto in which he, Groznyy, was the star soloist.

Cesare gave new toady Brad Gable, Lorraine Boe's ex-husband, the exacting post of director of operations in the president's office. Promoted by Lorraine, hard worker Brad Gable had risen from being a humble security guard. Brad's main interest was in promoting singer Holly Wood.

To Carpenter Cain, whom Groznyy had met on vacation in the Adirondacks, he gave the pivotal post of head of the Alumni Bureau. This job had the power to collect and disburse dollars from former students.

The cover story of the way Groznyy and Cain had met was

not edifying, but it was credible to foes of the president. In fact, Groznyy was being manipulated twice over, first by his own ego that had led him to take on a casual acquaintance and then by that acquaintance whose meeting with the president had not been by chance.

The seedy cover story of Cain's appointment unintentionally covered Cain's involvement with the half-secret Oryx Party run by Ace Ferrari, the dean of psychology.

What Groznyy still did not know was that among some professors' extracurricular interests was this secret Oryx Party. It was part benevolent club for Afghan and other Arabs within and outside the United States and part cheerleader for Hamas, the Palestinian organization determined to bring down Israel. To this end the Oryx Party at BCU provided cover for young Arab foot soldiers with multiple aliases. Some worked or studied in Babel City and Norse Hoven Universities. Their visas came in part because Ace Ferrari and his ally, Don Fatale, chair of chemistry at NHU, presented them as their nephews.

Cain enjoyed playing a double game in this scenario.

Born Achmed Mechtal to Syrian and Iraqi parents, he was a youngish forty-year-old who had lost his hair prematurely. It was good fortune for him to look older than his years. It helped him get trusted in WASP and Jewish American society on the supposition that middle age was a guarantee of respectability. Cain was full of inner fire against Israel yet old enough to know he would be more successful blending in than venting vocal hysteria over Israel, Palestine, and the West.

In his official role at BCU, Cain had a brisk wise-cracking manner that made him well liked at parties. He also had a kind of Yankee can-do bent for money-spinning enterprises—anything to make a fast buck. Indeed, he had served as dean of business at more than one low-profile college. His light fingers on behalf of Afghan Arab funds had often been found out, but he was always a step ahead of his investigators and moved on before getting caught.

Impressed by the immaculately kept grounds, Holly was surprised when she discovered that the ground staff numbered only four men, including the manager, Johnnie Jaundice, Lorraine Boe's brother. Johnnie Jaundice was a money-grubbing, self-made contractor, notable for his sleazy wheeling and dealing. Superficially a bluff fellow, Johnnie had a short fuse. He was super-good at cap-doffing to the governor. He could tolerate the endless presidential vocal foreplay in the Monday morning cabinet sessions when he joined the Chosen Council with their minimum forty-five-minute opening speech by the president. Meeting the president regularly gave him access to decision-making. Even when Groznyy was at his most boring, it was preferable to Bikers Island, the offshore prison where Johnnie had recently been an involuntary guest.

Politically attuned professors understood that the Chosen Council would act as a cabal of heavies who would exert pressure through threats of negative career consequences to those who disagreed with "the party line of Dr. G.," the diminutive term his office staff used and his enemies parodied.

Groznyy's one undisputed professional ability was to create an aura around himself: personality as power.

The more they went around newly acquired NHU with Provost Lucy Kaye, the more depressed became Cesare, Holly, and Larry Dawdler.

They did not see Don Fatale, chair of chemistry at NHU, appraising them: the svelte blonde jazz artist now looking as stylish as any star in the golden age of movies; the dumpy woman known as the Commodore, hovering like a myna bird; the pretentious president with a roving eye and trousers flapping at half-mast; the fleshy lawyer with broad enough shoulders to make middle-aged spread look good. Don Fatale said nothing. The visitors said plenty.

"These two administration buildings are by Richard Morris Hunt," said a proud Lucy, the new provost who had led the campaign to make Groznyy president.

"Dear lady, they certainly have grace and favor—at least on the outside with their Colonial style."

But when they went inside, it was a raggle-taggle of dirty corridors.

"It's as horrible as a drunk's hairstyle on a Saturday night," said Larry.

"Yes," said Holly, "but the offices could be redeemed to make a better feature of their windows—really elegant."

The Richard Morris Hunt building ran from east to west. The ground floor had its own West Wing, wherein lay the offices of president and treasurer. By sealing the interior entrance passage with an elaborate glass-screen security door and laying a deep-pile carpet along its length, Groznyy created a presidential corridor of implied status.

But there tradition ceased. For, in his office, the president's table was hard glass, a desk without drawers because, as he told Steve Sharp, rising reporter for the local *Norse Hoven Courier* newspaper, "I always process correspondence pronto—no time wasting—no delay—no hiding things in drawers. Drawers are for procrastinators. I speak. I act. I move."

Later Groznyy copied his adaptations to the NHU presidential corridor and office for the comparable corridor and office at BCU.

Groznyy wanted to make his presidential inauguration the most glorious day of his life. Inauguration it may have been to his chattels, his serfs in all but name. But to him it was a coronation, although he dared not use that word.

Among power details important to Groznyy for his "coronation" was the creation of a red staircase as there had been in the Kremlin in Moscow for hundreds of years. It had been used for ceremonial occasions until it was demolished to facilitate the creation of a Grand Palace for Nicholas I in the 1840s. Since then the staircase had been recreated but demolished again in Stalin's time as an embarrassing relic of the tsarist past. Groznyy guessed that in changing times, Russia would rebuild the Red Staircase.

Groznyy wanted one for himself at little BCU. He cajoled Parthy Burnable for funds to create his own version. There was no space for an interior red staircase at BCU. Groznyy had to be content with an outside side staircase from a second-story balcony window at NHU whence it descended like a common fire escape.

As with the crowning of the tsars in the old Russia, it was not the actual ceremony that mattered most but the parade to show the tsar to the people and for the tsar to show off. Groznyy wanted his coronation to be an epiphany. He would show them who was boss at BCU. But some details were so minute that the serfs would not notice—just like a coronation.

Most significant to Groznyy was an addition to his university robes, a vest over his white shirt and under his president's gown. It had a pattern in gold thread with rose symbols copied from a nineteenth-century portrait of his model, Ivan the Terrible, in the Tretyakov Gallery in Moscow.

As he passed by the various university buildings—the absurd library looking like a church organ standing on one leg, the paltry galumphing science building—he imagined them as the imposing cathedrals of the Kremlin and the bell tower of Ivan the Great.

Then Groznyy had his chauffeuse drive him to Norse Hoven University where he repeated the parade. There he minced down the new red staircase. Another difference was that at NHU he had processional music blaring from the loudspeaker of a hired ice-cream truck. There was a tocsin motif with three peals and a brass fanfare.

In his early months as president, students and alumni and some professors, albeit grudgingly, found themselves charmed by Groznyy's magnetic persona and his statements delivered as if by a Delphi oracle—especially after a lavish buffet supper. In his initial meeting before everyone, he forecast change—the "unlimited academic possibilities" of the newly conjoined universities and the need for "adventure and risk-oriented enterprise." He told rising journalist Steve Sharp that he would make the combined schools a gathering place for the world's leading intellectuals.

Serious trouble began when, having bought time with his bank deals and zero-based budget, Groznyy settled down to true academic work. Student enrolment at BCU–NHU was in decline—by 34 percent in his first three years. The Chosen Council said the problem was beyond Groznyy's control as the number of high school graduates in their area had begun to shrink in the baby bust of the 1980s.

Groznyy had a plan that had wowed the trustees: change the focus of BCU and NHU's undergraduate programs from applied subjects such as business, nursing, and social work to concentrate on arts and sciences courses, what some called "great books" classes and others derided as "from Plato to NATO."

But Groznyy and the trustees were dealing with a culture and academic system already in place and with entrenched interests hostile to reform. Professors recognized that Groznyy's strategy of trying to increase enrolment and raise academic standards at the same time was most risky.

Mordred Stickleman told his history colleagues at a department meeting, "When a college sets out to increase enrolment, the academic level of students usually declines."

"That's true," said the chair of history. "And sudden fundamental changes in an educational institution risk alienating students already here. We used to be successful in attracting students with our professional programs in nursing, social work, and business."

"This isn't a recognized liberal-arts college like Amherst or Swarthmore," continued Stickleman. "If you're going to become like them, you must have a massive infusion of funds from outside sources. Besides, we are in the same city as Milhous College, a leading Ivy League school. If students want arts and sciences, that's where they will go—not to BCU."

Stickleman made sure that Steve Sharp received a copy of the minutes of that meeting. And Sharp quoted him as an anonymous insider when he produced his next press article, "Disease in Academia."

Ever the man to woo new trustees with big ideas to stir women's blood, at a Saturday night dinner at the Golden Cockerel restaurant in Manhattan Groznyy announced with a flourish to Veronica Veneer, the ambitious new trustee whom he planned to make chair of the board, "I plan to bring to BCU and NHU a wide variety of experts to teach our administrative staff new skills, notably IT skills that are essential for success in the modern world. Together, you and I, dear lady, must also attract distinguished foreign academics to teach as guests and bring us academic diversity and refreshment."

Then he drew Mrs. Veneer ever nearer to his face and even nearer to his terrible breath in order to entice her into calumny of people absent. As she now learnt, worst was Groznyy's hatred of Jews, immigrants, and refugees. Well into his cups that Saturday night he spluttered, "Don't you agree that the worst thing about these two damn universities is that there are too many lick-spittle Jews everywhere—in the lawns, in the lecture halls, skulking in labs and lavatories alike?"

Veronica Veneer, self-made entrepreneur of an African-American construction company, Blackthorn Buildings, disliked competition with companies from a different ethnic group. But she was taken aback by Groznyy's remark nevertheless. If Groznyy was this blunt in his bigotry against Jews, what did he really think of her?

Groznyy continued regardless. "These Jews d'esprits, they are like the rotting carcasses of the unburied dead in a horror movie. They pollute the air with their foul stench. I wish I could repay them with unclean meat—not Jurassic Park but Jew-rassic Pork."

In the background, restaurateur Benny Vincenzo and his assistant, Hermione, did not need to exchange glances. But Groznyy's tirade was a wake-up call to Veronica Veneer. She would have to rethink her priorities if Blackthorn Buildings was ever going to profit at BCU. If Groznyy was going to use her and disparage her, she could do the same to him.

After he had sobered up on Sunday morning, Groznyy realized he had made a terrible mistake. To deride Jews was far worse than simply misspeaking in an alcohol-fueled rant. It laid bare Groznyy's deep-rooted anti-Semitism. If someone complained and exposed him, his career really would be over. And his jibe cut at the heart of the integrated mission of his two colleges. To have spoken as he had to an African American princess—a symbol of how people from minorities could participate in the American Dream—was crass.

As Holly made filter coffee in the kitchen that morning, she heard Groznyy whining over his revelatory mistake:

"There was a sound moral purpose behind NHU when it was still Lazarus College with Gentiles and Jews together—merging the honorable Hebraic tradition in which culture is a universal birthright and the honorable American aim of nurturing an educated democracy. We support this at BCU.

18

Although what I said is true, my enemies will make hay. But I will never apologize."

Holly still said nothing.

Groznyy remembered that Sunday very well. First, he had the earliest of what proved to be a series of sporadic headaches—stabbing pains across his temples. They would be sharp. Then they would disappear.

After his headache passed that Sunday afternoon, Groznyy once more displayed his genius for bending a random event to his advantage.

"Mr. President, I'll tell you."

Gus Revisor was an expatriate Czech opportunist who had turned up on Cesare Groznyy's doorstop. Groznyy was pacing around endlessly. His new wife was out.

"Your friend, Franklin Miller—I met him at the Yale Club on Vanderbilt Avenue, the night before he flew out as ambassador. He said you were looking for a personal assistant. I have degrees from Harvard in Comparative Literature and Creative Writing."

That was what Augustus Revisor said at the front door.

Cesare Groznyy stared at the long face with short-cropped, receding curly hair. He thought, "He looks like Prokofiev before Stalin. Which of us is Peter and which is the wolf?"

Having heard so much of the power-dressed president of BCU, Augustus Revisor had not expected to see him at play. For leisure what figure-hugging, black-leather blouson jacket and trousers Cesare Groznyy sported! Everything emphasized that this mutton-dressed-as-lamb edifice was crumbling within. Underneath the skin, Revisor thought Groznyy looked as if he were being eaten alive by maggots— his psychological fears. It was very far from the hipster pretensions Groznyy intended.

What Gus Revisor did not say was that he had set off from Gloversville in upstate New York with a naïve belief that, once in Manhattan, he could launch himself on a brilliant career; that American society would immediately recognize him as a gifted person whose destiny was to perform a great service for the city. But no one in the Big Apple wanted him.

What had saved Gus Revisor from being engulfed by the vast bureaucracies of Corporate America as he toiled away in a few dead-end jobs in department stores was his skill as a flaneur. He had recognized Franklin Miller's face from newspaper photos when, by chance, he had seen him in the bar of the hotel opposite Penn Station. He had quickly ingratiated himself by helping the old guy with his luggage. Then he had traveled with him to Vanderbilt Avenue and the Yale Club near Grand Central Station.

The advice he had gleaned was to go north to New England.

Now seated over a low polished glass coffee table in the mansion of the president of Babel City University, it seemed that Augustus Revisor had as dramatic a childhood story to tell as had the former Nemo Groznyy.

"Where do you come from?" Groznyy asked.

"Czechoslovakia. I was born in World War II. When I was a baby, only one week old, I was smuggled out of the Nazi show concentration camp, Terezin—Theresienstadt."

Deeply anti-Semitic though he was, Groznyy always responded to a buccaneering story. Anything that smacked of intrigue sent his nostrils aquiver as if he had just sniffed poppers.

"My family has some Jewish blood," said Augustus Revisor.

With that evasion, Groznyy sensed a poseur and someone whom he could present as his front of Jewish credibility.

"My father was a violinist. My mother was a pianist. They were safe from death—even in the extermination camps—for as long as they could play for time and the Allies were still only on the perimeter of the Nazi Empire.

"After I was born, my parents bribed one of the guards by giving him my father's precious Bergonzi violin. Through this man, my parents made underground arrangements with the partisans. I was to be left not far from the camp in a breadbasket. My parents gave me to the guard and he left me as arranged. Partisans found me and smuggled me to safety. Later, they got me doctored papers so that, after the war, they could take me to the American zone in Austria."

Groznyy was mesmerized. His old friend, Franklin Miller, was right indeed. He was looking for a personal assistant who could be his eyes and ears and could penetrate the damnable professors of Babel City University and get them to bow before him. Here was the answer to his prayers, an unimpeachable refugee story from that most precious commodity, a Jew who was not a Jew. He may have been Jewish by birth, maybe by religion, but Augustus Revisor was a partisan in spirit, a resistance fighter by choice, and a survivor by temperament. And he had survived the Holocaust!

Even his name was perfect: Revisor, Russian for inspector, and the original Russian title for Gogol's satirical comedy known in English as *The Government Inspector*. Before any scurrilous story about his unfortunate anti-Semitic remark could circulate, Groznyy would have Gus in place as a symbol of his solidarity with the Jewish people.

Moreover, Gus Revisor had the nerve to tell Cesare Groznyy upfront about his nickname—something that might otherwise have been a drawback.

"Dr. G.—"

"Cesare, please."

"Cesare, my first name, Augustus, is usually shortened to Gus. Over the years it got adapted by playful friends into Bogus."

Groznyy saw this as a way of making Bogus Revisor approachable to people at work, a trivial way of giving him a human face. Using it would be a way of lightening the harsh connotations of Revisor, Regulator, Inspector, or whatever. Bogus Revisor would be his creation, his flea, like the bug in Modest Mussorgsky's song that rises as the king's favorite and soon has the whole court scratching. Cesare loved the adept flattery of this super flea.

"Your flea, my flea, my grandmother's flea," he said to himself.

Together, they would bask in a show of mutual adoration—the prince and the parasite. Bogus Revisor would work as Cesare's personal assistant, be his eyes and ears around the chattering classes of the stale professors and sometimes act as his intermediary. Moreover, Bogus Revisor would show his credentials as a supporter of Jewish interests.

"He's a prince. He's a prince," Cesare told Holly when she came back. Before she even met him, Holly realized that this Bogus Revisor was already responding to Cesare's insatiable need for adulation.

"If only you knew," she thought, as Gus turned his attention onto her, "why I am here and what I am going to do. It's not that behind every great man there is a greater woman, as Dr. Chicago thinks. It's what the princess says—behind every bad man there is an even worse woman."

Now Bogus was in her presence, having seen and heard her first when he had sat behind Modest and his girlfriend at the jazz club in Greenwich Village. Since then he had tortured himself about the president's umpteenth wife, twisting the screw of his addiction into an ecstatic obsession.

Holly herself looked lovingly on the pleasure that Bogus Revisor could give her. She saw that he was a driven hunk eager for a leg up the social ladder.

Groznyy was thinking ahead. He decided he would test Bogus by getting him to organize his next formal meeting with the deans.

When Bogus Revisor started to meet the deans and the professors of Babel City University and its sister colleges in the science consortium that linked universities and colleges in Norse Hoven County, he soon made a literary comparison. From Bogus's perspective, faculty meetings were like a free activities class for kindergarten kids and the president and provost were the kindergarten cops. The club feeling and its hostility to improvement were among the enduring facts of BCU, especially when faced with outside winds of change that President Groznyy represented—supposedly.

To Groznyy, BCU was an extension of himself and a means of making money. The professors were squabbling anarchists to be detonated into oblivion. But to Holly Wood Groznyy, who was not unaware of its limited resources and the all-too-human failings of its professors, BCU represented a gateway to learning. For it had a library, its professors held the keys to ideas as well as facts. Inside books, professors, and students lay ideas and knowledge.

For Holly, there was also a distinctly erotic undercurrent to life at Babel City University. She soon grasped how university professors with time on their hands were always up for illegitimate sex. She knew from Groznyy's stories that in novels and plays men who wooed women inappropriately had to avoid discovery by husbands or families. Such opportunistic swains might be forced to leap out of high windows, or bury themselves in piles of manure, or do something equally comic and repulsive.

Treasurer Parthy Burnable's head was brimming with ideas as to how to maximize the by-now liquid cash flow of the combined universities. Single-minded financial executive or not, she knew a handsome man when she saw one. But she appreciated sub treasurer Darko Delizio more for his wizardry in moving funds undetected, in amassing considerable sums from leftover trifles, and for the imaginative use to which he could put everything.

When she spoke with Groznyy ahead of Monday's meeting of the Chosen Council, she took Darko along so that Groznyy could see that she could build a formidable financial team and not just work alone.

She came straight to the point.

"We can do better with our investment portfolios if we target specific profitable areas."

"Such as?"

"There's the growing IT revolution. Companies always need more and more investment. If you invest in IT stocks, your yield will be high."

"Where will this lead us?"

"Darko has a good business plan."

Groznyy saw in Darko a personable Iranian or Iraqi or maybe Serb.

Darko said, "If we utilize our tiny endowment, invest the combined reserves of BCU and NHU, and manage our running costs prudently, I predict that, given the continued interest in communication technology, you can expect more than a tenfold yield over the next years."

"That would bring us?"

Parthy answered, "We could go from $4 million at present—that's counting everything—to $40 million in five years, more later. But it needs revenue management."

Darko nodded. Groznyy saw all three of them were of a mind.

It was to be said of Treasurer Parthy Burnable later that three university presidents had served under her. Groznyy did not realize it, but he was only the first. He did as she and Darko suggested.

Under Parthy—even better than she predicted—the two universities' assets grew to $115 million in five years. Under Darko, prudent management of the universities' combined revenue increased it from $15 million to $69 million.

With the extra funds, Groznyy oversaw first the introduction and then the wider use of computers across the campuses. He and Parthy also made physical improvements by way of better, modernized labs and dormitories. And he planned a hospital extension to be named after him.

As to control of the trustees, by his second year, Groznyy had already eased sharp-eyed and sharper-tongued trustee chairman Tiberius Brown off the board to be replaced by pushy but pliant Veronica Veneer. She was only too happy to become chair and advance the interests, first of her construction company, the up-and-coming Blackthorn Buildings, and then of her insurance company named Bentlegs, by getting lucrative contracts from BCU.

This helped Groznyy personally. He planned to get his salary raised by taking full advantage of the accountancy sleights of hand by treasurer Parthy and by persuading new trustee chair Veronica to raise his pay, first by small leaps, then by larger ones.

Veneer was a willing accomplice, glad to make the implied assumption that BCU would award profitable contracts to her own companies. Both sides benefited. Veneer's companies secured university contracts; Groznyy and Burnable gained ever higher salaries. However, within these maneuvers, Groznyy was unintentionally laying land mines.

TSAR AND STAR

Once he felt little BCU was safe from financial collapse, Groznyy began to shuffle administrators around, giving some new jobs. He was wreaking havoc with the morale of the people he needed most. His worst abuse was to the deans and their assistants, many of whom did not have tenure—a secure job for life—like the professors. So they relied on him solely. Every time he needed to distract them from making constructive suggestions or showing any spark of originality, he had an assortment of tricks to send these puny lords a-leaping. Out would pop a command that would set them on a back foot. He thought, correctly, that they would be in no position to object to his tantrums and abuse except to one another in private. Victims of Groznyy's early purges included the deans of business, social work, and of the center of education for mature students.

The provost—the highest academic administrator—soon followed.

Lucy Kaye felt unsettled. She had never even considered that her rise to provost would make her unpopular with her former colleagues, the professors. But now she began to receive anonymous notes. One slipped under the front door of her home read, "Get your big, brown nose out of Groznyy's sweet, slurpy ass and start to behave like a real provost." Another arrived in the internal office mail at BCU. Wrapped in tissue was a tiny hard piece of human excrement. A slip of paper said, "Up the shitty."

This was only the beginning.

One Monday the Chosen Council met at breakfast as usual. Groznyy looked at Lucy with contempt, despising her dreary dress, hoary hair, weary face, and self-satisfied look. Before the provost had even drafted proposals that Groznyy had ordered the previous week, Groznyy announced, "We are to establish a state department to target endowments from overseas, a land office to oversee buildings and grounds, and offices of faculty recruitment and student enrolment, under a new dean of admissions. Madam Provost, please make arrangements. Larry, who shares my excessive burdens of state, has a list of prospective candidates to assume office under your good self."

Provost Lucy was already behind in her work. She could

not even stutter a reply. However, when Groznyy paused, she realized it was now or never.

"Mr. President, aren't we moving too quickly? With all these new proposals and new appointments, there will be more opinions to hear, more employees to confer—let alone pay—more meetings in which to debate matters and to make decisions. Surely the present number of administrators is large enough so far as the prompt conduct of business is concerned. All these innovations will entail extra work—not least in the provost's office. And there is no proposal for extra clerical staff to shoulder the burden."

"Ah, Madam Provost, I've already thought of that and have taken care of your need. Let us, as the English saying has it, kill two old birds with one stone, oh yes."

The provost was not sure which she disliked more, the way the president relished the verb "kill" or that he was calling her an "old bird."

"In an effort to curb the self-interest of deans appointed before us, we insist that they share their tasks with our own representatives, oh yes. Both the old deans and my new representatives will help your tender shoulders bear your work."

None of this did Provost Lucy want to hear—neither the interference nor the threat of more unwelcome scrutiny.

"Don't be impotent; be important," Groznyy urged her, while making it impossible for her to do her job.

Her confidante was Zenocrate Cohen, the associate provost. She had come to America as a young refugee after World War II. A careworn administrator in arts and sciences who was about to retire, Zenocrate had been persuaded to stay longer to help Lucy learn how to run the provost's office. She commiserated with Lucy: "It's made worse because he's temperamentally incapable of delegating responsibility. He holds on to power until he throttles it. The deans can't act because he interferes so much and they have to watch their backs."

It was gradually dawning on the provost that Groznyy had an unstated plan for controlling senior administrators and this included her. Her associate spelled it out.

"Haven't you wondered why he moved so many administrators from their original offices into the main administrative building?"

The provost was silent. The associate answered her own question.

"All the better to spy upon us. Everything has been done to strengthen the power of the president. First, he raises us by promoting us to senior positions—something he does to puff up our pride and hype our hubris."

The provost did not like any reference to pride and hubris.

"When you were dean of nursing, you angled for, and got, the provost's job. Then, having detached you from your power base, Groznyy set you the impossible task of turning deadbeat professors into cutting-edge scientists or pioneer philosophers."

"And if I fail?" Lucy was not sure if she heard herself—openly considering failure.

"When—not if—we both fail, he will denounce us before the Chosen Council."

"Then he will fire us—"

"With deadly dispatch—like Joseph Stalin."

The new provost's sense of purposelessness deepened. The result was intense fear and chaos in her office. Routine administration was left undone. It took weeks for the provost's office to process simple requests, to reach ordinary decisions, and people who asked for help went unanswered.

In addition to problems with office politics, her doctor warned Lucy that she might have a heart attack brought on by the overdrive of Groznyy's micro-management and aggravated by smoking too many cigarettes.

Sensing Lucy's distress, Lorraine Boe, manager of human resources, went to see her. Seated in the outer office alongside the associate provost, she surveyed the cascading piles of letters, memos, and circulars around the room.

"Lucy, dear friend, you really must see to the backlog of papers," she said.

Associate Provost Cohen said, "Lorraine is right. No matter how bad all this looks outside the office, it's far worse inside. There's no proper order or routine. For years they managed all the routine business in this office without a hitch. How on earth could this have happened?"

"Don't worry," answered Lucy as she stubbed out a cigarette. "I'll get down to it. I'll come in over the weekend and work my way through it."

How and when and what she did, the associate provost could not be sure. But when Zenocrate arrived for work on Monday, the layers of correspondence had certainly disappeared. Following Lucy's cleaning of the Augean stables, there was no correspondence for her secretary to type, or file, or complete in any way.

Meanwhile, as Lucy and Zenocrate surveyed the emptied scene, Mordred Stickleman, associate professor of economic history, burst into the room. He had a rucksack slung over his shoulders.

"You denied my sabbatical leave in revenge for my political views," he told the astonished provost. "I will not leave until you get the trustees to grant my paid sabbatical leave."

He flung his rucksack to the floor so hard that out tumbled hastily made sandwiches, three apples, two bottles of squash, and a cascade of fruit-and-nut bars. He swept them back up into his treasure-trove hamper, almost, thought the associate provost, like a fox savoring a basket of chicken pieces.

"Here I am and here I stay. You made this sabbatical leave not happen. Now you make it happen."

The provost was guilty of many things (according to her critics), but she was entirely innocent of this.

So, this was it: a sit-in, a sit-down, like a mini civil rights or anti-Vietnam demonstration. To look into the matter, Lucy's associate, Zenocrate, went into an inner office and started to make phone calls. She discovered that Stickleman was due for leave next semester and he had already applied for it. Zenocrate learned from Bee Flute in the president's office that Groznyy and the trustees wanted to put down Stickleman for his continuous sniping. The trustees had, indeed, cancelled Stickleman's forthcoming sabbatical leave. Zenocrate also learned that Groznyy had kept the provost out of the loop of information on sabbaticals.

But Stickleman was still alive and kicking in the main office. Suddenly and without even her knowing it, Provost Lucy took command—not by barking orders but by becoming calmer. Lucy knew she had to keep Stickleman steady and still. She understood that he was not only livid but also emotionally disturbed. His pent-up hatred of all things Groznyy had contorted his face. His psychological distress was more pressing than the physical inconvenience of having someone in her office with enough rage for twelve angry men. She forgot about her cigarettes.

Lucy knew that the important thing was not how she felt but to keep order in her office. She started to get Mordred to explain how upset he was. She appreciated how his distress mirrored her own. As she talked, he grew quieter. The office secretaries marveled at Lucy's presence of mind—no longer the tremors of career failure but steadiness like the center of a hurricane.

By chance, the chairman of the history department came in to discuss the costs of stationery. He did not want to deal with this sit-in but he was trapped. He tried to explain things from Stickleman's point of view.

"He wants to write his great history on President Andrew Jackson's War on the Bank. This sabbatical may be his last chance just to get started. He feels he has right on his side in his criticism of the president and the trustees, and that, like student protesters of the 1960s, he is being punished for expressing viable democratic opinions."

The more Mordred heard this sympathetic explanation, the faster his stamina for a sit-in evaporated.

By the time Zenocrate returned from her inner office with a verbal assurance from Bee Flute that Stickleman would get his sabbatical leave after all, Stickleman was ready to shake hands with the provost and leave feeling deflated. But he was also elated that he would soon be away on his precious academic mission.

Zenocrate gave Stickleman's forgotten fruit-and-nut bars to the secretaries.

Although she had handled the little crisis expertly, the Commodore was far from secure. Inwardly, she was still in a state of outraged confusion. With matters Groznyy, she was like a never-before-questioned matriarch. Her world had been turned upside down by a man representing forces of change she was unable to understand, even though she herself had unwittingly unleashed them.

It was another two days before Lorraine and Zenocrate had worked out what the provost had done with the cascading piles of correspondence—and why the skips in the refuse yard were spilling over with discarded paper. Bee said to herself, "Well, no one was going to do anything constructive with all that correspondence anyway."

There followed a stream of little rumors around campus circulated by presidential aide Bogus Revisor: that Lucy was not up to the job, that every time she spoke she made a gaffe, and that she was on the firing line.

"The fucking cunts are trying to stitch me up," exploded Lucy.

When she accosted him, Cesare denied everything. Indeed, he agreed to speak up for her in public. When he did so at a meeting of science consortium managers, it was in the past tense: how she had once helped prepare NHU and the consortium for its great period—his presidency; how she had "manfully shouldered" extra duties to receive him at BCU. With that, implied Groznyy, her special contribution was over.

However, when the Commodore failed to parry opposition from professors, he rounded on her in private.

"You should have gone in there fit to be tied. Make them afraid for their lives. I expect a provost to be so majestic that these puerile professors will shit themselves before getting through the door into your presence."

Behind her back Groznyy wrote a letter to the chair of the trustees pouring venom on the self-interested lives of the deans, the chairs, and the professors. With trenchant sarcasm he described their supposedly luxurious lifestyles in what was meant to be a gracious citadel of academic asceticism—Babel City University and Norse Hoven University. His main point—and all the more telling for being implied rather than stated—was that Lucy Kaye had done nothing to curtail the professors' hedonistic abandon.

Ever the mordant wit, Bogus Revisor quipped to Lorraine Boe: "It seems that Commodore Lucy is going down without her ship."

In a drowsy stupor one night at home, Lucy took a late call.

"Hi! Lucy, Bogus Revisor here. Cesare wants you to give up the provostship. Your services are no longer required. You can expect a parting handshake—bronze, not golden—if you resign with immediate effect."

He put his phone down.

Then Bogus went to Cesare for a drink-fueled rant to ridicule Lucy.

"We've got her fat ass stuck in a barrel," said Bogus.

"Fat ass? What lovely boobs she's got, oh yes," answered Groznyy, venting his pent-up spleen against the ladder he had used to scale the towers of BCU. "And what a nose she's got—big enough for seven, oh yes. And her ass—seats eight."

"I'll say," added the parasitic flea. "She's got the sort of legs you could make into chops."

Lucy fumed through her sleepless night. Next day was Saturday. She went round to the president's house. Summoning up courage almost equal to her weight, she burst in on Groznyy and his wife at their chilly breakfast.

"It isn't the impossible you expect of your deans. It's their destruction. You would never admit it but you think a mushroom cloud is beautiful, provided it's you who presses the button to detonate it."

Groznyy yawned. Recalling another phrase from one of his second wife's favorite operas, he said, "Sing your tired old song wherever you want, oh yes. You're finished here. Kaput."

This taunt goaded the rejected provost even further.

"You want to make everyone fall in love with you—men, women, and children. You, a poisoned dwarf if ever there was one! A petit Napoleon dangling titles like jewels from a crown, promising power but delivering ashes that taste like bitter gall!"

This time Groznyy did not yawn. He heard little of what Lucy said. Sharp, flashing pains struck his temples.

"You survive because the people you terrorize would rather be the last pitiful survivors still standing than any one of your victims. They would rather live with failure than accept death."

With this parting shot, Lucy opened the front door behind her, but not before she heard Holly whisper, "It was nice she could drop by."

At that, Lucy was back in the breakfast room, larger than life and not nearly so beautiful.

"I'll expose you, Groznyy, your past, your secret love child, and the money the university paid to keep your ex-girlfriend, your discarded mistress, the horrid Esther Vashti, quiet when you were running for office."

Lucy thought she had triumphed even in defeat. She wondered why the third Mrs. Groznyy was not taken aback that Groznyy had fathered a secret love child that she surely knew nothing about.

With immense composure, Holly decided to take over. "Isn't that risky for you—representing the university supposedly paying off a shady lady? If you squeal after doing the deed, won't you look stupid? You went along with the cover-up, helped paint the whitewash. If you speak now, won't it be your reputation that's in the gutter?"

"I don't care. I don't care as long as he falls along with me."

Holly decided to play her trump card. She had been saving it. She could only play it once. She had someone else to think of—someone not in the room. Groznyy knew what was coming and he admired her audacity.

"I don't think you understand, Ms. Kaye," Holly said simply.

"Don't understand? I know a cheat when I see one."

"No, you don't understand fully. You see, I'm Esther Vashti."

Incomprehension.

"It's true. Cesare and I had a love child. We were both very young. Once obstacles to our marriage evaporated, we did get married. That you know."

The scales had fallen from Lucy's eyes. She spared no thought for the passing reference to Anna Stasinova, Groznyy's second wife whom everyone respected, as an "obstacle." Lucy looked back at Groznyy. His face was inscrutable. In fact, his head was smarting with stabs of intense pain. What Lucy interpreted as moody defiance was simple determination to stand up by grasping the side arms of the breakfast chair as tightly as he could.

Lucy looked from husband to wife and back again.

"What I told you is true," added Holly. "You can tell all—all you know, at any rate—but now we are married we fear no exposure. The only person you will hurt, besides yourself, will be our child raised safely by my family away from here."

Lucy wanted to explode, to rain blows down on the head of this Esther Vashti, or Holly Wood, or the Misses Lee Aisons Dangereuses, or whoever else she was. She wanted to kill Groznyy. She knew this chit of a girl, this white-trash chant-tootsie, this never-has-been, had outsmarted her. Lucy's face contorted into a red bulge. She had been ruined, first by this dreadful man who had seduced her into leading him like a Trojan horse into the hallowed academic stockade of two universities, then by the false woman who had laughed all the way to the bank with BCU's money.

Suddenly finding a form of majesty now she was no longer provost and that would have served her better in office, Lucy shouted at Groznyy, "Your punishment is your unfulfilled life—imprisonment without end while you still breathe."

With that she was out, banging the door with a slam so loud as to awaken the dead.

"So long, dearie," thought Holly. "Unfortunately for you, Cesare still has his assortment of tricks. Every time he's cornered, out pops a command that sets his toads on a back foot."

But when she turned round Holly saw Cesare crumpled on his chair and his head over the leftover breakfast.

Indeed, this political crisis, in which Groznyy had deliberately provoked uproar to deflect anger through chaos, had come to an end not with the firing of Provost Lucy Kaye but immediately after.

Groznyy had a bad attack of shingles that struck him across the temple and upper face on the right. In desperate pain and with the possibility he would lose his sight, he was confined to bed, his eyes covered with shades. It was touch and go whether he would survive.

News of Lucy's exit and Groznyy's brush with death was all over campus. But the sensation was Holly's multiple lives.

"The barefaced audacity of it," Lucy told anyone who would listen to her. "She has a secret child by Groznyy, then she gets pregnant by his first son. Then she blackmails the university over the secret son. Then she marries him. Venus and Mars in conjunction again? I don't think so. She's worse than shameless. It's worse than incest. It's—she's a white devil. You think she's got the voice of an angel? She's got the hide of a rhinoceros—and then some. She's a white devil in a little black dress."

Holly had neither the education nor the composure to make a statement. She consulted her offstage allies, Princess Glinskaya and Benny Vincenzo, who drafted the right words. Then presidential aide Bogus Revisor circulated a sympathetic announcement about the president's "only temporary ill health," adding to it a codicil that "President and Mrs. Groznyy have previously had a child together whom Dr. Groznyy has supported from birth and who will now become a regular family member."

Groznyy was ill, indeed. Any scandal that might have broken was now submerged in a wave of artificial sympathy for his serious ill health.

Circulating a discreetly worded account of her personal life across the two universities was one thing, but Holly thought she had better open up to Hermione if she was going to keep her new friend onside. They met in the restaurant's upper room.

"You've heard?"

Hermione nodded.

"Yes, it's true. I am Esther Vashti. Lee Aison was another stage name. That night our paths first crossed, I knew I had to close one chapter and open another. Choosing a better name helped me reinvent myself."

Hermione swallowed.

"My mom had been an amateur blues singer. She thought I had a talent that deserved to be heard. She told me, 'Your gift is greater than mine. A careless man used you. I will look after your child. You get regular work in a university where there are showbiz contacts. Then seize every artistic chance you can.'"

Holly paused. She wanted to give Hermione a moment to reflect.

"Now it's out in the open. It can't be used to hurt either of us. He didn't marry me to make things regular. He married me to buy my silence."

"Silence?"

"Silence over Modest."

"Because if you were married you couldn't be forced to give evidence against your husband?"

"That's the way he interprets the law. It makes bizarre sense. If I exposed him, everyone would expect me to explain how I married him, knowing what he did. If I went to the police, I would be an accessory."

"I don't think that's the way people would react. I did hear about another child in another state. Modest said his half-brother was also visually impaired—that was why Groznyy had such a horror of disabled people."

"Luke, my son, has a serious eye condition—pathological myopia. In time, he may lose his sight. I wanted to protect him from his father—the savage rages. Dr. Chicago says it's a narcissistic character disorder."

"The story going the rounds was that you were blackmailing him and that the university paid."

"That's the way it looked to them. I was fighting to get Luke recognized. He has my mother's original last name—Reader. It's an American form of the Russian name Rurik or Ryurikid. My brother, Boris, wanted to make sure my mom had enough money to bring him up, see him through college. In his position, Groznyy couldn't avoid maintenance payments."

"But he wouldn't bother to find out what the real problem was?"

"Right. Luke would be safe from a very disturbed man. Boris said that, whatever the problem, Cesare would regard it as a slight on himself."

Hermione realized she had only just peered below the surface of the complex person who was Holly Wood. This woman with no college education and no intellectual airs could run rings round the man with the degrees. He had enough intellectual pretensions to fill three universities but he was a cynic who knew the value of nothing that mattered. Holly could lead a double life. Hermione wondered if, in another context, the FBI might have recruited her as an agent. But Holly had a tremendous talent. She was becoming an incandescent musical star. That was her destiny.

"So, you married Groznyy to sink your differences?"

"To stabilize things. Luke is safe. There can be no blackmail over Luke now from anyone who hates Groznyy. And our marriage leaves open the possibility that, if he wants it, Luke can be Cesare's heir."

"Does Luke know?"

"He knows the bare facts. The way my mother and my brother have brought him up, he doesn't want anything to do with his father."

"So, when Modest brought you here to meet his parents?"

"They were horrified, aghast, any word you want to choose."

"Did Modest know?"

"No. Not at all."

"Didn't he suspect?"

"He thought the trouble was that, from their point of view, I was older, that his parents considered me a stage has-been. And that wasn't wrong. Some years I'm the coolest rising star. Next year, everyone is over me and I'm invisible. Of course, Modest's mother couldn't tell him about Groznyy and me without provoking more questions. That's where I had them."

"I have no right to ask, but—"

Holly knew that Hermione would ask one particular question. She had her answer ready in advance. "Were we intimate? No."

"So, you were proposing to become the partner, the wife of the son of the man who had given you a child and abandoned you?"

"That sums it up. But it doesn't take account of feelings, emotions, and love. I loved Modest for his kindness and generosity—just like you did—and he loved me. Cesare was beside himself—that I had been with him and then taken his son from him."

"Was that part of the reason why he was so furious when Modest tried to reason with him about the science survey and possible terrorism in the college?"

"Probably."

"Does that mean that you—unintentionally—roused Groznyy to such a fever pitch against Modest that he was beside himself—out of control—and that led him to kill Modest?"

"That's a possibility," answered Holly as if she were giving evidence in court under strict guidelines from her lawyer.

"A possibility!" Hermione almost shriveled with anger.

Holly broke down.

"Don't you think that all the time I am tortured by this—

that I might have incited Groznyy to do it, the hope that I can prove he did it? I hardly sleep. Not—"

"You don't sleep with Groznyy?"

"What do you think? Do you think he can? They say power is an aphrodisiac. But that's not true in his case. Don't you think I'm relieved? Besides, if the marriage isn't consummated that will probably give him a reason for an annulment, or a way of reducing any separation settlement. I may not have been an ideal mother. But I had Luke's interests at heart."

Hermione was silent.

"That's enough secrets for one day," said Holly. "I need to rest before rehearsal."

Hermione wondered if this was how Holly survived. She put her outsize talent into her art and shielded herself from the mess of her personal life by putting her psyche on hold in the wings while she used her perfectly honed gifts onstage before her adoring fans.

Indeed, throughout her confession to Hermione—no matter how open—Holly was keeping a tight rein on the information she gave and the emotions welling up inside her. But when she was alone it was more than she could do to keep her balance. Having to talk about her earlier life with Groznyy brought back her tender sexual urges as little Esther Vashti.

She tried not to think about it.

But their first time together came flooding back. They were making love on her mother's bed while she was out shopping. He had kissed her gently on the cheek. When she stayed still and did not withdraw, he kissed her insistently on her lips. She kissed him back, opening up her mouth to his tongue, hugging his shoulders, and digging her fingers through his blue shirt and into his back. Then he eased his hand under her blouse. He touched her supple young body, exploring and caressing her until she started moaning in ecstasy.

When he had undressed her, Cesare marveled at the globules of enticing moisture shimmering between her supple thighs. He licked them. She lifted her slender legs and spread them. He fell upon her, kissing her head and shoulders, her breasts and stomach.

First she caressed his penis to make it hard and drew it inside her. Then, just as suddenly, she panicked. He thought she was going to stop. But she let him continue. She gasped, "I'm coming."

After they had sweated themselves into climax, she said matter-of-factly, "Can we do this every single day?"

For Groznyy this was a jolting déjà vu. He had heard the same words and made the same reply the night before when he was in bed with one of Esther's girl friends. He could run Esther's script over and over in his mind.

"We'll do this every day until I finish high school," she said. "Then we can get married."

"Yes."

In Groznyy's mind, the two girls' words ran into one another seamlessly. He had thought—dashing fellow that he was—that he was the director as well as the leading man in this scenario. Esther was so defenseless against his magnetism.

Fate and family had other ideas.

That was a lifetime ago. In the present Holly wondered which was worse: marriage to Groznyy when she was a teenager or now when she was a woman of the world. But as first lady of BCU, Holly did not want Cesare to die of shingles. That was not the plan. She had no faith in the specialist at the hospital. She phoned Dr. Squires, the one true friend of Groznyy's late second wife. He came back from vacation to minister to Groznyy.

Even sedated, Groznyy was greatly agitated.

41

"Everywhere I'm surrounded by conspiracy and sedition. In the meantime, students, yearning for enlightenment, roam without academic progress as if they are stricken with paralysis."

Since Lucy Kaye had gone, Bogus Revisor became interim provost but without Zenocrate Cohen. She had survived Hitler's Holocaust and experienced the horrors of brutal wartime dictators as tragedy. She did not want to live under their puny imitator at BCU—a mini Hitler—this time as farce. She retired gratefully.

Bogus knew Groznyy had got rid of so many of his administrators within their first twelve months. How would he survive? Bogus had an acute political sense for self-preservation but his communication skills were undermined by his offhand rudeness, his detachment from the foot soldier experiences of the deans, and his determination to remain the last man standing. Administrators disliked his way of polishing his eyeglasses when he talked at them or interrupted their verbal flights with such dismissive exclamations as "Right!" and "Next!" Professors were angered by Bogus's habit of abruptly rising from his chair in his office and leaving them in mid-sentence when they still had points to make.

Bogus's gushing and fawning over Groznyy in public was always depersonalized for grandeur. He always made clear his identification of The President with The University and The University with The State, and, further, with Inevitable and Progressive Reform.

Behind the scenes, however, it was different. For, with his own staff and cronies, instead of "the Esteemed President," it was "Fucking Cesare," or "Shit-Faced Cesare," or "Motherfucker Groznyy." These were in response to Groznyy's abrupt shifts of policy or his outrageous lies. The epithets might be about Groznyy's false promises to make professors or donors believe he would reward them.

Despite his severe illness, Groznyy never gave up power. He summoned the trustees to a sickbed moved to the porch. They arrived like choristers with a refrain of hypocritical groveling: "Don't leave us, Mr. President. Without you, life at BCU would be dreary. Any success would not be real success."

But when Groznyy asked them to swear an oath of commitment to his reforms, it was a different matter. Some declined because they thought he was going to die.

A temporary housekeeper brought out special cushions for the president and plumped them up. She went back inside and returned with treats to eat. These comforting touches soothed the trustees, who now sang Groznyy's praises like so many pet parrots.

This two-faced behavior infuriated Cesare. It added to his distrust of the fawning trustees. His restless mind moved over how he would continue to reshape the board. He thought about people in the public eye on whom he could rely. In some cases this was because being a trustee would promote their careers through extra publicity.

Thus, among new trustees, he chose a post-modern vernacular architect, the failing editor of a failing right-wing magazine, and an aggressive self-publicizing physicist whose specialty was magnetic imaging. They coveted the limelight. Each one he drew in through flattery applied as liberally as drama coach Paula Strasberg had to needy film star Marilyn Monroe. All they had to do in return was mouth right-of-center platitudes about pioneer education.

When he joined the board, new trustee Abraham Ripemoff of Visually Impaired People's Services told the *Norse Hoven Courier*, "I'm here to balance some of the more outspoken conservatives on the board. My credentials as a spokesman for disabled people are impeccable. You have to hand it to Cesare—the way he emphasizes the importance of the great books of western civilization for college kids without getting ensnarled in controversies over race or gender or class: absolutely brilliant."

Upstairs in the green baize room of the Golden Cockerel now adorned with cityscapes of New York in the Gilded Age, the Dominican waiters provided seamless service.

When Hermione joined them because they were short-staffed, she wore the same white shirt and black bolero jacket as they did. Head waiter Bernardo guided her. Guests thought she was his wife helping out. Hermione realized that, because what few words the waiting staff spoke to one another they spoke in Spanish, the guests assumed they knew next to no English. And that included her. Thus the guests' conversation was as open and unguarded as aristocrats might have spoken in ancient Rome before their slaves. Their carelessness gave Hermione insight into the mindset of Cesare's cronies as they babbled away their secrets.

There were four of them whom Benny identified for Hermione: chair of the trustees Veronica Veneer; Georgie Lucre, owner of a PR firm named Lucrative Lucre; Carpenter Cain, head of the alumni bureau at BCU; and the ubiquitous Brad Gable.

Having recently discarded her outsize Afro wig for a sleek bob, Veronica Veneer felt empowered by her new cut.

"The university hospital extension is our next golden opportunity. Yes, it's one hell of a building complex that has many special features—offices, labs, reception rooms, equipment, furniture, carpets, flooring."

Veronica put two fingers to her lips to signal that silence was always golden and that a nod was as good as a wink.

Indeed, the Chosen Council had appropriated an initial $3.6 million from alumni gifts garnered by Carpenter Cain as BCU's contribution to the consortium. Groznyy had taken great pleasure in reporting this to journalists to enhance his preferred image as dispenser of university largess. He basked in what he assumed would prove reflected glory—his first of all.

Mrs. Veneer's interest was more practical. She knew that Brad Gable was a bustling, energetic person with a glib tongue about how quickly he was applying university funds to getting the new hospital wing built. She wanted to shape his maneuvers.

"Since we are all honorable men—ladies included—everything has to look above board. We have to demonstrate that everything we do is for genuine need. Relish your work. Be creative with your payees. Use straightforward names like T.C. Cash. Other examples? Remember we're in a cosmopolitan society."

"Mark. Frank. Pfund. Yuan."

Bringing up the rear, Brad suggested "T. Hee."

And so it was, not only in construction but also on the stock market.

As the US economy began to soar alongside expanding IT and communications, there developed a profitable market for fixers. These were intermediaries who could get a private organization with a public function—such as a university—to provide financial opportunities to people wanting to make a fast buck. In the BCU version of this scenario, Brad Gable was the satellite of trustees Veronica Veneer and Georgie Lucre and alumni boss Carpenter Cain. All three had the ear of Groznyy. Brad was in a state of exaltation at the prospect of making money as an intermediary. Everything was balmy. The only problem was his old physical one of type 1 diabetes.

As Groznyy replaced the trustees one after another with his own men, Veronica would ask Brad to wait in the lobby of the Golden Cockerel, ostensibly for security. While the trustees dined upstairs, Brad would stand at the foot of the staircase, with the lapels of his dinner jacket spread open to reveal a red cummerbund that covered a girdle that compressed his stomach. As the trustees went up the narrow staircase to the upper room, Brad would call out to them with a wink, "If you're looking for some business, come on over." Out of his gaping mouth with its gleaming new porcelain teeth would pop something like a hooker's invitation to a big spender to have a good time.

From their deluded perspective, other trustees besides Veneer and Lucre were local New England businessmen and women with an eye on the main chance. There were elderly, do-good dollar millionaires mightily afraid of the next world in case they had not been sufficiently conscious of the poor in this one. There were also public servants who regretted lives devoted to public concerns in order to make themselves important. They were now anxious to mingle with the inconspicuous rich who might give them a stock-market tip or a well-paid sinecure to make them more comfortably off. And there were always trustees who simply wanted to be on the inside of deals.

Thus it was that such trustees sought out Brad Gable and he loved it. One might ask Brad to put in a good word for a tender. A second sought a concession for on-campus trading. And a third needed a special student immigration application visa for her brother-in-law endorsed by someone with a respectable job at a university.

In return for his services, trustees and contractors would offer Brad complementary token compensation. At first this was no more than a large bottle of a rare whiskey, or a tip on the expanding stock market, or an invitation to a business banquet at the World Trade Center. Such trivial fees that Brad accepted for dubious services opened the path for larger fees for services even more questionable.

There were also trustees who were not looking for immediate financial gain. What they wanted was a decent forum where they could negotiate delicate matters away from prying eyes. They might be lawyers with an awkward

46

civil case so they wanted to meet officials for prior negotiations—to achieve a done deal in a smoke-filled room.

All this set the tone and the script of what was to follow.

Having levelled with Hermione, Holly wondered if she would falter in her resolve with Groznyy's colleagues.

Once she realized that Bogus Revisor was in her sights, she changed the time and route of her morning jogging schedule.

When the commuter train carrying Bogus arrived at the suburban railroad station, Holly would be there to run aside it as if by coincidence. She had to get her timing right. She paced herself by marking her progress through select staging posts. A group of birch trees was her favorite, a sliver of Russian silver on American soil. She also liked the dense grass alongside a tiny spring that disappeared underground ten minutes after it appeared. At last, there was the slender suburban station of Babel City with its steel railings and arc lights. But there was no train. Today she would have to go round a block again since she was early. And when the train arrived, there she was, jogging nicely to show the men that she was fit.

Bogus certainly noticed. As the days passed their brief salutations became short conversations. Bogus was sure Holly was drawing him in. His words turned into a hesitant courtship.

When Groznyy was getting better but was still confined to his home, Dr. Squires encouraged him to spend more time in the garden. Still with bandages over his eyes and guided by his charming wife, Groznyy sat in the paltry shade of the wasted pear tree.

Holly sensed another opportunity. She had her seductive dialog ready. She borrowed from Modest's treasured words in their brief past together. This made her ashamed and her sense of shame put brakes on her emotions. She had her plan: get Groznyy's close aides to squeal on him and then embarrass him whenever possible.

So she invited Bogus Revisor over to the house.

Groznyy was dozing.

"Aren't you afraid, just a little, when I stand near you that I may give in to my feelings and caress you?" Holly asked.

Bogus thought here was another poseur just like himself. "What about your husband?"

"He's as cold as a fish. You can signal with your eyes if he wakes. If he takes his bandages off, I'll have my answer ready."

Groznyy was, indeed, woken by the noise of their love fumbles. Suspicious as ever, he tried to rise, protesting with flailing hands. He tore off his bandages. Blinded by the sunlight, he fell back into his chair. "What's that on the ground? A man's belt!"

Holly was ready for him. "I found it on the sidewalk and used it to fasten my skirt tight."

Groznyy was about to explode.

"Dearest Cesare, you cannot be sure what you see. Our dearest friend, Dr. Squires, explained that, when you started to see again, your sight would be fuzzy, unreliable. All I have been doing is pouring my heart out to Bogus, your closest ally. Dr. Squires said that the trouble we have—you know what I mean—was because I have been so uptight since—you know—the terrors of Modest's tragic death. Dr. Squires said that if I broke down before your best friend this would unlock my passion for you and all would be well physically between us. I'm not complaining, dear, because I know you're doing the best you can."

Part blinded by glaring sunlight, Groznyy stared in outraged disbelief. Bogus scuttled away as fast as a cockroach racing into a cupboard.

"Take care, Miss Holly Wood Groznyy, my third wife—or is it my fourth? Take care!"

Groznyy had been out-maneuvered. Ever so subtly, and in front of a witness, Holly had referred to two dark sides of their marriage: the sinister mystery of Modest's death and that their marriage was unconsummated. And these she had referred to before Bogus—a prince of thieves.

Bogus had only just got his foot in the door. What should be his next move? How would Holly react when they met?

The next time his path crossed hers, Holly Wood simply said, "Hi!" as if she were acknowledging a neighbor. Before he could reply, she said sweetly, "You know what they say? You can die of encouragement in Hollywood." Then she passed by.

When Bogus had recovered his composure and thanked whichever god he prayed to for his escape, he had a lingering doubt. It was clear that Holly Wood, this bloom in June, was as much a match for him as for her old husband. Bogus felt older than he was.

Shingles or not, embarrassed or not over his wife's supposed sex life, Groznyy was not going to hide away. His next ruse to defuse the gathering storm of university opposition was to organize a special academic meeting. Ignoring medical advice and with all the avenging force of his royal conviction, he devised an off-campus retreat for the deans and department chairs about teaching and research in the changed political landscape.

Scandalized to the point of convulsive hilarity over Holly and Bogus, the deans and chairs were still apprehensive about what to expect from the stricken tsar. They knew they had better be up-to-date academically for their forthcoming retreat with President Groznyy. Even those whose diet of information came from the *New York Daily News* understood that 1989, the previous year, had brought political upheaval overseas and this probably would be the topic for discussion.

49

Dean of Psychology Ace Ferrari took charge at a private meeting in advance at his house: "He will expect us to know everything: glasnost and perestroika, Gorbachev and Yeltsin, protest in Tiananmen Square in Beijing, tearing down the Berlin Wall, Soviet withdrawal from Afghanistan, etcetera. We can't all do everything. We must take individual topics."

Like a lizard ready to lay her eggs, he produced an old felt hat and strips of white paper, each one with a typed slogan. He put the slips of paper in the hat. Then he invited his guests to dip their hands into the hat and retrieve a slip of paper with such subjects as "Tiananmen," "Berlin Wall," "Gorbachev," "Perestroika," "Glasnost," and others.

"These are your individual assignments. Get the facts. The town library is ideal. No one else goes there. If anyone stumbles at the retreat, I will cover for us."

The guests scurried away, half trembling, half expecting that they might learn something new.

After their homework, the dean coached them at another meeting.

"When he asks you to sum up the two sides of the East–West conflict, what will you say?"

Back came the chorus: "D and M: Dictatorship and Marxism versus Democracy and Materialism."

"And when East Berliners finally got into West Berlin last year, what did they do?"

"Went shopping!"

No matter how clever the dean was, the president of Babel City University was ahead in mind games. His off-campus BCU retreat met in a large hired room of Milhous College in the shadow of its famous Crown Tower.

His eyes still shaded, Groznyy first overwhelmed everyone with a profusion of insincere compliments. No one was more uncomfortable than Bogus, who knew he was on borrowed time. Unused to ecstatic good wishes from Groznyy, the dean of the library whispered to Bogus, "He can be nice and welcoming—seductive, even—sometimes brimming with good humor. But be warned: it's all show."

Sensing the general apprehension, but not fully understanding it, was the new dean of nursing. Wendy Pretzel was a mid-forties Midwesterner with a mid-1950s perm who tried to give the impression she was a mid-thirties sophisticate. Charmed by the president's seductive manner, she had campaigned through her interview process to become dean as successor to Lucy Kaye by oohing and cooing about Groznyy. Now she was peering beneath his veneer.

Groznyy began to use his verbal scalpel to turn his deans' innards to Jell-O.

"We need to review our academic priorities. Communism in Europe has collapsed following the dismantling of the Berlin Wall. There must be something in the numeric or political atmosphere of years ending in 89. What do you say, Mr. Dean of Arts and Sciences?"

"You're referring to the English Revolution of 1689 and the French Revolution of 1789, before perestroika and glasnost last year, 1989, and the uprising in Tiananmen Square against the Chinese government—the massacre in Beijing."

"More."

The dean of arts and sciences was stumped. Groznyy decided to embarrass him by posing the question to his deputy.

"Mr. Assistant Dean of Arts and Sciences, you recently came back from a conference. Tell us about it. This is the most formative event of 1989—more than anything in Germany, Russia, or China."

Wendy Pretzel shifted uneasily. She recognized college mind games, knew she was out of her depth, and thanked God that, as a newcomer, she did not have to take part in such mental Paralympics tests—yet.

"Well, Mr. President," began the assistant dean, "it was the Chapman conference at San Diego, organized for the American Geophysical Union to discuss Gaia."

"The Greek primeval goddess who lends her name to?"

"Gaia. William Golding suggested using the name Gaia for the theory that our biosphere regulates the Earth's environment to sustain life."

Most of the deans and professors were at sea. They had prepared the wrong material: politics, not earth sciences. Some glared at Ace Ferrari.

The president adjusted his bandages as if he could see through them. "William Golding, oh yes? The novelist who wrote *Lord of the Flies*?" Groznyy's emphasis on "flies" made it clear whom he considered the flies. "Please no more sheepish despondency."

The dean of medicine spoke to help out. "What we call the Gaia theory is a result of research by many scientists."

Wendy Pretzel was more uneasy. What on earth could she contribute? What kept her going was the thought of buying her own condo.

Chair of Chemistry Don Fatale stepped in. He gave a simplified account that saved the deans from more embarrassment but angered the president, who hated anyone else being articulate.

"The Gaia hypothesis proposes that the physical components of the Earth—our atmosphere, hydrosphere, and so on—together make up a complex, interacting system that keeps the climatic and biogeochemical conditions on Earth in balance: homeostasis."

"More."

"It's the accumulation of work of several people—most of all, James Lovelock, an English scientist who began with research into the dead atmosphere on Mars, which is dominated by carbon monoxide. He compared it with the dynamic mixture of the Earth. To another scientist, Guy Murchie, things we think of as dead—such as metals and sand—are also living organisms."

Groznyy interrupted: "Dead atmosphere, oh yes. Does

that sound familiar? When threatened by an extraordinary life-threatening crisis, change or die. We are in a difficult situation, oh yes. We need students. And first we need to improve our professors. This is what I ask of you—to inspire the professors to academic greatness."

Don Fatale tried to go back to general principles. "The Gaia hypothesis proposes that living and non-living parts of the Earth form a complex interacting system that is also a single organism."

The president had had enough.

"Yes, we know—Strong Gaia, Weak Gaia, your Gaia, my Gaia, my grandmother's Gaia—the permutations are endless. Some scientists call the Earth the Blue Planet because we are two-thirds water. It's a pity that astronomers had already named Neptune. It's the Earth that should be Neptune—or Poseidon—for Gaia is a ball of water with deep, limitless currents. Now, listen, all of you," continued the president. "This is what we at little BCU need to do. Experiment. Challenge any outdated assumptions. Look beyond contemporary politics. Forget about the invasion of Kuwait by Iraqi dictator Saddam Hussein. And forget about the US-led coalition to defeat him. In the wider context of geopolitics, both are inconsequential."

Dean Ace Ferrari was glad of the president's flippant remarks on a subject near to home, but at the same time he wondered if Groznyy was being dismissive because he did not want to be compared to another megalomaniac.

"The Gaia theory shows us the path to the future," continued Groznyy. "We at BCU–NHU are in a stable academic environment. But it is dying through lack of the oxygen of new ideas that young minds seek. We don't have enough students. What we have too much of are outdated academic assumptions. We should be playing our part, oh yes. Woods Hole can do it. Cambridge can do it. It is your duty to make our professors do it. There are Nobel prizes to be won. They should be ours—yours and mine."

The chairs and deans were silent. It was as if the ground had opened up beneath them. Groznyy sensed their nothingness.

"Let us pause for lunch. Mr. Dean of the Library, I hear you have brought excellent strawberries from your garden to follow our veggie sandwiches. Will you allow me to try some?"

"With pleasure," mumbled the dean of the library, as he took the president's arm to guide him, wondering where this pleasantry would lead. He escorted the president to the buffet lunch of crumbly dry sandwiches, sticky buns, and curdled coffee in the next room.

Groznyy knew the sort of thing the deans and chairs would say about him behind his back. Backbiters all, they would never fail him in that respect. Indeed, as soon as he was gone, Ferrari said to the group, "All this is Groznyy's way to tell us we are not good enough. He says he wants ideas and imagination. It isn't true. He wants worship—and Nobel prizes conjured up out of thin air."

The dean of arts and sciences asked, "What about his rages? There's this story that he killed his son—whom he was supposed to love to death—killed him in a violent fit, following a row about the way his future daughter-in-law was dressed. Imagine."

"That was just a bizarre rumor. The culprit was that arsonist."

Groznyy was back among them. His mood was thunder black.

"Who said this about me? Which of you?"

The silence was mortifying.

"Is that all you can say? Nothing? Don't think I don't know what you are up to. My eyes may be bandaged but my brain is still alert, oh yes."

Groznyy tore off his bandages. The chairs and deans were so startled that they wondered if his eyes had seen them all along.

Groznyy staggered slightly and raised his right hand to his face. "Some of you think you have discovered the secrets of my sex life—my loving wife's and mine. Well, I have a little—no, a big—surprise for you. Don't think I'm alone. Neither are you. Not for a second. You have your spies. I have mine."

Bogus felt the president's eyes boring right through his skull.

"I know exactly what you do in bed."

Cesare turned to Don Fatale, whom he hoped must be cringing.

"Don't shake. When I'm ready, I'll make you void your bowels and follow through. I'll do it. Yes, I know what you do in bed. I'll call a press conference and get it reported in the papers. In the press! Understand? Class dismissed."

Thus roused, when he recovered, Groznyy proceeded on another periodic bloodletting with the summary firing of two associate deans and intrigues against three trustees whom he disliked. Dean Wendy Pretzel was scared. She knew she had better take notes.

Don Fatale took some comfort in his belief that, like Gaia's stewardship of the Earth, human compassion and the natural checks and balances of society could, in time, redress the disorder of Groznyy's rule at BCU.

Ace Ferrari gave a sigh of relief. He had attended a conference on Islam in Dallas the previous year. Fortunately, it had gone undetected at BCU.

"Benny, I think we're asking too much of Holly. All she's been able to find out—and that was from a casual remark from someone in the treasurer's office—was that Groznyy has bought a graveyard plot two towns over for himself and his second wife who's already buried there."

"It's not Holly's fault. I think she needs backup," answered Benny.

As the princess was speaking, adopting her most charming style, Hermione, who had sat silently through this, now realized where it was going.

"Hermione, you're a skilled pianist. We all know that Holly has the chance of rising as a jazz singer. I suggest you offer her your services as an accompanist. In this way, Holly will get the support of someone she trusts both for her artistic career and for our mission to expose Groznyy."

Hermione reddened.

"Benny will give you time off work. We will pay you." Benny rolled his eyes. The unflappable princess continued, "You graduated from Milhous. They don't know you at BCU. And Groznyy won't recognize you with your new hairstyle."

There was no denying the princess's whim of iron. And it was off to the beauty salon for Hermione that afternoon.

Next day, it was much easier than Hermione expected. Without saying anything in advance, Hermione, with her new hairstyle, got off the commuter train at the Babel City substation just as Holly arrived on her daily jog. The two women fell into one another's arms. Holly took Hermione back home for coffee and croissants.

Some time before, Groznyy had authorized the renovation of the university theater to commemorate BCU's famous prewar innovations: a school of dance and schools of nursing and social work. All these had been rarities in the 1930s. Groznyy joked over dinner at the Golden Cockerel how impressed he was with the design for the new postmodern theater façade— a glass curtain wall, designed by Postnik Yakovlev.

"If I could, I would have the architect blinded, so that never again could he design anything as marvelous for a rival college."

There was a suppressed sensation round the table.

Yakovlev heard the anecdote on the grapevine. It alerted him to his potential earning power. Realizing the president's jealousy, he knew he had to act quickly. He promoted his theater design on the local television station, Network News Norse Hoven. Thus he secured commissions from BCU's college rivals in the state.

Aggravated, Groznyy brought Yakovlev back to design a fountain aside the steps of the BCU library to commemorate BCU's pioneer male students in World War II when BCU had been primarily a female institution. Cesare's critics said this St. Basil's Fountain was just like him—saying prayers for the souls of his past victims, including his own son.

ONSTAGE AND OFF

"What do you expect in a gala performance: a sense of occasion? Stars? Popular numbers? Interesting music? All these will be on offer next month."

This was how Groznyy, now recovered from shingles, introduced his next stage show at a meeting with the deans. To open the renovated theater, he told the music and drama departments to perform a version of *Cosi fan tutte*, the last Mozart–da Ponte opera.

"My charming lady wife has agreed to advise the artists."

Holly had done no such thing. The idea for the opening gala had come from a Texas oilman. Bogus Revisor could recall how he had made them an offer they could not refuse.

"See here, Mr. President—"

Groznyy loved that.

"I'm willing to make you an outsize donation—outsize— for the opening show of the renovated theater."

Groznyy and Bogus were all ears as they danced attention

on the Texas oilman before them. He sat all bronzed complexion and beige leisure clothes. His eyes were hidden by orangutan shades. He had come as a suppliant. But Groznyy and Revisor knew it was BCU and NHU that were the real beggars. This was the man who had already paid anonymously for the renovation of the theater, for the new fountain, and had helped BCU over the scandal of Groznyy's old sex life.

Now he wanted to come out of the shadows.

"Here's the thing: one condition only."

Groznyy groaned. Experience had taught him "one condition" always meant several.

"My daughter, Ruby—we call her Roubles—takes the principal soprano role."

"She's sung in opera before?" asked Bogus.

"You bet. Here's the thing. Juilliard turned her down. They said that, in the world of classical music, whatever audiences want, commercially speaking, there are too many sopranos, too many pianists, and too many violinists. They can't all be headliners."

"Was there more to it?" asked Bogus, as he tried to sidle up to the oilman. "What kind of soprano is your daughter?"

"She says dramatic coloratura. They say lyric spinto. They said she's pushing herself. And—"

"And?"

"She doesn't do thrills."

"Thrills?"

"Decorations."

"Trills?"

"That's your word. At the audition, they asked her to do her showpiece again with trills. She said, 'Must I?' They said, 'Can you hear yourself? If we were at any music conservatoire anywhere in the world and we asked a wind player to show his trills, and he said, "Must I? Do I have to?" what would we do? Show him what the door is for.'

"That's what they did to Roubles, sure enough. I know what you're thinking. Spoiled rich kid. Lives on daddy's dough. She's never worked. Well, you'd be wrong. She practices way beyond the call of duty. She's a star. Just needs a break. I'm going to make sure she gets it in your opening production of *Cosi fan tutte*. I hear Mozart is all the rage."

Groznyy groaned inside.

"Do you know the opera?" asked Bogus to keep the peace.

"No," answered Big Daddy.

Groznyy wondered when the oilman would ask for his name in lights.

Bogus was in another world. He advised Groznyy how to turn the invitation and the opportunity it offered to create an artistic shrine for Holly. He was still thinking about how she might reward him.

Whom did he dislike more, the president with the verbal diarrhea or the self-serving provost? Eddie Walker, chair of performing arts at BCU, knew where he stood. Like others, Walker detested Bogus's snooty style.

"Anything wrong?" Revisor asked haughtily after he had outlined the president's requirements for *Cosi*.

"A lot," said Walker. "We may be a department of performing arts but we're not large: no orchestra, no conductor, and no singers. What we have are actors and dancers whom this show will not be using."

"Improvise. Big Daddy has made sure that you have a splendid renovated theater."

"Not exactly. It's been turned into a lecture auditorium for our esteemed president to make speeches before a captive audience. It's not a space where drama can be played, far less a space that's accessible for disabled people."

Bogus glared at him, not risking any hostages to fortune over Groznyy's known dislike of disabled people. "Put on the show or face the consequences."

Eddie Walker drew breath. On second thoughts, he was ready to take part himself and play Don Alfonso, the dry old cynical bachelor who sets the plot of *Cosi fan tutte* spinning. He would talk through the role and sing a note here and there. As to the conductor, Walker had heard that Milhous College had a Japanese American wunderkind, an aspiring maestro ready to try anything to get noticed.

Hermione had heard of this rising Japanese American conductor when they had both been students at Milhous College. Now they were introduced for the first time—he with a flurry of Japanese names. He said simply, "Call me Goro. It's easier. It's the name my manager wants me to use. Just Goro."

Surely, thought Eddie, there must also be a tenor among students at Milhous College who could sing the leading man, Ferrando? Then Eddie himself could always co-opt high school seniors for the offstage military chorus and any onstage silent servants. It might just work.

Because he had heard Holly perform one of Despina's arias at the fundraiser after the fire, Eddie agreed with Bogus that she, with her unerring ability to adapt her voice, could get through any female role and promoted her to the flirtatious sister, Dorabella. Holly agreed, provided Hermione played piano for rehearsals.

Like everyone who heard her play, Holly was impressed by Hermione's pianistic dexterity. Mordred Stickleman's wife, Pauline, told her, "My dear, the way she tickles the ivories, it gives me goose bumps."

Holly thought, "There's way more to it. She can color the notes and it's always the right color. She senses the meaning of every phrase."

At the first cast meeting, Eddie Walker explained the opera.

"*Cosi fan tutte* is usually translated as 'So Do All Women.' I would call it 'Everyone Pretends.' *Cosi* is an insightful drama about female constancy. But it's the men who get the worst of it.

"In Naples two soldiers bet an old bachelor friend on the faithfulness of their fiancées. The young blades pretend to leave on duty with their regiment. But they return dressed as Albanians and start to woo the young women. Encouraged by their maid, Despina, who is being paid by the cynical bachelor Don Alfonso, each woman falls for the charms of the wrong suitor. So each soldier has the other's girlfriend—offstage.

"Don't you hate it when that happens?" he added as a New York aside.

"Don't they recognize their own boyfriends?" asked Holly.

"Well, the soldiers are dressed as Muslims," said Hermione.

"What is there to say about any opera plot?" Groznyy observed when he heard about the discussion. "The tenor and the soprano want to make love and the baritone wants to stop them. What else is there?"

However, there was more to all this. The fresh component in the Oryx Party at BCU was another of Ace Ferrari's nephews. This was Darius Esen, recently arrived and with a thought-through backstory.

"You sang in Turkish opera. I know it's different," said the dean of psychology. "But it's opera. We must find a way to bring your skills to distract the ladies, especially Holly Wood Groznyy."

In addition, the dean recommended that sub treasurer Darko Delizio should become tenor hero Ferrando opposite Roubles as Fiordiligi.

And everyone liked Roubles, the soprano whose father was bankrolling the show. Hermione could see why her father adored her for her generous manner and outsize natural gifts. But Hermione could also guess why Juilliard had turned her down: true dramatic coloratura, possibly—

but how incomplete. Yes, she had steely high notes and a prodigious chest register. But in performance for Roubles near enough was good enough. That was her limit.

As for who could play Despina, the manipulative maid, there was a sprightly African American soprano, trustee Veronica Veneer's daughter, Pretty. Eddie Walker had once heard Pretty sing "He's Got the Whole World in His Hands" at a student party. It had been memorable not least because Groznyy, who did not know it was a spiritual, thought that the song was about him. Eddie thought Pretty could sing the part of the calculating servant, mistress of disguises. Pretty had a small but penetrating soprano voice that could twinkle merrily above the stave.

Eddie wanted to distance himself from the success or failure of the show. So he decided on a guest director: he would entice the chair of chemistry back into his former off-Broadway career.

What Hermione told Holly about Don Fatale was, "He never wanted anyone outside show business to know his origins. He wanted to be taken as part of Broadway aristocracy—never complimented for his rise over difficult hurdles. No one can fill an ordinary stage with such color and light, fluid movement and exciting effects—and all by the simplest means."

Holly was intrigued. At first she hardly noticed him, this small, self-contained African American. He was just someone you would never notice in a diner or remember on a train. Then she remembered that she had seen him before and where. It was in Dr Chicago's clinic. He had played a trick on her insecurity and programmed her to get Modest into trouble. When he caught her gaze in the rehearsal room, Don Fatale looked back with flinty silence. But when he opened his mouth to call the rehearsal to order, he made Holly and everyone else feel they were the sole objects of his attention. He did this simply by asking questions and responding with a warm smile that lit up the room.

To her surprise, Holly knew they were on the same wavelength when he asked Hermione to play, first gently, then friskily, the melody to "Rahadlakum," the suggestive praise of Turkish delight from *Kismet*. When they started working on it together, Holly and Don Fatale exchanged the spoken pleasantries between Lalume and the Wazir's other wives about lip service to virtue. It ended with the tart remark about virtue being its own reward. The enticing lyrics of the song rippled across the rehearsal room like a pretend orgasm, suggesting the endless rapture that awaited Arabian lords from their ladies.

Just before the final few phrases, they were surprised to hear an offstage baritone singing the words with a glorious rock-hard cantabile. Only her sure technique sustained Holly to the final note.

He stood perfectly framed in the open doorway. To Holly, he was physical perfection. She did not know what height he was, only that he had toned biceps and broad shoulders, tapering to a trim waist. When he strode through the door, offering to shake hands with singer and pianist, he did so with compelling purpose. Then Holly realized that Don Fatale must have planned it all this way. He said, "This is Darius Esen, our Guglielmo."

"I'm from Turkey," Darius said. "I'm doing post-doctorate research in engineering."

When he spoke Holly melted further.

"Haven't you noticed his face, his eyes—what flashing bed-room eyes—his perfect, sculpted body?" Holly's friend Carmine asked her after she had seen them in rehearsal together.

Holly had noticed but said nothing.

"You could shoot a movie set anywhere around the Mediterranean. And as Latin lover or Arab steed, Darius would look perfect—and he would also stand out."

The master puppeteers inside and outside the opera production knew what they were doing.

"It's the American way, all right: forge an identity. When you have used it, change your name and reinvent yourself. Americans have been doing it ever since the first settlers arrived," said Ace Ferrari to Don Fatale.

Darius Esen knew that the chair of chemistry could provide materiel assistance to some supposed great cause. But it took Darius time to work out what a dean of psychology had to offer instead of, for example, a professor of military studies. Little by little, he had begun to understand. Psychology was a natural academic partner of military studies, providing the whys and wherefores to assist the how-tos of destruction. Except that the dean would rather postpone than act.

Despite his mission and his reverting to Islam, Fatale had not left his old western showbiz romanticism completely behind. He thought the dean was mistaken in getting Darius to know Holly.

"Don't you think you're playing with fire by throwing these two at one another?" he asked the dean.

"No," said Ferrari.

"How can you be sure? There's always the danger that their relationship will get the Oryx Party more noticed."

"Here are two people who think they're going to have an idyllic future together. However, they don't understand that they will make one another miserable. It will work for us. You'll see."

Grishka. The last person Cesare Groznyy ever wanted to see again—besides the disappeared princess—was his younger brother. He had not seen or heard of him for decades. It was not that he had forgotten him. He had suppressed any lingering memories of him. That was a deliberate part of his re-invention of himself as Groznyy, Man of Destiny. After all, Groznyy's true past was not known, certainly not in any detail, allowing yet more invention when convenient. And this let both the Groznyy Gang and the Opposition Party fill in the gaps with their own assumptions. But Cesare Groznyy's discarded brother re-emerging from the failed Soviet Union might put paid to all that.

First came a telephone message scrawled by secretary Bee Flute on pink notepaper. It simply said, "I am back from the dead and ready to spend, spend, and spend Russian style."

Cesare Groznyy would never admit to gulping. He had no feeling for his long-lost brother beyond irritation. Then a phone call came through. He took it. He simply did not recognize the middle-aged man's voice with such good English, albeit in a heavily coated Russian accent.

"Hi, Nemo, it's Grishka. I got into Manhattan today. We arrived in Kennedy behind schedule. The traffic into Manhattan was awesome—almost as heavy as in Moskva."

Groznyy kept a tight grip on himself. "Where are you?"

"Waldorf Astoria, Park Avenue."

Groznyy was still thinking.

"Nemo, bro, let's meet tomorrow night. Do you know a select restaurant where we can meet and catch up as we dine?"

Indeed, Groznyy did know such a place, somewhere discreet with enough tawdry glitz to impress his backwoods "bro." And it had a Russian name.

Groznyy went to the restaurant with bad grace with his new wife, Larry Dawdler, and two untrustworthy trustees in tow. He had coached them to present the modest nouvelle cuisine of the Golden Cockerel to his backwoods relative as Manhattan high style. But when they arrived in the lobby it was Groznyy who was taken by surprise. Bernardo and another waiter were folding expensive furs.

"It's like a furriers' convention," said Bernardo.

It looked as if Grishka had taken over the entire restaurant. The dining room had been rearranged for an elaborate cocktail party with the tables set against the walls. The room seemed full of Russian expatriates and their companions. Some were Russian immigrants living in New York. Some of the girls were Polish. Every shake of the ladies' coiffured tresses showed off cascades of diamonds on ears, necks, and décolleté bosoms.

Larry Dawdler kept abreast of international news by reading the *Wall Street Journal*. He had explained Russia's new economics to Holly Wood and trustee Veronica Veneer as they traveled into the city together.

"Since the fall of the Berlin Wall, Russia has been going through big changes. Russia is moving faster economically and socially than many countries. There are some parallels between the Russia of Ivan the Terrible and the Russia of today. We are about to meet the product of one of them.

"In 1990 Russian leader Boris Yeltsin, faced with national bankruptcy, sold off Russia's oil and gas companies and other assets to businesses created and run by former communist apparatchiks. The recent rise in energy prices across the world has led to Russia, the world's biggest oil and gas exporter, being overwhelmed with petrodollars on a scale that could never have been imagined. The downside is that the Russian government has had to watch this wealth pour into the grasping hands of the new oligarchs who bought the concessions when Russia faced bankruptcy."

As they entered the reorganized dining room, Larry explained to Holly and Veronica, "The new Russian rich don't try and hide their wealth. They've taken on the style and swagger we used to associate with Arab oil sheiks. Nothing is too gilded, nothing too covered with jewels for the new breed of Russian oligarchs. It don't mean a thing if it don't have that bling."

Veronica was making mental notes, playing with the

words she heard from Larry for future use in her catalog of phony signatures. She particularly liked "Ollie Garch" and "Cal Ashnikov."

Music came from the gallery. Grishka had hired a string quartet. Hermione, who helped serve the canapés, recognized the scherzo trio of Beethoven's second opus 59 quartet. She told Benny it was dedicated to Count Razumovsky, Russian ambassador in Vienna. "Do you think Grishka Groznyy is giving us a hint?"

Three burly men with shaved heads and wearing expensive dark suits stood brooding as they watched guests mill around their boss. They kept their shades on. The bodyguards were sporting the sort of glitzy watches seen on Hollywood A-list stars in glossy magazines. Grishka introduced the bodyguards as his "associates." He told Larry that their names were Gryaznoy, Bomelius, and Sobakin. He added that Bomelius was a Dutch name and that, in Russian, "Sobakin" meant "dog"—as if this were as much as his guests needed to know. It was not what the heavy named Sobakin wanted to hear.

When the Groznyy brothers came face to face neither recognized the other. When they had last been together, they were both scrawny kids, Cesare in early adolescence, Grishka still a boy. Then the Second Great Patriotic War separated them. Now they were both middle-aged. They looked sated with the pleasures of both the flesh and the bottle. But Grishka looked more than prosperous. Was he just one of the new oligarchs? Or was he a Russian mobster on his way to the top of the heap? Cesare sensed that the latent menace from Grishka's heavies could be ratcheted up with a flick of his brother's eyelashes. This was someone who had served the Soviet army as an officer in Afghanistan. And, as a new oil oligarch, Grishka was already experienced in the capitalist world. It was clear he disdained anything inexpensive. Groznyy was consumed with envy. It seemed to churn in his bowels.

Worse, Grishka's sharp memory of things unfortunate could pierce the paper-thin façade of the quicksilver sophist Groznyy had become. Hermione had now had several chances to observe Cesare Groznyy and the way he operated. But she had never seen him made so uncomfortable, and by someone who was not his intellectual equal.

Groznyy had planned a well-worn script of self-presentation to show his upstart relation how successful he was as a living embodiment of the American Dream: how a penniless immigrant could arrive stateside and rise from rags to riches and become a big player in America. But Grishka could trump him. His script cut Cesare to the quick: Russian oligarch sets out to impress the whole wide world with his magnificence. Grishka was in charge and he enjoyed it. As he said, "There is rich, and there is super rich, and there is Russian rich."

Of course the two brothers did as their audience expected them to do—fall into one another's arms. Cesare liked to pride himself on his display of graciousness in his supposedly impromptu speech of reconciliation:

"Dearest friends and colleagues, you see here a happy reunited family after years—no, decades—of enforced separation by the terrors of war and the cruel disorder of communism. We are so happy. Words cannot express how much."

Benny quipped to Hermione, "It's like that song in *Oklahoma!* 'The corn is as high as an elephant's eye!'"

But the reunion was essentially a pseudo-event: an event taking place so that it could be reported. And reported it was to be. Indeed, Cesare Groznyy was outraged that Grishka had arranged a press conference. He recognized reporters Mickey Garnier and Steve Sharp from Norse Hoven. This deepened his unease.

Without saying so to one another, the two journalists liked to think of themselves as the Bob Woodward and Carl

Bernstein of Norse Hoven County whose exposure of academic rifling and fraud on a grandiose scale could make their names nationwide. Both were tousle-haired youngsters when they began, Garnier dark with darting eyes, Sharp fair-haired with a fulsome manner. They complemented one another in person and print.

It looked as if Mickey Garnier had gone over—defected—to the East, if only temporarily. Not content with being an impartial journalist, Garnier seemed to be making a good living as a temporary fixer, attending to the super-rich Grishka. As he dashed about, he made a more than plausible lackey. Garnier acted as if no task were too excessive, too ridiculous, or too degrading. Later, Groznyy parodied him: "You want a solid-gold cell phone? A jewel-encrusted saucepan for your grandmother? I'm your man."

But when Grishka spoke to the press that night, he added salt to Cesare's psychological wound of being outsmarted by his kid "bro."

"Nemo was a naughty little boy. He exasperated our mother, Elena Glinskaya, when she told him to do his math homework. Mama's wheedling got on his nerves. She used to say to him when he was wayward—as if to prove she was a good communist—'Lenin would never do that.'"

Grishka Groznyy made good copy. His English was as polished as that of any Russian diplomat. He was in his element. Out of his mouth tumbled more complaints about Cesare, the ingrate child.

"Nemo goaded mama. He threw a bowl of borscht across the room. Everything was spilt—the beetroot soup—and the bowl broke on the wall. This was too much for her. She left him alone for hours, hoping that he would reflect on his bad behavior. But no. Nemo threw a tantrum, bashing his toys about. He kicked mama's armchair so hard that he tore holes in it. Through his tears, it looked like the other chairs were moving away like a magnetic pulse in reverse."

Cesare was speechless. Grishka was only a toddler when this was meant to have happened. And how could Grishka know where all this existed—his nightmares? Had he spoken in his sleep? Had Holly told Grishka?

Grishka was more alert than Cesare and moved things along. "Sadly, in the 1930s, our mother disappeared in one of Stalin's purges. We think she died in a gulag."

This melancholy moment was enhanced by a violin solo from the musicians' gallery. Hermione had some sense of pitch. She guessed that the opening phrase alternated B minor with D flat major. The cadences sounded Russian. Hermione thought it might be by Rimsky-Korsakov. It was exquisite. Guests stopped to listen.

One of the heavies showed his overcrowded teeth as he almost snarled at Bernardo, "Serve champagne. Not look. No eye contact."

Bernardo did not know what to say. The bodyguard repeated the order: "Insist: do not look guests in eye when serve champagne."

"That's going to make topping up their glasses tricky," Hermione whispered to Benny.

"These people think they can do whatever they want. Probably because they can," Benny observed laconically.

Grishka now moved onto the conversational offensive. "How much did you pay for poor Nemo's tired tie?" he asked Holly.

Holly plucked a figure from thin air: "$500."

"You fool! In Moskva I know places where you could pay twice that."

Afterwards, no one could specify the moment when the atmosphere began to change. Larry made his excuses and left to be up early next day for a business trip. The journalists and the photographer also left. Then there was a gradual shift from stilted chitchat—punctuated by outrageous boasts by the Russians—to something more raucous as they downed Smirnoff vodka and revved up their boasting.

First came a banal assertion: "Moskva has huge traffic jams. We have more stretch limos than Broadway." Then Grishka had the nerve to tell Benny, "You could improve the décor of the restaurant, go up market, like one of New York's best hotels—marble and polished chrome—perhaps with a swimming pool on the roof."

Grishka and his cronies started to order more shots of vodka, proposing bawdy toasts, downing the shots, and shattering their glasses in the hearth below the ornamental fireplace. It was like a parody of an old Hollywood movie about roistering soldiers in the days of Pushkin or Tolstoy.

Cesare Groznyy was not going to be outdone. To keep up his image, he ordered a bottle of a rare brandy, a favorite of the other token trustee besides Veronica who was there. This was literary editor Fulton Carter. It cost $700. To get it, Benny had to go plodding himself to a classier restaurant farther up the block, nearer Third Avenue.

The Russian men started singing broken snatches of "America" from *West Side Story*, ruffling their girls' skirts in a parodic imitation of Anita and the Shark girls in their big dance number. Then the men riffled under the skirts while the Polish girls squealed with excitement.

Hermione sensed she was the object of the heavies' brutish attention.

"We show you who dog now. Down, bitch!"

With that, the heavy named Sobakin put his hands on her shoulders and thrust Hermione to her knees.

"Down lower, dog bitch."

Bomelius, another heavy, set a tray of canapés on her back. They expected her to crawl on all fours, staying level, as they dined off her back. Terrified, Hermione turned her eyes to Holly. Holly signaled helplessness. Groznyy set his face grimly. Hermione's fear deepened. She felt Groznyy was

71

appraising her. It seemed he wanted to throw away his social inhibitions and take part with the bullyboys undressing and taking her. Shock, fear, sexual foreboding—all flooded her body.

Unseen, chef Imelda let herself quietly out of the front door.

"We want topless service!" called the Russian men.

"They want topless service," repeated Grishka, not as a half-hearted apology but as a command.

The heavies echoed him: "Topless! Topless!" "*Ochin horosho!*" Gryaznoy began to drum his fingers on a side table. The molls guffawed. "Topless! Topless! We pay extra."

"In Russian language *Gryaznoy* means something dirty and servile," said Grishka to Hermione with a leer to increase the tension.

The cascade of bizarre Russian commands grew more insistent. The palpable fear of the shallow Manhattanites was more paralyzing.

"Topless now. Service us later! Russians coming! Russians coming!"

One unzipped his trousers. Hermione was afraid they would strip off her clothes and take her in front of everyone. No one would help. Her heart was pounding.

Just then, someone cracked an outsize umbrella loudly under a table heavy with idle crockery. The plates juddered. It was Benny back with the brandy and in full self-righteous mode. Imelda skulked behind him.

"I also like America," said Benny, "but I like it my way!"

With that, he brought the umbrella down from above the table again with all the feeble force he could muster. It landed on top of the crockery, which broke and scattered. The tottering crash brought the scene to abject silence. Benny raised the closed umbrella horizontal to the ground, pointing it around. Holly bent down to raise Hermione up. Benny's glare signaled that the party was over.

While he was settling the bill in the lobby, Grishka turned and said to Benny loudly enough for his brother to hear, "Like I said about Russian wealth, this is only the beginning of what you are in for."

Groznyy heaved a sigh of relief. No matter what he had put up with that night, at least it was over. Soon Grishka would be out of his hair.

At home later Holly was leafing through some magazines. The TV was on. The channel was playing *Gone with the Wind*. Groznyy heard Vivien Leigh as Scarlett O'Hara telling earth and sky that she would do whatever it took but she would never be hungry again. This speech, after Grishka's arrogance in the restaurant, crystallized Cesare's thoughts. He would do whatever was necessary to get richer than his half-assed brother.

The Russian tease party made Hermione review her situation in the cold light of day. She was not simply going to put the rowdy intimidation down to experience and continue her life as if nothing had happened. It was a turning point. In her fascination with Manhattan and the restaurant she had put off her studies and let things Groznyy take over her life. The jolt forced her to face the fact that, if she continued, she would never get to grad school. And she would be left empty inside with nothing in material terms. She would have to make a clean break with the Golden Cockerel and the Groznyy family.

Hermione barely knew her great-aunt. And shortly after she had moved into her aunt's house in New England, her aunt had moved into a care home. It was no surprise when her aunt died. Hermione felt slight sorrow but nothing more. The surprise came with the will in which her aunt had bequeathed her her own Plumfield—a house to do with what she wanted, as Aunt March had done for Jo in *Good Wives*. This gave Hermione an escape route, a sense of security, and a choice. Now she had a house and a base for a studio to teach piano.

Steve Sharp had never wanted to be a society reporter. However, his editor placed his story, "Groznyy Brothers' Reunion Defeats Time," on the society page of the weekend magazine of the *Norse Hoven Courier*.

It attracted interest in unexpected quarters.

It is central to communications theory that it is the context that defines the meaning of any message. And the people who were the "contexts" for Steve Sharp's story about Grishka in the Golden Cockerel had a hostile interest in all things Groznyy. One was the Opposition Party. Another was the Oryx Party.

A third receptive audience was the Norse Hoven and the Babel City police, who still had a mysterious death to resolve. They came to any new evidence with their private supposition that a death in Groznyy's house had been murder.

Detective Leo Guerra read Steve's story when McSweeny handed it to him.

"This may be the break we need. Groznyy's brother may be able to help us by giving us some background. But we have to move fast. As soon as Grishka Groznyy goes back to Moscow, we've lost our chance."

Guerra and another colleague took an interpreter with them to New York. But this was not necessary. Grishka's English was fluent. And he had his own score to settle with his brother. When Guerra met him in the Waldorf Astoria, he was more than eager to cooperate. Guerra handed Grishka a photo of the victim.

"We never met. But, good looking."

Then Guerra showed him photos of the Groznyy family together: father, mother, and son.

"How can I help?"

Guerra explained that his colleague had a special field: psychological profiles. The profiler said, "In no way are you implicated in what happened with the fire or afterwards. All we ask of you is to think hard about when you and Cesare were kids together—before you got separated in World War II. Can you tell us about Cesare's early years?"

Indeed, he could. Grishka was so smooth it was almost as if he had prepared his speech.

"Back in Irkutsk in the 1930s our dwindling family's rivalry over lost estates evaporated in Stalin's collectivization of agriculture. I was too young to remember. But people told me later. My dear brother, Nemo, was forced to witness horrifying things. He saw and heard physical and verbal abuse on a regular basis. It was disturbing. It seemed Nemo might be showing telltale signs of future madness. Incapable of striking back at state tormentors, he took out his frustrations on pet animals. He tortured them in the fantasy that he was inflicting pain on men who had terrorized our people.

"Fortunately, all this is in the past," Grishka concluded knowingly to a deafening silence from the police officers.

The interview ended with a simple question.

"Do the letters KAZ have any significance? They were on what was left of a car registration plate found in the embers of the fire."

Grishka did not think long. He said, "KAZ could be the first letters of Kazan—a strategic city in Ivan IV's campaign in the East."

"Torture, fantasy, pain," Leo Guerra observed to his profiler colleague on the journey back to New England. "And this is the way he remains with his colleagues—and his nearest and dearest."

Groznyy now concentrated on plans for a secret accumulation of wealth to exceed his oligarch brother. As he grew bolder, Groznyy saw his salary grow to a cool half million dollars while securing his extras. These went beyond what people called "perks" into real perquisites: eventual ownership of the new presidential seaside house outright after he retired from the university and permanent ownership of the art treasures he bought through the university.

The trustees were letting their giant ape out of the jungle. And he was not going to be captured, felled, and killed by the forces of public opinion. He was the monster who ensnared all he surveyed, including the trophy wife whom all men desired. There was no stealthier capitalist predator than Cesare Groznyy.

Groznyy thought he was safe. It did not occur to him that his lavish lifestyle would excite aggrieved envy among his court and beyond. He might just as well have been an advertising plant of Corporate America, set down in small-town suburbia with a supply of Arabian Nights riches. These made his incredulous neighbors want as many consumer durables, as much valuable art for their own collections, as Groznyy had. Of course, what he had was beyond any realistic expectations of his neighbors. They could not afford them, but then how could he? There was only one way their resentment could express itself. That was in a widespread conclusion: "There's something rotten here! There must be corruption!"

While the police were trying to assess the fragments of hearsay and evidence against Groznyy, and while Groznyy was trying to take stock of Grishka's reappearance, the cast of *Cosi* was also reviewing its interpretations.

Producer Eddie, director Don, and conductor Goro wanted the cast to focus on the finale of *Cosi* and why it was what it was.

"The guys and dolls have put one another on pedestals," began Don. "When we meet them—first the guys and then

76

the dolls—they are singing exaggerated praises about the physical perfection of their loves."

"But love is different from adulation," added Goro. "Men and women revere gods. But it is only living and imperfect human beings who can be loved. When men revere women, they cannot love them."

"The four lovers sign a marriage contract—the two fiancées with their supposed new love interests," said Eddie. "The men think it's a bittersweet joke and they'll split their sides laughing."

"So the women are only there to be made fun of?" asked Holly.

"When men discover that women are not goddesses, their love can turn to hate. It's a sort of self-loathing," explained Don.

Stage soldier lovers Darius and Darko felt distinctly uncomfortable at this insight. They were relieved that the others were too absorbed in the argument to notice them.

"However," concluded Eddie, "the wedding ceremony is interrupted by the offstage sound of a march signaling the return of the original soldier lovers. Pretending consternation, the false Albanian husbands hide. Then they return—very confident—as their former Italian selves. They expose the charade, prompting accusations, indignation, and, finally, pardon. The boyfriends are reconciled to their errant fiancées. Or are they?"

"Is this believable?" asked Holly.

"Nowadays audiences find deeper meanings in the plot," answered Eddie.

Hermione understood Holly's feminist stance but she delved deeper. "In the nineteenth century *Cosi* almost disappeared. People thought it was either too silly or too risqué—or both. Its success now comes from recordings. When the opera exists in sound only, the psychological insights take over."

Don had thought long and hard about what the show would look like. He decided to take a chance. Instead of pretty eighteenth-century costumes, he decided they must perform in modern dress with the soldiers in combat fatigues to emphasize contemporary parallels. This time it was Dean Ace Ferrari who thought his partner was taking a risk. He asked, "Won't this expose us?"

"It's a risk worth taking," came Don's answer. "After all, they couldn't work out the meaning of 'KAZ.'"

To the cast all he said was, "The problem in staging *Cosi* is how to make the audience aware that serious issues are at stake under the romcom plot—without upsetting the entertainment. What we need is an enticing image to conjure up the inner eroticism of the opera while doing justice to the locale—Naples cradled by the volcano, Vesuvius."

Both Holly and Hermione knew where to look. Next day they showed him one of Modest's art books and a reproduction of a painting by contemporary artist Tom Wesselmann: *Big Brown Nude*. Don was transfixed.

In the painting an African American woman lay asleep. She leant to the left. Her left breast protruded with erect nipple, making a hillock among the landscape mounds of bedlinen, dark pink satin duvet, and turquoise pillows. Eddie Walker told them there was a whole series of Tom Wesselmann's nudes, all openly erotic with languorous mouths, swelling breasts and vaginas, accompanied by romantic paraphernalia—flowers and bottles of perfumes.

That was it. Don knew what to do. He said, "When the soldiers return as Muslims we shall see them enter Vesuvius and enter the women."

Cast and crew may have been absorbed in *Cosi*. The Opposition Party was still simmering with resentment of Groznyy but doing nothing effective. But in the Oryx Party the dean and the chair were keeping their nephews on side.

"Islam has never been a creed of violence but a creed of

peace and respect," Ferrari told them. "Yet for centuries it's been linked to a struggle between the western nations and the Muslim East."

Fatale took up his argument: "All this must come to a head with our campaign against the oppressive policies of Israel."

Darko Delizio asked, "Do we meet force with more violence?"

"Well," replied the dean. "If you are saying that terrible crimes have been committed in the name of Islam—that is true. Terrible crimes have also been committed in the name of Christianity. Extremists—Muslims and Christians—both have tortured and even massacred millions of people. They have destroyed civilizations that they—in their arrogance—deemed ungodly.

"Here's the thing. The Cold War was wonderful for lazy political thinkers because it eliminated the inconvenience of thought. It was simple: US good, USSR bad. And, for leaders of the USSR: vice versa."

"Now, with the end of the Cold War and the end of the Soviet Union," said Fatale, "the map of Europe is different."

It was back to the dean.

"But the end of the Cold War is to our advantage—provided we don't play by their rules," insisted Ferrari. "Keep up the good work and we shall all be together in paradise. Every suicide is a martyr. Every successful detonation is a publicity victory in the war of the worlds.

"Revolutions burst when people with pent-up grievances rise against their oppressors—just like the American revolutionaries and the civil rights activists did. Revolutions turn violent when the people in charge are ready to kill to retain power. The people who are protesting are ready to give their lives in the cause of freedom."

The "nephews" thought that their "uncles" were just talking the talk.

After the young blades had left a Jeep drew up outside the dean's house. Alumnae chief Carpenter Cain got out and pulled a heavy rucksack from the back seat. He went into the house by the kitchen door. He flung the rucksack on the kitchen table.

The dean said, "Thank you, Amir."

Cain did not point out that his Arabic name was Achmed, not Amir. He simply said, "That's it for this month."

Ace Ferrari said nothing. He unzipped the rucksack and pulled out bundles of used dollar notes of mixed denominations.

Cain left as discreetly as anyone in a Jeep in a suburb could.

During rehearsals for *Cosi*, Holly found herself carried away by Mozart's music that made the artificial situation psychologically plausible. Don alerted her to the historical backdrop to the opera—how Ottoman Turks had advanced on southeast Europe, and how they were sometimes near the gates of Vienna.

"They were always about in the southern Mediterranean," he said.

This set Holly thinking. If her husband was this modern petty Ivan the Terrible, was he confronting a modern mini Asian horde of political extremists? Holly recalled how disturbed Modest had been by his discovery of some bomb-making plan in Science Park. He had found the plan of a tourist plane with the fuel tank highlighted in red. Holly could not help thinking that her Ivan the Terrible might do better to cast his eyes to the East rather than being so absorbed in the petty intrigues of university politics.

Then there was this handsome stranger who said he was Turkish. He told her that he and Mukhtar, Modest's old friend who had not been forgotten by Holly or Hermione, were cousins and also more nephews of the dean. Holly did not know if it was true. She knew she was falling for Darius.

Darius blended in everywhere—in rehearsals and in offstage chitchat with the cast. He could make inconsequential jokes about "my poor English, *come il mio povero italiano goffo.*" Everyone laughed along with him. And when he made a mistake, such as a mis-sung word, he was self-deprecating with such sure throwaway delivery that he could have charmed the birds off the trees. This songbird, too.

When he walked Holly home, he delayed saying good night. His caresses, his mouth on her cheek, her neck, and her breasts filled Holly with ecstasy she had never known. She succumbed next afternoon. She blushed at the very idea of her body betraying her love for Modest, maddening her with pleasure, making her cry out. Modest's affection was gentle and lacking desperate passion. This was different.

In the languorous aftermath of their first lovemaking, Holly asked Darius, "Kiss me so hard that my blood rushes to my head."

"Yes, angel. Of all treasures on offer, I chose the best."

No matter how head-over-heels she was, Holly had enough showbiz experience to know how actors sometimes fell in love with their drama partners. They were living the stage illusion of their characters falling in love. There were backstage stories about Bette Davis and Gary Merrill, and Laurence Olivier and Vivien Leigh, falling in love when they were playing lovers and subsequently living unhappy marriages. But Holly let Darius continue. Darius's words of love, his tender but insistent foreplay were so sweet. For minutes on end it was as if they were one person. And that was before he entered her. Holly had never had such luxurious orgasms.

Holly could escape the sexual aridity and psychological fens of her marriage to Groznyy with this love affair. Darius was not in awe of her, her status, her talent, or her husband.

There was no break between his performance onstage and his performance off. Holly was too satisfied physically and emotionally to think this seamlessness might be a problem and also a clue.

Until he met Holly, Darius had only known the mechanics of sex, nothing of the emotional realities of love. With his all-but-forgotten absent wife and his many one-night stands, sex had been nothing more than sharp ejaculation, followed by loathing. Afterwards, he and his partners had just wanted to get away from one another—and fast. Now Darius understood that romantic joy came in a glowing expansion after climax. After sex, he and Holly basked in the illusion that their two souls were fused like one.

But there was a persistent problem. When they could spend the night together, after they had made love and Holly went to sleep, she would wake and see him moving about. He made furtive phone calls, some long-distance. She mentioned it. Darius thought too much of Holly to pretend she had got it wrong. He put his index finger up to his lips and said, "Angel, don't try and work out the dark art of politics."

As she watched the magnetic pull between Holly and Darius, Hermione grew uneasy. Yes, Darius was drop-dead gorgeous, sure enough. But she saw more. His face—and Darko's face, too—had such beckoning, almost pleading, eyes. But they had almost feral expressions as well. And she could not forget Darius's diatribe against America and Israel in his little talk at Milhous College not so long ago.

In rehearsal Darius's seamless performance unnerved her. She wondered if she was being jealous of Holly because Modest had left her for Holly and because Holly was the center of attention. But it was not jealousy. An inner voice was warning her that Holly was being played upon.

One evening, Hermione sat on the BCU library steps near

St. Basil's Fountain, watching professors and students come and go. The flow of human traffic gave her perspective as she heard snatches of conversations.

Behind her Don Fatale was speaking to Darius Esen.

"The professors go on and on about irony, dramatic irony, political irony, and the rest. But they never mention the supreme irony of themselves as pawns of the American state or of Jews becoming like the Nazis who oppressed Jews in the 1930s and then killed them in the 1940s."

Don and Darius had not noticed Hermione. Don continued.

"Now Jews in Israel use the same means against the Palestinians, first marginalizing them and then putting them in what are concentration camps in all but name. And the American people support all this."

Then Don cracked a joke. But was it to lighten the tone?

"What do you call a dead American?" he asked Darius.

Back came the smart-ass answer: "A good start."

After a moment, Darius spoke again. "Aren't we going too far in the production with all this emphasis on a woman's body as a landscape to be penetrated by occupying troops with us as Muslim soldiers in army fatigues? Aren't you in danger of pressing American buttons too hard?"

"I don't think so. We're engaged in a war in pieces."

This jolted Hermione. Someone was indeed playing games with them.

No one noticed Bogus Revisor walking nearby. He had been instinctively jealous of Darius being close to Holly. Now he remembered that he had seen and heard him before when Darius had given a diatribe against America and Israel under the guise of a lecture at Milhous College perhaps a year ago. This recollection deepened his surly resentment.

In fact, Darius was discovering that Mozart's music and the experience of positive collaboration among everyone at rehearsals to make their interpretation of the opera effective onstage was softening his original harsh political view of America.

Although he gave nothing away, under his professionalism and charm, director Don Fatale was, perhaps, the person most changed by rehearsing *Cosi fan tutte*. The overriding humanity of Mozart and da Ponte and their ability to present the vivacious outer personalities alongside the inner turmoil and conflicts of the four lovers gave everyone involved the perspective that there should always be room for another point of view. And the goodness of humanity was in such sharp contrast with the one-sided, hard-driven mission of the double-dealing, puritanical dean. A theater animal to his fingertips, Don Fatale was bound to be swayed by Mozart's insights. It was as if, in Don's mind, humanity was creeping and changing his priorities away from blinkered vengeance to humanity and tolerance. What the dean wanted was hateful and wrong. There was no escaping that. True Islam was not about that.

Later in rehearsal, the singers found the ending for *Cosi* unsatisfactory.

"How could the girls go back to their original lovers who have set them up?" asked Don.

"But how could they stay with the new lovers, who have tricked them?" added Eddie. "Both sets of lovers are the same men."

Conductor Goro asked, "Don't you think the guys are dupes just as much as the dolls? The real officers pretend to go to war. When they return, they play this hoax. They're in Muslim costumes. It's important for them to stay within the characters of their aliases. But their male egos get the better of them. They can't resist the sexual urge to score."

Hermione noticed that Darius colored and Darko winced.

Don said, "Anyway, it's a letdown when the four lovers

simply say they will learn from experience and go back to their original partners."

There was a stir. Cesare Groznyy had arrived with his coterie, including the high and mighty young treasurer. No one said anything. The snatch of conversation he had overheard gave Groznyy his cue.

"And so?" he asked. "Since the last words of the opera are ambiguous, why not have the men called away to a real war?"

"That's true," said Don, surprised to find he agreed with Groznyy about anything. "We could have a brief reprise of the offstage chorus about war being beautiful. Then an officer comes in. Silently, he hands the soldiers new marching orders. The four lovers read the papers ordering the two officers to rejoin their regiments for a real war with growing frustration."

Groznyy had made the decision for them. They knew what Eddie would say. And he did: "Don't you hate it when that happens?"

"So," said Hermione, "now love has to face the test of a real separation. This makes their discomfort more bitter."

On the first night, Hermione watched from the wings. She had all sorts of ideas about *Cosi*: that it was romantic, mildly amusing, and always ironic. But until then she had never thought it was sinister. At the close of the famous trio, the stage lighting darkened with the rippling orchestral music. Now everything moved from the external and artificial to the interior and claustrophobic.

The set was minimal, with just a few chairs in front of a backdrop of the Bay of Naples cradled by the volcano Vesuvius. As the stage darkened, by a trick of lighting and one diaphanous drop cloth in front of the other, Vesuvius became an outsize Tom Wesselmann-type reclining nude ready for the men's brazen exploitation of women. One part of a conversation she had heard earlier in rehearsal came back to Hermione in a sharp burst: "a woman's body as a landscape to be penetrated by occupying troops."

Hermione felt more uneasy than ever before. For, in this production, two Arab men—or were they Pakistani, or Palestinian, or Turkish?—had made a show of being assimilated into American society. Yet the part of the opera where the Christian soldiers are disguised seemed to liberate them. The false selves of Darko and Darius as Albanians revealed their inner characters as Middle Easterners—make-believe, exotic, manipulative. They were "blending in." And behind them were master puppeteers, the dean and the chair.

In the front row, all Big Daddy had eyes and ears for was his darling daughter. And onstage Roubles was like a force of nature, a Niagara Falls of a dramatic soprano from whom Holly learned the importance of spontaneity. Holly could not help wondering if some promoter would tempt Roubles into roles beyond her range and then find someone else in five years' time.

Moments after the lights dimmed, Groznyy slid into sleep. During the applause at the end of the first half, he turned to Lorraine Boe sitting beside him and said with no sense of irony, "I have, in my time, attended all the great operas. None of them tells us anything. Besides, they prevent me from talking."

There was a snort of derision from behind. Groznyy turned round but his glare was useless. It was his brother, Grishka, who said as he chewed gum, "Hi, bro! Great show. Not as good as Bolshoi, though."

Grishka stopped chewing, took the gum out of his mouth, and stuck it on the top rim of Cesare's seat.

Fortunately looks could not kill.

As people milled around the lobby during intermission, Mordred Stickleman failed with his putdowns of Holly.

"The production doesn't work," he said. "You can lead a whore to culture but you can't make her think."

However, literary critic and BCU trustee Fulton Carter said to Don Fatale, "Absolutely brilliant!"

Stickleman tried again. Supping water from the fountain in a paper cup, he said, "This water tastes like shit!"

"I've never tasted shit myself, so I don't know," Grishka said.

Grishka did not know Mozart or *Cosi*. But he knew Tolstoy and *War and Peace*. And he knew when an artist was using silly girls and their predatory fiancés as metaphors for society unravelling.

In the second half, things became even more uneasy onstage and backstage. Accomplished pro that she was, Holly could sparkle through Dorabella's aria about love being a little thief. But inside she felt uncomfortable because words and music told her more keenly than ever that she was being played with.

Just before he was to sing "Tradito, schernito," leading to the aria about betrayal, tenor Darko Delizio scoured the audience. When he saw a former Russian officer sitting in the second row, he thought he would jump out of his skin. But had the Russian man recognized him?

Hermione noticed something that escaped everyone else but Grishka, Darius, and Darko. They looked at one another and looked hard. Darko quickly looked down. Grishka held his gaze. On one side the look was bleak. On the other it was dread—terror of the past and fear of the future.

The singer-soldiers' real-life alarm deepened their onstage reaction to the unwelcome news that their musical characters, Ferrando and Guglielmo, were being called up to fight in a real war. It aroused in agents Darko and Darius reactions and emotions they had learnt to suppress—their forlorn experience as freedom fighters on the plains of Afghanistan. Their trembling at the prospect of being exposed was real enough. They were shaking.

Afterwards, Groznyy arrived at the reception with his court. There were those members of the Groznyy Gang deemed the "beautiful people"—some trustees, his pets for the night, and his infuriating brother.

Everyone waited for the star: Holly Wood in all her glory. This was not what Stickleman and the Opposition Party wanted to see—especially Groznyy basking in the aura of his charming wife.

"It's a fake through and through," began Stickleman to his own wife in a voice penetrating enough to carry across the room. "A plot as unreal as anything in Jane Austen, the silly novelist with the always-repeated second chance in love. And this is not BCU. Imported conductor, director, and orchestra! The show is just a vanity display for Groznyy, his wife, and for Big Daddy and his precious daughter."

Stickleman's wife, Pauline, had been moved by the opera but, out of loyalty to her husband, did not want to admit it. So she asked Don Fatale, "How do we all get like people in the opera—everyone pretending?"

"It's because we live by illusions. And our illusions about sex and love, and consumption and wealth, serve those in power. Men have power over women. Rich men have power over poor men. To keep going, this system requires fantasies about political leaders, about the beautiful people, about the benefits of capitalism, and sex. In the end, these fantasies don't fulfil us. They make us unhappy. But, without them, our political leaders and the gnomes of Corporate America would lose control. And they will not give up power."

Stickleman did not want to admit that the show had been a success, mostly because of Mozart's music, lovely and disturbing, and because of its undercurrents—the very ideas the guests were talking about at the reception.

Stickleman and his allies had planned to send up Holly to make Groznyy even more ridiculous. Stickleman leant across the lobby piano and tried to croon grotesquely, "When roses are red, they're ready for plucking. When Holly's in bloom, she's ready for—"

Holly moved forward, all smiles. One of the Opposition Party whom she did not know—and most cowardly, she thought—pushed his ten-year-old daughter forward to do something he did not have the guts to do himself. The little girl presented Holly with a bouquet of root vegetables from her father's yard: a marrow, zucchini, and soiled carrots still with some tendrils of dirty green shoots.

Groznyy said nothing. Grishka decided to steady Holly.

"If this is the worst thing that happens to me, I can put up with it," she thought. Holly did not want to admit it but she had learnt from Groznyy's manipulation of words. Aloud, she said, "If only you knew," then, correcting herself, she continued with, "If only you knew how much pleasure your vegetables give. I shall think of you every time I smell them. What courage your little girl has!"

She smelled the vegetables. Grishka took the bouquet with its barbed intentions from her. He passed it to the reluctant hands of Bogus Revisor, first caressing his cheek with it so that a stray nettle stung him.

This time, when Eddie Walker spoke his tagline to Stickleman, it was a putdown: "Don't you hate it when that happens?"

It was clear that the reception was going to be labored. The two Arab stallions were anxious and their nervousness spread. Groznyy and Holly thought that the palpable tension was generated by the intense feelings of the Opposition Party. But the tension between Grishka and the two pretend lovers was of a different order. The only outsider who guessed what it was about was Ace Ferrari. He was too much a charmer to show it. But the frisson he noticed between Grishka, Darko, and Darius jolted him.

As the party continued, each man in the discordant trio—Darko, Darius, and Grishka—put on a false smile and allowed other guests to lead the conversation. Each time Grishka moved from one little group to another to face his former adversaries close up, Darius and Darko edged away.

When they heard trustee Veronica Veneer in a nearby group repeat a stale joke on the lines of, "If life is supposed to be a bowl of cherries, what am I doing with the pits?" that final word, "pits," hit them hard.

For Grishka, Darius, and Darko that tiny word sent them back into the pits of Afghanistan. That had been the setting for their interdependent roles in the 1980s as interrogator, prisoner, and interpreter in the Russian War.

As she saw her husband move around the assembly with a kind word for this person, a scolding look to another, and smiles to others, not to mention ogling Hermione, Holly had a tugging sensation that Groznyy was appraising young women as if he were preparing a list of candidates for future wives.

Hermione took a risk to calm things down. She played the intro to the famous *Cosi* trio, "Soave sia il vento," when Don Alfonso and the sisters sing for prosperous seas for the supposedly departing lovers. This tempted Holly, Eddie, and Roubles to reprise the trio. The sinuous beauty of the melody and the women's slinky performances in this farewell to innocence broke the tension, as did the alcohol.

Don Fatale slipped away unnoticed. He needed time to think. He knew it would not be easy to get out of the pernicious oyster shell of the Oryx Party. He was going to have to choose his time and the means skillfully.

COURTS OF TRIUMPHANT LIES

Next day when Groznyy went to his office, there he was again: Grishka, chatting amicably to Bee Flute in the outer office, delighting her with an elementary lesson in Russian. *"Kak dela?" "Kak doma?" "Kak mama?"*

Bee giggled. "Oh, Dr. G., your brother, he's got real charisma."

To Cesare Groznyy, it was sickening. Besides, the mirror in the hall told him every day that no one had more charisma than he did.

Before Groznyy could extricate himself, Grishka said, "Big bro, I've come to help you. And, boy, do you need it. You're in trouble here and now."

The last thing Groznyy wanted was his best-forgotten brother's advice on how to handle the Opposition Party. But when Grishka mentioned Franklin Miller, Groznyy took him into his office.

As they went in, Grishka patted the small Picasso sculpted pot in the shape of an exotic cubist bird as if it were his personal pet. Without asking, he went into Groznyy's private toilet in a half-hidden cubicle cut into the dark paneling. This tiny gesture of control angered Groznyy and set his mind against listening to what Grishka had to say.

"You have two men here in Babel City," Grishka began. "Both have imagined names.

"One has studied in England and the United States. He calls himself Darko Delizio but he has other names. Darko Delizio wasn't his name when he first hit our radar. He called himself Barak Ali. As I said, he has aliases. Don't we all?" Grishka gave his brother a hard look. "We can't be sure of his origins, maybe Pakistani, maybe Palestinian, maybe Iranian, but I think he's from Serbia or Kosovo—from one of the states of the disintegrated Yugoslavia, maybe Christian, maybe Muslim."

Grishka produced a few photocopies of photos and some documents of a college in Oxford in England that was outside Oxford University. "The other is Darius Esen. What we know of his background is also contradictory, maybe Turkish, and maybe Kurdish. He wanted to be an engineer. European countries did not want him. The USSR offered training in engineering and technology to students from countries in Eastern Europe—you used to call them satellite states—and to students from some countries in the Middle East, like Syria. For Darius Esen this meant a year learning Russian in Minsk and then four years studying engineering in Moscow.

"From the point of view of your not-so-secret Oryx Party—it's committed to the liberation of the Palestinian people and hates Israel with venom—these two young guys are two precious, highly trained commodities.

"Afghanistan may be a mountainous country, scorching in summer and like Antarctica in winter. Romantics like to think of such countries as lands of mysterious beauty with snow leopards, golden eagles, and bar-headed geese that fly higher than any other bird.

"But, when what you're doing there is fighting, you forget the raw beauties of nature. You think you're in a psychological dungeon with unending tunnels, twisting and turning. It's true that the harsh environment strengthens family life. You have to work together to survive. Even predators from different species hunt cooperatively. And it's true of different fighting forces with a common aim.

"In 1986 the Afghan mountain village of Jadji was under attack. Our headquarters there were, as you say, rude. Our soldiers were, as you say, uncouth. We had taken the one who now calls himself Darius Esen. We thought he had been laying land mines.

"We were applying our techniques to get him to speak. This was not your good-cop-bad-cop approach. It was—how do you say—nasty, brutal, and as short as possible?

"'Where is your base? How many men are there? We know whom you work for and you know that we do. Don't you know it will be easier if you cooperate?'

"But for first time, it was me who felt uneasy. The one you call Darko Delizio was also there. He was supposed to be on our side, on the side of the government we came to

Afghanistan to support. He worked as an interpreter. We thought he believed in the old Afghanistan. As we asked questions and the interrogation moved through Arabic and Russian with snatches of English, I felt it was not just the prisoner who was evading our questions but also the interpreter."

As he told his backstory, Grishka was back in the caves, the temporary shacks, and the rocky compounds of Afghanistan—torrid in unforgiving summers, Siberian cold in harsh winters that did not melt into springs. Above all was the relentless roughness of the Soviet army, tireless in its demands on soldiers, exacting in its discipline. He remembered the dirty scared faces of the Afghan Arabs caught by his Russian comrades.

"What we got from both men were evasive answers. We expected that. I also suspect that they already know one another. Not by anything said. Not by gesture. Just involuntary way of reacting."

Grishka was getting excited. He was no longer playing the role of Russian benefactor. His cultured English became more like Russian, without the definite and indefinite articles.

"Then, during break while I scan notes, I heard him you call Darko Delizio mumble, 'What do you call dead Russky?' One you call Darius Esen knew answer: 'Good start.'

"Now Darko is one of your accountants. He puts on a mild manner—almost contrite. I bet treasurer finds him creative in way he moves monies around the university without true owners realizing. Underneath veneer of blend-in charm, he's hardened fighter with a specialty."

"A specialty?"

"We think he's a silent assassin. Like you. You with your rapier tongue; he with curved Bedouin blade."

"That's the specialty?" asked Groznyy, sneering at the comparison.

"There's twist. Darko is right-handed. But he always

administers his *coup de grace* with his left hand—a special twist that's his calling card. It's intended as warning."

Darius and Darko sipped dark coffee together in Darko's apartment in Babel City. The unexpected and most unwanted reappearance of Grishka Groznyy in their lives was not simply like a stab in the dark. It was like a thunderbolt opening up a fissure in the ground beneath them through which they felt they were about to fall.

Darius had suppressed the way he had been interrogated by his Russian captors in Afghanistan. Now it flooded back in a sharp spurt.

Two heavily built guards had come into his cell after Grishka had questioned him. One slapped his face. The second punched him hard in the stomach. One named Bomelius said, "You are charged with being a terrorist. Is this true?"

"I claim it. I am proud to be."

The other, named Sobakin, held Darius down on a crude table while Bomelius strapped him to it. Like Grishka, they asked the names of his contacts and what his instructions were. They pulled his socks off. They took rushes to lash the soles of his feet. He squirmed. When he fainted they brought him round with lashings of cold water. They pulled down his pants and underwear and lit cigarette lighters against his testicles. They stopped and disappeared. But this was so that he would think it was all over.

The torture, however, would start all over again.

Darius was now desperate. After mumbling or screaming various Arab names, he barely croaked, "Just kill me off."

"So that the pain will stop? Think again."

Darius passed out once more. He came to when a middle-aged doctor of indeterminate nationality was changing his dressings. The doctor bandaged not only his feet but also his hands.

Darius awoke lying on a rough pallet. He was too weak to

94

move. But someone came in, gently bandaged his eyes, and, without explanation, carried him away. He did not dare to hope. But it was the first leg of his escape.

Darius did not break down in Darko's room in Babel City as these bitter memories of the late 1980s flooded his brain. But he froze into near immobility. Darko and Darius had both known what had seemed like unending darkness, bitterness, and rank despair that was becoming unforgiving hatred.

"What happened next?" asked Groznyy of Grishka in his office at BCU.

"Next day, Darius Esen was gone. Guards gone. Disappeared into mountains. Interpreter Darko Delizio—also gone. Like you say, 'Over the hills and far away.'"

"What did you do?"

"What could we do? Order came from Moskva: move back. Help consolidate Russian forces. Whatever military explanation, I knew there was loss of confidence in Kremlin. There, retreat—failure, like American exit from Saigon. And, just like Vietnam War, withdrawal of superpower was not end. Now you have old-school Fifth Column. Like your *Cosi*. Lovers play soldiers but get called up to real war."

"So Russia, the mother country, failed?"

"Rugged mountains with pitiless glaciers have much to teach us about power of nature. Nature is in charge even when we damage it with heavy industry, barbaric wars—even civilized canals, dams, and highways.

"When Darius and Darko disappeared into night, someone—I don't know who—left a scrawled message in poor Russian: 'We can cut off twin heads of Russian eagle. You see. And we can behead single head of American eagle, imperial despot.'"

Groznyy grabbed the phone and summoned Bogus Revisor: "I don't care what you're doing, just get Franklin

Miller on the phone, wherever in the world he is. Then get the fuck out of your office and into mine!"

Grishka changed tack and started giving his interpretation of Bogus.

"You think he's like irritating flea in song, flea that gets everyone scratching. They think he's your eyes and ears. But he thinks something different. He's like the nose in the story by Gogol, who gets away from face of hero and thinks he's superior to him. Watch your back, big bro."

Grishka paused to let Groznyy digest this unwelcome interpretation.

"These young guys, they're on mission here."

"What do you expect me to do?"

"Ivan Groznyy pushed Russian boundaries to east. He was visionary. You cast yourself in his mold. Rise to occasion. If you don't, you may not have university to quarrel over."

"Why should I believe you? America and Russia aren't allies. In the Cold War we were on opposite sides. You're asking us to dance cheek-to-cheek with the Russian bear. These men were your enemies in the Afghan War. But they were our allies. How can they be a danger to us after we supported them?" Having decided to shoot down Grishka's arguments, Groznyy was not going to concede any point now. Above all, he did not want Grishka to sense what he was thinking. He simply said, "Darko Delizio and Darius Esen? Your Darko, my Darko, my grandmother's Darko."

Bogus came in. Without saying a word, he handed Groznyy a scrap of pink paper with a hastily scrawled message:

"Franklin Miller won't come to phone—doesn't want information overheard, intercepted, etc. An assistant, a woman calling herself 'Almond Eyes,' tells us to get Todd Carter, the ex-CIA man, who will give us background. That meeting has to be away from BCU."

Grishka smiled to himself. His brother did not trust him. The Cold War had lasted for over forty years but it might be decades before American politicos recognized that the Russians and the Americans were now on the same side.

"What you have here, big bro, is a war in pieces. The Oryx Party gave you a sign with the bomb in the basement and its telltale calling card with the letters KAZ."

"Why would they do that—give themselves away?"

"They're like you. Ego gets in the way of cover—like fake lovers in your show. They can't resist showing off and scoring. Here was another sign. Your director took his cue from Tolstoy's *War and Peace*. In the novel there's a romantic plot around heroine Natasha, who represents spirit of Russia. Slimy sexual predators groom her and distract her from her nobleman fiancé. It's sign that Russian society is unraveling even before Napoleon invades. Natasha is saved from a terrible mistake by the generous-natured Pierre, a great bear of a man, like Russian Field Marshal Kutuzov who saves country from Napoleon.

"Your director has taken this idea and imposed it on *Cosi fan tutte*: woman as sexual object, victim, and psychological landscape. Your enemies in the Oryx Party can't resist showing off any more than you can. It's no surprise that your other enemies in the Opposition Party hated the show. Like you, they also don't want anyone else to be clever."

As ever when he had been bested intellectually, Cesare Groznyy's face contorted first into a bulbous pink pig's face and then contracted into a hollow ashen specter. All he could do was bluster like a mini Mussolini. But Grishka was having none of it.

"You are so immersed in your private war with Mordred Stickleman that you don't hear the Asiatic tiger at the gates.

"The unofficial leader of the Afghan Arabs is Osama bin Laden, the moneybags of the enterprise. He has a virtual army of some 5,000 terrorists. Darko Delizio, who works for you at BCU, is a prototype of his terrorists. Then there's a rabble-rousing fanatic, Ramzi Yousef—a firebrand with multiple aliases. Yousef and other foot soldiers are determined to bring terror to the West.

"These militants are skilled in modern methods of death. They will attack us, we in the East and you in the West, with bombs as lethal as anything America used against Japan in World War II or Vietnam in the 1960s. And you taught them how. Osama bin Laden had a relationship with the US government in Cyclone, the code name for operation against Russian forces in Afghanistan. The US let him buy weapons at rock-bottom prices. He has the materiels."

Grishka smiled again, showing perfect new teeth. He got up. As he opened the door to leave, Grishka looked back and added, "Did I mention jumping spider in Himalayas that uses wind to travel—something like our supposed great-aunt, the self-disappeared Nadezhda Arachnova Glinskaya?"

Then Grishka cocked his lower left leg at the door. Groznyy wanted to throw a book at him. But with this parting shot Grishka was gone.

But for how long?

When Darius explained to Ace Ferrari how he and Grishka had met on different sides in Afghanistan, the dean told him, "It's too dangerous for you here. Go where you will not be noticed: Little Cairo in New Jersey."

When Ferrari told Don Fatale about Darius leaving, Fatale said, "Darius and Holly won't give one another up, whatever the obstacles."

"No, but it will work for us."

"How so?"

"It's a classic of the uncomfortable human psyche. As time passes, these lovers will go from ecstasy to despair. When passion is spent, Darius will tell himself she's just another loose white woman. That will make his disgust more painful. Then iron will enter his soul. And he will be ours—firm, resolute, unwavering."

"And Darko?"

"His financial skills are too important for Groznyy to let him go."

Cesare Groznyy had to persuade Benny Vincenzo that, when he met with Todd Carter in the upper room of the Golden Cockerel, there would be no repetition of the gross behavior when Grishka had been there with his heavies.

Todd Carter was formally dressed in an inconspicuous gray suit and had an inscrutable manner when he met Groznyy and Larry Dawdler there. Out tumbled the familiar history of the Afghan blowback revolutionaries, information still new to Groznyy, who never looked beyond his immediate interests.

"American strategy during the Russian war in Afghanistan was not based on democratic principles. But it did have a humanitarian dimension. After all, three million Afghanis were killed or wounded during the Russian invasion. Six million fled to Pakistan or Iran. Once the war was over, tens of thousands of the young militants, the Afghan Arabs, were left to their own devices."

"Who are they? Where do they come from?"

"These Afghan Arabs include Egyptians, Saudis, Yemenis, and Algerians in thousands. There are also men from Tunisia, Iraq, and Jordan. They will continue the Afghan jihad in guerrilla movements against Arab countries where they think the government is not sufficiently Islamic. Radicalized by their experiences and very well trained—in part by us—they are fueled by extreme political views and religious zeal. They have replaced the target of the defunct USSR by taking on new enemies in their own countries and across the world. They are committed to the elimination of Israel."

"What are you doing about it? Hasn't the CIA been part of the problem?"

Todd chose his words carefully. "During the Russo-Afghan war, the CIA funded and trained Afghan Arabs—that's true. Now it's a shock to the CIA that their 'assets' have turned on us. We call this—the way Afghan Arabs have flipped—'blowback.' The trouble is that the Afghan Arabs are neither disposed of nor disposed to think the way America wants them to do."

"What do you ask me to do?"

"The INS is holding a man in New York who gives his name as Ajaj, says he's part Swedish, part Pakistani. He arrived with someone named Ramzi Yousef—that's one of his many names. He's at large, possibly in Little Cairo in Jersey City. Inside Ajaj's luggage, which the INS confiscated, officers found several passports—Jordanian, British, and Saudi Arabian. This Ajaj also had books and videotapes. They contained directions on how to make big makeshift bombs. There was a videotape of a suicide bombing; handbooks on how to make explosives and improvised armaments; manuals on catalysts, detonators, and ingredients for big bombs.

"That's not all. Other documents included a paper urging violence against the enemies of Islam, declaring: 'Facing the enemies of God, terrorism is a religious duty and force is necessary.'

"We have a double agent—yes, I know, unreliable, but we have to take the risk. From him we think this Ajaj keeps in touch with Ramzi Yousef in phone calls made through a third party. Here's the onion: a judge decided that Ajaj could have his tell-tale documents back."

"Some judge who thinks he's funny?"

"Think harder."

And Groznyy did just that. "The INS wanted to see what Ajaj would do. Would he collect the dangerous documents—"

"—Or send them on so the CIA could follow this up?"

"So, what did this Ajaj do?"

"Nothing. He hasn't sent them to Yousef—either to protect Yousef or to try and throw us off the scent."

"Again, what do you want me to do?"

"You have your Oryx Party at BCU. Is it a front? Is it active? One of its members left BCU all of a sudden. I'll take instructions from my people and get back to you when we're ready."

Hermione, who was helping serve the meal and had heard snatches of the conversation, was now clear in her mind. She remembered how Modest had worked out everything. And the bomb in the drain in the basement that had finished him off was surely the work of Middle Eastern fanatics who wanted Israel gone and America damaged psychically. Deadly though it was, Hermione thought that the bomb in the basement of the provost's old house had been a trial run.

She recalled how, when she and Modest had gone to the police, the police had drawn a blank. But as she served lunch she knew it was now or never. When Benny called Groznyy away to take a phone call from some journalist, Hermione took her chance.

"Sir," she began.

Todd saw she was nervous. "You'd like an autograph? Sure."

"No. I don't mean that I wouldn't like your autograph. But there's something I have to tell you.

"I have a friend," she began. If Hermione half expected Todd Carter's eyes to glaze over as if she were going to say her friend had problems, she was mistaken. For as a former CIA agent Todd had learned never to leave a stone unturned. Even if a witness were incoherent or motivated by anger, there would always be some crucial detail, a nugget of important information.

Hermione took a deep breath.

"I think there's a bomb plot."

Groznyy returned. Todd signaled with his eyes that he understood. After he and Groznyy had left and gone their separate ways, he was back within ten minutes to hear more from Hermione.

Hermione had had just enough time to think through what Holly had told her more than once about Darius being on edge and how he tried to make light of snatches of his telephone conversations that Holly had overheard. Hermione sensed the unseen but controlling hand of Ace Ferrari, a constant presence when there was political trouble. Hermione had heard references to the Oryx, an Arabian antelope and the Arabs' name for some co-operative organization.

Then her words to Todd cascaded out like Niagara Falls: the mysterious bomb in the provost's old house; the brazen boasts but furtive behavior of the Arab contingent during the science survey; the blueprint of the plane.

"I know all this is in the past. But my friend, Holly Wood Groznyy—this has to stay secret until she's safe—has seen a friend of hers—Turkish, we think, but maybe Palestinian— become increasingly nervous about his friends. I think they're in New Jersey. Everything she hears spells trouble."

Then Hermione produced not evidence but an incriminating impression. She had had time in Todd's brief absence to retrieve from upstairs Modest's bizarre cartoon of Ace Ferrari, Mukhtar, Saleem, and Darko Delizio as fanatics peering into an Arabian cave of perverse treasures—not gold and silver and precious jewels but pipe bombs, beakers labelled "nitric acid" and "filtered urine," and bottles containing explosives. And out of this Aladdin's lamp came forth a mighty explosion.

Todd was mesmerized by the liveliness of the drawing and the perception behind it. He promised to keep it carefully and to use the portraits for help with any future identification, since they went further into the minds of the subjects than could any regular ID photos.

The feds set Modest's elaborate sketch aside. Todd thought it was worth more than that.

Days later when he was in a meeting, Groznyy had to take a phone call from Todd Carter. He did not like being interrupted when he was in full flow.

"I repeat: what are you asking from me?"

"We think your former BCU man, Darius Esen, is in Little Cairo; that he knows Yousef, who will try and use him. I hear young Esen is a skilled engineer. One of your deans knows him. Your wife is cordial to him."

Groznyy stiffened. Todd did not care.

"You must not do anything to alert the Oryx Party. But anything they say in conversation, let slip—no matter how casual—you let me know."

"How do I do that?" asked Groznyy.

"We need to monitor Darko Delizio, Ace Ferrari, and Don Fatale. We need an observer in Babel City and Norse Hoven. You know the general reasons but not the details. And that's for your protection."

Groznyy did not resist.

The sudden appearance of the splendid Todd Carter at BCU, out of nowhere but highly recommended as a new star professor of communications from somewhere or other, alerted Ace Ferrari to the fact that he was being watched.

Ferrari wondered what Groznyy was going to do. By now, the damnable Grishka must have given Groznyy the background to Darko as well as Darius. Ferrari still wanted to use the tug-of-war between the Opposition Party and the Groznyy Gang as a shield. He guessed that Groznyy did not want any exposure of Darius at BCU to cast light on his own subversive financial dealings. Yet Ferrari could not be sure if the Oryx Party at BCU was safe or not. In any case, any bomb plan was now firmly with some black devil in New Jersey.

In fact Groznyy was as inward-looking as any US president who finds an intrusive press scrutinizing him adversely. Whatever his words about future academic paradise, Groznyy kept his eyes peeled and set on his immediate prospects.

The wonderful Todd Carter had inexhaustible charm and he also believed in his own charisma. He had sailed through the CIA in his early days as an operative. He had made a name for himself when his tender conscience would not allow him to do unconscionable things for the CIA. He had excelled as a circuit speaker with selective critical memories to stir any audience. And—wonder of wonders—he had managed to finesse, if not a return to the CIA when the money and fame ran out, an informal deal. He had become a secret team player who could be eyes, ears, and subtle spokesman for the rightness of American policies.

Todd's academic subject was communication studies—not the doing it for film and television but the theories underpinning the subject. His academic gods were communications pundit Marshall McLuhan and the man behind him, Howard Gossage. Todd excelled as a platform lecturer, especially in the core introduction course, Communications 101, teaching freshmen basic theory.

It was who you were, how you thought, your socio-economic background, and your expectations that determined how you would interpret information. Moreover, information was conveyed not only through obvious channels of communication such as human speech and the written word but also by gesture, custom, and costume.

You could say Todd was in tune with the times. He saw the 1990s as a "best time" economically and socially because the United States was on the crest of a wave of information technology that would not only broaden communication but also stimulate trade and industry.

Todd's words flowed easily and his presence intrigued students. He counted on his native wit to be able to do his two new jobs at once: teaching communications while pursuing a secret fact-finding mission and reporting back to DC. To Todd the Oryx Party at BCU was the tip of a wider and deeper problem. For Todd also saw the 1990s as a "worst time." This was because the United States was unwittingly harboring devastating schools of terrorists. They were the new jackals. He feared some deadly blasts would ripple worldwide. And though he was at BCU to be the secret eyes and ears of the CIA, he heard little. Todd was not a happy man.

Before her first meeting with the Chosen Council of BCU, chic Manhattan publicist Kelly Danson reread an old letter from Groznyy when he had first tempted her to leave Columbia University for BCU:

Dear Lady,
From our meeting a few short years ago, I learned to esteem you as a noble soul with considerable talents not sufficiently appreciated at your alma mater, Columbia. The grace and charm of your presence showcase your skills as a publicist and copywriter. Your profound insights into marketing can place Babel City University at the forefront of American colleges.

With your help, I will take my art, my ideas, my insight to the sleeping stone of the faculty and give them human form. As with Picasso and Shostakovich, the hammer of my artistry will beat things into academic shape. I am the reason students want to come here: my academic integrity, my art.

I look forward to our joint initiative. We shall have such fun.

Yours in splendid anticipation,
Cesare Groznyy

Kelly Danson would need every grain of comfort in that letter that morning.

Bogus Revisor, the new provost, began by telling the Chosen Council that BCU and NHU still faced a serious problem with falling student enrolment.

"The number of full-time and part-time students has declined between 25 and 40 percent. Whichever figure is right, this is a fiscal disaster. Already BCU has had to close one dorm and spend less on such resources as library books."

Then Treasurer Parthy Burnable gave a bleak summary of declining student enrolment.

"Are we making the most of our resources, applying funds to best advantage?" asked Todd Carter, who was at the Chosen Council as a token representative of the professors. "Isn't it true that while the number of professors has declined, the number of administrators has risen?"

Groznyy and Revisor glared. But they did not answer Todd's question.

Kelly Danson had her big new idea to resolve the enrolment problems. Her slide show was ready. She knew she must begin with flattery.

"As our respected president has explained, we have a rare opportunity—thanks to his guidance—to present BCU's future achievements as positive assets that already exist. First we must make people aware of BCU as a center of academic excellence rooted in arts and sciences. Second, we know that the secret to student enrolment is parental approval and purchasing power."

Groznyy could not stop himself interrupting. "We have to rank little BCU with the best: Harvard, Oxford, Cambridge, and the Sorbonne. These parents are scared. The world is changing and the academic world with it: IT, Earth sciences, the Gaia theory—all new. Colleges have to incorporate these developing fields into their academic offerings. What parents want is an assurance of comfort and convenience. Not all Americans are travelers across the world or into new academic disciplines. Those who are timid need someone to hold their hands."

Kelly made sure the august Groznyy had finished before she resumed.

"Thank you for explaining it so cogently, Mr. President. This is where BCU comes in. Our campaign is based around one buttressing slogan, 'BCU has all the answers.'"

Kelly began flipping through slides on the portable screen.

"It all comes down to the three letters: BCU.

"What is the college word for IT? BCU.

"What do you say when you want to understand Earth sciences? BCU.

"What do you ask for when you want to study foreign languages? BCU.

"How do you say 'academic excellence' in Chinese? BCU.

"Who gives you your visa to Oxford and Cambridge? BCU."

While she ran through her list of variables, all with one common destination, Kelly could sense growing amazement around the room and a grudging approval of her daring slogans. She thought that, when she came to publication targets for the slogans, she was preaching to the converted. She finished with a flourish: "It's a great idea, capable of infinite variations. They all bring us back to the central message: the greatness of BCU under President Cesare Groznyy."

Todd was impressed by Kelly—by her poise, her all-purpose slogan, and her ability to play Groznyy like a lyre while maintaining her integrity as a PR expert.

But Kelly's sense of victory, silently acknowledged by Todd and trumpeted before everyone had time to digest the information, was not the end of the story, as Kelly now discovered. For it was the great Groznyy's principal strategy to divide and rule—to have his officers compete for the same resources, to let them squabble, and then for him to enter the fray when their words against one another were most bitter.

When he had wooed her to come to BCU, Groznyy had told Kelly Danson that she had funds of $100,000 to spend on the publicity plans they would dream up together. In fact, $30,000 of Kelly's money had already been allocated to student recruitment. And that very same money was in the budget of Nellie Garter, dean of admissions, for such recruitment essentials as mass mailings and open-day presentations. Another $20,000 of Kelly's budget had already been assigned to the budget of the pre-med recruitment program of Barney Lichtenberger, the pompous biologist useful for his skill in placing undeserving students in med programs in graduate schools.

Nellie Garter had the lissom figure and stylistic hauteur for the university's crucial front woman, the dean of admissions. Her picture-perfect cosmetic self-presentation included a commanding strut as if she were a cheerleader about to belt out a raunchy games chant. Her Irish American husband liked that; he was a skilled firefighter.

Kelly only discovered Groznyy's double dealing in the course of this, her crucial first meeting with the Chosen Council. For, after Kelly had spoken, Dean Nellie Garter gave her own presentation detailing how she had already spent some of Kelly's funds. Kelly was first surprised, and then angry at what seemed to her unwarranted presumption by Nellie. In return Dean Garter was ready to give full vent to her Irish temper to show she was the better prima donna. The two had a spat in front of everyone around the table.

Human resources manager Lorraine Boe nudged Kelly silently, almost like saying, "Shush." Kelly took the cue. Later, in a brief break in the meeting, Lorraine said to Kelly, "Remember, Nellie Garter's husband has a high-up job in the fire service."

This remark meant nothing to Kelly at the time. It was months before she worked out its significance.

Groznyy's way of handling the spat between Kelly and Nellie was not to explain and calm things but to exploit the situation by putting yet more demands on Kelly Danson. It transpired that Nellie Garter did, indeed, have prior claims to the disputed $30,000, as did Barney Lichtenberger for another $20,000. Worse, Kelly was now expected to use these same previously allocated funds for the plans she had already made with Cesare Groznyy. She was expected somehow to conjure up the spent money from nowhere or be shouted at for incompetence even though the fault was Groznyy's.

Groznyy eventually entered the fray as a *deus ex machina*, the god who could arbitrate everyone's problems. Only the high-and-mighty He could resolve the situation and his toads must bow low.

Kelly retired in confusion, knowing she had unwittingly made an enemy of the powerful dean of admissions and that this was not her fault. She knew she would have to put on a brave face in the face of wilting support from her colleagues.

Sitting down in the corridor outside the presidential suite, Kelly could not help herself. She broke down. A stranger also sitting there moved beside her and took out his handkerchief. He put his arms round her shoulders.

This man was immaculately dressed. She guessed he was a lawyer. Even the handkerchief he offered her was so pristine it was almost as coiffed as his sleek black hair.

"My name is Boris Goodenough," he said. "I'm a corporate lawyer."

He was pleased that his name meant nothing to her. He did not tell Kelly that his social call on Groznyy had an unspoken message—that he had not forgotten his sister, Holly, or her interests.

Boris saw distinct possibilities in this Manhattan damsel in distress—diplomatic, career, and erotic. He could utilize her both for his career and for sex.

Troubled though she was, Kelly could see that, with this steely, groomed man suddenly taking an interest in her, one thing would lead to another. That evening, she opened up to him.

"I can't make any headway. It's as if a thicket of body-guards protects him. The campaign idea is strong. The slogan is great. Why doesn't he see this?"

"It's easy to guess what Groznyy would have preferred," answered her prospective boyfriend. "What's the answer to every single academic problem in the whole wide world? Cesare Groznyy!

"Of course, even he wouldn't dare say it before his Chosen Council since you are all supposed to be supporting 'little BCU.' But that's what he wants—everything personalized, centered on him."

The scales fell from Kelly's eyes.

Boris added, "To keep your job in such a corrupt court for any length of time is going to be a major achievement. You're in the loop, sure enough. And that does give you immediate access to the president. But it also exposes you to the contin-uous glare of unreasonable expectation."

Kelly was still too upset to work out why this guy under-stood BCU.

When they heard about the spat between Kelly Danson and Dean Nellie Garter, critical professors spoke informally.

Ace Ferrari said, "Groznyy thinks his presidential robes give him the right to deceive everyone. Yes, he frightens people, but he doesn't see that his reign of terror makes them inactive. Therefore, it also renders them useless."

Stickleman was typically mordant. He said, "He sits like a spider spinning yarns of hope in his poisonous web, but it is he who is the most infected."

When Bee Flute told her husband, he said, "It seems that President Groznyy has shaped the environment in his own image with brutal rigor. It must be like living under a mini Mussolini. So far, he isn't facing up to the consequences of his actions. But they will come back to haunt him."

This was also Todd Carter's private view. As he watched and listened to pro- and anti-Groznyy forces, he saw matters with fresh eyes. He heard the president's party declare that they wanted greater academic rigor. He heard that Groznyy wanted professors to return to their research origins and to undertake new research and get it published. Todd saw an insuperable academic gulf. What reputation Babel City University had rested on subjects with a practical application: nursing, psychology, pre-med biology, and social work. Groznyy was convinced that the fundamental principles of core arts and science subjects were the most important even for students who wanted to study a subject with an immediate practical application.

As Todd saw it, neither the president nor his opponents had the least ability for thinking outside the comfort zone of their untested convictions. Both sides were prisoners of inward-looking self-regard. Conflict was inevitable.

Another watcher and one who was also a player was new provost Bogus Revisor. Bogus noted that BCU was no different from other organizations in being torn with conflicting opinions. There was no end of foul voices: dyed-in-the-wool, sexist, racist, homophobic—even criminal. It was a mixed spectrum of blinkered humanity, all in need of wider education. To Bogus, the professors' protests were like a revolt by medieval peasants against a self-obsessed king.

However, among these peasant protesters a hard group of professors was raising issues of academic governance.

Todd quickly learned about this group of protesters. Among their hated targets was the "Statute of Professorial and Professional Conduct." As its self-identified victims complained, this statute prevented revisions to labor contracts. Todd saw that the Opposition Party wanted a protectionist system in which all had won and all must have prizes. And the Opposition Party did have a winning card. By their rhetoric, the professors could widen protest and disturb the trustees.

Todd also grasped that the president's powers—by his control of the budget, his own formidable rhetoric, and his manipulation of the deans—were considerable. A president skilled in diplomacy could have wielded these powers to his advantage. Was Groznyy such a president? Todd did not think so. Groznyy's psychological baggage made it unlikely that he could overcome the hatred of the deans, the chairs, and the professors.

Indeed, Groznyy was shackled and he knew it. As Todd saw it, Groznyy made things worse for himself. Instead of putting out minor political fires, he preferred continuous skirmishes and an inner court of favorites.

Todd interpreted the situation as a feeble parody of what commentators on Soviet Russia called the Court of the Triumphant Lie. The fears of Groznyy's colleagues shivered like a malign aura around BCU. Todd could tell that people were circumspect about what they told their co-workers. He saw that none of these enforced cowards had any hesitation in belittling one another. Groznyy was training a generation of sneaks modelled on the stereotype of the *stukach*—the informer—a staple of Russian life before, during, and after Stalin. Fear infiltrated every floor of BCU's administration buildings. Administrators feared an unexpected knock at their workstation. Deans feared someone informing on them.

Todd had come to BCU to do a job independent of Groznyy matters. But he sensed his professional energy being sapped.

And he was not alone.

Report and rumor about the controversies swirling around

Groznyy spread across Norse Hoven County and into New York. At the Golden Cockerel Benny Vincenzo was in full vocal flight while he, Hermione, and the princess waited in the upstairs room for diners to arrive for lunch. By now Hermione had been fully welcomed into Benny and the secret princess's confidence.

The princess said, "People like Nemo Groznyy are devils."

"Well," said Hermione, "Groznyy is not got up in red like Mephistopheles with a goatee beard and a tail."

"But," said Benny, "he does have the head of an ill-tempered pig."

The princess was off in her own world: "Like witches and wizards, he has the power of swift flight. Witches fly across the sky on broomsticks for trysts with the devil. Groznyy's speed comes in the way he uses words."

"It's true no one speaks more seductively or for as long. He scoops his victims up in his flights of fancy—Modest told me that," said Hermione.

"Then he dumps them hundreds of miles away," said Benny. "By then they've lost the plot. When they wake up they're in a snowdrift without shelter. This is what happened to Provost Lucy Kaye."

Not the least interested in others' misfortunes, the princess was still in her imaginary Russia of myth and retribution. She twisted her gnarled hands.

"There's a Russian story about how, when the devil had to hide, he jumped into a basin of dough that some peasant woman was kneading. She made a sign of the cross to make the dough rise. And so the devil found himself stuck fast. No matter how manipulative they are, little devils like Groznyy are always in a hell of their own devising."

Indeed, nothing was plain sailing on the good ship Groznyy.

The BCU professors' senate was increasingly fed up with Groznyy and his arbitrary management. Convinced that his arts-and-sciences vision lacked substance, they asked the board of trustees to remove him.

Todd Carter heard Mordred Stickleman joke to Ace Ferrari in the staff canteen, "The good news is that it's Cesare Groznyy's funeral tomorrow."

Ferrari quipped back, "The bad news is that he's cancelled it."

The angry professors heard nothing back from the trustees. What most frustrated them was not that the president, his provost, his treasurer, and his fiddlers three disputed their opinions but that they simply ignored them. Letters, position papers, faculty resolutions, and motions of censure—everything was to no avail. Nothing was more cutting. Stymied, Todd felt he had no choice but to cast his lot in with the anti-Groznyy faction.

Well-wishers around the president wanted his presidency to be enhanced by the most fashionable form of human resource management instead of the mom-and-pop system of Lorraine Boe. When alumni bureau chief Carpenter Cain persuaded Cesare Groznyy that a top-notch HR executive from Manhattan should supersede Lorraine, Groznyy agreed. He also reluctantly agreed that, as her most loyal supporter, it was he who should break the news to her, his most loyal fan.

Groznyy could break the spirit of any dean but he habitually left dismissal arrangements to others. Now he could not bring himself to tell Lorraine. She took a surprise call from a junior secretary in the president's office when Bee Flute was away. Lorraine hastened to this hastily arranged meeting. Cesare began at his most enticing. She sensed nothing.

"Lorraine, my dear, I've always thought how lovely your name is. Still do. Ever since Noah's Ark, rainbows have delighted people. Wagner built a musical bridge with one. Judy Garland peered over one. Broadway gave another one an Irish Gaelic spin. Other people have used the rainbow as a political symbol"—then, sensing her confusion, he clarified—"as in the Rainbow Coalition."

Lorraine could not see where these compliments were leading.

She left none the wiser.

But she did learn, and in a cruel way. The original intention had been for Groznyy to tell Lorraine of her demotion. Then, officious provost Bogus was to come and explain to her the form of the press ad announcing the vacancy to replace her.

Bogus did appear in her office as planned, believing she already knew she had been demoted. He simply handed to Lorraine a previously drafted advertisement about the vacancy for her successor.

"You know about this," said the bogus confidante. "Place the notice in the *New York Times* two Sundays hence. Get it set on the recto page, outer corner at the top."

Lorraine stared. She read: "Babel City University has a vacancy for a fully qualified professional to manage its expanded human resources office, beginning a month before the fall semester."

So the way Lorraine learnt she had been demoted was when she was instructed to place an advert for her successor. She was uncontrollable even before a comparative stranger. Todd Carter had come to her office to collect some special mail he did not want left in his own department office.

"I've been fired. I've been fired," was all she could mumble to him.

Her eyes were streaming.

"You don't want to work at a place like this where they would do that to you," Todd said as he took her out for coffee and she broke down again. Todd considered what sort of an accessory that made him. The day before, he had watched yet another British TV import about Henry VIII. He said to himself, "Whether in real life, or plays, or films, even in operas, Henry VIII never does the deed himself. It's always his servants."

Todd knew that Lorraine had been Groznyy's most loyal supporter, his most affectionate fan, and the person anyone in trouble would most readily turn to. Todd felt ashamed. Would the CIA at its most impersonal have behaved with such careless spite?

And he was not the only one who was ashamed. The Chosen Council and the deans assumed that, if Groznyy would do this to such a loyal ally, no one was safe.

Kelly Danson knew everything her new boyfriend, Boris, said about life under Groznyy at BCU was true. Over the nine months she was there, with her hopes of forging ahead in tatters, Kelly was simply waiting for the inevitable: getting fired. And when it came, as she knew it would, she was surprised at how bitter she was, how angry she was for not going earlier and leaving Groznyy in the lurch.

Boris tried to comfort her.

"For almost a year, you've always come home exhausted, never had enough sleep. They've never acknowledged you at work, let alone thanked you. At BCU, all around you are false witness, deceit, and calumny. Not one of these can you keep under lock and key—but neither can he. In time, they will engulf him. That will be his comeuppance."

"He's already had it," said Kelly plaintively, repeating an old wisecrack. "He's the president of Babel City University."

"For our relationship, it's for the best. But he will get his just deserts. You will wear the tsarina's slippers yet."

Kelly could not fathom this remark.

"Everything I told you about me is true—my life in the boondocks," Boris said.

Kelly sensed a shift. "But you've been economical with the truth?"

"I left something out. Holly Wood Groznyy is my sister."

Why did Kelly now think Boris was using her?

*

The man chosen to take over Kelly's role and who was already a trustee at BCU was Georgie Lucre. He had a mean streak in petty literary theft. Turning over old papers left by Kelly, he saw how good her ad campaign would have been.

He had a corker of a slogan he wanted to push: "Study at BCU. Succeed anywhere."

But he knew that in the corporate and university world—just like the military—people reported upwards. And he knew Kelly's slogans could be adapted to satisfy the one person who was paying his company Lucrative Lucre. Instead of coming back to Kelly's slogan and response of "What do you say when you want to understand Earth sciences?" "BCU," he made a simple direct change. Thus it became, "How do you say 'academic excellence' in Chinese?" "Cesare Groznyy." "Who gets you into Oxford and Cambridge?" "Cesare Groznyy." And so on. The new answer was always "Cesare Groznyy."

Todd winced at Cain's audacious theft. But it was neither more nor less than the beautiful people on the Chosen Council expected of a Groznyy toad.

Groznyy took the slogan as no more than his due. He did not see how ridiculous it made him even as he put on a show of undeserving modesty about it. Yet he wanted more. The published ads proclaimed that both Groznyy and BCU were great. There was a niggling doubt. If, in his mind, Groznyy thought he had solved all the academic problems of BCU, then why was BCU so manifestly third-rate?

As the PR campaign spluttered on without any positive results, Dean of Nursing Wendy Pretzel found herself besieged on three fronts: having to defend cuts in the nursing budget that the almighty treasurer insisted on, trying to discipline her fractious professors who wanted her to resist the cuts, and having to show Groznyy that she was an intellectual star.

117

Smarting for Lorraine over her demotion, Todd could no longer escape a bitter conclusion. Whether they were members of the Groznyy Gang, or the Opposition Party, or the Oryx Party, the various factions in BCU were no better than pretenders in their power games. They were neither true movers nor shakers, yet they wrapped themselves in a comforting cloak of professional purpose. And Todd, who had come to BCU with such high hopes for his secret mission, cursed himself that he had been drained by it all and had achieved none of his secret aims.

What he had learned from a sociology text when he had been a college student must be true—that social culture outlasts body and mind. He who had always despised the pettiness of someone like that bottled-up tank of spite Mordred Stickleman had now become not a critical observer but a stalwart of the Opposition Party. Was he no better than Stickleman?

1993

HOUSES OF DEATH

From the start Darius Esen enjoyed the streets of Little Cairo in Jersey City, in the Garden State but close to New York. After the surface quiet of a college town in New England—despite rough edges of deprivation in Louvre Ville and constant back-biting and bickering at BCU—the streets of Little Cairo seemed like a rollicking thoroughfare. He liked the smells of Middle Eastern cuisine, the hawkers and traders, the mix of Middle Eastern and western clothes as European America and Asian America seemed to mingle. True, some people from the Middle East could be surly. The occasional furtive look, the suspicious glance of people around inconspicuous doors added sinister excitement to the breezy atmosphere. And Darius no longer had Dean Ferrari yapping at his heels. And he and Holly continued to meet in secret.

Darius was little swayed by rabble-rousing rhetoric against America and Israel that he heard in a makeshift mosque. He saw something absurd in the fact that Afghan Arabs continually charged American leaders with acting dishonorably to the Palestinian people when there was ample proof to the contrary. He knew that successive presi-dents and secretaries of state had tried to mediate between rival Middle Eastern groups who were intransigent to one another. The American politicos were continually trying to make a case for judicious compromise while keeping the American electorate onside.

Darius thought that, with their continual calling young men to arms, rabble-rousing Muslim preachers showed superstition and fatalism that made them ridiculous as well as sinister.

When one prayer meeting was over, a young man in a white T-shirt and slashed jeans with a dark, straggly beard said to Darius without any introduction, "Can I ask you a question?"

Darius said nothing.

"I think you're an engineer. You were moved by the words. Help us. We need you."

Darius's look was uninviting but the young guy went on.

"Here is too open. There's a coffee shop on the next block."

When they sat down away from the griddle and the cut-price breakfasts, another not-so-young man in a caftan and with bushy fair hair came over and said, "You don't remember me? We were in Helmand province fighting the Russians. You're a skilled engineer. The Russkies took you in for questioning. When they took me in, we couldn't speak. I know you're on our side. We have the same destiny."

Darius felt cornered. Was this a set-up?

Darius had not listened for long to the second young man before he realized that these young jackals with their as yet unstated malign plan left the supposed doctors of death at the university at the starting post.

The young guy in the coffee shop asked a routine question on land mines. Then he asked a question on explosives. The meeting fizzled out.

But two days later Darius was at a street stall, flipping through an outsize book with what, to him, was a bizarre title: *The Poor Man's James Bond*. The book amounted to a catalog of homemade weapons. Out of nowhere the first young man was again beside him.

In another coffee shop Darius's new acquaintance asked more questions, this time on chemicals such as urea, nitric acid, and sulfuric acid, and how they might react together. Then Darius found himself facing questions on his political allegiance. It was almost like a job interview. He felt himself being appraised from another table by a pair of dark haunted eyes. He saw a young man with big features in a scarred face, who looked old beyond his years.

Darius had heard rumors about a young man, sometimes known as Ramsay and sometimes as Rashid. He heard that this man had multiple identities but a fixed conviction: destroy Israel; damage America.

One afternoon Darius heard two men talking at a newspaper stall: the owner and a customer, a well-dressed, preppy type.

The friendly customer said, "I hear he got into the US, first by bribing officials in Karachi to get a visa. When he arrived at Kennedy Airport, he put on a show of being contrite for the immigration officers. He asked for asylum. He acted the supplicant perfectly—not only by what he said and how he said it but also by how he looked when he said it. He was wearing Pakistani Muslim clothes—blouson-style pants, vest and jacket in orange, brown, and olive-green Afghan silk.

"Well, he may have been wearing Pakistani clothes but I heard he had an Iraqi passport. He said his name was Yousef. He said Iraqi soldiers had persecuted him. He said he would be oppressed if he were not allowed into the United States. I heard that the immigration officer wasn't convinced but her superiors overruled her. It seems there weren't enough detention spaces in the INS center."

The next turn of the conversation drew Darius up sharp.

"I tell you, a sure sign that this supposed Iraqi is not on the level is his poor knowledge of Iraq," said the vendor. "Someone in the apartment block asked him a simple question about Baghdad, but he knew nothing about Baghdad, and that's the capital. My wife manages the building. She searched his room for his passport because she thought he was lying about his nationality. She doesn't want to get caught up in any enquiry. She's afraid of the police and anything to do with government."

"Another thing," said the customer. "The guy who arrived with this Rashid was belligerent. He had a fake Swedish passport. He claimed he had a Muslim father and a Swedish mother. He used the name of Khurram Khan. The INS officer peeled off the photo in his passport. It was stuck on top of the photo of the previous owner. Even when he was confronted, this guy went on shouting at the INS people."

Darius wondered if the scenario was different from what the two men were saying—if the newcomers, rather than being two immigrants who just behaved differently from one another, had been staging a show for the INS, with one being deliberately antagonistic so that the other guy, who was more important, would seem reasonable and would get in.

Such scraps of conversation Darius heard in markets seemed to coalesce into a narrative with deadening certainty. There were stories about chemicals, storage, vans, and this charismatic leader with several identities.

Darius now understood that whoever was running the young man who had first spoken to him was not interested in his being a trained engineer, unless "engineer" was some code for "explosives expert." It was as if someone wanted his expertise not to discover what to use but to check his knowledge against their own ideas. However, when Darius tried to find out more he found he was up against a brick wall.

"You don't need to know that," the intermediary said. "Stick with what you know and do best. It's safer."

Darius deduced that whoever was in charge ran his cells by restricting information. Sometimes his intermediary would give him something specific, like the address of a meeting place but no more. "We give information to individual cell members on a need-to-know basis."

Was this a primitive safety net? If things went wrong, it would be difficult for investigators to trace leaders. It was like computers sending out information by breaking up messages into particles to be reunited on receipt. Here the particles were kept apart. However, Darius was well aware that everything he had said about chemicals had found a ready home in someone's mind for future reference. Darius guessed that the unknown man who had stared at him— perhaps the widely known Rashid or Ramsay—was making pipe bombs. Darius knew he had said enough to help would-be bombers make bombs. He had compared roadside bombs, land mines, and car bombs detonated both by remote control and by suicide bombers. Was he becoming an accessory?

Darius realized there was another twist to the way he was being questioned as an expert. Ramsay or Rashid wanted his operatives not to be as clever as him but, rather, to be subservient. And the operatives he knew seemed neither imaginative nor creative.

Darius formed a mental picture of the militants around this Ramsay. They were loose cannons with a warped view of the world. Whereas the little group had initially made contact with Darius because of his scientific expertise, the last thing their leader wanted was someone who was his intellectual equal.

He could not tell Holly. Holly—that was it. The cell leader was like Holly's detested husband: no one could be as clever, as charismatic as him.

Indeed, bomb-maker Ramzi Yousef had insinuated himself into America. He was living in Little Cairo and planning ahead. In the Al Kifah refugee center, he had met Mahmud Abouhalima, an old comrade from the Russo-Afghan war. Abouhalima had worked as a chauffeur for blind cleric Sheik Omar Abdel-Rahman, widely known for his diatribes against America and Israel. Abouhalima suggested to Yousef that he should wage a pipe-bomb campaign in New York.

Holly felt trapped in her claustrophobic marriage. She had a worrying recurrent dream that she was in a shabby vaudeville theater. The curtain rose to disclose celebrated escapologist Harry Houdini. He was looking into a glass box where she was being held captive in chains. The curtain fell. There was no escape. When she awoke, it was a relief.

Holly was usually ready to sing at fundraising events for rebuilding town and gown in Norse Hoven County after the fire. When an invitation came from Badger's Sett for such a gig, her promoter, Brad Gable, assumed she would accept. But the gig was for a day Holly had planned to be away in Manhattan with Darius. She told Brad and Larry Dawdler that she did not have enough time to prepare new material and did not want to repeat her repertoire. They suspected nothing. Brad did not want to tell the fundraisers what Holly had said in case this implied she was running empty. Larry suggested they just say Holly was not well. Holly did not like this but she knew if she vetoed it Brad and Larry would question her further, so she said nothing.

Darius's interest in the terrorists in Little Cairo became more focused when he and Holly, on that stolen day together, went on a boat trip to Ellis Island.

Ellis Island had once been a famous northeast gateway to the United States. In the early twentieth century, immigration officers there had processed a million immigrants every year. But Ellis Island had long been closed and had lain derelict for several decades. However, it had recently been re-opened as a national monument, its buildings scrubbed clean and sandblasted, the halls shiningly restored as if they were architectural treasures as well as historic curiosities. Ellis Island had never looked this good when it had been a processing center, with its mythic story now emblazoned on signs and in screen projections. The familiar story of the heroic march of immigrants to the United States, many poor and dispossessed but all with ambitions and expectations of the American Dream, was now a legend.

That sun-kissed winter day Ellis Island was a perfect cover for America's new enemies within, determined to undermine that dream and cause havoc. They were, indeed, new dogs of war.

Darius was not sure if Holly noticed the few groups of Middle Easterners around, but he sure did. In New York City, renowned for multiple ethnicities, no one would pay more than a passing glance to people who looked foreign. By their style of modern dress, younger men from the Middle East with designer-casual jeans and jocular T-shirts, and older ones in bourgeois leisure outfits of slacks under worn winter coats, proclaimed themselves men of today. To onlookers, two older men in indistinguishable Muslim dress with caps simply added picturesque detail.

One older man with a beard and wearing Pakistani clothes mumbled, "It's better we didn't meet in Brooklyn in Atlantic Avenue. Too many out-of-towners asking for directions— that would certainly get us noticed."

Some Arabs made a half-hearted survey of the immigration buildings. Like regular tourists they took in the view. There to the north was Corporate America thrusting its symbolic power upwards with the twin towers of the World Trade Center. Around the towers a court of smaller financial buildings stood like attendant dwarves paying homage to these totems of capitalist supremacy.

Some of the new jackals were appraising the very buildings they were targeting for a future attack, using phrases culled from the *New York Times*.

"It's true what critics say," said one. "The World Trade Center has nothing to offer but height. The towers deaden the skyline. Just look at the bleak box shapes and flat desolate tops."

Darius overheard the remark. When Holly looked at him,

he said, "It's funny. I've always thought they looked like giant tombstones."

After the return journey, when the boat docked at the pier leaving subversive thoughts unresolved, the new jackals parted as inconspicuously as they had met, moving eastwards along 42nd and 43rd Streets.

The fresh air of the boat trip had made the various travelers hungry. Some new jackals stopped at a Tex-Mex fast-food outlet named *La Fuerza de Sino*. Darius and Holly had arrived first and were eating enchiladas.

"Hello and welcome," said the owner. "Spicy Mexican food to build up strength. You're welcome to bring wine from the liquor store on the next block."

A group of happy-go-lucky American students were downing red Chilean wine and about to rip into chimichangas.

"We should thank God," said a student from Union Theological Seminary. *"In nomine Patris et Filii et Spiritus Sancti.* Amen."

The host said, "My wife doesn't speak Latin but she sure can cook."

"You can say that again," said the trainee priest. "This asks to be eaten."

Three sailors on shore leave came in with their arms around two girls. When they took off their winter coats the girls showed off frocks with cabbage rose patterns. While the guys were giving their order, one of the girls said to the students, "It's their last day before they go off to the Gulf— off to make their fortune. Death to Saddam Hussein, I say," she added carelessly.

Holly started to repeat "Saddam" as a question. Darius cautioned her with a glance that said, "Later."

Holly wanted to speak seriously to Darius before they were alone and his insistent caresses took over. But she had to wait. When the Arabs arrived, Holly could tell they were torn between wanting to blend in with the innocent Yankee merriment and wanting to say something provocative.

"That's right," said one of the Arabs who had heard the girl's jibe about Saddam Hussein. "Hurrah for war! War is beautiful!"

"You can laugh, but our war will bring us honor," said a sailor.

The older guy who was shepherding the Middle East contingent was sardonic. "Oh yes, give us the sound of drumbeats. Don't let it be said you will die cowards." He mimicked the cheeky girl as if she were a recruiting sergeant. He spoke to each of his men in turn and flicked his sleeve at every salacious *double entendre* like a hooker to privates on parade: "If you let me sign you up, you'll be a corporal" (to one), "and you'll be a colonel" (to the next), "and you'll rise to general" (to the last). "And, when you've risen through the ranks, I'll reward you." At this he raised his clenched right fist.

The merry students at the other table joined in the fun. "And what do you have for us students?"

The imam put on his serious face. "So merry, gentlemen? You shall pass through horrible times—interesting but horrible. You can ridicule just wars. But it won't make you men." Indicating the uneven beards of his young followers, he added, "The only way you'll pass for men like these is if someone paints mustaches on your faces. And they'll wash off tomorrow."

The Arabs grinned.

Just then the diners heard a Salvation Army band tuning up outside. The organizers said their own prayer.

"Have mercy on us.

"Lord in your goodness, save us from Hell."

While other diners stopped to listen, Holly did something she had not done for years: she prayed—silently.

"Dear God, save him from his brothers and this thirst for blood. I can't help him. If you don't, nothing can save him."

Darius did not want Holly's mood soured anymore, so he tried switching the subject. He raised his glass of Coke. "Good health. Glory afterwards."

"Are you already with the angels, Darius?" asked the older Muslim man.

A Salvation Army officer outside was rousing his troops for the coming march: "Brothers and sisters love one another more than you do your own lives. The Holy Spirit entrusts the seed of life to us for love of God."

Inside the takeaway, one of the sailors said, "This hot gospel is too much. We're off to the Moose to meet up with other guys who aren't BAs and where we can use our monsters, get laid, and sleep for an hour."

"What, in a hell like that?" said one of the girls, as she buttoned up her overcoat. With a collective giggle, guys and dolls were gone.

Two other Middle Easterners came in. One, Holly thought, had a face like a horse. The other had straggly red hair. They arrived a minute or so apart. Both ordered tortillas. Without looking at one another, they left abruptly. Darius's mood darkened.

"What's with this?" Holly asked uneasily. "They came in and then left straight away. Why didn't they stay?"

"I don't know."

When other diners were preoccupied with their meals, Holly asked the question Darius had known she would ask.

"Who is this Saddam Hussein and what does he want?"

"Saddam Hussein is the corrupt dictator of Iraq. The guys and dolls were referring to the recent war in the Persian Gulf region waged by US-led coalition forces against Ba'athist Iraq to repulse Iraq's invasion of Kuwait. Some people called it Operation Desert Storm. America still has forces in the area."

Although this was a concise and dispassionate summary, Darius immediately knew he had opened a floodgate of questions from Holly. But he was nevertheless startled when Holly said quietly, "I know your secret. You and your friends are preparing some sort of bomb. If you go ahead, you're making a living grave for yourself and a living death for me."

"Shush!" he said. "There are informers every step of the way."

Then the Arab leader spoke to his followers with a frankness he would not have used on Ellis Island.

"Day is over. It's night—the New Yorkers' day. Notice the change in smell? The tawdry glitz of neon lights casts devilish shadows. These New Yorkers have the souls of thieves. But"—and here he changed subject abruptly—"in future, we cannot meet together. We must stay in our cells. We must not lose our greatest weapon—surprise—by giving ourselves away to casual observers."

"Let's go," said Darius, still shaking at the memory of the horse-faced man.

Holly was not an adoptive New Yorker for nothing.

"Good night," she said to the Middle Easterners as if to indicate, "No fear."

Darius remembered one of the dean's mind games at BCU. Ferrari used to ask his "nephews" to quote a famous Chinese saying. When they answered, "May you live in interesting times," he would say, "Here's a better one: 'The tigers of wrath are wiser than the horses of instruction.'"

Darius got the point. In this scenario this Ramsay and his tools were tigers who acted. Back at little BCU, the crafty dean was NATO: No Action, Talk Only.

Of course, the refurbished Ellis Island was open to people besides errant lovers and Afghan Arabs. Other pairs of eyes had followed Holly that afternoon.

Next day Larry Dawdler was waiting for Groznyy in the president's outer office. Stickleman was also there with a candidate for an assistant professorship in history.

Confident of his attack, Stickleman said to Larry, "I understand that Mrs. Groznyy has recovered from her recent illness."

Larry answered, "Yes, Mordred. And it's nice of you to ask after her."

"Don't say that. I wasn't asking. My wife saw her at Ellis Island yesterday afternoon."

Larry wondered what on earth Holly was doing there. She must have gone there to get away from Groznyy. But Larry was not going to give Stickleman any satisfaction that Holly was playing away. "Holly is trying to get to know as much about New York as she can, since her singing career will be centered there."

"You don't say. Was that why she was with a man?"

So, thought Larry, the rumors must be true. Cesare has a rival.

He tried to keep a lid on his irritation.

"Who is he?" asked Stickleman.

Larry decided to wing it. "Some Manhattan agent."

"I don't think so," said Stickleman. "This guy looked like he was from the Middle East. And they were with some older guys wearing Pakistani clothes. My wife followed them around. She said they had horrible breath."

Muslim clothes? Older men? Horrible breath?

Who could these men be? Didn't Holly think about her own reputation even if she was being careless about Cesare? How close to the Arab men did Pauline Stickleman have to be to know the men had horrible breath? Did the Sticklemans have no life of their own? Was that why they were always trying to mess up other people's lives? Was this their substitute for living? Sick or not, Stickleman could damage Cesare with all this.

"Whoever the younger man was, I hear they were holding hands," added Stickleman, this time showing his chipped teeth. "Pauline said Holly looked like she'd been slept in," he added as an afterthought.

Larry could no longer pretend everything was fine and dandy. He got up abruptly. What had Holly got them all into?

Sure his barb had unnerved Larry, Stickleman continued. "I heard that at some Hollywood ball they needed nothing at all, but we are at a university in New England in an Ivy League town."

"But we're not living in Colonial times. This is the 1990s." Larry left.

Muslim clothes. Holding hands. Older men. Looked like she'd been slept in. This would humiliate Cesare. The Pakistani clothes meant these were angry outsiders determined not to assimilate. That they were older meant they were randy old goats. Holding hands suggested they had already hit the jackpot—as did Holly's reported appearance.

Canny though he was over legal matters no matter how murky, Larry was at sea in affairs of the heart. If he confronted Holly she would have an answer ready and there might well be an innocent explanation. If he told Groznyy there would be a voluble explosion and that would make matters worse when the press was sniffing around. If Larry wanted damage limitation, he would have to keep his own counsel over this.

What he had seen on Ellis Island and heard in the Tex-Mex takeaway set Darius's mind racing. Holly's comments made it speed up even more.

Outside Ramzi Yousef's tiny terrorist cell there was a world of kindly common sense with decent people going about their daily lives, earning their living and loving their families. Inside the cell Yousef and his pals lived in a tiny parallel universe of personal demons and nightmares. They were living a destructive fantasy. The mercurial, shifty Yousef now changed his original plot to set off a series of pipe bombs into a big attack on the World Trade Center.

*

"I've been president for several years. Everyone says my presidency has been prosperous," Groznyy announced to his wife over dinner.

"But your soul is tortured," she answered.

He knew this was not sympathy, not even the tart words of a Job's comforter. No, it was unmistakable reproach.

Holly was still playing her cards close to her chest. But sometimes her natural feelings got the better of her. "And why do you have to fire people so easily, as if they're nine-pin skittles? You're blind to people's good points. Hate students? Despise professors? Loathe your office staff? Repulse everyone even when you've already turned them into toads or they've refused to trumpet how much they adore you?

"But you can't do the most obvious, the most necessary thing—face up to your own self-hatred. Face facts. Face the future—instead of pretending you want to climb mountains, swim oceans, all the time carrying the pitiful Babel City University to the peak of the highest mountain in the Himalayas: the Bestest Everest!"

Despite himself, Groznyy could not but admire Holly's acquired fluency. He gave himself full credit for that.

Holly continued with a killer putdown. "But that's not what drives you, is it, honey dearest? In your case, what you want is to fail. To fall forever! When are you going to face your own inadequacy, Mr. President, you who judges others?"

It was true. Cesare's little court had started to turn in on itself, members trying to blame one another as the farrago of his presidency unraveled.

Once Lorraine Boe, now working as an aide in the president's office, caught her ex-husband, Brad Gable, rubbishing her brother, Johnnie Jaundice, on the phone. She yelled, "What the fuck do you think you are doing?"

"Just what Gus Revisor told me to do."

This provoked Lorraine into an all-out verbal attack on her ex-spouse. The two screamed at one another until Bee Flute warned them that she would have to call security guards to separate them.

Lorraine and Brad appeared for work next day as if nothing were amiss. But many relationships were poisoned by this kind of fracas.

Lorraine did not know it, but her ex had started to take financial advice freely given by his new contacts among the untrustworthy trustees. He began to invest in the stock market. Convinced that greed was good, his casual business associates opened accounts for him with two stockbrokers. But winning on the stock market was not as easy as taking a backhanded bill. When Brad lost, he took more advice and continued to play by borrowing more money to compensate for stock losses.

Brad was naturally spontaneous. He simply could not handle dark secrets. His debts multiplied. Conscience and fear made him sick to the stomach. When he collapsed suddenly with severe abdominal pains after a drink-fueled supper at the Golden Cockerel, he was carted off to the emergency room of St. Vincent's Hospital on 7th Avenue and 12th Street. He had appendicitis. After the otherwise successful operation, the surgery wound did not heal properly. What with his uncomfortable physical condition and gnawing mental distress, Brad got increasingly disturbed.

So wrapped up in his inner psychological turmoil was Groznyy that he did not recognize Mickey Garnier when the cocky investigative reporter appeared to interview him. Garnier reappraised the mahogany-paneled presidential room dotted with minor works by major artists. Groznyy's appearance was not a work of art, however. Under his greasy mop of matted hair streaked with white and gray danced untidy eyebrows.

"Is it too much to say that BCU is in crisis, turmoil, even?" Garnier asked.

"Not too much, simply wrong. BCU is on the rise. It will emerge stronger from the challenges. My academic vision will prevail." After that pithy remark, delivered with his indeterminate European accent, Groznyy shifted his scrawny butt on his stuffed chair and bounced uneasily on the cushion.

"Surely it's one thing to have a vision but another to make it materialize?" asked Garnier.

"Of course. 'Near enough is good enough' has never been my philosophy."

"Much of the controversy seems to be centered on the difference between your approach and the traditions of BCU and NHU. Both have traditionally been commuter schools teaching practical subjects—business, nursing, social work, and so on at BCU; medicine at NHU. Your preference is for arts and sciences. In a period of economic straits, should nursing and social work students be required to take great books courses?"

"Are you saying these students are less gifted, less important? We cannot tell students, 'You should just study accounting.' The opposite is true. The opportunities are infinite! The world outside academia values value."

"Isn't this grandiose?"

"My ideas aren't grandiose. They're grand."

With that, Groznyy thought that his endless charm had won over Mickey Garnier.

But Garnier was an ideal hustler-hawker. Encouraged by his editor in Norse Hoven, he phoned one of the tabloids in New York. It ran his article as a weekend feature, "Debacle at Babel City University":

The college looks like a lovely idyll of university life. Students frolic on the Cross Campus Green, capturing the welcome rays of the waning sun. They are passing time between classes by socializing or throwing Frisbees. Because the great Milhous College is nearby, local colleges have the same social pretensions as Ivy League schools. Students here enjoy the same pranks as English students at Oxbridge, like climbing turrets to leave chamber pots and ladies' underwear aloft.

But "little BCU"—as its beleaguered boss calls it—is in the eye of an academic storm between President Cesare Groznyy and his outraged professors.

What are the bones of contention for these minuscule forces, each beside themselves with grievances? The central issue is about who should determine the academic curriculum. The professors are convinced that BCU along with its annex, NHU, is a commuter school with a base in practical education—business, nursing, and social work. However, the self-described visionary president is trying to make BCU change its identity into a major arts-and-sciences college like Amherst, or Brandeis, or Reed.

Both sides like to think of themselves as liberators. The president and his supporters claim they are cleansing the university of outdated academic assumptions and bringing it into the light of inquisitive knowledge. The professors claim they are making a stand for academic independence against dictatorship. Yet, as time passes, the only thing that moves in the university is an invisible hedge of pedantic stubbornness. Its thorny tentacles block out more light month after month.

As well as thorns, the hedge has pretty flowers: the open faces of its students who've come for education.

As for the professors, they can't go on and they can't break free. It's an impasse and their careers die as they are caught in the hedge. With student enrolment falling, Babel City University is groping toward extinction.

What do you think?

Todd Carter was the first professor to phone Garnier and congratulate him.

"This is a fight to the death over university governance and the proper way to use limited resources—and you can quote me."

When he read the article, Ace Ferrari told Don Fatale, "Our tactics remain the same. We must be like monkeys high up in the trees, throwing down pits and stones onto two giants sleeping below. They will blame one another. Then they fight until they are both dead."

In the Golden Cockerel in Manhattan, when Princess Nadezhda Arachnova Glinskaya read the article, she decided to amuse herself. Donning one of the disguises Hermione had found for her, she left the townhouse through the barber shop next door and hailed a taxi. She went to Grand Central Station. She turned off the main concourse into a deserted track on the lower level and picked up a payphone receiver just inside. She had the telephone number she wanted. She got the voicemail of Pauline Stickleman. She just left an expletive. Then she dialed again.

"Is that you, Liberty Belle? I thought it must be you. Aren't you some extremist communist, toilet organization trying to destroy university education? I want you out of BCU, not President Groznyy."

The princess laughed herself silly. She could hold herself back no longer and let rip. Her water cascaded on the track. A little dog that had wandered from its owner stopped to look and wonder. A man from the maintenance crew also stopped.

"Lady, look what your dog has done."

"Bullshit, sir. That was me."

A suburban train that had been diverted to the lower level arrived. When the doors opened, it seemed like an eruption of passengers burst forth. Unlike the little dog, they wanted not to stop and wonder but simply to get upstairs and out as quickly as possible without getting spattered themselves.

Some averted their eyes. Others looked with disgust at the aberrant old woman wetting herself.

Later, Mordred Stickleman's wife, Pauline, was checking voicemail on her answering machine at home. Half drowsy at the end of the day, she was brought up sharp by what sounded like a man's voice with a Russian accent saying, "Fuck you!" The second unidentified message came from a woman assuming some other unidentifiable foreign accent.

When Pauline played the messages back to Mordred, he was incandescent—with outraged joy. He thought the caller might be Holly Wood, using one of her stage voices to threaten his wife. But when the Opposition Party hired a voice analyst to expose the ruse, they drew a blank. The specialist said that the caller was not Groznyy's wife. They were stymied. It was galling to Stickleman and his cronies.

At the restaurant, Princess Glinskaya was still in hysterics at the consternation she had caused. Again, she could not control herself. She wet the upstairs carpet. While Imelda was cleaning up the mess, Benny told Hermione, "*Macbeth* has the witches. Invisible to the naked eye, BCU has Princess Glinskaya."

Holly had no reason to feel that her trysts with Darius would end or that her feelings would lessen. Even though he was in New Jersey and she was in New England, they went on seeing one another secretly in New York. Holly did not see that her fragile state was something that Darius worked both to satisfy and to intensify. His declarations of love were genuine enough. He was just as immersed in their passion as she was. But it was not enough. Now when he touched her she felt somehow that he was molding her; for what she did not know. Holly had never felt like this before: intense sexual panic with intense fear—for him, for her. This made their lovemaking ten times more exciting, as if the danger Darius had put himself in somehow multiplied the ecstasy. It left her in a state of perpetual and agonizing bewilderment.

What they both wanted was escape.

In her case it was to escape the dreary terror of her marriage. She also wanted to get away from the princess's sporadic needling. To Holly, the princess was like a never-satisfied spider, locked in her claustrophobic Manhattan townhouse.

For Darius it was to escape the tendrils of the raging clerics in New Jersey's Little Cairo with their incessant diatribes. The clerics' words amounted to an insistent demand that young Muslims should immerse themselves in a noble destiny to destroy the great Satan.

"We can make a life together," said Darius. "It is realistic. I have my degrees. They will help me get work teaching in a private school."

"And I can go on singing and make money," said Holly.

Larry Dawdler had lived through Groznyy's controversial tenures as provost and then president. He thought it had made him hard-boiled. But now Dawdler was sick at heart. He had never liked the onerous work of BCU and the pressure he felt Groznyy put on him.

One afternoon while Dawdler was taking his regular, never-to-be-disturbed nap after his usual liquid lunch, across the campus, Brad Gable took a phone call from some bigwig who insisted on seeing Mr. Dawdler. It was the know-all from the UN who knew them both from the restaurant.

"He's resting and I can't disturb him."

"Don't bullshit me. This is essential business. It can't be delayed."

"It's more than my job's worth."

"I'll make it worth your while."

That was enough. Brad went over to the presidential suite

and woke Larry, who was fit to be tied after a weary night of phone calls from Groznyy. He flew off the handle and swore at Brad. This unsettled Brad.

Meanwhile, Bee Flute had to field another phone call from Mickey Garnier. He wanted to ask questions about the relationship between trustee chair Veronica Veneer's insurance company Bentlegs and BCU. And was it true that BCU employee Brad Gable had invested heavily in Bentlegs on its stock market flotation and that he had borrowed funds from the university to do so?

When he heard this from Bee, Groznyy knew he was going to have to face the stubborn fact that Brad had been keeping open company with trustees whom he should only have met briefly on formal occasions. It seemed that Brad had, indeed, used university funds for his personal gain by investing in Veneer's insurance company, the same company that the university also used. Groznyy had already known some of this—not the details but the general outline. He and Veronica had instigated it. However, Larry Dawdler did not know it because Groznyy had kept it from him.

With Garnier snapping at his heels, it was no longer possible for Groznyy to keep a lid on such matters. Groznyy now owned up to Dawdler about knowing something—but not all. Confronted by Larry's questions, he told him simply to send Brad away.

Larry gave Brad the bad news as gently as he could. By now Brad was shot with nerves. He burst into tears. Before he could calm him, Larry had to leave to take another phone call from the UN know-all. Alone and with tears still streaming down his face, Brad left BCU and hailed a taxi. He traveled by Amtrak to Penn Station in Manhattan. There he took a train on the Long Island Railroad. He went to a gunsmith and bought a gun. The gunsmith also advised him about cartridges and which would fire best. He bought what he needed.

Suddenly he was afraid his courage would fail him. He called at a liquor store and bought two large bottles of Smirnoff vodka. They also had glass tumblers for sale with nice fluting and the words "Crown Royal" in gray at the top rim. They were going for a dollar apiece. He bought two. The clerk asked, "Two?"

"Yup, misery loves company."

Brad put the two bottles and glasses inside his travel bag alongside the gun. God damn it, the bottles were heavy.

He drank so steadily at the lonely suburban station that he was drunk when he boarded the train. It was already dark.

It was now or never. He knew that. He felt submerged by shame. The shame of being a failure as a husband with a roving eye who could not keep his wife in the dark and his songbirds high in the trees; the shame of hitching himself to a rising academic star with mighty pretensions and falling off as the star faded. Brad had no career prospects, no future. He was shrouded by the stigma of failure whether he chose life or death.

After the guard on the train checked his ticket, he fell asleep.

When he awoke, he did not know where he was. It was pitch black. He could see nothing. He started to grope around himself. Then it came back to him. He had gone by train to Long Island and bought a gun. That was it. He felt round the seat and into his bag. He knew the cold globular shape was the half-full bottle of vodka. The train was not moving. He put the bottle and glass back into his case. Then he stumbled along the aisle to the exit doors on either side of the train. They were both locked. That must be it: the train had arrived in Penn Station. Everyone had left the train. They had left him asleep either because he was just a drunken heap or because they were too busy with their own affairs to have noticed him.

His pitiful situation hit Brad hard yet again. He sat down,

opened his case, and poured himself another drink. He felt alone, betrayed by Larry, by Groznyy, but not by Lee Aison, whom he had courted, promoted, used, and allowed to get away from him.

"There has to be a way out," he said aloud.

Twice he walked the entire length of the train, back and forth, banging open the partition doors and letting them close behind him with an even louder bang. But all the side exit doors were shut. They were closed as tight as the clenched teeth of an animal that had gobbled up its prey and was waiting for its juices to soften up its meal—him—before it digested him.

Did it matter which way he died?

Then Brad realized that, although it was dark, it was less dark at one end of the train. From the last end window of the last carriage he could make out blurry lights. One of the lights was swaying gently and also getting closer. Someone was coming toward him. He began to bang on the window, first with his fist, then with the bottle.

He shouted, "Help! Help! I'm trapped!"

A man from the railroad was standing outside, below the end window.

"Help! Help!" was all Brad could manage.

The man disappeared and then reappeared through a side door. He held his lantern at shoulder height and said, "Steady, my friend. You're safe now. What happened?"

"I fell asleep on the journey from Massapequa. Where am I?"

"You're in the yards west of Penn Station where the trains stay overnight."

The man held out his arm to assist Brad down the steep steps and finally the jump from the last step to the tracks—very steep since there was no raised platform in the yard.

"I'll get you back to the station."

Together, they walked along the track to the main station. Then they climbed steps to a raised platform.

"Thanks for saving my life."

"You're welcome, my friend. From time to time, someone falls asleep on a train, misses their destination. But you're straight now. Let me get you to the main concourse."

"Thanks a heap," was all Brad could mumble. He knew that Penn Station beneath the planet of the apes was ugly. It was inhospitable to passengers and workers alike because it was cramped and claustrophobic. Modifications over the years had done little to soften its hardness or make it a more efficient public space for moving people upstairs, down-stairs, and along. But late that night, its hubbub seemed to be mellowing as if human beings were moving contentedly about.

Brad went up to the main east exit on 7th Avenue. He stood for a moment by a newsvendor's stand. Then he crossed the avenue to the grand hotel opposite. He was stumbling and he reeked of booze. The security guard would not let him enter the hotel and told him to get lost.

As Brad stood at the northeast corner, he was surprised to see Cesare Groznyy come out of the hotel and get into a yellow taxi. The president must have been at some business meeting. Brad wanted to run up and press his face onto the side window of the cab. But he froze. It all came back to him. He had gone out of his way to buy a gun on Long Island where no one knew him. He began to cry inconsolably. He went back to Plan A. He walked a few blocks up 7th Avenue. He turned to the left, took another swig from the bottle of vodka, and walked along a side street and across 8th Avenue. He turned right into 9th Avenue. He finished the last of the vodka in the first bottle and dropped it, letting it roll off the sidewalk.

By chance he saw two old jazz cronies go into a midtown bar. He joined them. He seemed upbeat, as if he had found his old self again.

"Are things all right?" one of them asked him.

"Sure, everything's fine."

Brad was putting off his great final gesture.

When he decided he must go before he had no money left, he and his friends parted. Brad went to the Moose. This was the murky hotel on 42nd Street—a flophouse on the Deuce, the block between 8th and 9th Avenues.

Brad paid the Indian clerk with his last dollars, stumbled up the stairs and into a room on the third floor. The bed was minimal, a thin mattress on a shallow ledge with a pillow and a white sheet. There was a tawdry blanket of gray crochet wool. In the corner there was a tiny washbasin into which he urinated. Then he fell on the bed. Before he reached for the second bottle, he noted two broken syringes in a dirty corner.

He wanted to drink so as not to think and to drink in order to screw up his courage. Worst of all in his terrible situation, he, and he alone, had discovered this singer with tremendous potential, a flexible voice, strong and sweet. She was also capable of hard work so that she could develop while maintaining a rock-hard technique. And she had such powers of interpretation. But he had not appreciated her until it was too late! Brad gulped down another swig of vodka. He felt dizzy. Then it all came back to him, his failures and his inadequacies. He repeated the little cycle of misery again.

Brad had never been so terrified. It was as if the drab, off-white surroundings of the decayed room in the grungy hotel were deteriorating further into an all-encompassing gray fog. Then, worse, it seemed he fell into a psychological pit so black that it was like an oozy crater of such corrosive pitch that his senses reeled. He knew if he was going to do it, he had to take a last grip and just get on with it. But he could not. He fell back onto the rotting bed. He lay immobile. Was it for a few seconds? A few minutes? Or a bad quarter of an hour?

He sat up. He reached again for the bottle and sucked the juice out of it. He raised the gun to the side of his face. But he could not shoot. It was now or never, he told himself again. He wanted oblivion more than salvation or peace. This time when he drank, his lips caressed the lip of the bottle. Was it empty? It was not the bottle. It was the trash basket. Get on with it, he told himself again. Better my mouth, he thought. He put the nozzle firmly into the side of his mouth and pressed hard. It felt like a raging toothache. This time he pulled the trigger.

Blast, terror, nothingness.

Larry Dawdler felt bad because of the way he had spoken to Brad. When he called him at home there was no answer. He wondered if Brad might be drowning his sorrows in his favorite Manhattan watering hole with some old pals. He drove into Manhattan, went to the bar, and got the name of the hotel where Brad had gone from the drinking buddies who were still there carousing. He went to the Moose. The receptionist directed him to Brad's room.

Coming along the shabby corridor he heard a noise like something metallic being dropped into a washbowl. Larry knocked twice. When he got no response, he opened the door—which was not locked—and found Brad slumped on the floor. His head was in a trash basket and he had a revolver in his hand. Brad seemed not so much dead by violence as drained of life by exhaustion. The empty bottle of vodka rolled on the floor toward Larry.

After the shock, a nagging thought pierced Larry's brain—perhaps to lessen his own sense of guilt. It was a thought he would never have said aloud: "This is another casualty of the modern Ivan the Terrible—more collateral damage. Someone tossed aside without scruple or remorse."

Brad's suicide in a flophouse in midtown Manhattan might have passed unnoticed by the press but for the dead man's association with President Groznyy of BCU and the dark rumors swirling around him. It was not big news nation-wide. But it was most unwelcome to the Groznyy Gang because the bald facts hit at the worst suspicions about Groznyy. They included financial irregularities, construction site thefts, drunken suicide—as well as seedy flophouses. Out tumbled accusations, counter-accusations, truths, half-truths, and inventions.

Mordred Stickleman was in full flight at a faculty meeting, so emphatic in his venom that his colleagues were silenced as he read out his prepared speech.

"Brad Gable, the trimmer and recent suicide, was open in taking backhanders and pocketing plunder. He used a Manhattan restaurant, the Golden Cockerel, and its upper dining chamber, for his murky acquisitions.

"Recent press revelations have now exposed Brad Gable for embezzling funds assigned to build the new hospital extension. Arguing that the original appropriation of $5 million was unworthy of the science consortium of Milhous College, Babel City University, and Norse Hoven University, Brad Gable had proposed a façade in post-modern vernacular style with a green glass curtain wall. He secured an additional appropriation of $5 million from the BCU trustees and various public sources, plus a further $800,000 two years later, then another $500,000. By now Brad Gable and his master, President Cesare Groznyy, have spent squillions altogether on a building that is still incomplete. It's like the Tweed Ring of the 1870s or the Ohio Gang of the 1920s."

The professors agreed that the abuse had been so flagrant as to merit a special senate investigation into the contractors and their deals.

"Chief," said Larry Dawdler in the president's paneled room, "Brad's suicide has to be our wake-up call. The press has shifted from disputes about academic matters to the university's business affairs. They won't rest. It's best that we try and defuse this crisis."

Groznyy knew that Dawdler meant trying to turn the two young investigators, Garnier and Sharp, who were bent on raising their own profile as they damaged his reputation. He said, "We will buy them off."

"You mean a bribe?"

"Nothing so blatant. Nothing that can be cast back at us! These guys are supposed to be hot shots at communication. We can make one of them a visiting professor in communications theory and bring the other into our publicity team."

Groznyy picked up his phone. "Bogus, call the journalists in—not here—invite them to hear my side of the story at the Golden Cockerel."

Turning back to Dawdler, Groznyy added, "A good meal can work just as well as an honor. It's cheaper and it leaves a happy afterglow."

"And it will compromise them."

"Exactly."

So Groznyy had a plan: either get the journalist troublemakers onside or embarrass them by exposing them at lunch with him in his secret nook.

What Veronica Veneer and Georgie Lucre and other shady trustees took from Brad's suicide, however, was not that the game was up but that they had to be more skillful.

Journalist Steve Sharp declined Groznyy's kind invitation to lunch. He had already committed himself to going to a lunch Todd Carter was giving at the World Trade Center for his kid sister who had just graduated from college.

"So much the better," thought Groznyy. "Bribe one and make the other jealous."

Benny recorded Groznyy's booking in the restaurant diary for the planned compromise of Mickey Garnier. The princess recognized an opportunity.

"Holly hasn't got anywhere. What we need to do is to jolt Groznyy. This journalist isn't going to be bought off. That's the moment for us to strike—when Groznyy realizes the danger he's in. What's the word you use when families unite to force a problem member to face reality?"

"Intervention."

"Intervention, that's right. Just when Groznyy realizes he's failing with the journalist, let's—how do you say?— sock it to him. And let's get it on TV. Who will help? There's the chic Manhattan PR chick: Kelly Danson. Here's the script: Groznyy finds the journalist isn't a pushover. While he's stumbling, I appear—my long-dreaded resurrection— hand in hand with Holly to show we mean business."

Kelly Danson, urged by boyfriend Boris Goodenough, accepted the princess's kind invitation to hire a TV crew to put pressure on Groznyy at the Golden Cockerel.

The princess was on emotional fire as she planned her reappearance as Groznyy's nemesis: "I have another iron in the fire."

The princess asked Hermione to meet her upstairs. And there Hermione recognized the books on the table before them. They were illustrated books of American history. At their side was a stack of tracing paper.

"Modest taught you how to draw cartoons as he would— or, anyways, to cheat at it. We have to do what it takes to bring matters to a head. You live opposite a journalist, eager for news about Groznyy. You don't need to speak to him. I'll call him. The press isn't impartial. They're on our side."

The princess pushed the little stash of books toward Hermione. Benny shook his head. Indeed, it did not fall out as the princess wanted.

At home that weekend Hermione skimmed the history books. One cartoon caught her eye: a satire of President Warren Harding and the corrupt Ohio Gang of the 1920s, a satire based on an old nursery rhyme. Hermione set herself to work.

While he was waiting for Holly for another not-so-secret rendezvous, Darius sat in a lowly Irish bar on 42nd Street opposite the Moose, the flophouse where Brad had died. Near the window of the bar two youngsters were playing fruit machines, the guy in a red tank top and his girl in a white halter top.

"Just like an angel and a devil," thought Darius.

Darius thought he was caught between two devils: the devil of carnage in the name of fanatical purification and the devil of Christian conscience and guilt.

"The fanatics want me to help them destroy Manhattan."

His conscience reminded him that the American people had welcomed him stateside and educated him.

"Yet the fanatics say Americans are devils. But it's the fanatics who are devils hell-bent on destruction. It's true what they say. Men will swear that white is black when they're in the grip of an obsession."

Inwardly, Darius felt he was crumbling because he understood that Holly had fallen in love with him as her projection of an ideal lover, a grown-up Modest. But he was only the outer case of that person. He was just pretending to be a compassionate man. He realized he could not tell her about his past life, nor the Afghan Arabs' unfocused but malign plans for the future. If he went with his conscience, he would stay with Holly and rescue her from her marriage. But he had never told her that he already had a wife in the Middle East and that it was a comfortable marriage. If he helped the bombers more, he would be a partner in their crime and violence.

"If I squeal, I will expose my brothers in arms. Whatever I do, I'm damned. And whom could I tell? And who would believe me?"

It was as if a chilly and weighty hand had got inside Darius and was pressing hard on his heart.

When Holly arrived after a delay on the Times Square Shuttle, Darius put on a brave face. But she sensed something was wrong. The more she was with him, the more wary his inner misery was making her.

However, the suicide of Brad brought forward Darius and Holly's decision to escape. It was now or never. Holly would go to Brad's funeral in New Jersey by herself. Groznyy would not be suspicious. It would be right for Holly to attend because Brad had been her manager and because, by implication, she would be Groznyy's representative. By not going himself Groznyy would avoid questions from the press. After the funeral Holly would travel discreetly back to the PATH station in downtown Manhattan. There Darius would be ready for her. They would go to Penn Station and then disappear.

There was also the cover of the princess's intervention plans in the Golden Cockerel. Holly had agreed to attend but that was just to keep the princess quiet. By the time everyone was at the restaurant, Holly and her lover would be up, up and away.

They made love in the afternoon more intensely than usual.

When the phone rang in the middle of the night, Darius was suddenly afraid even before he picked up the receiver. He did not know who it would be for sure but he felt a wrenching in his gut as if disaster were looming for him, for Holly, and for others unknown. Even before the caller spoke, Darius guessed from the background atmosphere that it was Ramsay-Rashid's intermediary. He was not surprised that they had his number or that they withheld their own.

The young man spoke feverishly and in a muddle. Darius had to fill in the gaps in the information. There was something about another minor auto accident in New Jersey—more Keystone Kops antics from one of Ramsay-Rashid's bumbling accomplices whom Darius now knew was Mohammed Salameh. Salameh could not drive safely and yet Ramsay was using him for precarious missions. The accident had left Ramsay-Rashid on his back in hospital. But it was clear Ramsay-Rashid was still running things from his hospital bed.

What the caller wanted could hardly have been more specific.

"Ramzi wants some confirmation. If we get more hydrogen tanks, will that boost the bomb enough to be worth the risk? He's also thinking of using hydroxide gas."

Darius was unnerved. He did not want to wake Holly. He answered quietly and hurriedly. "Sure. But if you go ahead with such extras, you'll need a larger truck. And the larger the truck, the greater the chance of discovery."

"Guess we'll have to go ahead like we first planned. One last thing: if the bomb is detonated inside a truck, will it show afterwards or will the bomb obliterate everything the same way?"

Darius sensed Holly moving. In the brief moment when he was distracted—and without even a token "Thank you"— the student caller put down the phone. This made Darius's panic worse. He felt that he had given away too much. He tossed and turned. It seemed he was back under interrogation in Afghanistan. The psychological ticking inside him was endless. Round and round it went like the thudding of repeated kicks in the groin. The pain was debilitating and piercing at the same time.

When he managed to tear his mind away from the terrors of Afghanistan, he could not help calculating what amounts of destructive chemicals Ramsay or Ramzi and his cell had bought; how many pounds of urea, how many gallons of nitric acid and sulfuric acid. And were they going through with this? How had they funded things? And how had they laundered the money to cover their traces?

Round and round it went in his head.

Holly did wake. She stayed still but attentive to every move of her troubled lover.

Abruptly, yet still asleep, Darius sat bolt upright, staring ahead, and said something hard in a foreign language.

Holly turned on her side, thinking back to Modest. He was lying beside her. He whispered, "See? Blood guilty, step by step."

When Holly stared harder, Modest was gone. Which was worse—the past ripped apart like a torn curtain or the tortuous present with its insecure future?

By morning Darius was soaked with sweat. There was nothing he could do to hide his apprehension. When he and Holly parted with a sworn undertaking to meet in the PATH station after Holly returned from Brad's funeral in two days' time, they had no energy left for a tender farewell.

TWIN TOWERS

In the early hours of February 26, 1993, Ramzi Yousef loaded the explosives he had cooked in his bomb factory in Jersey City into a rented Ryder Ford F350 Econoline truck. His restless mind turned over and over again what he had done and what he had to do:

"I've packed the cardboard boxes into the back. Each has a mix of paper bags, newspapers, urea, and nitric acid. I put three red cylinders of compressed hydrogen next to them. The hydrogen in the cylinders should magnify the destructive power of the explosives. This will make one tower crash into the other and bring them both down.

"A crucial thing. I loaded the four big containers of nitroglycerine into the center of the van. I connected Atlas

Rockmaster blasting caps to each one. I reckon the bomb contains 1,500 lb of urea nitrate. That should work.

"We're off. First I collected everyone—all three vehicles. We'll have a short meeting in midtown to make sure we work together.

"As we drive I keep my crew in order with putdowns of the Big Apple: 'Welcome to the New Yorkers' morning rush hour. Take a good look. There won't be a sight like this tomorrow, for there is no tomorrow for these suckers. Everywhere you look it's just a noisy, senseless rush without pleasure. Look at them, hundreds of faces with such dull western features that you can't tell one from another.'"

But Yousef was mainly communing with himself.

"The streets from midtown to downtown are jammed with cars, taxis, and trucks. I'm excited. It's almost like being high—but that abomination is behind me now. Some neighborhoods are busy with market porters carrying groceries to Korean convenience stores. Poor working stiffs.

"There are more working stiffs living a stupid illusion of superiority: office workers—the support staff in durable clothes for their daily grind—the clerical staff in the standard uniform of dark suits and dry-cleaned shirts. Poor fools, they know nothing. Nor do the gaping tourists around them—all colors and in all sorts of clothes. They stay focused on their sightseeing plans as if simply looking at tourist attractions is living the American dream. Short-sighted fools. Their eyes gaze without really seeing. They're no better than gawking monsters, as curious to look at as the sights they've come to see. And all around them hustlers on the make: street peddlers selling everything from knickknacks to disposable razors to ballpoint pens—even fake subway tokens that are really slot-machine tokens.

"The din is enormous. That helps hide us. When the traffic gets stalled at cross streets, drivers just going on hooting together, it's like the backing group of a rock band thundering in unison. But it gets them nowhere. Yet everyone is so determined to get somewhere, anywhere, nowhere in particular. If I had my way, they would get nowhere today. Today of all days, their lives are going nowhere. Poor deluded fools, they deserve everything they're gonna get."

"Well, we are about to play such a trick on them in their favorite city, these vermin with the souls of thieves."

As his mind raced ahead to finishing off his great mission by setting off the bomb, it did not occur to Yousef and his bomber pals that these people whose lives he wanted to destroy would prove to be survivors. It never crossed Yousef's mind that the raw disorder of New York and the flotsam and jetsam of humanity, rich and poor, would eventually pool their resources to ensnare him and his terrorist plans after he had tried to bring down Corporate America.

Yousef had assembled the chemical ingredients to blow everyone into eternity and beyond. But the human beings around him were going to be brought together with great emotional solidarity by his outrage. This was something that Yousef in his excessive and stultified fanaticism could not imagine.

On that fateful February day the terrorists drove their yellow Ford Econoline truck into the twin towers' entrails underground.

Later Yousef replayed in his mind what he had done and what had not happened.

"To the side of us was a concrete wall. I knew it separated a workers' lunchroom from the ramp to the public parking lot. Inside the truck I lit four twenty-foot-long fuses. Then I dashed into our red getaway Chevrolet.

"Just as I planned, the gunpowder ignited at 12:17 pm.

"The blast wave roared upwards. It raced through five reinforced concrete floors. The explosion dislodged a twelve-foot-long diagonal brace that bound the supporting steel columns of the twin towers together.

"I had planned to increase the destruction by adding aluminum azide, magnesium azide, and bottled hydrogen, plus a container of sodium cyanide, to the mix. But there were two problems. The cost of these extras was beyond our budget. Then, more ingredients would require a larger truck, and a larger truck would have been more noticeable. The crucial ingredient in our great mission was surprise. And it was a surprise—big time."

The explosion shot through the basement of the towers where workers were having lunch. Six people died instantly: John DiGiovanni, Robert Kirkpatrick, Stephen Knapp, William Macko, Wilfredo Mercado, and Monica Smith. Monica was a thirty-five-year-old immigrant from Ecuador, widely liked for her charm. Her death was the most grotesque because she was carrying her unborn baby whom she had named Eddie.

Around the victims the bomb created a hole 150 feet in diameter that ran five floors deep in the parking garage.

The twin towers were plunged into darkness.

Up in the North Tower, people were jolted from their office tasks as the entire building shook. Overhead lights flashed off and on. Computers went down almost immediately.

A group in a brokerage firm on the eighty-fifth floor noticed smoke beginning to sweep through the door. They closed the door. One man threw up at his desk. Someone suggested using towels from the rest room to block the smoke seeping inside from under the doors. They wet the towels and banked them up against the doors to the entrance lobby.

In the tremendous shock of the explosion, many people thought they were facing sudden death. The sense of terror was palpable. Panic spread up and down the floors as workers rose to head for the nearest stairwells. All they could think about was how to get down and out as fast as possible. But the stairwells were pitch black. Few people had flashlights. The people behind were pressing down on those in front. It was as if they were kicking their way downstairs. It seemed the people lower down might be crushed by this mighty tsunami of humanity.

Since it was lunchtime the World Trade Center was also bursting with workers and visitors. Among guests that day was communications professor Todd Carter, who had come with his ally, journalist Steve Sharp, for a lunch for his disabled sister who had just graduated from college.

Their special event was interrupted by the explosion. Todd and his guests were trapped in the surging downwards wave of terrified people. Todd went into his default CIA rescuer persona. He called out, "Enough. Our only chance is to keep calm and do everything in order."

The hubbub ceased.

"Now," barked Todd, "form a human chain by putting your hand on the shoulder of the person in front of you."

People followed the impromptu command and made a twirling and fumbling human chain in the stairwell. It was getting hotter with each step.

Todd hoisted his small sister onto his shoulder. With Steve guiding them, they edged downstairs.

When they reached floors in the twenties, instead of simply fumbling forward, the human centipede turned an emotional corner and quickened its pace. It was no longer a sluggish marathon but a race, a dash to the finish: open door and light. Although he was just as keen as everyone else to get down and out to safety, Steve Sharp's default mode was the eyes-peeled, always-observant journalist. He could not stop himself taking mental notes:

"When the people in the tower got outside, some looked back. Through the smoke and flames they saw the shapes of two men who had just carried a wheelchair user down sixty stories.

"In the subway station below the World Trade Center on Level 2 the blast had blown a hole in the side of the wall. It spanned 180 feet by twelve feet. Concrete and warped metal flew like malign birds of prey, tearing some commuters' arms and legs and lacerating spines.

"Disaster was a great leveler among survivors outside. Throngs of firefighters, police officers, and paramedics around Ground Zero who had come to aid the victims of the explosion saw no visible signs to distinguish the staggering wounded—apart from age. Their faces were blackened—stained, really—by soot and filth from the explosion. They belched the debris onto the slush and snow."

During the bomb crisis Todd was so busy taking charge of frightened New Yorkers and making sure that his disabled sister was safe that he had no time to check himself. When the immediate danger was over, he recognized with a mix of shame and elation that he had secretly enjoyed being immersed in such clear and present danger. He knew this sort of action was where he belonged.

Holly Wood was returning from Brad Gable's funeral in Jersey City. She was preparing herself for her getaway with Darius Esen.

The homeward journey through New Jersey was all the same—the raggle-taggle mix of buildings on downtown strips, the dreariness of the stations—until she reached the gloomy tiles, dull walls, and drab atmosphere of the PATH Station below the World Trade Center. As she started to make her way out of the PATH station there was an almighty crash. Jolted, Holly did not know what to make of the rumble. The noise was deafening.

She saw rescue teams crawling under pipes that seemed to have fallen like mighty redwood trees in California. The smell was overpowering. She knew instinctively what the isolated flickers meant—that there must be a fire. Rescue workers were calling to encourage sufferers, saying help was at hand.

At the end of the track Holly saw paramedics moving toward some poor man who had just come out of a volley of flames. It was a horror movie, all right. A man with his clothes off lay crumpled aside a victim she was trying to tend. His flesh was peeling from his torso and fluttering in the swirling smoke.

Holly seemed to see everyone around her frozen still as in a tableau. It was not just the commuters and transport staff in anguish and panic in front of her but also the men and women in her own life. She thought of Modest as an ever-present shadow at her shoulder; of her brother, Boris, the legal eagle with his eye on the main chance; of her friend Carmine with her old Hollywood quips; of selfless Hermione keeping everything in order and her own emotions in check. She thought of the ogre who had taken her and had then left her alone for years and whose small shape cast such a giant shadow of menace with his toadies, willing and unwilling. There were those who wanted to be Cesare's pet and others who hated themselves as much as they hated him.

Holly felt dizzy. Everything seemed to be swimming around her. But, as she fainted, she thought of the beautiful Darius.

When she came to, a woman was cradling her. This woman's hair stood out all around her head like flames of fire. The woman's husband raised Holly to her feet. He said, "It's like the world's coming to an end."

They walked with her to an exit and then up into the cloudy daylight.

Holly knew where she and Darius were to meet. The confused scene outside with its bizarre mix of debris and soot spun round in her mind. The makeshift first aid centers, the jumbled assortment of fire engines, police cars, and ambulances. It was like the horrors of Groznyy's collection of war paintings come to tangled life.

But there was no point in trying to find Darius. The confusion was so great that only the fanciful scenario of a B movie could arrange a reunion in such circumstances. Holly knew that. Even if she had let go of her feelings, she had not left her common sense behind. She would have to go back to the loathsome Groznyy house until Darius found a way of getting in touch.

What did escapee terrorist Ramzi Yousef think as he made his getaway?

"Workers and tourists, capitalists and politicians alike—they all feed on fraud and self-delusion. The American people are accursed. Now they and their capitalist society will perish. May eternal fire consume their remains!"

But his botched plot had other ideas. From his vantage point on the Jersey shore Ramzi Yousef now saw that the towers were still there. Now his entirely different thoughts were most bitter:

"What went wrong? Perhaps the explosion incinerated rather than vaporized some of the chemicals. Perhaps I should have gone for broke with a bigger bomb."

Yousef could fume but he knew what he had to do next—and do fast. That very day he flew to Karachi in Pakistan using his real name: Abdul Basit Karim. He went first class.

Although he had thought something was coming, something destructive, Darius Esen was just as shocked as everyone else. When he emerged from a downtown subway early that lunchtime he heard the rumbling and saw the repercussions of the bomb all around. He did not need to work out where the bomb had struck. Darius felt events were driving him out of his mind. He wanted to hurl himself from the precipice of the towers, shrieking curses on the blowback terrorists.

He knew that it spelt the ruin of his dreams. He was not a bomber. But he was an accessory for sure. If he did not want to face prison, this time he really had to disappear. He tried to tell himself that he was a victim of fate. He tried to convince himself that his honor was dearer to him than life. He had not committed himself to terrorism. And he had not betrayed the fanatics of Little Cairo. He had not forsaken Holly. But it was no use. He would be a villain to the country that had welcomed him and given him more education and economic chances. He would be a villain to Holly, first for not trying to prevent the outrage and then for running away. Yet that was what he had to do.

"Holly will reject me."

Perhaps he had always known it would come to this. What surprised him was how keenly he felt the worst sting: "Her contempt is the most acid part."

To begin with, all that staff and guests at the Golden Cockerel restaurant knew from the radio was that there had been some explosion at the World Trade Center and that, in the aftermath, there was widespread disruption of traffic across New York City. Diners heard no noise above the clatter of the traffic. Later some said they had sensed something underground as if there had been a small earthquake.

An Arab sheik at a table near the window blanched. He tossed his headdress slightly, signaling to his henchmen sitting separately that they must settle the account and leave immediately.

"I see his sheikness has left," Benny Vincenzo muttered to Hermione. Her mind raced back to the way Arab men at the universities in Babel City tried to make themselves scarce at the slightest hint of inspection.

Benny wanted to appraise the actors in the princess's plan. But only Groznyy was in place. Benny assumed that Kelly

Danson was ready offstage for her entrance with a camera crew. But, since the bomb had disrupted downtown Manhattan, Benny guessed that the usual cast in a Groznyy crisis—the toady-cronies and the favored reporters—would not come.

As Benny circulated around the half-empty dining area, Groznyy thought Benny was like Ursula, the outrageous sea witch octopus in Disney's version of *The Little Mermaid*, plumped up with seafood delicacies that she plucked peremptorily from underwater plants, all the time protesting how she was wasting away. Groznyy wondered if he, too, was to be eaten alive.

Slightly comforted by his bizarre comparison between big Benny and overbearing Ursula, Groznyy ate his meal in morose silence downstairs in the main salon with the *hoi polloi*. He skimmed the surface of the lentil soup and picked at stray leaves in the green salad. The dark circles around his blinking eyes made him look like a giant panda. Would he eat, shoot, and leave?

Later, when people were able to travel cautiously around Manhattan, news became more precise. The bomb blast had opened a 100-foot hole through five sublevels of the North Tower. The worst damage was on levels B1 and B2 but there was also significant structural damage on level B3.

A latecomer at another table in the Golden Cockerel said, "There are news reports that six or seven people have been killed in the explosion."

When Benny came back into the dining room he handed Groznyy a hastily scrawled note on a slip of pink paper. It told Groznyy that his reporter guest had called to say that he had been delayed in the confusion and might not be able to make the meeting.

Suddenly the notorious Russian dragon appeared out of nowhere. Groznyy sensed that she must have emerged from some half-hidden door on a pre-arranged cue. Princess

Nadezhda Arachnova Glinskaya inclined her head slightly and said, "*Zdrazvitye*, little prince, *tsaryevitch*.

"Just as you thought I was gone. Yes, how desperately you must have wanted to persuade yourself that some old woman's sodden body pulled from the East River that you identified as me really was me."

The princess sat at his table uninvited and unwanted. She thrust a copy of the day's *Norse Hoven Courier* at him. It was open at a page with a large cartoon insulting him.

The cartoon boasted an outsize boot, out of which protruded an old woman: a harpy in a frilly frock with her hair knotted in a bun and with ringlets. She was raising her fingers in shock-horror. Her face was that of Cesare Groznyy. He was "The Old Woman Who Lived in a Shoe Who Had So Many Children She Didn't Know What to Do."

Out of the old boot burst a flock of repulsive old men, bearing placards to identify them: "Kickbacks," "Backhanders," "Deceit," "Betrayal of Academic Standards," and "Pedantry." The old men looked surprisingly like his cronies Bogus Revisor, Larry Dawdler, Georgie Lucre, and Veronica Veneer. Under the boot expired the wretched souls of "Academic Freedom" and "Scientific Integrity," the latter looking like the late Brad Gable.

For the moment all Groznyy was interested in was his dead son's signature in the lower right corner. There it was— not "Dare Devil" as in the student paper but "Modest Groznyy." Not then nor later did he recall that Modest had never used his own name while he was alive.

"What do you think of that?" the princess asked. "You can order your minions up and down your college greens. You can terrify them and impoverish their weary minds. You can leave your exhausted employees in the prison of their failures, but their silly jokes and jibes pass through the strongest bars."

He looked hard at his wine glass, knowing what she would say next.

"It's not poisoned, if that's what you think. The poison's in you. Your heart is overflowing with poison. Chance may have saved you today. But that is not the end of it. Your guilt is eating you up inside. Whatever your fine words, guilt and pain will hammer in your ears. Curses are going to suffocate you."

They could now hear another radio from the upstairs kitchen: "Early estimates suggest that 50,000 workers and visitors to the World Trade Center have been left gasping for air inside the 110-story North Tower. Many trapped inside have to walk down dark stairwells because the Center has no lighting for this sort of emergency. For some the perilous route to safety will take two hours."

The princess turned to Benny. "He's psychologically sick. Didn't you know that, *caro* Benny? And the upshot? Two universities, one murder, two suicides, one fire, one death by exposure. Quite a tally for little Ivan the Terrible. And the personal climax? Imminent career death. And the best joke is: Cesare Groznyy, our modern Ivan the Terrible, has become Ivan the Terrified. And he's still wondering what he did wrong."

Groznyy exploded with such a violent temper tantrum that he overturned the table with its cutlery and crockery and what was left of his food and drink. Groznyy went for the princess. She fell back just as two photographers burst in with shoulder-held TV cameras capturing everything.

Groznyy's two consiglieri, Larry Dawdler and Bogus Revisor, arrived late and were as surprised as the other players.

Fifteen minutes later, Princess Glinskaya was outside the restaurant in front of a small TV crew, being ordered about by Kelly Danson. Touching the rising red weal on her cheek, the princess gave her rehearsed speech condemning Groznyy and his methods.

"Supposedly, in World War II Cesare Groznyy supported Russian partisans against the Germans, facing down Nazi soldiers with machine guns. He's still facing down enemies—but this time with his considerable rhetoric. At least that's what he thinks. In reality he's pulling faces at them."

When everyone had left, the princess exploded at Benny and Hermione.

"How dare they bomb the World Trade Center and upstage me? To throw the dice and find we will be buried in today's TV news and tomorrow's newspapers! Damn them all to hell."

As Holly struggled with her tears on the crowded commuter train going home, dreaded thoughts nudged her more and more insistently. She recalled how Darius had suggested that he should spend the night before their getaway in Manhattan.

"We can't be seen together beforehand. It's best I travel to Manhattan the night before to be sure I'm there whatever happens."

Had Darius known something was going to happen?

Then it hit her with deadening insistence. Darius was not going to meet her now or ever. He had gone. And he had gone because he was mixed up in this bomb outrage. She knew she had to steady herself until her emotions calmed down.

No lover, no intervention, no future.

Later, Holly sat listlessly on the bed in the Groznyy house knowing she had tried and failed to escape. She did not know what anyone at BCU guessed about her affair with the now-disappeared Darius.

The only thing that united Darius and Holly now was their separate misery. She had given in to her emotions, in to her most tender need for companionship and love. She had expected Darius to be her savior. Instead, he had run away when the mystery bomb had exploded. Holly felt ashamed because she had begun to understand what this bomb was— not an isolated incident but an attack on America.

At her most wretched moments, the unseen but deeply felt presence of Modest gave her comfort. She kept photos of Modest in a drawer. Fumbling because she was still shaken, she took out a photo and sobbed onto it: "You were the best. You gave me something to live up to. I failed."

Still talking to Modest, she added, "These names—Darius Esen and Darko Delizio—why do I think they're not on the level? No one has had more names than me."

A few short months ago, she had been with them in this stage show about assuming false identities, making false promises, and allowing sex to rule heads and hearts with bittersweet consequences. And her husband, damn him, so contemptuous of the stage, had hit upon the bitter crux of the climax of the opera and found a resolution more psychologically daring and convincing than any ordinary production. It came down to the destructive consequences of playing games. Holly knew she had been played upon like a clarinet, the way she caressed the songs she sang. It hurt her deep in the gut. She clutched the photo until her fingers were sore. Modest's so simple words came back with murmuring insistence: "You are the Scheherazade of song."

Modest was silent as well as still.

Darius knew that whatever he wanted, he could not go first to Turkey in case they were looking for him at airports there. He had to choose an identity from his small collection of alias passports: Carlo Corrado, Pereda Vargas, Francesco Moor. He selected one with a mixed religion name: Manish Gupta. Recalling some overheard terrorist advice, Darius travelled first class.

As he tried to doze on the plane to Karachi, Darius seemed

to see Holly's accusing face reflected in the window to the side. He stared at the ghost face. A terrible agony welled up inside him. He wanted to whimper.

"I lied to her. I made love to her and ran away."

Unnerved as he had been by the unexpected resurrection of the Russian intelligence officer at BCU, worse was to come. Stunned as he was by the bomb under the World Trade Center, he faced an immediate threat. Sudden fear burst inside him. For ahead of him on the plane to Karachi, he saw the back of someone's head. First he suspected, then, as it inclined to the right, he was sure. Unexpected dread knocked his shaky composure. It was him; it must be him— the man known as Ramsay, as Ramzi, and as Rashid, the man who had supervised his "interviews" from behind the scenes. Darius was terrified of exposure and then terrified that the plane itself might hold a cargo of death with a hidden bomb. When the man rose and moved to the lavatory, Darius was gripped by panic.

Ramzi Yousef saw him. Recognition was instant. The horse face with scars from burns and huge liquid eyes did not have to give Darius a second glance. The first glance was enough. Without seeming to register anything, Yousef looked at him only briefly. On the surface the glance seemed to be indifferent. Darius knew better. The apparently unin-terested look carried a veiled threat.

Darius gripped the slender arms of the seat. He stared ahead. To make a show of indifference must be part of the unwritten terrorist code. He was more frightened than he had ever been under fire in Afghanistan. He could not think clearly enough to plan ahead. He waited anxiously for Yousef to return from the lavatory.

Then Yousef reappeared as inconsequentially as he had gone in. This time, just after he moved two seats ahead of Darius, he looked back. The liquid eyes stared and the lids closed a little. Darius read this unspoken message loud and clear: "I know who you are, where you're from, about your wife and kids, and how you've been gallivanting around with the loose jazz singer. You think of me as a fanatic. You underestimate me. I have your number, my pseudo-American buddy, more than you have mine. I can hide. You cannot."

Yousef turned away. Darius was petrified. His face flooded with fear. He had faced down Americans and Russians in Afghanistan; how could it be that this guilty man could conjure up such fear? Darius knew the dread he felt was fear of open exposure, condemnation, and elimination. Was there a bomb on the plane?

The passenger next to Darius noticed his agitation and said kind-heartedly, "It's just a spot of turbulence. It will pass."

Darius managed a nod to acknowledge this fleeting kindness. But his terror was palpable. He tried to rationalize what Yousef could and could not do. He was a man on the run whose priority was to disappear! That would require all his energy and skill. Musing thus, Darius passed a troubled night.

Yousef told himself he was still going to his great destiny.

Yousef knew he had to be composed, to assume a well-heeled identity. He always had escape routes and escape personas prepared in advance of any discovery. But although his expression was inscrutable to outsiders, inwardly he was turning over and over in his mind reasons why the bomb had exploded but not done its work.

"I should never have persisted with Salamch—that boob. I should have fired him after the first car crash—not taken account of his dumb loyalty. All those auto accidents. We were lucky he didn't bring us down. Then what went wrong with the bomb? I had done my research. Years of studying. Months of experimenting. Was the balance of the urea and the sulfuric acid wrong? Was there something about the construction of the twin totems of Capitalist America that I didn't understand?"

Then another fear nagged Yousef on the overnight flight.

"Did the explosion wreck the truck beyond recognition so that it can't be traced? Or will its remains lead the Feds to me wherever I go?"

Round and round went such disturbing self-accusations of incompetence in Yousef's overworked brain.

When the plane landed in Karachi, Darius Esen went through immigration like an automaton. He kept a wary eye on Yousef, seeing his distinctive head bob and weave and then disappear, which was what Darius had to do.

First he breathed a sigh of relief in the baking sunshine. But as the weeks passed into months, wherever he went, Darius could not shake off the nagging fear of exposure made worse by his inner shame. He was an accessory to the bomb that had caused havoc in Manhattan. As he crossed and re-crossed the Middle East, he began to hate himself.

HEROIC INVESTIGATIONS

The outrage at the World Trade Center sent lasting shivers across almost everyone who had been there that day. But this was not how Todd Carter felt. A psychological fire burned inside him. He yearned to be a player again, to join in the Feds' dangerous investigation into the whats, hows, and whys of the explosion even though, as a renegade CIA man, he might not be trusted. Todd's gut instinct was that the outrage had been caused by a bomb and that Ramzi Yousef was the principal culprit.

Others were not sure—or needed convincing.

Despite the rage of the explosion, the twin towers had absorbed the detonation. Neither tower had crashed to the ground. However, besides the toll of six lives and one unborn child, 1,042 people had been injured. Moreover, the bomb had undermined the inner construction of the twin towers' defensive bulwarks. One of the crucial concrete slabs protecting the towers had slid down. Engineers worked to support the lower concrete slab and stop water getting in and rusting the structural columns. Had that happened, it would have forced demolition of the World Trade Center on straightforward grounds of safety

The debris—massive and small—was thrown every which way with all sorts of metals twisted around one another. There were 6,000 tons of debris.

As the conspirators scuttled away, the FBI and its partners began staffing a command center to ascertain the damage and find who was responsible. The principal agency investigating the outrage was the JTTF: the Joint Terrorist Task Force. It had been first formed in 1980 to pool resources of the FBI and the New York Police Department. Later, it included the State Department and the Immigration and Naturalization Service.

There was no end of suspect organizations for the atrocity, ranging from Balkan extremists to Serbian, Croatian, and Macedonian nationalists and Colombian drug cartels. Because they had been tracking Islamic fundamentalists in New York, the Feds' instincts told them that this terrible bomb was, indeed, the work of Islamic terrorists with a wider mission.

Todd wanted to be part of the action. But he knew he could not. He could, however, keep his eyes and ears and instincts peeled. He knew that the JTTF was preparing a team to enter the bombsite when it was safer to do so. The task force eventually numbered 700 people.

The area under and around the twin towers—what came to be known as Ground Zero—was potentially lethal for investigators. The atmosphere was toxic. The team of investigators wore white jumpsuits, helmets, respirators, and gloves to protect themselves from harmful chemicals, asbestos, and leaking sewage.

With such persistence, whatever the hazards, Todd believed that the investigators' stamina would yield a lucky break. Indeed, it seemed the bombers had miscalculated, assuming that their explosion would blow apart the truck that held the bomb and render it indistinguishable. Whereas other vehicles had been damaged from the outside, a single truck was ravaged inside out. Surely this must have been the one that had contained the bomb?

Todd continued to take a keen interest in the way the JTTF explored and unfolded the secrets of the bomb. From time to time Todd met Steve Sharp, sharing such secrets as he knew with him on the strict understanding that Steve kept everything between them until Todd ever—if at all—gave him permission to use them.

If they were in New York they decided to meet not in the Golden Cockerel but in locations where they were not known. When they met in the Tex-Mex fast-food *La Fuerza de Sino* on the West Side near the docks, Todd was almost on fire with his news, interrupting Steve's reverie about the fast-food outlet's name. *Fuerza de Sino*: power of fate.

"Inspectors found a gear assembly and two parts of its forged-steel casing ripped apart, just below the bomb," Todd said. "They ran gloved fingers over the metal and found the series of dots and digits that makes up the VIN."

"The vehicle identification number?" Steve asked, wanting to be sure.

"Exactly. And having found the VIN, they soon discovered that Ryder—the nationwide vehicle-hire company—had bought this van and that the current lessee was one Mohammed Salameh."

Steve knew that Todd was using him, getting him to take notes for a book or perhaps to collate information to show the CIA or the JTTF that, whether he was in the loop or not,

Todd still knew what was going on. And Steve wanted to stay in Todd's career scenario even as a supporting player. Just as Steve sensed that Todd was auditioning him for some unspecified role, Todd surmised that Steve was considering him as a career ladder.

Todd went on.

"Salameh had already reported the vehicle missing. He almost gave himself away by cheekily asking the leasing company for a refund of his $400 deposit. He wanted the money to upgrade an airline ticket for his own getaway from New York.

"An FBI agent posed as a Ryder employee, an invented 'loss prevention analyst,' when he met Salameh to trap him. He played simple with Salameh, giving him compensation of $200 for the loss of the vehicle and letting him leave. Salameh's rental documents were covered with traces of chemical nitrates commonly used in explosives. He was arrested outside the building but away from the prying eyes of journalists."

As they left the fast food café, Steve cast a quick glance at some of the posters on the walls, including reproductions of classic patriotic posters from World War II. He said to Todd, "Funny, it's almost as if Osama bin Laden is standing right behind you."

What Todd told Steve Sharp was only the beginning of the dragnet.

Soon three more suspects were in custody: Nidal Ayyad, Mahmud Abouhalima, and Ahmed Ajaj, the terrorist with the crudely falsified passport who had been detained by the INS at Kennedy Airport when, albeit with sharp misgivings, they had let Yousef in.

The JTTF had other telltale evidence. Investigators began scouring phone records. They discovered that the now-absent kingpin Ramzi Yousef had made thousands of phone calls to terrorist contacts in the Middle East. It seemed he had founded a small cabal of militant extremists. He was traced through flights to Pakistan and Afghanistan. The CIA offered a reward of $2 million for Yousef's capture.

From safety in Asia—and having partly regained his composure—Yousef sent a letter to the *New York Times* that declared his motive for the bombing: "We declare our responsibility for the explosion on the mentioned building. This action was done in response to the American political, economic, and military support for Israel, the state of terrorism, and for the rest of the dictator countries in the region."

The World Trade Center catastrophe was a botched bomb. That was not at all what the dean of psychology at BCU had wanted. It had caused extensive and horrible damage. It might alert Americans to the dangers facing them, whereas the secretive Oryx Party wanted more time to prepare—always more time.

"However, it will consume the men who investigate it. It will all but kill them. We wait," Ace Ferrari told Don Fatale. "We have to learn what we can from the Feds' discoveries that the press will release drip by drip."

In pursuit of Yousef and his cabal the Feds also used informers, sometimes insiders to the terrorist plots. This was not only for their special knowledge but also for their emotional empathy with the victims rather than the perpetrators. The Feds thought the insiders' empathy was a guarantee of loyalty to the Feds and to the US.

Todd was still giving Steve Sharp such information as he knew. They sipped coffee in the diner in Norse Hoven where Muhktar had once provoked Todd after Darius's lecture on Israel and Palestine.

"One of their double agents is Emad Salem. At one time,

he had a high rank in the Egyptian army. And he was close to Afghan Arab dissidents even while working as an informant for the FBI. It seems Salem is genuinely appalled by the murder of six innocent people in the World Trade Center—truly shocked by the gross barbarity."

"I heard on the grapevine that the FBI now pays him a salary of $1.5 million," said Steve.

"Maybe; they've certainly set him to work. The FBI fitted Salem with microphones so minute they could be hidden in the zipper of his trousers when he mixed with Middle Eastern immigrants. Through recorded conversations Salameh showed the FBI that there was a series of bombs planned against American targets.

"This was a second terrorist plot to bomb a series of New York landmarks simultaneously; also to bomb some major passenger conduits: two in the Holland and Lincoln tunnels, one at the George Washington Bridge. Other targets were American icons like the Statue of Liberty; also the UN and Federal Plaza, site of the FBI office."

Steve was astonished but suppressed a low whistle.

"Other targets were against Jews, such as the midtown diamond district where many workers are Hassidic Jews," Todd said.

"They don't limit themselves, do they?"

"That's for sure. Well, still working undercover, Salem rented an old warehouse in Jamaica, Queens. This was to be the springboard for the FBI sting operation. It reached its climax two days ago when scores of marksmen and assault teams cornered twelve conspirators inside the warehouse. Can you believe it? They were using wooden spatulas to mix fuel and fertilizers into bombs."

These various discoveries became the current big story for New York media.

On September 14, 1993, two months after the JTTF

discovery of the wider terrorist conspiracy against New York, the first World Trade Center bomb trial opened against Mohammed Salameh, Mahmud Abouhalima, Nidal Ayyad, and Ahmed Ajaj. Scores of witnesses gave evidence. Much of it pointed to the young mastermind, the phantom menace yet to be captured.

The judge, Kevin Duffy, was an experienced, mainly respected but sometimes controversial judge, skilled in negotiating the legal snares of legally complex and socially toxic cases. The trial continued until March 4, 1994, when a skilled summary by US Attorney Henry DePippo drew together the threads of the thirty-eight separate charges against the four defendants. The jury convicted them of all charges. Judge Duffy sentenced each of them to prison for 240 years. They were later taken to the high-security US Penitentiary at Lewisburg, Pennsylvania.

When the *New York Post* covered the verdict and Duffy's sentencing, it described Duffy as "Avenger."

Now pressure was on to capture Yousef.

Mid 1990s

ENDLESS CONSPIRACIES

For some time Holly was too listless to sing. Her nerves were shot.

Although she and others at BCU did not know the reasons for Holly's dejection, Lorraine Boe, with all the warm-hearted kindness she felt naturally and the business acumen she had developed in human resources, knew what to do to help the talented muse of her late ex-husband. She came every day to prepare a modest meal, took out Holly's diary, and called managers at various venues across the tri-state area. She made diplomatic excuses and took decisions as to which scheduled gigs Holly would fulfil, given time. Later, Larry Dawdler offered to take over bookings for Holly's engagements. Holly knew his presence would protect her. But she also knew that Dawdler's unpaid help was a way for Groznyy to control her.

Never had Holly appreciated Dr. Chicago's support so much. Holly did not have the learning of her university friends. For her, the torture was the continuous fear of discovery of the aborted getaway and the continuous sniping by her husband's enemies. In her eyes Groznyy was far from a prince. He would never be anything more to her than an envenomed toad—as he was to his enemies.

Almost in despair she visited the grave of Anna Stasinova, two towns over. Anna's grave with its Russian Orthodox decorations was in a plot large enough to hold Groznyy's body when the blessed event of his death swallowed up his mortal coil. Holly was not the first person to think that the way the sheltering boughs of the trees seemed to intertwine made them look like protective crosses. But they were no comfort. Tears of rage, helplessness, and inconsolable grief burst like a dam.

She felt—but she could not speak about it—that Anna's grave somehow held a clue to the dark secret she wanted to expose. She heard someone whistling. Trying to place the tune distracted her for a moment. It was "Someone to Watch Over Me."

But Holly left without comfort. She did not see two men in overcoats at the side of the church. They had the same suspicion as she did about the grave and its secret. Her presence confirmed them in their interpretation.

At the cemetery gate Holly turned slightly to brush away her tears. And there he was. By some rose-colored stone pillars with Egyptian hieroglyphs was Modest with the hyacinth curls. He was sitting on a bench with his sketch-book and drawing. He looked up at Holly and smiled.

"You were right. Mama took the secret with her to her grave. It's there. Still."

Holly stumbled. And in that moment, Modest was gone.

Of all her new friends, it was selfless Hermione who coaxed Holly back into what to her—ever the romantic artist—was surely Holly's destiny. Hermione had the skill to do something imaginative, first by playing the soothing music of Chopin and Bizet, then the songs of yesterday, and then more spiky jazz numbers.

Hermione realized that, however much she resented Holly for having stolen Modest, here was a major stage artist. She had an idea that would break down any lingering coldness between them and also help Holly artistically. She went to the music library of Milhous College and asked for help identifying a tune. Next day, in a break in rehearsal for another fundraiser concert, Hermione played the tune that the string quartet had played at Grishka Groznyy's reception in the Golden Cockerel.

"That tune is going to stay with me all day," Holly said

when Hermione had stopped embroidering it and brought it to a happy close.

"You bet. It's the first aria from an opera by Rimsky-Korsakov. The title is a mouthful: *The Invisible City of Kitezh*. Fevronia is the heroine. She lives near the river Volga. She is ecstatic about the beauty of nature. To her the woods are like a great temple."

Hermione knew that Holly would respond instinctively to the music. She began to play the aria again. This was to indicate to Holly that she should take up the score. Again, Holly was touched by the plaintive melody.

Hermione said, "It would be a good song for you. The tune is as immortal as any modern classic like 'Summertime.'"

Hermione rapped the tune out gently. Holly found herself joining in. As the other artists drifted in, they listened spellbound. Holly sensed why Hermione wanted to coax her onto a new artistic path.

"Sing it again, Holly," said a stagehand.

Her reply surprised them.

"I don't think so. I never sing the same song twice for nothing."

Holly had read a tale Hermione had shown her in *The Thousand and One Nights* about a magical singing bird that repeated the same answer to a frequently asked question. Carmine had suggested Holly use this as a default line every time someone asked her to sing an impromptu encore.

Watching from the wings was sub treasurer Darko Delizio, the former Ferrando, tenor soldier lover in *Cosi*. Holly knew he had always wanted her. Hermione and the princess also knew. But it was the princess who decided to turn his unrequited love to her own advantage. She knew that the Opposition Party's campaign was at best sputtering on. Any political opportunity that might have been come from the scandal of Brad Gable's suicide had disintegrated in the media conflagration over the World Trade Center bomb.

Reverting to her imagined role as a canny New Yorker, the princess said to Benny, "They need a kick up the ass."

"And I bet you're going to give it to them."

Benny wondered at the princess's tenacity. Even at her advanced age—whatever that was—she was not going to set aside revenge on Groznyy for the death of his son—not to mention her own back catalog of past slights. Benny wondered what the princess would now dredge up from the dark recesses of her manipulative mind.

She tapped her lips with her spindly index finger. "Groznyy wants to be as rich as Croesus—to exceed his brother—right?"

"Right."

"Well, since all his businesses are part-owned with other people, they're not going to give his game away."

"Right."

The princess saw that any Groznyy financial irregularity would cause more uproar at BCU. And the glare of more press coverage might make all the difference. "We have to find him out through his salary and his perks."

They had to devise a way of getting certain documents with incriminating details to where they could provoke tumult without Groznyy being able to trace the paper trail.

"I don't see how I can reach them," said Holly when the princess called her. "I don't have access to his private documents. He keeps them in a bank vault. There are some locked in the treasurer's office. Parthy Burnable is utterly loyal to him. She owes everything to him."

"However we do it, we have to target the treasurer's office. Aren't you friendly with Darko Delizio? He's a sub treasurer. Doesn't he want you?"

Holly was not a natural conspirator. But she agreed to try.

"I'll do whatever I have to do for you, my dear," she said aloud, thinking of Modest. "I have to vary my jogging schedule," she added.

It was true. Darko had always wanted Holly. He had been startled by, and jealous of, her relationship with Darius. When by chance Holly ran near the small suburban train station where he got off the commuter train, his emotions got the better of his common sense. On successive days Holly's initially casual greetings at the station were followed by generous smiles and welcoming remarks, leading to slight physical touches—a handshake, the unnecessary brushing away of a stray hair on his shoulder. One day their brief conversation was longer and Holly was walking toward Babel City University with him. He could not stand the tiny distance between them. He embraced her with all his pent-up passion.

"I've always wanted this, to have you. It was torture to me when you were cast opposite Darius in *Cosi*. All the time you were making love to Darius onstage, I was racked with jealousy. I loved you. But you believed him and his words offstage as well as on it. And he ran away. I never will."

Holly wondered how often Darko had spun such a line. They agreed to meet that afternoon.

Darko was following his emotions and his own mentor's script. Holly Wood was following her desperate desire to unmask Groznyy according to the script the princess had dictated. He lived to talk of love as a prelude. She wanted to speak of practical matters.

When Holly phoned him at his desk in mid-afternoon, Darko thought she was going to cancel their rendezvous. His heart sank. In fact, Holly asked him if he could come to the house an hour later than they had first agreed. He also heard Groznyy in the background almost yelling at her, "What are you, eh? You're nothing but a nightclub singer." Then Groznyy went out of earshot. Holly could not have planned such an outburst from her husband better if she had tried to show Darko what she had to put up with.

When Darko came to the seashore house by the back

veranda, he found Holly clearly shaken. She plunged into her sorry domestic politics.

"I'm at his mercy. You must have heard what he said. I'm a prisoner in my own home."

Holly really was in a state of emotional turmoil.

"His deliberate insulting me is part of his system of control. He doesn't want me to have any artistic freedom. This lovely house is like a morgue. Look around you at the mangled limbs of people in the paintings. It's like he's still in World War II. I need the tenderness of a free spirit like you—someone strong enough for us to be able to escape together."

All this was true about how Holly felt. But she was also economical with the truth. Holly did not mention her past, her past with Modest, and the reason why she was opening up to Darko. Darko would have given her anything he could to make love to her. And he knew she knew it.

"You remember the little prank I played with Mukhtar—the chemist—pretending to drink poison when you sang at Badger's Sett?" he asked. "That's how silly I was. But my feelings were sincere."

After a few days, Darko was ready to fall in with Holly's stated plan. If they were to go away together, they would need money.

"He keeps me completely in the dark about money. I don't know what there is. I don't know if any of what there is is mine. If we are to plan ahead, we need to find out, to be certain. Can you help?"

"Yes."

Darko arrived on a designated day at the president's seashore house in deliveryman's clothes hired by Benny and left for him in a janitor's closet by Hermione. His face was partly hidden by a peaked cap. As he rang the doorbell, he called out, "Special delivery for Mrs. Groznyy."

Groznyy was in his study having coffee with Larry Dawdler.

Holly was dressed to go out and was wearing gloves. Benny had told her, "No fingerprints."

"Hi! I've been expecting these," she said at the door without giving Darko a second look. She asked him to wait in the hall while she opened the package in a side room.

"This is just what I asked for: *Pajama Game*, *Les Misérables*—just like all of us at BCU." She reeled off some other titles. "Thank you."

She pretended to sign something. With that, Darko was gone.

Without looking at Groznyy and Dawdler, Holly took out photocopies of Groznyy's tax returns that Darko had made from Parthy Burnable's secret files. There were also other receipts folded into the scores. Her hands were trembling. She put the photocopies in two brown envelopes.

"Good to see you, Larry," she called back as she left the house with the various scores ostentatiously piled on the hall table.

Holly drove to first one and then another suburban post office where she was not known. With a pre-typed address label and using a phony dispatch address, she sent the two precious envelopes separately by regular mail to the Golden Cockerel in Manhattan.

"This is what you need," said Benny when he and the princess opened the envelopes and scoured the contents.

Benny hid one set of copies while handing over the other set to the princess. In themselves the documents were as dry as dust—simply records of salary payments and tax returns. What they implied was dynamite in university politics.

"Invite Norse Hoven's answer to Bernstein and Woodward round," suggested the princess. "Reporters will do a lot for a good meal—especially one cooked by Imelda."

"They've moved on," answered Benny. "Mickey Garnier

now works as an editor in publishing in Manhattan. Steve Sharp has moved from the local rag in Norse Hoven to the local TV station, Network News Norse Hoven."

"That might be better—two outlets. Do you think they'll come?"

"You bet your bottom dollar. I think they both keep their contacts well oiled. And this could be their big break."

Indeed, new careers they might have in TV and publishing but Sharp and Garnier still had an inner core of muckraking journalism. To be the agents who helped topple a university president mired in double-dealing and wrapped in pretensions would secure their credentials across the northeast—not to mention guarantee future incomes.

And so, after a free lunch, the two journalists departed with copies of the telltale documents. As they left, they held the front door open for Golden Cockerel chef Imelda, who was leaving for two weeks in the Philippines at her hometown of Cebu City on the island of Cebu.

Sharp and Garnier worked through that night and the next polishing their prose. Their first instinct was to drop accusations like bombs as soon as possible. But then they agreed they should find out as much as they could, get as much hard evidence as possible, and refine their prose. They would let fly when their words would carry most weight.

None of the players in this little anti-Groznyy scenario cared about Darko—that he and Holly would not escape. Holly told Darko that the probable ruckus over the secret accounts meant that they would have to postpone their getaway. The princess told Holly, "Don't worry—every time you drift by, his knees turn to water. He won't complain. He's just more junk male."

Neither Holly nor the princess knew then how far Darko was prepared to go. No matter how smitten Darko was with Holly, he was ruled by a bigger attraction: his part in a great destiny—to liberate the Middle East from the capitalist West.

Music now enveloped Holly. She could not get Fevronia's aria out of her head—just as Hermione had intended. First it came to her all of a sudden. Then she started humming it, then singing it as a vocalise until she began to play with the melody, embroidering it until it fitted her voice like a glove.

Moving around southeast Asia, Ramzi Yousef was at his exercises again.

He was on an ecstatic personal high. Not only had he got away with murder, but also sub-Arabian and southeast Asia were his as he swanned around Pakistan and swooped down as predator onto Thailand and the Philippines. It was an Arabian Nights of excessive pleasure with easy local girls who squirmed with delight when he called them bitches. He smiled as he thought of his conquests:

"Not every girl—western, Pakistani, or Filipino—is easy. Some don't think I'm good-looking enough. Some sense I'm dangerous—and I am. But those who do find me attractive find me irresistible. My sense of danger is a powerful aphrodisiac and I use that.

"What more could I want? I have almost instant access to mayhem and death via those great modern genies of the skies, the airplanes. I do not need to be a Middle East oil millionaire to take what I want when I want it. For those who bother to read them, the Arabian tales of *One Thousand and One Nights* are as full of cruelty as they are of intrigue and sumptuousness. And I can move seamlessly between all three."

Yousef proved toxic and dangerous to all who followed him. His accomplices might have heard of parallel universes and virtual realities, but not of parallel underworlds. Now it was as if they had been kidnapped and they were living in a subterranean dungeon of psychological hell.

Without scruple or remorse, and using and discarding accomplices like so many worn dolls, Yousef embarked on sporadic acts of terror, stirring up intense fear when he performed, and later boasted of, atrocities. Over two years Yousef considered but aborted assassination attempts on Pope John Paul II, President Bill Clinton of the US, and Prime Minister Benazir Bhutto of Pakistan.

Yousef would recount his planned or aborted crimes not as a far-fetched Arabian horror fable but as guerrilla strategy with a high moral purpose. He bragged how he had organized the Mashhad ("Place of Martyrdom") bombing on June 20, 1994, in Iran, a massacre in which twenty-six pilgrims died. The Sunni Yousef salivated as he recalled the crisis:

"Murder in the mosque? That huge old chandelier crashed onto the heads of people as they prayed. How I hate Shiites! I told them I had done it but they could not track me down."

Yousef's most bizarre and biggest plan was to bring down eleven American airliners simultaneously over the Pacific.

For that he needed trial runs:

"Using an Italian name, Armaldo Forlani, I bought a one-way ticket for a Philippine Airlines flight in Manila to Cebu. On December 11, 1994, I walked through the X-ray machines in Manila with a nine-volt battery hidden in each of my shoes. Nobody noticed anything. Nobody suspected anything. Then I boarded flight 434 to Cebu. I sat near the back in seat 35F. Then I did what I had to do."

Every time New York chef Imelda traveled home to the Philippines, she was on tenterhooks. First she had to swap her gender-bending turn as a chic Manhattan crossdresser and go as a man. In the enclosed hermitage of the Golden Cockerel restaurant, Imelda's tongue was as sharp as her kitchen knives. In New York she was free from provincial life. Manhattan allowed her to live like a caged exotic bird and entertain New Yorkers like a bizarre trinket on a charm bracelet. But now she was traveling beyond her comfort zone of the Golden Cockerel and its immediate neighborhood. She felt hesitant before eyes prying into her male outfits.

The princess and Benny paid for her journey because her father was ill.

At present Imelda was on the short flight from Manila to her family home in Cebu City. She felt more uncomfortable than ever. She thought an Arab passenger with a scarred face and bulbous nose was staring right into her, contemptuous of her androgynous appearance. She had heard him say to a flight attendant at check-in that he was an Italian MP visiting the Philippines.

She thought he had almost spat at her when they had boarded the plane. Then she realized there had to be a reason why he held himself back. When the flight was airborne, she heard him ask another flight attendant if he could move to seat 26K in the economy section of the Boeing 747-200.

"You don't mind, do you? The view there is better."

Imelda noticed this guy again. She could hardly help it because he kept changing seats. Surely he could not have moved four or five times? But that was how it seemed.

The plane landed at Cebu. Imelda shuddered when she got off. So did the Arab man. Imelda scurried out of the airport, glad to be free of this specter. Whatever she thought, she could not know that what her fellow passenger had done was going to rip apart the peace of the Pacific when the flight resumed for its final leg to Narita Airport, Tokyo.

At home with her family, Imelda dismissed her fears. She was now a New Yorker, was she not? She could face down prejudiced stares. Then the news came through. When the PAL plane on which she had traveled had been over Minami Daito Island in Okinawa Prefecture, a bomb had exploded. It had been packed under the seat of a Japanese man, splitting him in two, although he had died almost instantaneously. Another five passengers were seriously injured. The blast had blown a small hole in the floor and severed the aileron cables that controlled the plane's flaps. TV and radio accounts paid tribute to the valiant efforts of the captain to steer the plane to an emergency landing at Naha Airport in Okinawa on the southern tip of Japan and to the crew who had to keep the 292 people on board as calm as possible in such an emergency.

From another hidey-hole, Yousef rang Associated Press anonymously and claimed responsibility for the explosion on behalf of yet another militant group.

What he thought was:

"It was all so easy. Halfway through the first leg of the flight, I went to the toilet. I took off my shoes, withdrew the necessaries in them, and assembled my bomb. I went back to my seat and waited while the flight attendants served their silly snacks. Then I tucked the newly made tiny bomb into the life-vest under my seat. They didn't notice a thing. Poor fools.

"What do I care about what they call tragedies? The Japs and Filipinos have served the Great Satan like toads, and like toads they will come to a sticky end. It's a trial run for the great Bojinka plot. That will make everyone take notice."

Terrified by news reports of the midair explosion, Imelda was riddled with nerves throughout her vacation. Two weeks later when she got back to Manhattan, everything she had seen and heard tumbled out before Benny.

"Terrible, yes," said Benny to the princess. "But this guy leaves his clammy fingerprints behind with every crime and that's how they will catch him."

Nobody in the US could then guess what this horrible single outrage pointed to: a projected campaign of midair explosions across the Pacific.

News of Yousef's airplane atrocity proved a wake-up call to Todd Carter in Babel City. When he overheard an off-the-cuff remark Mordred Stickleman made about him to another professor, it struck him like a winged arrow.

"Todd is too clever for his own good. He can analyze the malign panorama of things Groznyy but he can't see his own situation. He sees how manipulative Groznyy is—but not how clever the master puppeteers in the CIA who control him are."

Todd did not want to credit the envenomed Stickleman with any insight. But he could not dismiss this remark. He now saw himself as the butt of a cruel joke. He had thought he was doing the federal government a favor by observing the Oryx Party at BCU undercover while teaching communications there. He had thought he was back in a chase for America's most bitter enemies across army camp and college campus. But it was not so much a randy and rowdy campus as an emasculated cloister. Franklin Miller, clever devil that he was, had placed Todd at BCU to sidetrack him.

As to the Oryx Party, it was no more than a distraction for more proactive Afghan Arabs elsewhere. Perhaps Todd acted as a brake on them since they must have known they were being watched. But Todd himself was no more than a reservist. And for al-Qaeda, "the Base," the Oryx Party was also a reserve battalion, a cover to shelter the "nephews" of the dean at BCU and from which any terrorist group could find recruits when necessary. Todd saw that Yousef's continued atrocities showed that the action was elsewhere.

What cut Todd to the quick was that now he knew for sure that he was just a pawn—just a working stiff put on hold until someone in DC wanted him. And if he wanted to survive economically, he had to remain trapped in this dried-up well. It was he who had been disposed of, not the Afghan Arabs.

To escape and remake a productive career, he would have to strategize, to use his talents to get out and forge ahead. He realized that this was what Franklin Miller had done—used BCU as a base to become ambassador—and what Cesare Groznyy was still doing—using BCU to make a personal fortune. Todd did not want to compare himself with either of them. Yet he had his contacts, his charm, and his energy. There were other patriotic institutions besides the CIA, including TV channels. At BCU he would remain Todd Carter. Outside he would start by adding an extra name to his other two: "Fox," like the TV channel.

In Norse Hoven County the two enemy parties were now waterlogged in the most difficult campaign of their puny war. For the slightly renamed Todd Carter Fox it was like frozen tundra in some northern clime, as if he and the Opposition Party had to trudge across a wasteland clogged with impacted snow and ice, punctuated here and there by bright bursts of hope when some hot geysers erupted with bursts of scalding water. This happened when yet another scandal broke in Groznyy's court: the unexpected firing of deans popular in their schools and therefore not to be tolerated by Groznyy the supreme narcissist.

To Mordred Stickleman the stretch of hopelessness was not frozen cold but more like some overheated tropical swamp in which you got so entangled in foliage that you never knew if you were predator, prey, or pest. Stickleman swore never to give up, no matter the cost to his blood pressure or his heart.

Groznyy himself was more than ever the self-deceiver. He believed that all he had to do was wait: wait for his foes to die of exhaustion; eliminate more deans to stave off more rebellions; act as if he were in charge because he was king of the jungle, lord of the enchanted rings, top of the heap. After all, he was leading a double life. He was no longer the emissary of great academic change but the grasping miser of an ever-growing stash.

Two people detected parallels in the Cesare Groznyy and Ramzi Yousef scenarios. They had seen enough of the two worlds—petty university politics and frightening terrorist feuds—to draw deeper conclusions from the shock-horror of press coverage.

Hermione saw the blinkered professors of BCU and the fanatical fundamentalists of New Jersey as products of comparable cultural revolutions, although they came from different generations. She knew from college courses how youth culture had developed. Rock and roll in the 1950s had led to the pop explosion of the 1960s when the cultural eruption of a young generation shook arts and politics. The new power of young people was to culminate in student revolts across Western Europe in 1968. It made its presence felt stateside in civil rights, black power, and protest against American involvement in Vietnam. It seemed that the affluent society had nurtured children who were happy to bite the hand that fed them.

Hermione considered the professors of the Opposition Party at BCU as relics of student protests. She saw the terrorists as their bizarre heirs.

Sub treasurer Darko Delizio saw this, too. But he also saw his old friends as protesters against repressive liberalism. He recalled from college classes on sociology how radical Herbert Marcuse had used the term "repressive liberalism" to express the idea that liberal democracies fostered mechanisms that stifled free expression and forestalled political change.

The BCU professors might have agreed with this when they were young students, but they had long been co-opted by repressive liberalism into maintaining their comfortable bourgeois lifestyles.

The Afghan Arab fanatics wanted to disrupt American global power because they saw it as an enemy to the rights of their cherished Palestinian people. Like student activists of the 1960s and 1970s, fanatics in the 1990s such as Ramzi Yousef and his followers liked to think that western society was ignoring them in order to avoid facing their radical views.

To Darko the fanatics were a terrifying form of the most destructive heirs of the hippie movement. However, like some protesters of the 1960s, Yousef's allies could not play their parts properly. They kept forgetting the scenarios as dictated by Yousef and Osama bin Laden, the moneybags of the malign enterprise—hence the bizarre malfunctioning Keystone Kops actions such as their mixing bomb ingredients in places where they would be discovered, their amateurish car collisions, and their penny pinching on telltale receipts and bank accounts.

Whereas both sides in the academic dispute at BCU said they stood for academic freedom and for liberation from oppression, what they had come to represent was dictatorship, whether of the absolute master (as the Groznyy Gang maintained) or of the professors' leaders (such as Stickleman).

Caught in the intense dramas of the Groznyy family but also interested in the dramatic troublemaker bombers, Hermione always came back to her core characterizations of Groznyy, Yousef, and Holly: the red devil, the black devil, and the white devil in the little black dress.

She detected disturbing similarities in the malign deeds of Groznyy and Yousef. They were comic-book devils all right. When they spoke with dazzling vigor, their words soared. Whereas Groznyy liked to imagine himself as someone working for higher academic good, his methods were destructive.

Ramzi Yousef was a diabolical, illusive figure. The paradox of Yousef was that he supposedly hated western lifestyles but that he had also lived an indulgent western lifestyle to the full. Yousef may have pretended that he was working for the good of the Palestinian people, but his route was destruction. And his destruction inspired tireless investigators across the world to identify, capture, and contain him. Yousef's evil provoked good in other people.

189

It showed the healing and cleansing capacity in decent human beings.

Where was Holly in this? She could not get any closer to the truth of Modest's death. Holly had some independence through her stints as a jazz singer with a widening fan base and an emotional outlet of artistic achievement. Hermione advised her that Groznyy's waiting game with the Opposition Party would come to an end with a political climax. Then her flourishing music career would provide not only her escape from BCU but also her future as a great singer.

If the princess could program her, Holly Wood could program others.

She called Dr. Justin Squires, explaining how concerned she was at the way things seemed to be turning against her husband. The week before, Dr. Squires had heard something at the hospital—a casual remark from a nurse whose husband worked in construction—that alerted his suspicions. It was something about BCU and "jobs for the boys," then "toys for the boys," then "who was going to pay for whose vacation in Hawaii." Then he overheard the name of Carpenter Cain again and again in different contexts.

When he drove over to the twin towns of Norse Hoven and Babel City, Dr. Squires noticed construction signs around the new hospital extension with the name "BLACK-THORN BUILDINGS." He linked these to trustee chair Veronica Veneer. Then Dr. Squires drove by another construction site at a field hospital that was also part of the consortium. This time the name on the placards was "VENEER."

Dr. Squires took his discoveries and suspicions to Larry Dawdler. Larry said little. But his controlled response said much.

"Thank you for your advice."

Larry Dawdler knew what Dr. Squires was thinking. And

it confirmed what he dreaded public opinion might say: that the late Brad Gable had had shady dealings with contractors who were trustees of BCU.

Dawdler went over to see Groznyy while he was having his portrait painted. He had to wait for the sitting to end. This gave him time to reflect.

There had been two stages to his disillusionment with Groznyy. First he had discovered that Brad Gable was involved in financial finagling with the trustees. Now he realized that Groznyy himself had corrupt deals with the trustees. This was unnerving to Dawdler. However, when he got the president by himself, Dawdler was surprised to find he was lost for words. He hemmed and hawed until Groznyy, exasperated, ordered, "Fire away."

Dawdler told Groznyy what he had heard from Dr. Squires and then what he had checked up on. It was that Carpenter Cain was supplying nominally disinterested BCU trustees led by Veronica Veneer with building contracts and that he was probably being rewarded with kickbacks.

Groznyy went red in the face. He said it was the very first time he had received any complaint about lack of propriety. In fact he thought he had covered his tracks. After all, he was a seasoned trouper and a born liar.

Dawdler repeated that both he and Dr. Squires had already looked into the matter—examining the list of trustees and comparing it with the list of contractors and the names of guests at banquets. He tried to persuade Groznyy that there should be some internal investigation before the matter became public.

Groznyy told Dawdler he would let him know about it later. And he dismissed him without his usual invitation to stay for dinner. As soon as Dawdler was out of the room, Groznyy had the hotline telephone link between them cut off. He wanted to think without interruption.

He was incandescent when he heard that the *Norse Hoven*

191

Courier was about to lead its next day's edition with a catalog of alleged financial wheeling and dealing among trustees. He summoned his grand vizier, Bogus Revisor, who told him that he was ready to refute the claims.

"The paper is to quote me as saying, 'These malicious stories have no foundation in fact,'" said Provost Bogus Revisor.

However, faculty opposition, led by Todd Carter and Mordred Stickleman, was seething—again.

Two days later, Cesare Groznyy invited Dawdler back.

"Dear friend, did I unintentionally offend you two days ago? You are my best, my oldest ally. Acting on your excellent advice, I have ordered an internal enquiry. If it confirms what you've reported, then together we can take action and heads will roll."

Dawdler now became part of Groznyy's default plan for Carpenter Cain. Cain was to go to England on special business—to see if BCU and some Oxbridge colleges could institute student exchange programs. That was the cover story. After initiating negotiations, Carpenter Cain was to travel on vacation to rural Scotland—the Highlands. Once there, he was to report back that he had discovered a serious health problem. He could choose which. After a few days, having learnt the results of a non-existent medical examination, he was to resign from BCU on grounds of ill health.

Cain now knew the sort of desperation that Brad Gable had experienced before him. He was no longer one of Cesare's pets and it hurt. Instead of England or Scotland, Cain asked to go to Canada, supposedly to look over colleges in Toronto and Montreal and there discover his mystery illness. In other respects, he would follow the Groznyy–Dawdler script. Dawdler agreed. He counted on the fact that Cain was only a bit player in the unraveling tapestry and that Canada would serve just as well as Scotland to deter the press.

The press, maybe, but not other interested parties.

Dean Ace Ferrari, so sluggish about terrorist scares, moved fast when it came to money—or more precisely the loss of it, since he regarded Cain's misappropriation of alumnae funds to the Oryx Party as his due. He was angry partly because funds would now dry up, partly because he suspected Cain had already held on to some Oryx Party monies. He summoned Darko.

"It seems we cannot trust Achmed. He has disappeared with our money. We cannot allow anyone to take advantage of us and betray the great cause."

Darko knew such open anger from the dean was most unusual.

"Before Achmed came to BCU he moved around college towns in New England near the Canadian border," Ferrari said. "He still has a sideline in local businesses there—small hotels, guesthouses, and convenience stores. I'll track him down. You sharpen your special skills."

"Consider it done," answered the accountant with many talents.

"We need to protect you as well as eliminate Achmed. You ask for leave of absence. As a patriotic Serb—or is it Albanian?—you want to give your services to your homeland in its new hour of need as the old Yugoslavia disintegrates and the West comes to the rescue of Kosovo. The treasurer won't refuse. She has other things on her mind. She would rather let you go for a short time over a national emergency than lose you completely.

"You take a secret detour to northern New England first. By the time Achmed has disappeared for good, you will be out of reach in Europe.

"Another thing. You will need cutlery for your journey. Try somewhere in New York. What about stalls on West 14th Street? We have to leave a telltale warning to any insiders who transgress as well as handing the police a weapon since this must look like suicide. Get ready and go when I give you the signal."

Long used to the hurly-burly of university squabbles, Larry Dawdler had limitless stoicism for commonplace reverses. However, he felt surprisingly wounded inside by Groznyy's wheeling and dealing. It was as if something irreparable inside him had broken. It was not his heart, however.

After a brief meal at a diner in Norse Hoven with his niece, Larry went with her to a bar in Babel City and sat at the counter. They tried to watch a movie on the overhead TV. It was a relief to divert themselves with this stale chick-flick. A customer on the next bar stool, sensing their gloom, observed to the bartender, "I guess it's true what they say. TV proves people will watch just anything rather than look at one another."

Groznyy's adversaries among the professors discovered that he had made arrangements to sell one of his less favored Picasso sculptures for a cool half million—twice as much as it was worth. The buyers were trustees Veronica Veneer and Georgie Lucre. The implication was that the sale was a cover—the trustees' way of giving Groznyy money for favors rendered.

Things were more ominous elsewhere.

A survey in a weekly glossy nationwide magazine disclosed presidential salaries in colleges, high and low, across the land. Groznyy, president of one of the smallest universities, had one of the highest salaries. BCU professors looked on with pretended outrage and inner delight. They relished two paragraphs:

Rumors have circulated that Groznyy has brokered salary deals with the trustees from his initial $60,000, to $80,000 in his second year, then $100,000 and up to $200,000 by his fourth year. After several years, his salary is supposed to be above $400,000, way more than presidents of Harvard, Yale, and Princeton might expect.

Alongside this, insider sources say that he has been spending university money on a lavish lifestyle with expensive suits and expensive dinners in Manhattan where bottles of wine cost over $200 apiece.

The inside information in the national survey had come courtesy of Sharp and Garnier. Once the bald facts had been published, their background story in the *Norse Hoven Courier* broke big time.

It's well known across Norse Hoven County that Cesare Groznyy has really cheesy taste. His ideas of high-class décor would make the late Aristotle Onassis and his bar stools covered in skin from a whale's scrotum look refined. While not yet in the same Russian oligarch class as his younger oil-tycoon brother in Moscow, Groznyy likes to spend, spend, and spend as if there is no tomorrow.

He has a specially commissioned auto: a scarlet Rolls-Royce; a collection of modern art with works by European masters Pablo Picasso and Piet Mondrian and American artists Jackson Pollock and Mark Rothko. His seashore house painted red, yellow, and black, when completed with turrets adorned with Russian stars and Russian eagles, will make robber barons' mansions in Rhode Island look like grubby English country cottages.

And how does he pay for all this?

The answer is simple. He doesn't. Who pays? Why, "little BCU," as he calls the undistinguished New England university that employs him.

The ripples of the salacious article spread ever wider and raised academic eyebrows nationwide.

Still working away, Steve Sharp and Mickey Garnier now uncovered evidence of gross fraud at BCU. They fed the

Norse Hoven Courier precise facts and figures. Thus the *Courier* began a series of exposure articles. Its first headline was "The Secret Accounts: Proofs of Undoubted Fraud Brought to Light." The articles were widely syndicated.

The BCU senate investigation was taking evidence about construction contracts. It heard from Groznyy's enemies that Brad Gable had embezzled close to an estimated $2 million, mainly in connection with the building of the hospital extension and kickbacks from contractors.

The senate called in state prosecutors.

Groznyy was in the presidential car on the highway when he learnt on his cell phone from journalist Steve Sharp, pretending impartiality, what was to happen. A special state commission—an oversight body that had been agreed to establish the part-public, part-private science consortium— was going to investigate both Groznyy and the board of trustees for misappropriation of funds and conflicts of interest.

As he heard the news from Sharp, Groznyy stopped making notes in his pad. He jabbed the pen into the back of the driver's seat in front of him. Then he pummeled his fist into the upholstery. The driver was afraid he would be forced to stall in the middle of the highway. Cowering, he just managed to pull the car over to the hard shoulder and avoid a crash. When the driver cleaned out the car later, he found that the grey upholstery was punctured with indigo perforations and flecked with splashes from Groznyy's pen.

"There is an unexpected silver lining in this," Larry told Groznyy later. "The state has appointed Boris Goodenough as legal adviser to the investigating panel."

Groznyy wanted to let out a whistle of exasperation but he did not have the skill.

"He's not our friend," he said.

"Maybe not. But, because he's your brother-in-law, your interests are the same as the interests of his family—his sister and his nephew. Whatever regrets he might mouth in public, he won't kill you off."

Groznyy was not convinced. But he knew better than to accuse the panel itself of a conflict of interest. That would mean opening up old psychological wounds to more adverse public gaze.

Groznyy and Dawdler had reckoned without Boris Goodenough's ambition.

"Gentlemen and other deans, we are now at war with the scurvy professors. I will use every weapon at my disposal, every weapon in my arsenal. And so must you."

Groznyy had called the deans to an emergency meeting in response to the announcement of the hearings to investigate him and the trustees for mismanagement. The possibility that the special education panel would dismiss the trustees and that the president would also fall was now real. Groznyy knew he would have to harness his faltering troops seated before him in the room with the black swivel back chairs.

After his opening salvo, Groznyy shot a lingering look at each of his audience in turn. They looked as if they wanted to slide down in their chairs so that their heads would fall below the parapet of the table ledge.

"Forget the Geneva Convention. Forget the quality of mercy. Forget the Great Escape. Clean your machetes, polish your scalpels, keep your pistols loaded, and prepare your Molotov cocktails. This is total war. World War I, World War II, and Vietnam have nothing on this. The Cold War is over. Get ready to shoot your load.

"In case any of you are wavering, I've never failed. I've never lost a battle."

ADVOCATES

The great and the good of Norse Hoven County who had established the state commission to oversee the science consortium had never imagined they would have to examine the integrity of a college president and board of trustees. After to-ing and fro-ing between the various parties, the state decided to hold hearings in a courthouse in downtown Norse Hoven, using a panel of three members. The panel would examine documents and listen to the testimony of university professors and other workers. Since the president and board of trustees of BCU were being charged with civil offences, they could speak for themselves and through their lawyer, Larry Dawdler.

The state commission charged the panel to investigate two principal complaints against Groznyy and the trustees: that several trustees had conflicts of interest and had used their positions as trustees to get work for their companies, and that BCU was failing in its academic mission.

The professors, who thought they held the best cards, were angry that the commission panel was not going to investigate the trustees for wasting BCU funds in extravagant compensation for Groznyy.

"It's outrageous," declared Mordred Stickleman.

However, Todd Carter and others settled on cooperation with the panel. They also realized that if Stickleman ever spoke before the panel in court, his venom against Groznyy would damage their case. It was difficult for Todd and the others to dissuade Stickleman without wounding his hypersensitive self-esteem. So they suggested to him that, if he appeared in court, he could not also speak independently to journalists. And he would serve the Opposition Party best as a specialist who could explain things to journalists. Thus journalists would get their facts right and make the public see matters in the same way as the Opposition Party.

Looking for battle, as he entered the dark hall of the courthouse on the first day of the hearings, the president stumbled. Across the lower steps of the ornamental marble staircase, he seemed to see his two sons. The one who was alive was bending down, tending to his brother, the one Groznyy had killed and who lay crushed and splattered.

For its first witness the Opposition Party fielded an administrator who had turned against Groznyy. This was former dean of nursing Wendy Pretzel. She told the panel that she had resigned as dean in protest at the budget cuts of Cesare Groznyy, which she said were destroying her school.

"How was it that you came to BCU?" the chair of the panel asked her.

"The president enticed me to BCU from one of the Seven Sisters. He told me my task was to rescue the nursing program, which had been in decline under the former dean, Lucy Kaye."

"And did you?"

"I worked damn hard, twenty-four-seven, to reinvigorate the curriculum only to see President Groznyy thwart it with crippling budget cuts so that we couldn't move ahead with new courses, new professors."

"Were you surprised?"

"Sure. I came to BCU with high hopes for the president's vision. But, little by little, I got discouraged by the revolving door—"

"Meaning?"

"The high turnover of administrators across the university. Since I arrived a few years ago, he—Dr. Groznyy—has fired over seventy deans and associate deans. It's almost like a bloodlust in him. He has to do it—like making a habit of murder because you've found it's easy."

"I don't know he would appreciate your reference to the whodunits of Ed McBain or Raymond Chandler."

"I think that's the least of his problems."

"What was your relationship like with Dr. Groznyy?"

"At first he was all smiles and flattery. Then he turned. Whatever I did, it was never good enough."

"How did you cope?"

"Well, as a Noo Yoiker by choice and a New Englander by conviction, I've learned that to get along, you go along. I was naïve. I had no idea of the massive cuts that were to come, no idea whatsoever. When I started to express my concerns, my relationship with the president and the provost—his high and mighty grand vizier—became confrontational. The cuts got ever wider and deeper. Yet there was this pretense that everything was getting better and better all the time. It was like a parody of the old Communist party line in Russia. They made me sign memos claiming that the school was maintaining standards. It was false. He—President Groznyy—was as cruel as a crocodile."

Larry Dawdler wanted to skew matters in Groznyy's interest. "If it was as bad as you say, then why did you go along with this?"

"I did so partly to curry favor with the administration. I was in deep doo-doo over budget disagreements—make no mistake. I was afraid of losing my job. I had just bought a condo. I guess you could say I was trying to do damage limitation. I was forced to sign letters supporting the president."

"Forced?"

"Obliged, corralled—it amounts to the same thing. I signed letters supporting President Groznyy under coercion. It wasn't just me. The other deans were also forced to endorse statements supporting Groznyy. They told us we would be fired if we didn't."

"Did this bring your deanship to an end?"

"No. I resigned because I believed there was unethical conduct going on. While there were plenty of speeches and press statements about quality education, the behavior of the president, the provost, the treasurer, and the trustees certainly didn't reflect concern for the students. Too many words but no respect for the professors at all. Mortgage or no mortgage, I got to the point where I just didn't want to be associated with an administration of this kind."

"What did you do?"

"I resigned my deanship and started teaching full-time at BCU."

Dawdler now moved to his killer question intended to demolish Wendy Pretzel's credibility.

"So you chickened out when you faced hard decisions?"

Wendy blanched. Hitherto, she had avoided looking at Groznyy. Now she caught his eye. She trembled. There he was with his snowy white hair offset by a deep tan. She knew the tan came courtesy of a tanning bed and brown makeup. And this fakery, combined with Groznyy's studied show of being relaxed, gave her unexpected courage. There he was, dressed for the cameras in his couture navy blue suit and a blazing red power tie.

"There you are," she thought, "sitting cross-legged with your hands clasped in front like an English dandy—just like the double-crosser you are."

Recovering her composure, she said, "Mr. Dawdler's comment is not fair—and he knows it. My individual experience was part of a wider pattern."

She turned to the panel. "You see, another major bone of contention is the Imperial Presidency of Cesare Groznyy. It is this that has made him infamous—and I do not think that is too strong a word."

Rather than let Dawdler challenge this, the panel chair said, "It seems that when things got difficult, Dr. Groznyy fired deans who were trying to pursue his policies. And he did so to blame others and save himself."

Groznyy and Dawdler could say nothing.

The chair asked Groznyy why he was always hiring new administrators, then dispatching them with the ruthlessness of a communist tyrant. "Was it to divert the Opposition Party away from you and onto administrators whom you regarded as collateral damage?"

"Not at all. Let me give you a parallel. In South Africa, they used to inoculate oxen against 'lung sick'—cattle pneumonia that destroyed teams of oxen. The farmers would slit part of the ox's tail and bind onto it a piece of the diseased lung of a dead ox. The newly infected ox would get the disease in a mild form. It caused its lower tail to wither and drop off. But the process saved the ox from future attacks.

"It must be true," added Groznyy; "I read it in *King Solomon's Mines*. Does it seem cruel to rob the oxen of their tails—especially in a country with so many flies?"

"Well," said the chairman, "it must look odd to drive a team of oxen behind a score of stumps instead of tails."

"Indeed," replied the quicksilver sophist. "Surely it is better for an ox to yield its tail than its life? If deans at BCU cannot tame the beasts of burden of our faculty, then they will lose their jobs when the university fails. If they don't get infected with the truth and change, they will die."

When the panel retired for lunch, another panelist said to the chair, "It seems that Groznyy's administration, whatever its high-falutin' statements, lacks conviction, courage, and any cohesion except a desire to survive at all costs and to milk the university dry."

At the close of hearings every day, reporters found no shortage of expert analysts in the courthouse lobby to help shape their reports.

Stickleman was eager to be the first to bend TV journalist Steve Sharp's ear toward the professors' argument. Sharp's first broadside on the hearings was to be in the *Norse Hoven Courier*; his TV coverage was to come later. Wendy Pretzel's testimony about how Groznyy bullied the deans gave Stickleman an opportunity to canvass Sharp:

"Groznyy was in trouble almost from the very beginning. His erratic hiring and firing of senior administrators provoked turmoil in the administration. His capricious management caused havoc. Student enrolment at BCU started to drop."

This gave Sharp a cue for his press article that appeared next day, "A Crash Course in Major Rethinking at 'Little BCU'":

This is the scary tale of a mean-spirited university tearing its tarnished reputation into tatters. The proof comes in the testimony of professors and administrators called to give evidence to the hearings of the special three-member panel examining charges of misconduct by President Cesare Groznyy and his hand-selected board of trustees.

When he arrived at BCU, Groznyy, first as provost and then as president, wanted to refashion this commuter school known only—if at all—for vocational programs into a top-rank college favoring liberal arts. Critics allege that BCU was close to insolvency when it annexed NHU. Its academic standards were negligible. For example, it accepted eight of every ten high school students who applied.

Groznyy argued that BCU–NHU could be saved if it raised its intellectual sights and cut back on programs in practical subjects such as business, nursing, and social work. Colleges can take longer to debate smaller issues. It took decades and millions for New York University and Duke University to make the huge leap from being major regional colleges to becoming nationally ranked universities.

What do you think? Can BCU make that leap?

And can Groznyy survive the investigation into irregularities?

When he spoke to the panel later that first week, Todd Carter, who was the Opposition Party's best witness, wanted to show how far Groznyy and the trustees had ignored and alienated the professors.

The panel chairman asked, "Isn't it true that BCU has a long history of professors being opposed to presidents—that the professors would rather bring down a president than get on with the work of teaching and research?"

"Dr. Groznyy and his supporters have flung out this silly accusation," Todd said. "But it's just a ploy so that they can present their misdeeds as beneficial programs, their failures as successes."

Larry Dawdler leapt in. "Misdeeds? Failures? Isn't it true that Dr. Groznyy has made significant improvements, such as refurbished classrooms, attractive landscaping, and even championing sports programs?"

"Yes, I give him that, but—"

"No further questions."

Todd was not going to be silenced. He turned to the panel but spoke to the gallery.

"But there are questions of public interest and they have to be heard. Imagine. No students or their families will come to BCU or NHU for arts and sciences when there is the great Milhous College towering over us in the same town. As to his academic vision, Cesare Groznyy might just as well say he plans to turn any American suburban strip into Harvard, Yale, or Princeton."

Unlike Stickleman, Todd had a perspective that gave his words depth and a cutting edge. He turned back to the panel.

"It's not the Emperor's Clothes of Great Intellect that are invisible because they don't exist, even though his fawning courtiers pretend they can see them. It's something different: a physically invisible but psychologically true cloak of narcissism. It's invisible to the naked eye but it's as toxic as asbestos. While not immediately lethal, it will eat away the innards of anyone who comes near as surely as the venomous bite of a Komodo dragon."

When she gave evidence, Treasurer Parthy Burnable tried to counter charges against Groznyy.

"When President Groznyy started to improve the university so that it would attract top students in classics, philosophy, and public policy, the third-class culture of BCU's professors united against him."

The chairman asked, "Can you give us statistics about fundraising?"

"Sure. President Groznyy has raised about $13 million."

"That's average for comparable institutions."

"Maybe, but he also raised the college endowment from $4 million to $47 million."

"Isn't that because you, the treasurer, have taken advantage of a soaring stock market?"

Parthy was silenced. She could cut and dice figures, but dealing with the cut and thrust of court cross-examination was not her forte.

Age had not withered the next witness, Tiberius Brown, original chair of the trustees whom Groznyy had eased out. He told the panel that BCU's fundraising goals had proved elusive.

"The goals were not met. The 1994–95 target was $2.7 million but the collection was $1.6 million. Hopes for a $100 million fundraising drive during BCU's centennial year ran aground."

"This was after you had left the BCU board?"

"Yes. Being away allowed me to observe how Groznyy developed a repressive bureaucratic apparatus. By systematic mental cruelty to his colleagues he cut off any attempt at different ways of thinking from his."

In the afternoon recess, Kelly Danson, now acting as a TV journalist, recorded more than enough sound bites to fill an entire local news slot.

She said in her segment on the TV evening news, "Professor Pooky Shapiro of Social Work says"—and here the camera cut to the said Pooky Shapiro: "Everything the Groznyy Gang says is nonsense. President Groznyy doesn't have an educational philosophy. All he had in his old carpetbag of pretensions was a marketing strategy. Like him, it has failed."

The camera cut back to Kelly Danson.

"You're a senior in nursing?" she asked a girl with blonde hair cropped close.

"Right. And I agree with Professor Shapiro. I don't know what Dr. G. does but, if he does PR, it's nothing but bad PR."

The camera cut to a brunette who said, "Dr. G has shown nothing but contempt for the whole nursing program. Funds were so short that last year we had to have our maternity classes in a trailer without any heating."

Guided by Stickleman from behind the scenes, Kelly spoke to the camera: "Sometimes spats between professors (who love to think they are guardians of high academic standards) and administrators (who have the complex task of keeping finances stable) burst into public awareness. Rarely do they reach the furore that they have at BCU. So what is wrong here?"

She asked this just as Groznyy and Dawdler came down the courtroom steps. But they did not get far. For, as Kelly was wrapping up her TV recording, from inside the court-house there appeared thirteen BCU professors in college caps and gowns. As if to mock Groznyy's oracular pronouncements and his cape of narcissism, they assembled like Jesus and the Apostles at the Last Supper. They mimed eating crumbs of bread as if they had fallen from the master—as if his words were manna from Heaven. Then the professors moved like a menacing mob sashaying down the court steps. They broke into a Charleston routine, crying out, "Genuflect, genuflect."

Stimulated by media coverage, so many people started to come to the panel hearings that the authorities first ran out of chairs and then ran out of standing room at the back. They had to place a screen displaying CCTV footage in an adjacent court room to relay proceedings. This room, too, was so crowded that many people had to sit on the floor.

Todd might have felt he was on a winning streak. But the day after the little charade, Bogus Revisor summoned him to his office and said, "The president is angry that you have accepted chairmanship of the professors' senate. You are sadly mistaken if you think for a moment that you can heal the growing rift. You're just a dead man walking at this university. I'll see to that, little man. I'm gonna destroy your career. You pathetic shell! Hollow through and through! You've no business trying to lead the professors."

"I take that as a direct threat."

"You bet your bottom dollar it's a threat. Get the hell outta my office."

But now it was Bogus who was lost for words. Revisor knew Todd could run the Opposition Party and make it effective. That was why Groznyy wanted him fired. Revisor now learnt Todd had been playing a double game.

"Didn't you know? I thought you did," Todd said casually. "For some time now, I've been courted for president of a TV company with headquarters in New York. Franklin Miller recommended me. Yesterday they offered me a contract. Here's my card."

It read: "Todd Carter Fox, CEO, Network News Norse Hoven."

To his inner fury, Revisor knew that, in addition to his CIA background, Miller prized Todd Carter for his handsome appearance, winning manner, and core of administrative ruthlessness. Now the renamed Todd Carter Fox had outsmarted Groznyy. No one was more ambidextrous than this Fox: critical of the CIA and yet its greatest advocate. It seemed that the Groznyy Gang had been the inadvertent tool for placing the wily Fox in a position where he could harm them. Dispatching a new professor was one thing. Insulting the president-elect of a TV company was unthinkable. Yet this was what Revisor had done for Groznyy.

Hermione knew how interested Benny and the princess were in press coverage of the hearings against Groznyy. The princess devoured every morsel. There was something feral about her appetite.

Turning from 2nd Avenue into 50th Street for the Golden Cockerel one morning, Hermione stopped at a street bookseller. The cover of a softback edition of *Macbeth* caught her eye. The lurid drawing looked like a cross between the old film versions of Orson Welles and Akira Kurosawa.

Something Benny had once said as a throwaway line came back to Hermione: "*Macbeth* has the witches. Invisible to the naked eye, BCU has Princess Glinskaya."

With that the scales fell from her eyes. Hermione had always had an unsettled feeling that there was another unexplained mystery in the princess's hatred of Groznyy and her determination to make him suffer. After she had served the princess her morning coffee in the ersatz garden, Hermione sat opposite her and thrust the softcover copy of *Macbeth* on the table. The princess was startled. Hermione took a risk and challenged her.

"Didn't you once tell me that you have to be married to play the Macbeths? You weren't just thinking of Holly and Groznyy, were you? It was you, wasn't it? The wife of Groznyy's morning."

The princess did not answer directly. "You're too clever. I would have to get up very early in the morning to catch you." She paused and then said, "Set aside because I couldn't have children? That's not the half of it. Once Groznyy began to rise in the teacup world of academia, his first senior position was as a minor administrator in the boondocks outside Tulsa. It all went to his head—higher salary, office staff he could turn into servants, colleagues whom he could turn into a ragtag court of groveling toads."

"So, just like *Macbeth*," thought Hermione, "a childless couple driven by obsession over a missing child."

The thought of the pretentious fraudster president and princess even being good enough to play the Macbeths on stage struck her as so incredibly funny that she burst out laughing, something that mystified the princess who was on her high horse speaking Truth with a capital letter. But she continued nevertheless.

"Anna Stasinova was not only pliant but also ambitious. Don't let the memory of her sad countenance or her displays of dignified suffering fool you. There was more to her than a fading wallflower with neuroses. After Groznyy pulled her, he soon learnt how little there was to her brain except tenacity. At first, he didn't want to divorce me so he could marry her. He didn't want his career endangered by some murky matrimonial past. He wanted a front and he wanted pleasure.

"At that time it looked as if he also had a chance of becoming a star on the celebrity speaker circuit—even his enemies admit he has the gift of the gab—so, talks to universities and colleges, rotary clubs, and so on. It can be lucrative. It's also anonymous. You're in a town for a night, and then you move on. You're not forging permanent relationships with people you meet.

"So, what did Groznyy suggest? He wanted both his wife and his mistress. He wanted Anna to go round as his trophy wife. But he also wanted me as the aristocratic side of the big, happy family. So I was to tag along as his pretend mother-in-law—Anna's mother.

"But then his plan went wrong. Anna got pregnant with Modest. He wanted an heir and his heir had to be legitimate. By that time I was so disgusted that I wanted out of the marriage."

"And your feelings for Modest?"

"How could anyone who met Modest not love him—his open face, his charm, his loyalty—and his imagination? You know that better than anyone."

Hermione said nothing. The princess's remark hit her.

"Besides, over the years, my anger against Anna weakened. I realized that she had freed me. And her punishment for her affair with Groznyy was her marriage to him. She soon learnt that what she thought had been an affair was no more than a flicker in his life—not even a flame. The consequence was living hell. I pitied her more."

In Babel City daily press coverage was worse for Groznyy than any evidence in court. Outside the panel hearings, his mood was permanently black. His face seemed covered in globules of sweat. His eyes were clouded. Those who knew him well sensed that, underneath a veil of composure, they were flickering with fear.

"You know, people despise genius," Groznyy whispered to Bee Flute as he left for another day's embarrassing hearings. "However, whatever they like to say, whatever their calumnies, they're nothing without me."

One day there were no hearings so that the panel could examine the paper and digital evidence about the trustees in private. Boris Goodenough, the panel's legal adviser, told them, "The most powerful group on the board is its three-member executive committee with two members who have business dealings with the university. One is Veronica Veneer, who has both a construction company and an insurance company. Her business with the university is profitable and continuous. The other is Georgie Lucre, whose advertising and PR firm, Lucrative Lucre, was paid $100,000 for professional services in 1994 and $115,000 in 1995. This is according to tax receipts filed by the university."

Boris said, "Lucre's advertising company created an ad campaign for BCU. This was based on the motto that Cesare

Groznyy had all the answers to every problem in higher education. Neither Veneer nor Lucre told the other trustees that they were being paid by BCU. In fact, the other trustees were told that Veneer and Lucre were working free.

"It seems that the premiums BCU paid to Bentlegs—Veneer's insurance company—ranged from $700,000 to $800,000 a year, with additional commissions averaging $70,000 to $80,000 a year."

When former dean of nursing Lucy Kaye appeared before the panel next day, the chair asked her about missing funds in the hospital accounts.

"Where do you think the money has gone?"

"It's obvious. Brad Gable and the trustee auditors divided the money raised, with 35 percent going to contractors and 65 percent going in commission to certain members of the board of trustees." Lucy produced some papers. "The Groznyy ring has produced receipts. You've seen them. For example, for three tables and forty chairs, BCU paid $200,000. Carpets, shades, and furniture cost $1 million. What was it said of the Tweed Ring in New York in the 1870s—that the bills are not simply grotesque, they are also demonstrably fabulous?"

"Can you give details?"

"Can they? Here are some of the signatories: Tom Sawyer, Jay Gatsby, Scarlett O'Hara, Rhett Butler, Ma Joad, Yossarian, Randle McMurphy, Big Nurse Ratchet, Philip Marlowe, Billy Pilgrim."

"Would you like to add anything beyond this roll call of heroes from American literature?"

"Of course. It's back to the Tweed Ring. How much have the trustees taken? $5 million? $10 million? $50 million? Millions? Squillions? Who knows? Does the treasurer? Ask the head of the Alumnae Bureau—the self-disappeared Carpenter Cain.

"The incomplete hospital extension has cost twice as much as the purchase of Alaska from Russia in the 1860s. We can say, like the title of that old Cold War movie, 'The Russians are coming! The Russians are coming!'"

Lucy's ending, carried off with a flourish, earned applause from the groundlings watching on CCTV in the adjacent room.

Even though they knew the cards of evidence were stacked against them, neither Veronica Veneer nor Georgie Lucre was running scared. When he had to testify, PR man Lucre had his speech ready and he was ready to repeat it later to Kelly Danson's TV crew:

"The Opposition Party has indulged in an extraordinary exercise in rumor mongering, spreading calumny wherever the wind may blow. Some of its baseless allegations border on outright scandal. It has inveigled news magazines into publishing numerous hostile articles. These included one patronizing editorial suggesting that what students from modest backgrounds get at BCU is 'a taste of higher education.' The truth is that we believe that all students from whatever background are entitled to a complete and full education."

Groznyy might have expected his old friend, Dr. Squires, to back him—at least in public. But Dr. Squires had now had enough of Groznyy's wheeling and dealing. When they called him in after listening to Lucre, Dr. Squires told the panel that the board of trustees could resolve BCU's troubles but that "it lacks the will because of the trustees' business ties with BCU. It's simply outrageous. The board of trustees continues to place Dr. Groznyy and itself before the needs and future of BCU."

During the recess the panel chairman said to his colleagues, "Groznyy is trying to present himself as a progressive reformer. If that was ever true, he's slid from academic ideals into a flagrant abuse of power. He might try and argue that his getting a super salary augmented by extravagant perks was his right because of the stress of high office. But the fiscal evidence tells a different story: naked greed, pure and simple."

"I agree," said a colleague who already had enough. "Groznyy is a money-grabbing opportunist. And this pretense that he's an overachieving outsider rejected by a narrow-minded self-regarding society—that he's a revolutionary visionary artist—well, it's just that: pretense."

During the hearings each weekday evening Larry Dawdler steeled himself to watch the local TV news. None of it was favorable to Groznyy but Larry knew he had to be up-to-date on any developments.

Adding insult to injury, journalist Steve Sharp appeared on screen to report Milhous College's announcement of a major new exhibition in its art museum: "Ivan the Terrible and His Heirs in Art and Film." The fact that Network News Norse Hoven ran the story just after its report on the day's hearings about BCU gave Larry a big clue. Instinctively he knew who was behind the exhibition: Grishka.

After the initial announcement, the director of the Milhous Museum appeared onscreen and said, "The exhibition will draw together paintings about Ivan IV from museums across Russia never seen together before. They are by such famous artists as Repin, Serov, and Geller who captured the outer charisma and the inner torment of the controversial first tsar of all the Russias."

Back on camera, Steve Sharp added, "During the run of the show, the Milhous College Film Society will mount a season of films about accursed megalomaniacs, including Laurence Olivier's *Richard III*, Orson Welles's *Citizen Kane*, and, of course, Sergei Eisenstein's *Ivan the Terrible*—both parts."

Photographed outside the great library of Milhous

College, a Milhous history professor told him, "The exhibition and accompanying lectures on Ivan the Terrible in his time and after will show how continuous the reassessment of Ivan IV has been in Russia, as successive political regimes have sought to redefine the historical Ivan and what he achieved in order to justify their own current policies."

"Can you identify some of his heirs?" Steve asked.

"Where can we stop?" replied the professor. "Ivan's heirs include not only Peter the Great but also Russian rulers down to Stalin and beyond to such dictators across the world as Idi Amin, Robert Mugabe, Saddam Hussein, and Papa Doc."

From the discomfort of his own home, Larry Dawdler wondered when and how Grishka would make his appearance. It came somewhat blankly. But that did not blunt the cutting edge of Grishka's intentions. Steve Sharp said simply, "The exhibition has been made possible by a generous financial donation from a famous Russian oil consortium. We interviewed a spokesman earlier in his Moscow apartment near the Kremlin."

The camera cut to Grishka moving from a window, then cut to a glimpse of the striking russet red walls of the Kremlin, and back again to Grishka Groznyy at his desk. Grishka was his usual ebullient self. An unidentified interviewer off camera asked, "Mr. Groznyy, why are you doing this?"

Grishka smiled expansively and said, "Call me Craig—it's the English form of our Grigori. Why am I doing this? That's simple. To help Russo-American relations! I feel it is my duty to make some of our great artists available to our many American friends. And where better than in an Ivy League college town that cherishes Russia's great cultural legacy?"

Larry Dawdler wanted to explode. He yelled at the screen. "That's bullshit and you know it. You're doing it to hurt your big brother more than he's hurt himself—to show him up when he's down by forcing a compare-and-contrast of the great Ivan with Cesare Groznyy."

The phone rang. Larry knew it would be Cesare Groznyy and he dreaded having to say anything about the mocking exhibition. But Groznyy was in another world:

"What a mockery this court is. What a cast: a menagerie of timid bears and humble wolves—and that's only the panel. Then there are the self-styled, self-important witnesses: time-serving false friends, knaves and jacks of fortune! I don't believe they really are human. They've no more substance than the steaming vapor of a fog after snow in winter."

THE BLACK DEVIL IN COURT

The twin towers were still standing proud.

Although it was night, Ramzi Yousef could see them clearly through the window of the Sikorsky S-76A helicopter. There they were, rising like monoliths above the attendant dwarves of the lesser buildings of Corporate America on the southern tip of Manhattan.

But this was not a reconnaissance trip. Yousef was now a captive. He had been confined on a US Air Force flight from Karachi, Pakistan, to Stewart Airport in Newburgh, New York, blindfolded some of the time. After the plane had arrived stateside, security officers had moved their dangerous prisoner to the helicopter. As they neared New York City, the head of the FBI in New York took off Yousef's blindfold so that he could see the towers were still standing. The FBI intended this as a signal instructive act as if to say, "You failed."

Yousef got the message, although he would never have admitted it.

After so many attempts to capture him and so many near misses, Yousef's arrest in a guesthouse in Islamabad in

Pakistan had been dramatic enough. An accomplice whom he had bullied into a sweat of terror had betrayed him because he had no other option: it was either give up Yousef or go under himself.

"I was betrayed all right," Yousef thought during the long weary flight stateside. "There's no other possible explanation. But it's the guy who betrayed me—Ishtiaque Parker—who will never be free. He's a young South African Muslim. He was a student at the Islamic University in Islamabad. He likes to talk the talk of what our mutual enemies call fanaticism—undying hatred of things American—especially its foul support of that abomination Israel. To talk the talk of student protest in college is one thing, but for Parker to walk the walk on a path of constructive destruction was different.

"My next planned attack was the Bojinka mission—to detonate and down eleven American planes over the Pacific.

"To see how Bojinka could work, I needed to make trial runs after the Philippine jet explosion. I ordered Parker to travel ahead of me—like from Islamabad to Bangkok—to test whether airport security would allow passengers to take liquids (for bombs) aboard. I packed Parker's bag with two Casio Databank watches, batteries, and some incendiary cotton. I poured capsules of TNT and liquid nitroglycerine into small bottles made for contact lens solution. All I asked him to do was to go ahead of me to airports to find out what we could get away with—what materials we could take on board. Parker didn't take any real risk. Then I asked him to find out what sort of cargo airlines would ferry without a passenger on board. But, to use an English colloquial phrase, he bottled it.

"He may excuse himself by saying I'm too toxic and dangerous, but what it came down to was dollar signs—the $2 million reward on my head that he must have read about in *Time* magazine. Ironic, really—he got me kidnapped by the Feds but he himself will never be free, no matter how much money he has, whatever new identity he takes. He will be consumed by an edgy restlessness about who has him in their sights until the day he dies. That's what you get for being first an unfulfilled assassin against Corporate America and then a turncoat against me."

When the Americans had decided to kidnap Yousef they had had to move fast. The JTTF and the FBI had to assemble a SWAT-style team immediately with what resources were to hand in Islamabad, using agents from drug enforcement units to make up the numbers. They also had to secure the cooperation of the Pakistani government since there was no extradition treaty between the US and Pakistan. Prime Minister Benazir Bhutto understood the dangers of such terrorism as Yousef could deliver and agreed to his immediate extradition. US and Pakistani forces cooperated. The ISI (Pakistani Inter-Services Intelligence) and the US Diplomatic Service formed a team.

The SWAT-style team moved silently upstairs in the Grace guesthouse where Yousef was staying. As soon as they were on the second floor, the rear guard among them took the safety catches off their submachine guns. The vanguard drew their pistols. They edged forward with half-steps along the shabby corridor. They stopped on either side of the door to Yousef's room.

The men darted edgy looks at one other. The tension was palpable.

Yousef would play that moment over and over in his mind.

"I was sitting on one of the two beds when I heard the noise. I walked over to the door. When I swung it open, the posse pushed me back into the room. I have to say it was ironic. No matter how often I had worked out in advance what I would do if the Feds ever ambushed me, I was stunned. Not that I would ever admit that to them. One man kicked me in the groin. Two men bundled me against the wall, pulling my hands behind my back. One slipped handcuffs over my wrists as seamlessly as a magician. He must have done that dozens of times."

"Is this the right guy?" the SWAT team leader asked another agent. The Fed studied Yousef's face as the leader held it sideways.

"What are you doing? I've done nothing wrong," was all Yousef could manage.

"Shut it!" said the leader.

The Fed compared the scared, scarred face of Yousef squashed against the wall with a photo. He took in the features he had studied in fuzzy images from CCTV. Yes, there they were: the penetrating liquid eyes, the right eye framed with scars, the opulent, curled lips, and the globular ears. It must be him.

"Turn him round," said the leader.

When Yousef was facing the wall again, the Fed grabbed his fingers and checked for old burn scars and stains from chemicals.

"That's our boy."

The SWAT team tied his ankles together. They thrust his head into a black hood and pulled him out of the room along the corridor to the stairs. Yousef was shuffling and trying to kick. They hoisted him onto the shoulders of the burliest man and he carried Yousef downstairs and through the white marble entrance to some car outside. Still shocked but trying to recover, Yousef started yelling again, "I've done nothing wrong. Where the fuck are you taking me?"

On the plane from Pakistan to the US Yousef, trying to recover his bruised bravado, was expansive about his crimes to two agents, speaking on condition that they neither wrote down nor tape-recorded the conversation. After the shock of his unexpected arrest and the deepening, deadening feeling that he was never going to get out of prison alive, was it his irrepressible ego that made him open up? Or was it a bizarre, ecstatic high from this belated recognition of his skill? The ever-restless mind of this obsessive master bomber was already trying to plan his courtroom strategy for his survival. And ego got the better of this particular daredevil. Yousef could not resist showing off. To prove his know-all credentials, he asked for an agent's yellow-paper pad.

He sketched two diagrams of what he had originally planned for the twin towers. One was a vertical rendering showing one tower falling onto the other. The second was a ground plan of the site below ground level, marking the spatial relationship of the twin towers and the explosion.

The agent, astonished at Yousef's audacity, leaned over to tear the page from the pad to keep it separate.

"Just a minute," said Yousef. "Hand it back so I can add two details."

Yousef took the leaf of paper. In a flash he screwed it up and put it in his mouth, trying to chew it. The agent slapped him heartily on his shoulders to make him cough it back up again.

The repercussions of Yousef's arrest in the Islamabad guest house and swift extradition to the US rippled far and wide. Within days Pakistani authorities, trying to anticipate any retaliation, arrested over twenty of his supporters. Later they arrested one of Yousef's friends in Quetta, where he was trying to sell Yousef's house to raise money for Yousef and his family.

Yousef had other admirers in Asia. As a result of his arrest and extradition, there were some retaliatory attacks. Two consular workers and a consulate secretary were shot dead in Karachi and a postal clerk was wounded in the ankle. A suicide bomb attack virtually destroyed the Egyptian embassy in Islamabad. Fifteen people were killed and more than sixty others injured.

After his extradition to the US, Yousef was held under twenty-four-hour observation in the 9-South wing of New York's Metropolitan Correctional Center at 150 Park Street. This 1975 building was the first high-rise facility used by the Bureau of Prisons for criminals awaiting trial. Previous residents included crime bosses John Gotti and Jackie D'Amico and drug kingpin Frank Lucas.

Federal investigators knew that their months of grinding toil, of assembling, coding, and organizing evidence against Yousef were coming to a head. In his dealings with investigators before his trial Yousef was like a stage devil— arrogant, ironic, and alternately charming and melancholy. He thought this was as attractive an image for the East as fictional Brit spy James Bond was for the West.

Yet on one subject he was coy. His mind became as opaque as an oyster shell when they asked him about the chemicals he and the bombers had used to make their device in February 1993: "I wasn't there. I wasn't part of that scenario."

Evidently, Yousef was also thinking ahead.

"If I tell them exactly what chemicals I used in the bomb, the US will ban ingredients that could be used to make future bombs."

Prosecutors decided to have two trials for Yousef. One was for the Bojinka plot. This trial would also include the charge of the murder of Japanese passenger Haruki Ikegami on the PAL plane. The other trial was for the bomb inside the World Trade Center.

Both trials were held under Judge Kevin Duffy.

The preparation of evidence for the trials was a mammoth exercise for the FBI. It had conducted 5,000 examinations and put forward 1,000 exhibits.

The crucial bundle of evidence for the Bojinka trial came from a laptop police had seized in the Philippines when Yousef and his accomplice at that time had to flee an apartment building. Their chemicals had caught fire in the kitchen while they were cooking them in a pot bought at TJ Maxx. In the hands of investigators this laptop proved an Aladdin's lamp of incriminating evidence now Yousef was brought to trial.

In the shabby apartment officers had also found an assortment of chemicals and other evidence: sulfuric acid, bomb-making manuals, wire, timing devices, a soldering gun, a pipe, floppy disks, four small pipe-bombs. In a cabinet above the kitchen counter was a fragmentation bomb packed into a pipe already attached to a detonator.

But it was the laptop that supplied the most astonishing information. For, in the Bojinka plot, Yousef proposed to have five men plant bombs on eleven airliners to be detonated over the Pacific so that 4,000 passengers and crew members flying from Asia to America would be massacred. The entire US airline business would have been disabled. The laptop showed meticulous planning for the bizarre future atrocity with specific codenames for terrorists: Mirqas, Markoa, Obaid, Majbos, and Zyed.

At BCU Dean Ace Ferrari took a keen interest in the trial of Ramzi Yousef. What evidence would emerge? What would the jury decide about the various charges? And what were the implications for the Oryx Party at BCU? If Ferrari attended personally, he would be noticed and become open to speculation. However, he had the perfect plant in NHU chair of chemistry Don Fatale. For Fatale was not only a native New Yorker who was still a respected theater director but was also now on sabbatical leave from teaching to rehearse an off-Broadway production of Shakespeare's *Pericles*. Best of all, Don Fatale could become invisible and unrecognizable in a group of people.

Ace Ferrari made sure that Don Fatale had no difficulty in getting into court sessions to be his eyes and ears. As Ferrari expected, Fatale had the memory of an elephant and an artist's inner instincts for subtext—what might not be said in open court but might influence decisions behind the scenes.

But Ace Ferrari had miscalculated. Don Fatale was already undergoing a slow but insistent change of heart, increasingly disturbed by Ace Ferrari's ruthlessness—not on behalf of the Palestinian people but to keep control of his puny lieutenants for Paradise Postponed. Now Don Fatale saw Ace Ferrari not simply as an inflexible political puritan but rather as another narcissistic Groznyy. And Don Fatale was now in downtown New York almost daily. As a native New Yorker he felt strongly drawn to its high-octane American energy and sympathetic to its varied citizens and, above all, to the fundamental decency of American people.

While Don Fatale relayed the basic development of the court case and some important details and twists and turns in nighttime phone calls to Ace Ferrari—using different payphones—he said nothing and gave no hint about his change of heart. He guessed what fate Ace Ferrari would deal the slippery Carpenter Cain and thus the possible sort of revenge Ferrari would plan for him if he absconded.

With his usual mixture of empty bravado, flashes of courage, and long-term strategy, Yousef planned the outlines of his courtroom defense:

"When the first trial began on May 29, 1996, I had it all worked out. Next day I told the court I would handle my own defense. My strategy was to humanize myself to the gullible jury. That day and every day I made a show of being such a polite young guy. I was immaculately dressed in tailored suits with French cuffs, pristine shirts, and flashy gold cufflinks.

"I knew it all. I used to tell my stooges, 'When we're at work or play, we dress down. We look inconspicuous to fit in. When we pull cheap western girls, it's all down to our charm and flashing smiles that imply eastern promises—that always deceive. When we're out on a mission, we have to look like the affluent society—designer clothes, expensive accessories—and that includes the suitcases and, by no means least, first-class plane travel.'

"I worked it out from old Hollywood films and the star system. Outdoors, a film star must always be on show. We do that and we follow their maxim: dress to kill. Ironic, isn't it, because that's what we're in business to do? And that's how I conducted my trial. So, what with my cultured appearance and noble style, the jury had to reason that I could not possibly have committed the allegedly horrendous crimes of which they accused me.

"I could tell the judge was afraid that my persuasive talents would sway the jury. He said he would not let the court become an arena for my ego. That was a dead giveaway.

"But I was ahead of them. I was not going to be trapped by cross-examination. What I had to do was sow doubt in the minds of the jury. I did not testify at either trial. Yet I had a consistent line of defense: I was being made a scapegoat so that the US government could give the American people the impression that they were in control. And that was the uncomfortable truth.

"I laid the ground in advance. In a prepared opening statement at the Bojinka trial in which I referred to myself in the third person (which is correct legal practice), I told the jury, 'I want you to keep in mind that even though defendant Yousef is not a US citizen, and doesn't speak the way you speak, that he is a person just like you. Concentrate on the evidence. If you do so, the only just verdict is not guilty.'

"The lawyers didn't like it and they didn't like to admit it but I know, in their eyes, in this first trial I proved myself a credible defense attorney. I got an admission from a flight attendant on the PAL plane that she and her parents had relocated to the United States at the expense of the US government. In this way I implied that this was in exchange for her testimony against me. It was obviously true. But of course the American cards were stacked against me."

Don Fatale was intrigued by Ramzi Yousef's manner, his mixture of swagger and bravado. He appreciated Yousef's theatrical sense of dress style and contrite way of speaking.

As the trial took some curved turns with some particularly cruel detail about the explosion and the perpetrators, Don Fatale could not quieten a silent voice of reproach in his ear: "Have I got to sit through all this? Am I to blame? There is blood on everything Ramzi Yousef touches. And for all his fine words, whatever the dean touches, he kills."

Fourteen weeks after the start of the trial, on September 5, 1996, Yousef and two co-conspirators, Abdul Hakim Murad and Wali Khan Amin Shah, were convicted for their role in the Bojinka plot and were sentenced to life in prison without parole. Judge Duffy referred to Yousef as "an apostle of evil" before recommending that Yousef's entire sentence be served in solitary confinement.

At the second trial about the World Trade Center bomb in 1993 Yousef again tried to brazen things out, but this time he let his lawyers do the talking. As before, he tried to present himself to the jurors as a decent man who had nothing to hide. Stark testimony suggested otherwise. As is often the situation in a court case about atrocity, it was the individual human tragedies that were most telling. Jurors were deeply shocked by police photos of the mangled bodies of the victims. Then there was the sheer volume of incriminating evidence—disturbing enough. But more powerful still was one personal story: the murder of Monica Smith, the mother-to-be, and her unborn son.

In her evidence, expert witness Dr. Jacqueline Lee described the horrible way Monica had died of blunt impact trauma. When the huge blast ripped through Monica's office, it stamped the pattern of her sweater onto her shoulder. It killed her unborn son, tore her lungs, arteries, and other internal organs, fractured her pelvis, and broke her leg. Concrete blocks pummeled her head.

Hardened showbiz pro though he was, Don Fatale found himself moved by the grieving widower's plangent description of his tender wife's horrific murder. Others in the courtroom, whether experienced law officers or journalists, could not hold back their tears. It was only with great effort that Fatale held back his.

Ironically for someone who had meted out death remorselessly to innocents and had planned death to thousands more, Yousef now trembled at the prospect of facing death, even martyrdom, himself. Was this because he knew what death sentences were like? Was it abject fear of his methods?

However, President Benazir Bhutto of Pakistan (one of his intended victims) had saved him. Prosecutors in New York discovered that they could not seek the death sentence in the World Trade Center bombing trial. The US government had made certain assurances to Pakistan when seeking Yousef's extradition. These included that he would not be put to death. Thus prosecutors told Judge Duffy that they would seek a life sentence. Yousef became visibly more relaxed.

On November 12, 1997, the jury found Yousef guilty of masterminding the 1993 bombing. In 1998 he was convicted of "seditious conspiracy" to bomb the World Trade Center towers. Before he was sentenced, he boasted, "Yes, I am a terrorist and I am proud of it. And I support terrorism as long as it is against the United States government and against Israel, because you are more than terrorists, you are the ones who invented terrorism and using it every day. You are butchers, liars, and hypocrites."

The judge sentenced Yousef to 240 years for the World Trade Center attack.

When the judge delivered his vivid denunciation of Ramzi Yousef as someone who had betrayed the higher ideals of Islam, Don Fatale was not surprised to feel enveloped in emotional solidarity with all New Yorkers.

Don Fatale heard his inner voice, schooled as it had been by great plays he had read, seen, or directed: "It's true what they say. Whatever does or doesn't happen in men's law, our deeds carry their own judgement. It sounds a trumpet in our hearts that summons us to a higher judgement."

Traveling home on the subway that day, he was so immersed in his thoughts that he missed his stop. All he could think of was the gross brutality of Ramzi Yousef and his co-conspirators. Round and round it went in his head: "I thank heavens I was allowed to hear this dear husband and his pitiful account. It's because of him and the other witnesses that I will stay in New York to work with and for these men and share their burdens."

Don Fatale had made up his mind.

"So, my dear mischief-making dean, I'm leaving. For all your learning you know too little about what people need. You may commune with books in your study but what people set their hearts upon is hidden from you. You never take account of the huge cost the American people pay for everything or appreciate how every day they renew themselves like the phoenix and continuously raise themselves. All this is beyond you. But I belong to these people. You are not my kind."

Don Fatale's production of Shakespeare's *Pericles*, a shipwreck fantasy with action that roams around the ports and islands of the eastern Mediterranean and emphasizes the coruscating consequences of revenge and dynastic quarrels, sharpened his own interpretation of the political and religious divisions that had surfaced in the Ramzi Yousef court cases.

The success of his modern-dress off-Broadway production of Shakespeare's *Pericles*, followed by a flurry of offers for him to direct other shows, supplied both reason and excuse for Don Fatale's exit from BCU and his full-time return to the living theater of New York, away from the theater of death by degrees at BCU–NHU.

Because Don Fatale was a known figure in show business, his exit was public news and widely approved. Press publicity provided his guarantee of personal safety. Don could not be pursued by a Bohemian bear, a Berliner bear, or a North American grizzly, without an investigation that would surely lead to the Oryx Party.

Hermione saw parallels between the two cases, Ramzi Yousef's in New York and Cesare Groznyy's in New England. On her Monday morning journey into the city, Hermione read what the editorial in Sunday's edition of the *Norse Hoven Courier* had to say about the red and black devils, Groznyy and Yousef.

Forget the bizarre circus swirling around Cesare Groznyy that has turned BCU into an academic laughingstock. Yes, the usual suspects appearing before the panel appointed by the state education commission may be out to entertain us, but they're not as good as Gypsy Rose Lee or as perceptive as Stephen Sondheim.

Let's concentrate on serious matters that affect our lives and our democratic institutions. While Groznyy is being tried in all but name in New England, a far weightier case has loomed in New York.

The various verdicts and the sentencing of terrorist Ramzi Yousef for the airliner Bojinka plot and the bombing of the World Trade Center have spread themselves wearily over months. But this terrifying case is not getting the resounding attention in the press and on TV it deserves. Yet for the men and women in the FBI and the CIA or any alert politicians the events that led to Yousef's trials make it apparent that the United States has crossed into new political terrain.

The fanatics who led terrorism across the world until the 1990s were deadly. They developed dangerous explosives to detonate civic buildings, commercial centers, and planes and land vehicles. They left thousands of innocent people dead and injured thousands more.

But what Yousef and his co-conspirators aimed at is far worse.

Among factors that have brought the shift to the new terrorists are the breakdown of the Soviet Union and the Russian withdrawal from Afghanistan. Supposedly, terrorist leader Osama bin Laden has said that if Russia could be destroyed, then the United States can also be beheaded.

Another harbinger of change has been the Gulf War that we entered to expel Iraq from Kuwait. It has turned the heat up on things American and Arab hatred of Israel. Let's not forget the fact that we, the West, trained and equipped our potential enemies to fight the Russians in Afghanistan and then we left them ready to take on us.

Our best analysts caution us that other new jackals besides Yousef will not stop blowing up buildings and vehicles and killing people. What they now aspire to is to endanger entire cities or even to menace a whole nation. They are ready to use such weapons of mass destruction (WMDs) as biological and chemical weapons.

Osama bin Laden, the informal banker of al-Qaeda, 'the Base,' may think of Ramzi Yousef as a committed Muslim who has fortified Islam against America. However, such new jackals do not have specific political objectives like independence or separatism for particular regions. They are not interested in a place at a diplomatic negotiating table. What they want is widespread physical and psychological terror in order to dislocate government. They crave our downfall.

And what is the response of our elected government?

Rather than scare us—the electorate—politicians and law enforcement officers prefer to set our minds at rest, to bolster our confidence in them—that they have terrorism under control. But already there is a sea change. More insightful politicians now admit privately that scenarios of fanatics with toxic chemicals or a rough and ready nuclear bomb have moved from being overripe science fiction into problematic reality.

What do you think? What would you do about this new crisis?

Hermione could not help wondering who had written the editorial. Was it Todd Carter Fox, or Steve Sharp, or Mickey Garnier? All three had the chutzpah to tackle such a daring topic and to do it in an aggressive way. But only Fox would have the knowledge and hard-won military experience.

On her late-night Saturday return journey to Babel City after a week's work in Manhattan, Hermione saw next to her seat on the train a copy of that day's Norse Hoven paper that someone had left open at the letters page.

There it was: "Our readers' response to last Sunday's editorial was huge. We present a selection of letters chosen to represent the variety of opinions."

Hermione started to scan the letters.

As a Holocaust survivor and committed Zionist, I'm concerned about the way anti-Israel sentiment is solidifying in the Middle East and how certain groups are targeting the United States in their mission to bring down Israel. There is Hezbollah, mainly Shiite, which opposes Israel. There are the Afghan Arabs whose main vehicle is al-Qaeda. Al-Qaeda is a hard-line fundamentalist organization that is not only a threat to the West but also to fragile states in the Middle East and Asia, notably Pakistan. Not only does al-Qaeda insist on strict codes—such as separating men and women—but it also has a strategy of trying to destabilize relations between one state and another.

Zenocrate Cohen

Death by hanging? Electric chair? Lethal injection? They're all too good for terrorist Ramzi Yousef for his crimes against American humanity. What is even worse is that, since the death penalty is not possible because of a technicality, we—solid American citizens—have to pay for the man's upkeep for the rest of his miserable life. What a mockery of his innocent victims!

Sam Stone

How could the *Norse Hoven Courier* do it? Ridicule Cesare Groznyy, and, worse, imply there is some comparison between this misunderstood, visionary academic leader and terrorist scum of the lowest order like the gang that bombed the World Trade Center? Shame!

Georgie Lucre

The contrary groups at BCU—the so-called Groznyy Gang and the self-styled Opposition Party—they're like silly armies in a satire who will stop at nothing until they have fought one another to total destruction.

Donald Duck [verifiable name and address supplied]

Write all the diatribes you want. The twenty-first century will be the century of the Muslim. Remember, there are one billion of us Muslims worldwide. We shall have our new Caliphate yet.

Faisal Shah

The last letter was long. Hermione decided to save it for coffee and bagels in the morning. She looked up.

Steve Sharp was in a seat to the side. He winked at her. "You're tired. Let me give you a ride home."

Steve drove her back. As he dropped her off opposite his own house, he said, "It wasn't Todd, or Mickey, or me who wrote that editorial. It was Tiberius Brown. He's the former chair of the trustees of BCU whom Groznyy got rid of—to his cost. Brown's academic field is US foreign policy."

In the morning, Hermione went back to that final letter by Tiberius Brown:

Before we can tackle the new terrorists effectively, we need to have more information on how they operate. This includes facing up to some unpalatable facts. Gone are the days when bomb attacks were limited. The foiled Bojinka plot indicates that the new jackals prefer to target multiple targets simultaneously. Moreover, the new jackals do not care whether they kill their own people. They are religious fanatics without being truly religious in the sense of being compassionate. They teach hatred of America and the West generally—and even other branches of Islam.

Then there is the fact that what we consider among the benefits of society today—increased and wider communications—also excites our enemies. Al-Qaeda's ability to coordinate different groups is helped by the communications revolution.

Our strategy has to be: separate hardcore terrorists from their gangs and their recruiting pools. Governments should address legitimate grievances to steal the terrorists' thunder on such issues as corruption. Governments should also weaken the terrorists' pool of recruits by inspiring some harmony between East and West and should try to break down the barriers between religious groups.

Tiberius Brown

The paper's editor wanted to move the little community of the New England college town on. He added an imperial footnote.

The brouhaha at BCU is like a particularly horrid fairy tale. The only people who have behaved like decent human beings in the unsavory scenario have been the journalists and that great lady of song, Holly Wood. She's a real queen.

This correspondence is now closed. [Editor]

*

THE WHITE DEVIL IN THE LITTLE BLACK DRESS

As the educational panel against Groznyy and the trustees collected more evidence, spoken and written, they built up a detailed picture of the way Groznyy's administration functioned as a farcical parody of a totalitarian state. The local press gave readers the impression that Groznyy's way of running things at BCU was at once frightening and amusing. The implication was that the existence of such a grotesque administration was made possible by sinister intimidation of people stupefied by university work.

The Opposition Party had already shifted emphasis from Groznyy's alleged misrule to his interest in personal profit. And the panel followed suit.

Art professors at BCU had used their connections with Manhattan art galleries to explain that Groznyy was also using instalment-plan methods to acquire paintings by prominent modern artists—Picasso, Braque, Bacon— whereby portions of his monthly salary were used to acquire valuable works via an extended payment plan. These works were increasing in value as he paid for them so that they were worth two, three, and four times what he had started paying for them years previously.

After such intrusive, uncomfortable revelations, Groznyy was pacing up and down the reception room outside his inner office. He picked up the local paper peeping out from under the computer keyboard on Bee Flute's desk. What appeared inside was the unwanted visit of a dreaded ghost.

Groznyy had to steel himself over the day's cartoon. It stirred his faltering recollection of American history during Reconstruction after the Civil War. He recognized himself and Veronica Veneer. He was in doublet-and-hose as Iago whispering into the ears of Veronica. She was depicted with an outsize Afro hairstyle that she had not sported in real life for years and attired as a transgender Othello. As in Shakespeare's tragedy they were devils each with a vice the obverse of the other: Othello-Veronica was jealousy; Iago-Groznyy was envy.

Groznyy thought this was too sophisticated for regional readers. But the words that came out of his Iago mouth were not: "Treason is a crime and must be made odious and traitors must be punished."

Groznyy stared. The color drained away from his cheeks. There was also the unkindest cut that he knew was reserved for him alone. It was just like the cartoon the princess had taunted him with in the Golden Cockerel. The signature in the corner was again "Modest Groznyy." How could this be? Modest had died at his hands and had been burned in their house by the damnable Ashley Bedfellow Burns.

Still in the outer office but now flying into a rage, he hurled an orange from a fruit bowl into the central printer. The fruit got stuck and clogged up the feeder. Shamefaced, the president's staff had to use the printer in the treasurer's office until the one the president had damaged could be repaired.

As he sat before the committee one day, Groznyy heard one witness demolish his character. A mean-faced man whom he could not remember reported that guarding the president was the most unpopular task in the security firm because of Groznyy's mood swings: "One minute he can be friendly and the next he can turn into a screaming madman."

Then Groznyy remembered who it was. There followed the story of Groznyy hitting him when the car was traveling on the highway.

Another day Groznyy did not appear in the newspaper cartoon. He was torn between his vanity that he should always be the center of attention and relief that he had a reprieve. For this time he had been airbrushed out of his own story.

Whoever the artist was, he had shown people arriving for the panel's hearings as if they were footballers in a scrum, almost clambering upon one another to get through the courthouse door. There were old men and maidens, young women and children, in various garbs from *nouveaux riches* fashion plates to street people in rags. There were no bubble captions, merely a headline: "Artist's Impression of Public Interest in the Groznyy Hearings."

Who had done this to him?

Most bizarrely, Cesare began to pester the queen of England in hasty letters, enquiring about being granted asylum in the UK. Just as Ivan the Terrible had courted Elizabeth I through intermediaries, Nemo Groznyy decided he would court Elizabeth II through letters appealing for help:

> I know your birthday in April is close to that of England's greatest playwright but trust me when I say that I do not believe the scurrilous rumor that it was you who wrote Shakespeare's plays. However, I can help you with your great weakness, your highly nervous, frosty public speaking. I could ease your tenseness and give you the pizzazz you have always craved.

Such were his enticing words of love. He even told the queen that, like her, he was the only person in the palace who switched off unnecessary lights.

Holly's inner turmoil had settled into a deep but blunt emotional pain. She felt she had failed Modest. What was worse, she was beginning to forget him as clearly as she had known him. When he appeared in her mind's eye, his features were blurred even if she had a small treasure trove of photos to sharpen her memory.

"Sleep with the father, then give birth to his son, and then sleep with his elder son. Then marry the monster father that we think killed the elder son. What sort of white trash does this make me? A candidate for Jerry Springer's TV show?

Or"—thinking about her brief and incomplete education in classic literature—"is this the basis for the sort of highbrow drama they broadcast on *Masterpiece Theatre* on Sunday evenings?"

These troubling thoughts made Holly feel dirty. They cut like sharp daggers when she wondered if she should reward Darko or if another love affair with a mystery Muslim would make her feel even more soiled. Was that even possible?

"Both Carmine and Hermione would tell me to take charge of my own soap opera. At the moment, I'm just adrift."

When she took the surprise phone call, Holly was as calm as any wife could be when her husband's life was in turmoil. As soon as she heard the operator speak, she began shaking like a leaf.

"Al Binoni is calling from a correctional facility. Will you accept the call?"

Holly did not recognize the name but she could tell it was phony. And she knew it must be him. She felt a hurricane of contradictory emotions: surprise, panic, joy, and love. Her heart was crushed into powder. He had always been able to get under her skin.

After she mumbled, "Yes," half in expectation, half in dread, the dark chocolate voice spoke.

"Holly, it's me. Don't hang up, please. I'm sorry. I need you."

Chocolate still but somehow the voice sounded broken, nothing like the confident tones Darius had used when he was wooing her. Yet it exerted the same magnetic pull on her emotions. She tried to keep a grip.

"You left me alone in a disaster," she said. "You promised we'd go away together. But when I needed you, you weren't there, you'd vamoosed."

She was just mouthing words. She reflected on how she had reworked the tired scenario Darius had put her through when she herself had mischievously worked on Darko to get the tax documents. The difference was that, in the earlier scenario, she had been the victim and the escape plan had been botched; with Darko, she had played the predator with a steely hand and left him dangling.

Darius knew that this might be his only phone call to Holly and his only chance with her. He sensed she would not fall for any lame apology. Holly knew enough about men at universities to recognize self-deceivers. But she let him continue and he was determined to keep talking.

"I need to see you."

All Holly's thoughts about Darko disappeared.

Holly hated the shabby, winding route to the state correctional facility.

She was surprised when prison officers directed her to a medical wing. Although Holly felt she knew Darius's handsome face in every detail—the noble brow, the come-hither eyes, the neat nose and generous mouth with gleaming teeth—she knew she might find him changed. And he was.

He looked scruffy, not with a ragged beard or unwashed hair but certainly his now-furrowed brow seemed to have spread creases right across his face. He looked older, not with years but with experience. Sharp lines in his cheeks wrinkled his face. They suggested pain and hardship. And part of his upper body was bandaged.

Her first words were, "What happened?"

"When I tried to get back stateside, they didn't believe me. I couldn't tell them the real reason—to see you, to be with you. I said I wanted to finish my studies. My answers didn't stack up. The INS officers suspected my passport. My new name was different from my previous name when I was a student here."

"So they're holding you until they can determine your rights and let you stay?"

"There's more."

"Were you injured in prison? Is that why you're here?"

"No. There was a shooting incident in Karachi. This was some time ago. It may have been in retaliation against the authorities for Ramzi Yousef's arrest. I got caught in crossfire on a street. The bullet went through my upper shoulder. It didn't heal properly and it's affected my upper arm. It was the bandages that made me conspicuous in the airport. I tried to shift my story. I said I had been injured and had returned to the US for better medical services.

"This made the INS officers even more suspicious. They checked with Interpol. The Interpol records backed up my story to a point. But there were some inconsistencies—names—how I came to be shot." His voice trailed off. "So I'm being held until they decide. I think they want me out of immediate reach of other guys from Pakistan and Afghanistan. I'm also under suspicion of a crime not yet stated. Because some of my previous life was here, they sent me back to New England. And because I've been injured, I'm being held in the hospital wing."

All this confused Holly. It was too much information to take in. There were her troubled emotions—not wanting this old flame to disturb her life, crowded as it was with her husband's constant crises and her own determination to succeed as a singer. And underpinning everything was the hollow gap in her very being left by the death of Modest, whom she adored as she had adored no one else.

Darius did not want to lose her to this lost reverie. He rose from the table toward her. His restless mouth on her languorous lips was gentle and loving. She pressed her body onto his. There was a fire inside her. She shook. She took his bandaged arm and held his hand in hers, simply to have part of him to squeeze.

He responded with a brief gasp of pain. She gazed, mouth open and confused. He raised his hand to his lips. Holly realized that Darius had a cruel gash there and that, in her gripping his hand, it had started to ooze blood. In an instant he had changed. The magic charm of their love had snapped. He rose, turned away, and moved out of the visiting room.

Dismayed, she had to watch him disappear. Holly felt she was about to faint. She steadied herself on the hard edge of the table. What would Hermione or Carmine tell her to do? "Stay sympathetic but step back inside yourself, until you have sorted out what is best for you." She could also hear Benny's voice in her ear: "Nothing can bring Modest back, not this Darius. Do what is best for you—not us—you."

Mordred Stickleman had drawn two junior colleagues together. They did not yet have tenure and he was telling them what to do to earn his appreciation.

"It has to look like a student prank—something that a sophomore might get up to at Milhous College. But the subtext must be clear. This loose woman will go with anyone. People need to know. Understood?"

Stirred by her prison adventure, a light came back to Holly's eyes. Groznyy sensed it. He guessed she had been off with someone else. She was in the shower trying out Eliza Doolittle's farewell from *My Fair Lady*: "Without You."

When Holly came out of the shower singing a little ragtime phrase, he was fit to burst.

"How could you do this to me, you damn whore? Find Modest's drawings and sell them to the damned press?

"Al who was it? Al Fredo? Or was it Al Binoni and his friends in al-Qaeda? Your Al, my Al, my grandmother's Al? It was Al all the time."

In his fury, he tore at her bathrobe and towel. Then he grabbed her hair and pulled it out of its loosely tied knot. "You knew what you were in for when you had the nerve to marry me, didn't you?"

When Holly stumbled and fell, he dragged her over the bedroom floor onto the marriage bed.

"You ugly, cheating whore! Take that! And that!"

He cuffed her twice across the face with the back of his hand. A reddish weal spread across her cheeks where his ring had broken the skin. She felt her right eye smart.

Holly was terrified and yet strangely transfixed by his fury. Groznyy recognized abject fear in her eyes. Yet she said nothing. As it dawned on him what his attack might suggest about his murderous ability, he recoiled and sat on the bed.

Beaten though she might be, Holly was not crushed. It was as if she had a tensile backbone as supple as sprung steel. She clambered up and gathered her robe around her still-damp limbs. Groznyy expected her to lash out at him or even the opposite—to cower. He expected her to play a role based on one of her musical models. But no. She was suddenly collected as if she had deliberately overcome first-night nerves and was about to appear immaculate on stage. Suddenly everything she had absorbed as a club singer honed by experience at BCU came into play. By his temper tantrum, Groznyy had put her more in control.

"So, you think it was me, little man. You have even less common sense than I thought."

All this was said as if she were center stage with only her face lit by a blinding spotlight. Groznyy wondered if she was going to say something about a divorce and a lucrative settlement. He left.

Later that morning, Holly steeled herself further. Her makeup was immaculate. But she made no attempt to cover her swelling black eye or the weal on her cheek. In fact, she sported them.

Holly Wood Groznyy had not attended the panel's hearings. But that day of Groznyy's assault, she did appear, arriving an hour later than Groznyy. To bolster her courage, she sang Fevronia's song to herself on her nervous journey.

She wore a modest trouser suit, charcoal gray to be neither black nor white, neither bride nor widow, but like an office worker dressed as professional duty personified.

Holly timed her entry to be after the beginning of the hearings so that there would be no room for her in the main courtroom. She would have to listen in the annex with the CCTV feed. She squatted decorously on the floor with the junior journalists. Everyone knew who she was. Without saying a word, she was an abused wife. By her demure silence she had upstaged her husband, seeming both to support him by her attendance and to denounce him by her composure and her bruises.

She was in time to hear the testimony of Bogus.

Bogus Revisor still shielded his real opinion and his ambitions behind a façade of loyalty. He defended Nemo by saying, "Cesare Groznyy never likes taking no for an answer. He can be demanding of people. But it is always for the greater good of BCU. No one has ever said he's a shrinking violet—that's why he gets things done. That's why we're making progress academically.

"BCU was barely muddling along a few years ago, poorly organized, and in sharp need of dramatic revitalization. That is what President Groznyy has provided."

Such was the clarion trumpet fanfare of Bogus in public.

"Can you elaborate? Do you have any independent reference?" asked the chairman.

"Sure. The education research company, Wonder and Marvel, did a study just before President Groznyy arrived. Franklin Miller, who was acting as caretaker president, commissioned it. Wonder and Marvel said that BCU suffered from an inadequate central administration, feeble faculty with poor self-image, and faint-hearted trustees. President Groznyy wanted a unifying mission in BCU."

"Have your experiences as provost borne this out? Can you give us a before and after comparison?"

"Sure. When I started at BCU, it was difficult to work out how things got done there. The files in my office were in neither alphabetical nor any other order. Among other problems, there was no student orientation for freshmen. Documentation of peer review for professors' tenure was skimpy or non-existent. Departments carried out next to no evaluation of teaching."

"And this was the state of the provost's office?"

"Yes."

"Who were the two previous provosts?"

"Lucy Kaye, former dean of nursing."

"And?"

Bogus paused.

"We're waiting."

"Cesare Groznyy," Bogus said.

"So he was part of this scenario of apathy?"

"I wouldn't say that."

"You wouldn't or don't dare to?" The chairman let his point sink in. "And after you took over?"

"My attempts to make changes met with resistance. The professors were defensive toward anyone with higher standards—like me. When I tried to impose better evaluation of teaching, I faced stonewall opposition. It remains an issue today. The professors believed the quality of their teaching was high, but I did—and do—not. They awarded students inflated grades. Students scored an average of B at BCU. But their scores on national tests were way below average. The system of excessive self-regard was pernicious. The institution was inbred."

"None of this is a good recommendation for students or parents at BCU, is it?"

Silence.

"How does this square with BCU's advertising campaign to attract students with high claims? Were any of the glowing predictions legal?"

Before Bogus could stumble through a half-assed answer, Groznyy was on his feet and shouting.

"Legal? What's lawful around here? I never heard of such impertinence. My whims are orders. That's the law around BCU."

Stultifying silence.

In the early afternoon, when Holly left the courthouse near the green amid the spires and towers of Milhous College, the press was ready and curious. A reporter asked her about her future showbiz plans.

"What can I say? I'm like a Broadway gypsy. I'm open to offers—legitimate offers."

"Holly, does that mean you're thinking of widening your range?"

"Maybe. I'm considering making a blues album."

"Blues?"

"Yes, blues, why not, like Bessie Smith? You remember her lines? 'He blacked my eyes. I couldn't see. Then he pawned the things he gave to me.'"

Mordred Stickleman was ready to deflate her. "Mrs. Groznyy, hi! In that trouser suit you almost look like a man."

"Dear Mordred, so do you."

Stickleman smiled grimly. Holly knew what was coming next. Carmine had called her. She had also told her how to handle it.

Shielding his eyes from the waning sun, Stickleman looked skywards. Trying to sound casual, he said, "Strange where they hang out the washing."

Looking up at the great Crown Tower of Milhous College, the crowd saw a pair of pink panties tied up there and fluttering in the breeze. Holly knew they looked like hers but they surely could not be. They were embroidered with a large HW. The incident was meant to look like a student prank. But Holly knew how far the Opposition

Party would go to ridicule Groznyy through her. The little crowd gulped.

Holly stepped forward and sidled her arm into Stickleman's arm, gently moving him toward the tower.

"It makes the day so lovely when the sun shines like this," she began.

Stickleman felt uncomfortable.

"What do you want, Mrs. Groznyy?" he asked.

"Dear Mr. Stickleman," she answered sweetly, "I want you to take my panties down."

The pent-up feelings of the little group burst out in infectious laughter. Stickleman went bright red. He had planned ridicule on all things Groznyy. Once again, this damned chant-tootsie had got the better of him.

Holly bent down to adjust her hose. Drawing up a side zipper, she peeled up one trouser leg. As she swung her supple ass Stickleman thought she was going to break wind in his face. He moved to avoid her just at the moment she snapped a garter that sent a splinter of something sharp into his face. It stung. Then, inclining her head to acknowledge the spontaneous applause, Holly sang the opening of Fevronia's aria. This changed the mood of the crowd to instant rapture.

"Sing it again, Holly," said a journalist.

Her reply, as ever, was, "I never sing the same song twice for nothing. So long, dearie."

Disconcerted by media interest in Holly, anxious trustee Georgie Lucre, who had stood aside from the tawdry scene, corralled the TV crew as he took the high road of outraged propriety against the panel.

"There's mischief afoot. If the panel inside the courthouse acts against Dr. Groznyy, it will do the cause of higher education in the northeast serious damage. For weeks it has behaved like a kangaroo court and listened to nonsensical testimony from malcontents about President Groznyy's alleged misdeeds. This panel has assumed powers partly like a military court martial, partly like a secret police. But never for a moment has it focused on the fact that he has, practically single-handedly, saved a failing university."

No one was listening. The crowd had gone and the TV crew had left.

As Holly traveled home with her companion Dr. Squires, who had been to court that day, she mused on the limitless capacity of human beings to feud until they drew blood.

"We wound ourselves in stupid anger. Look at my husband. He's being driven out, yet he still thinks he's the hunter out hunting. He doesn't hear his own cry of pain. While he keeps digging into his own flesh, he thinks he is giving himself pleasure!"

That evening Groznyy returned home after Holly. Although he was exhausted he was still railing. It was as if nothing had happened between him and Holly that morning. He had not seen her at the panel's hearings and did not yet know the silent damage she had done.

"It was like rivers of blood today," he exclaimed, clapping his hands to summon Holly to dinner prepared by the cleaner. "There's no end to the gullibility, prurience, and fickleness of the public; the status-seeking of the professors; and the superficiality of the press. I will make the Cross Campus filthy with their blood."

Groznyy did not know Dr. Squires was in the next room.

When the doctor came in, he launched into an attack: "In the past, monarchies protected themselves with a corrupt court. The interest of the court was self-preservation—anything to retain power. In your case, it's worse. Your reign of terror prevents you from getting the information you need, despite your getting people to snitch on one another. Now it's all crumbling you have no friends."

"Faculty, what does your Shakespeare call them—'You common cry of curs whose breath I hate.'"

"Not Shakespeare himself but his character, Coriolanus, facing banishment from Rome on account of public fury at his pride."

Dr. Squires left without saying goodbye. But he cast a warning look as if to say, "Leave Holly alone."

Holly saw Groznyy wiping his face.

"It's not tears. I haven't survived this long by a weep in politics. Sorrow corrodes the ability to take revenge. I will throttle my enemies."

As Groznyy ate his moussaka, he could not stop talking, gulping the food, slurping it over his jacket, as he gave vent to his self-justification.

"Night falls and my enemies return to their silly conspiracies. These arts-and-sciences professors, their energies pent up with temper tantrums—they turn their futile anger into their own destruction. Look at the little critters. They march just like a column of ants. But I can retreat to my quicksilver mind."

Later Groznyy was afraid to look out of the upstairs picture-frame windows designed to impress his neighbors. He rehearsed another speech.

"It may be infuriating for everyone else that Night is eternally elusive, coming and going, expanding and contracting as it wants—not what humans desire. But you can use Night to prepare yourself for what lies ahead."

Groznyy had had the president's new garden surrounded by juniper and holly bushes. Although trimmed to create as uniform a hedge as possible, it looked as if the bushes knew how they could protrude and threaten. In his disturbed state Groznyy saw professors in the shapes of the skywards-jutting bushes.

He went outside for a closer look. In Groznyy's eyes the shapes of bushes and trees became ever more aggressive and as varied in height and girth as the hated professors—here there was a sturdy Lucy Kaye, there a lanky Mordred Stickleman, and, over there, a billowing Todd Carter Fox.

To Groznyy they might as well have been the sinister triffids of John Wyndham—perfect-oil-producing, mobile, hybrid plants with lethal stings. Groznyy knew he had played a crucial part in creating—in breeding—such greedy predatory professors, inadequate themselves but ever vigilant over their status, ever insistent on stagnant dogma over inconvenient thought. He had provoked them. They would retaliate. He had taught them how—through uproar. Now they were there in the bushes—phantom, green, dyed-in-the-wool ghouls. He was sweating.

The moon came out from behind clouds. In the garden it seemed that Nemo's would-be green tormentors were wailing with complaints against him. He sensed the little midges of a humid New England summer were heirs to the insects he had killed as a child years ago.

"I'm drowning and I can't swim," he exclaimed.

He saw Holly at an open upstairs window. Why did she not expose him? This could not be the loyalty of a tender spouse because each detested the other. Was it to keep the marriage going simply for her economic benefit? If she wanted revenge why did she hesitate? She surely knew the truth about Modest's death. Could she prove it?

It hit him. She wanted him ousted as president. He would leave in disgrace. He might have money squirreled away. But he would live as a pariah. He imagined Holly speaking to him.

"Death would be too easy for you. Even life in prison would be too easy because it would be a retreat. Your punishment is to face everyone around you. You've never produced anything lasting, just left messes—financial, emotional, and criminal. You don't have a conscience. But you fear shame. Everyone you meet will know who you are and despise you.

"You will always fear a knock on the door from a cop who has worked out how Modest died and can prove it. Of course, you could come clean about Modest's death. Face exposure. Go to prison. That would take greater courage than you have in your shriveled insides. And when Death does take you, it will take you in perpetual humiliation."

Groznyy did not know if Holly was speaking these words or if his mind was interpreting what she was thinking. He went for a walk on the beach of the Sound. It was past the middle of the night. Nighthawks might expect a dawn that would herald new hope. But there was no hope for Nemo. The moonlight was charmless.

He walked along the shore. He thought the gushing breasts of waves and the limitless expanse of ocean reaching ever farther across the Sound would put his own problems in perspective. In his darkened mind, the sea seemed to have corralled the secrets of Space and Time and Power. But it was, as always, indifferent to them. For Cesare Groznyy there was no harmony, only the dirty rags of human decay unravelling its relentless coils like Saturn plodding remorselessly to death.

In his troubled mind Groznyy interpreted the white ribbons, the crests of waves, not simply as slashes across the limitless ocean but as whiplashes on the backs of countless human cargo. He tried to distract himself by numbering the categories: immigrants, voluntary and involuntary, on States-bound ships: indentured servants, African slaves, and the huddled masses of the new immigration.

Greater than the sight, the sound of the sea was indomitable at night. Maybe the ocean united different countries. But that was a matter of political geography. Groznyy thought the sea merely separated rather than divided men. It called to intrepid mariners, always reminding these seafarers exactly who was Poseidon, who was Neptune, ruler of the blue planet. Diminishing waves seemed surprised to be engulfed by larger waves swallowing their bowels from behind. Groznyy thought the skies should cry out on his behalf till the Earth recognized his genius: "Wait! I am still president of BCU!"

DELIVERANCE

Disgraced alumnae chief Carpenter Cain had gone to Canada, just far enough to be out of reach of the press. But no matter how lush the forest north of the border, Cain was discontented. Notwithstanding his wide-ranging past travels, he was a softie when it came to New England. Following the Groznyy–Dawdler instructions about resigning after discovering he had a mystery illness, he crossed the border back into America by bus near Niagara Falls and Buffalo. Then he traveled across New York State into New England where he could hunker down.

As Cain traveled south, his assassin pursuer, Darko Delizio, traveled north. One bleak morning he arrived at Cain's modest guesthouse.

"The farther north you go, the more shanty-like the houses are," he thought. "Depression must be eating away at this town. Half the businesses on the main street are closed."

The guesthouse that Dean Ace Ferrari had told Darko to go to had a high wall on both sides. The yard at the back that served as a parking lot was like a courtyard and immaculately swept. The guesthouse was really a haven for summer tourists and a few out-of-towners in the winter on their way to skiing. This was off-season. Darko expected the house to be closed. He moved cautiously to the side and broke a window with a brick wrapped in a small towel.

When Darko climbed in through the window he found a ground floor suite painted white with a Colonial-style chandelier above the king-size bed. The walls were decorated with landscape and hunting pictures.

The next room was locked. Using a wire coat hanger from

the closet in the first room and sliding it between doorframe and door, and then jiggling it at the lock, he opened it. This room did not look like a bedroom for tourists. Here were no pastoral prints or hunting scenes. Instead it was furnished with floppy cushions and low coffee tables, hand-woven rugs of Tunisian design, and Arabian-style drapes. Above was an antique Spanish chandelier.

There was a low divan covered in satin with matching antique lamps on occasional tables at each side, and a polished desk with a blotting pad and inkwell. The telephone was not working. The elaborate bookcase held foreign and English-language dictionaries. But there were no personal documents or letters. All there was was a half-page of lined yellow paper with the end of some sentence: "I can't go on Monday." This took Darko back to an Agatha Christie murder mystery he had read when he was learning English. The room had not been used for some time, except for the closet that held American business clothes. There were two caftans. It was an Arab room in an American house.

A frosted door swung open into a bathroom with a power shower and off-white tiles with a rose-blush tint. Darko searched for a suitcase or rucksack or whatever holding stacks of mixed dollar bills that the dean wanted. Darko looked inside the closet, inside the bedside drawers, under the window ledges. When he thought he heard someone—perhaps a cleaner—about to enter the room, he hid in the shower. There it was: a wrapped packet in the bathrobe. But there was not enough. There must be more money elsewhere.

The person in the hall did not come into the suite. Darko decided to lie down on the bed in the other room.

Carpenter Cain usually enjoyed showers for the overwhelming thrust of the lukewarm water on his olive skin.

He felt somehow cleansed of all his murky financial deeds. But he knew he was on the run from some unspecified danger. It made him uneasy. Was Larry Dawdler no better than a crafty manager bent on damage limitation who was simply pushing him out because of his light fingers? Perhaps Groznyy and Dawdler knew everything about his laundering money for the Oryx Party. Were they torturing him with nagging doubts? Then there was the oily, vengeful dean of psychology with the rolling subversive plans. Carpenter's suspicions of Ace Ferrari were turning into terrifying fears.

When Carpenter Cain got out of the shower in his elaborate Arab room, Darko was waiting for him. Cain was naked apart from a towel, still wet. He was at his most vulnerable. Even so, he tried to be casual, as if he had been expecting Darko like an old friend.

"Oh, it's you, Darko, old pal. Come to rescue me. What a relief to leave this one-horse town."

But Darko, while never unpleasant, was having none of this. "You thought you could deceive us and then escape the consequences. Take our money. Forestall our great cause, Amir. I don't think so, Achmed."

Darko's use of two Arabic names was meant to twist a knife in Carpenter's innards. Darko was wearing gloves. He drew a small curled Bedouin blade recently bought on 14th Street—his pseudo-scimitar—from his breast pocket. It seemed to shine in his hand as his gaze met Cain's frightened stare. Darko's eyes glinted. Cain was scared stiff.

"Dry yourself," ordered Darko as he whipped Cain's towel from his waist and thrust it at his quivering frame.

Cain practically scrubbed himself dry with it.

"Put on this caftan," Darko said. "Now open your safe."

Cain was still quivering. He bent down by the bed, his flabby rump sticking out as he tapped a code into a drawer in the base. He was so nervous that his hands shook as he handed over bundles of bills. When he spilled some, he scooped them up abjectly and handed them to Darko, who shoved them into his own rucksack.

Cain's eyes shrank involuntarily as he stood up. He sensed his nightmare was not over. He could not speak. Darko clenched his right arm around Cain's torso. He turned his left hand and sliced deep into the tender tissue of Cain's trembling throat. Cain found his voice but his groan emerged as a blood-spattered babble. He gasped and died.

Darko had to work quickly, putting all thoughts aside apart from dressing the crime as suicide while the mind was disturbed. Thus Cain who had arrived at BCU with one false cover story, then told lie after lie to keep going, was to make his final exit with another invented by others. Cold to the last, Darko's only regret was in having to leave the knife behind aside the scrap of paper. He tore part of it so that it read, "I can't go on."

Waiting in a suburban railroad station outside Boston for an unknown intermediary sent by the dread dean to collect the rucksack, Darko's mind went dead. The exchange done, he flew to Europe and a new destiny.

The news of Cain's death did not reach Groznyy at BCU straight away. When detectives Leo Guerra and George McSweeny came to tell him and to question him on behalf of the other state, Groznyy was genuinely surprised. Any innocent man would have been surprised on hearing about the unexpected death of a former employee. But Groznyy's eyes visibly widened when Guerra said, "The fatal wound was unusual—a neat curved slit of his throat, twisted acutely. This was professional work—not like the hasty deed of someone who was distressed because he had lost his job and wasn't thinking straight."

Curved blade? Professional skill? Not suicide but murder?

That was the implication of the cop's words. These fragmented ideas raced through Groznyy's mind. A suppressed memory surfaced. Grishka's words came back to haunt him all through the panel's hearings that morning. He could hardly mumble "yes" or "no" to the panel's questions. The chairman knew why and did not press him—much to Larry Dawdler's relief.

Carpenter Cain's death had looked like suicide, sure enough, so it must be suicide. Another suicide in this tawdry scenario! That was more than enough for the state governor. The familiar pattern of things Groznyy repeated yet again, whether as tragedy or as farce, was more than enough to stifle independent thought. That was exactly what Ace Ferrari had intended. He had calculated correctly that the state would prefer to designate Cain's death as suicide rather than murder. That was the rub.

The panel in the courthouse thought it had already taken too long over the unsavory Groznyy business. Everyone in the state capitol felt that while people were laughing at BCU they were also laughing at a state that had allowed such academic shenanigans.

Governor and investigating panel alike now wanted to wrap things up as speedily as possible. This entailed arranging matters for BCU and NHU in the post-Groznyy era with an orderly transition of power under some caretaker manager who could return the two universities to their previous low-profile status. The panel's preferred candidate was to hand. He would become chair of the new board of trustees. The new board would then dismiss Groznyy as president (which the panel did not have the power to do). And the new board of trustees would then elect its new chair as interim president.

*

252

The police now had the right evidence against Cesare Groznyy to arrest him and charge him with murder. All they needed to do was pounce before their prey could escape. Detective Leo Guerra and Sergeant McSweeny had weighed up their options. They had followed press reports of the panel's hearings against Groznyy. They knew that the hearings set a time limit on their own ability to act while their suspect was within their grasp. If, as seemed likely, the panel found against Groznyy, the disgraced president might be up and away in the skies and beyond their immediate reach. Their last opportunity to catch him would be the last day of the hearings when the panel declared its findings.

Then Leo Guerra heard that the panel was going to make its ruling at noon in two days' time. He set everything else aside. They must arrest Groznyy as soon as he had made his official statement in response to the panel's decision. Everything had to be choreographed.

Someone else had the same idea. The princess called Holly.

"I'm asking your help again, and again it's for all of us. You don't have to say anything. Just be there when the panel posts its findings on the courtroom notice board. Don't go alone—no, not Dr. Chicago: someone else. Someone whose presence will jolt him. You know whom I mean."

An unknown young man was hesitant as he entered the Art Museum of Milhous College and presented his printed invitation to the haughty receptionist in the dark entrance hall. He was there for the private and press showing of the art exhibition on Ivan the Terrible. It was on the same morning as the expected decision by the education panel and ahead of the official opening. That was to be a swell affair with a lavish buffet and rounds of champagne and caviar the next day.

The unknown young man moved uneasily through the

dimly lit corridors and exhibition rooms of the Gothic-style museum.

Whatever his new responsibilities in publishing, Mickey Garnier was now the regular factotum for Grishka's American visits. Glib and bustling, no one was more adept at juggling the multi-tasking required of him. He had to ensure that all the pre-show arrangements moved easily and that guests, high and low, were met, shepherded, and even programmed into thinking they were attending something special: a newsworthy event, even though the way it would be reported was minor—a brief segment on local TV news and a curt mention in the society column of the *Norse Hoven Courier*. That was to plug the gala opening.

Mickey noted the unsure young man and thought he half-remembered him from somewhere or other. He prided himself on never forgetting a face, useful or otherwise.

"Don't I know you?" he asked invitingly.

"I don't think so, sir. I came because my uncle—Craig—invited me."

Mickey wanted to hear more but he had to move on to his targeted guests.

"Take this," he said, giving the newcomer his new business card from the publishing house of the great and the good.

Left alone, the young man was overwhelmed by the array of paintings and other pictures on Ivan IV. There was Ivan inspecting putative future brides, each dressed to the nines for court as the nineteenth century fancifully imagined the fashion of the sixteenth. Then there was Ivan dressed in an embroidered gold coat for his coronation. And here was Ivan brooding on politics, control, and revenge in his private chamber. Amid the sinister glitter artists conveyed of the flashy Russian court lay a bitter undercurrent of menace. This was obvious in the portrait of the recently dead Ivan being blessed by the metropolitan bishop as he raised him symbolically to the revered status of a monk. Most disturbing was Ivan cradling the limp body of the son he had killed in an insensate fit of anger.

Then there were Ivan's heirs, portraits of the accredited great rulers Peter and Catherine at their most regal. There was an array of workers' art and paintings of the young Stalin, the man of steel, usurping the hallowed position of Lenin as if he had always been intended for the supreme place in Russian and world history.

This section culminated in a cartoon by an American artist of Stalin as a benign but ruthless bird of prey. The curators had set it aside an outsize still from Sergei Eisenstein's fanciful film of *Ivan the Terrible*. Ivan was peering from a crevice in a rock on high. He was wearing an embroidered gown that echoed the winding pattern of his subjects below, who were supposedly pleading for him to return to power. More than the two pictures, striking in themselves, Grishka's nephew would remember how telling it was to set them side by side.

When it came to Ivan's so-called heirs elsewhere there were scabrous cartoons of Hitler and Mussolini culled from hitherto unseen German and Russian archives and simple, brutal photos of current African and Asian dictators.

But conspicuous by his absence among the guests and even more conspicuous by his absence from the subjects of the pictures on the walls was Cesare Groznyy. This did not escape anyone. It was as if Cesare Groznyy had become an invisible man to be ridiculed by being ignored even as the hearings against him were coming to their climax that very day. And the fact that the exhibition was timed to open alongside that climax told its own story of calculated insult: Cesare was not Groznyy the awesome, to be compared with the original Ivan Groznyy, but Cesare *le petit*, a minor cartoon figure, not even a fully developed human being. That was the implication.

In the exhibition hall, Grishka was in his element as self-declared new best friend to American culture vultures, dispensing instant jollity to all comers like any convivial barroom host. He asked all and sundry to address him by his new self-promoting Scots and English name: "Craig."

His nephew stood hesitantly at the side of Grishka's warm welcome to a group of arts journalists from the state capital.

"Don't be shy, come on over. Everyone, this is my favorite nephew."

"Hello, Uncle Craig," said the young man shyly when Grishka enfolded him in a bear hug.

As the little crowd applauded, Uncle Craig whispered affectionately to his nephew, "I know you can't stay now—that you have to be somewhere else. That's okay. We'll have lots of opportunities to play catch-up afterwards."

Grishka kissed his nephew. With that the young man left, already late for his next appointment.

Behind the scenes the avuncular Grishka was not so satisfied. He disliked Milhous College's practice of ultra-dim lighting of the paintings (on grounds of protecting them from light degradation) set on gloomy walls of muddy-colored coarse cloth. He had wanted something flash. He was also disappointed that Holly had declined his offer to have her (accompanied by Hermione at the piano) entertain guests at the lavish evening reception by singing "Send in the Clowns."

Grishka wondered if his not-so-subtle denigration of his brother might sit uncomfortably with this Ivy League college's deliberate understated approach to buildings, shows, and suburbs. None of the Groznyy Gang was going to give Grishka Groznyy the satisfaction of acknowledging his show, let alone of attending it. But in the end that did not matter. For what New England businessmen and their families hankered after was to be reported favorably in the society pages of the *Norse Hoven Courier* for having attended a small-town swell affair. That was something the Groznyy Gang had always denied them but which Grishka had now supplied: press photos galore, not of Ivan in art but of themselves as *bons viveurs*.

Because of rampant TV and press coverage of the education panel's hearings, the investigating panelists knew the numbers of people trying to get into court to hear their decision about Groznyy and BCU might be overwhelming. So they invited the principal speakers at the hearings to hear that decision in a court committee room while state marshals posted the ruling inside and outside the court building. It read:

> After twenty-seven days of hearings, today the panel appointed by the Commission has removed BCU's trustees.
>
> The panel's action is authorized under a special education statute since the two conjoined universities of BCU and NHU and the science consortium mix state and private interests.
>
> We made our decision on three grounds:
>
> First, the trustees failed to review the job performance of President Groznyy. The trustees failed further by showering him with extravagant perks. The record of written evidence and oral testimony demonstrates that the trustees failed to exercise due prudence.
>
> Therefore, they must be removed from office.
>
> Second, two trustees improperly profited by doing business with the universities. These trustees, property speculator Veronica Veneer and publicist Georgie Lucre, failed to disclose details of their dealings beyond the executive committee of the board. They used their positions to extract lucrative contracts from BCU for their own private businesses. The record shows that $1.2 million in fees went to the insurance firm of trustee chair Veronica Veneer for acting as the university's insurance adviser. And broker Georgie Lucre's advertising firm, Lucrative Lucre, received $155,000 in commissions for BCU ads. The other trustees were told,

wrongly, that these services were being provided free. By their negligence the trustees allowed these two board members to trade their personal positions for profit.

Third, there has been a complete breakdown of the principles of governance at BCU and NHU, which the board of trustees has countenanced.

We dismiss Dr. Groznyy as a trustee because he is one of the trustees who misused their power. We have no power to dismiss him as president. The panel has appointed new trustees to be chaired by state attorney Boris Goodenough.

Groznyy had expected the worst from the panel and yet had still counted on his charisma to survive. When the panel told him first in private, he said ironically, "The decision is worthy of you."

He came out of the private meeting unsteady on his feet. Groznyy did not need to rehearse his farewell speech. His skilled words poured out seamlessly before reporters on the steps of the courthouse:

"I feel no anger toward my assailants. The greatest moral critics—Socrates and Jesus, Dante and Cervantes—were all condemned by society for their moral insights. No matter how bitter my exile I am in good company. I could not share a better fate. Jesus and Socrates were executed for confronting the narrow prejudices of their closed societies. I'm with them."

When he had finished positioning himself among the philosophical greats, Groznyy scanned the crowd. There was Holly—damn her—come to gloat. But, no, her face was serene, inscrutable. And beside her was Modest! No, it was not a ghost. It was not a figment of his troubled mind. Modest had his hand in Holly's!

"Who's standing at the back? Who is it?"

People turned round to Holly and saw a young man with her.

"Don't look at me as if I'm raving."

258

Detective Leo Guerra stepped forward. The crowd was silent.

After he had spoken quietly to Groznyy, Guerra thought he had explained the reason for arresting him and given him the customary caution about Miranda rights. He was arresting Groznyy for the premeditated murder of his second wife, Anna Stasinova Groznyy. But then came two surprises. Instead of giving a hot blustery denial, Groznyy wrested a microphone from a TV man and raised it just as he had brandished the broken table leg to hit Modest.

"He's there! Look! No one else could have that shock of dark hair. He's still alive. There's proof."

There was movement in the eager crowd. Holly and Modest were still there. It was not a ghost. It was a living person. Groznyy could not stop his verbal diarrhea.

"How could I have killed him with the table leg if he's still standing there? You don't have any witnesses. I saw to that. Anna is out of the way."

Groznyy lost any sense and said, "Absalom, my son: I killed the best of me."

Leo Guerra had to think fast. His suspicions about the first unpremeditated murder had been true—that Cesare had killed his son, or at least injured him severely before the fire that had burned down the provost's old house. By coming to arrest Groznyy for the suspicious death of his second wife, Guerra and McSweeny had uncovered the dark secret behind Modest's death. With his eyes Guerra signaled to McSweeny that they must catch up with the third Mrs. Groznyy and the mysterious young man.

In a trice, Guerra's police backup was there to hustle Groznyy away. The crowd had come to rejoice at the fall of an academic charlatan. They had not expected police on the scene to arrest Groznyy for one murder and then overhear his confession to a second.

As the cops restrained him, Groznyy felt he was staring

into an abyss, as if unknown forces were shoving him to the ground. He blinked with abject terror.

"Take care. There, now, it's gone. It must have been my imagination."

A young cop said, "It must have been a trick of the light, sir. Don't be frightened by a shadow."

"But he was trying to scare me. I will never give in. I will never confess."

As the police car turned a corner, Groznyy peeped out at the Crown Tower of Milhous College and said under his breath, "Just let me take one last glance at the hollow tower that surrounds and protects the dried-up American educational establishment."

However, the police had not been fast enough to catch up with Holly and her young companion, the ersatz Modest. The pair had hailed a taxi. Holly told the driver to take them not to the Norse Hoven Railroad Station but to a smaller suburban station two towns nearer New York. In this way Holly evaded questions from police and journalists.

Unaware that the bizarre scene of Groznyy's arrest had upstaged the panel's announcement, ousted trustee chair Veronica Veneer was ready with her prepared statement. She read it in the comfort of her Blackthorn Buildings office to a *Courier* journalist.

"The so-called panel's announcement against the trustees of BCU is one of the most disgraceful and irresponsible rulings ever committed by a state body. On behalf of my esteemed colleagues, I say it is totally unwarranted. It amounts to a direct insult to the academic probity of, and threatens the independence of, every university in the northeast.

"Together, we—my fellow trustees and I—will go to the ends of the earth to reverse this hateful and undemocratic ruling."

The panel's statement was seized on by local press and

syndicated nationwide. The *Courier* reported it and more in next day's story under a blunt banner headline on page 3:

STATE PANEL OUSTS TRUSTEES
OF BABEL CITY UNIVERSITY
FOR NEGLECTING DUTIES

When the new board of trustees first met, their prime action was to dismiss Cesare Groznyy as president. In line with prior agreement with the state, the board appointed new trustee chair Boris Goodenough as interim president. Boris Goodenough wanted to comment that he felt honored. So was his PR fiancée, who would have the tsarina's slippers she deserved, just as he had always promised her.

But Cesare's arrest for murder had taken all attention away from Boris's rise without trace.

The Opposition Party had expected that the decisions by the state panel and the new board of trustees would be their triumph against Groznyy. But there was much to find fault with in the panel's ruling. The party believed they were the heroes of the hour, the idols of nationwide professorial probity. Yet no one praised them.

Speaking for the Opposition Party to reporter Steve Sharp, Mordred Stickleman said they were concerned that the panel and the new trustees had left top BCU officials like Provost Bogus Revisor and Treasurer Parthy Burnable—who not only had backed Groznyy to the hilt but had also carried out his policies—in power rather than firing them.

"Moreover, we feel that the panel and the new board of trustees have not recognized the Opposition Party's huge efforts to get Groznyy brought to book," said Stickleman. "Yet, without the Opposition Party, the new board would not have come into existence."

Performing arts chairman Eddie Walker repeated his default quip: "Don't you hate it when that happens?"

Reporters scoured the conjoined universities for other professors' reactions. A young journalist was not surprised to see Dean Ace Ferrari in his office stuffing papers into cases. Asked to comment on Groznyy's fall and the wider issue of academic probity, Ferrari replied, "This is the way it works. The students give us their money. Four years later we give them degrees. And what happens in between"—and here he held out his open palms as if to imply, "Don't ask questions."

The cub reporter took a chance and asked, "So, you're leaving?"

"Yes. I've accepted a chair overseas at a college with standards."

With that the Macavity of terrorism postponed was soon gone. The novice reporter did not notice the rucksack bulging with money that assassin Darko Delizio had collected from Carpenter Cain and then sent by a trusted intermediary to the disappearing dean. Nor did he guess what the dean's getaway implied about the future of the Oryx Party at BCU.

But Groznyy's arrest for the murders of his first son and his second wife and his breakdown in public upstaged all academic controversies. Notwithstanding the banner headline, it was not the panel's ruling on the trustees that led the news. It was the front-page headline that was on everyone's lips:

PRESIDENT GROZNYY ARRESTED FOR TWO MURDERS

*

"How did Groznyy do it—kill Modest's mother?" Hermione asked Benny.

"The princess thinks he substituted aspirin for Anna's penicillin and then made sure of her death with some small doses of arsenic. They will have exhumed her body and found forensic evidence."

"Why did he do it?"

"He couldn't trust Anna. She might recover from pneumonia. She might get her voice back or somehow let someone know how Modest died. But Anna was very ill, so her death was not unexpected."

"Why didn't he have Anna cremated to destroy any lingering evidence?"

The princess had the answer. "It was too big a risk. Two cremations in a few short months just after he had arranged for an elaborate family grave for Anna and himself? No."

Benny added, "Besides Modest's death, there was already the princess's supposed death and her burial—the burial of some poor unknown soul's body in Queens. Groznyy might have stared down adverse comments. But he also wanted the sort of ostentatious resting place for himself that a grave in a churchyard can provide. He considered an urn in a crematorium wall common."

That weekend in her home Hermione celebrated by playing Rachmaninov's Piano Sonata No. 2, making the most of its Russian bell-like undercurrents of terror and funeral peals.

The prison guard whose task was to watch Groznyy found him pacing up and down his cell.

"Put up barriers so that not a soul can get into BCU, barriers so sure that not even a groundhog can trundle home from Milhous College or a jackdaw swoop in from Louvre Ville. Did you ever hear of dead kids rising from their graves to confront their dads? It's funny when you think about it." Groznyy sensed he was being watched. He swung round toward his cell door and said, "Well, don't you agree it's funny?" Then more threateningly he added, "And if it's so funny, why aren't you laughing?"

Then Groznyy saw Modest sleeping on the prison bed. Modest was no longer an eager young man, far less a bloodied corpse. Groznyy saw him aged six after his first day at school. The features of his pretty face were still intact. It was as if he were sleeping calmly in his child's bed, with his tender little arms folded gently around a teddy bear. Then there was a whirling sound. Groznyy saw another toy in the cell, a spinning top.

"It's too painful to watch. Let me catch my breath."

The guard was transfixed. He saw Groznyy sink feebly onto the empty bench-bed and then fall onto his knees, holding his hands in prayer.

"Jesus. I'm not ready to die. Surely, you won't claim the life of a sinner. Have mercy on my soul."

The guard later told the prison governor, "I heard His Majesty groan, so I watched him closely. He was covered in a cold sweat. He was trembling and muttering incoherently. But his eyes were flashing, not just with anger but as if he was suffering from some inner distress. He was warding something off."

"Did he say anything?"

"Yes, something like, 'Stay away from me. Who called me "murderer"?'"

Hermione was going back to the restaurant after an errand. Then she got distracted. As she turned the corner from 2nd Avenue toward the Golden Cockerel, Hermione got the shock of her life. There, choosing blooms at a flower stall, was—but surely not? She and her allies had played an easy trick on Groznyy to unnerve him. She had traced the cartoons—just as Modest had taught her. They had made Groznyy think that these were drawings by Modest. And now there he was again on a New York street: Modest.

Hermione was trying to persuade herself that this must be some trick of the dappled sunlight peering through the scrubby trees on the sidewalk, when she got a second surprise. Crossing the street to the florist's to greet this unknown man came Holly. They kissed one another on the cheek. Hermione steadied herself again. Was Modest there after all? There he stood—preppy eagerness and unruly hair.

Then Holly turned from the florist's, recognized Hermione, and walked toward her with the new Modest in tow. Hermione was dazed.

"Hi, Hermione, this has turned out well. Here's someone I want you to meet."

Gently Holly nudged the strange young man toward her. All Hermione could think was, "Here we go again."

As he handed her the flowers, he said, "I bought these for you."

Although it was mid-afternoon, they sat like nighthawks at a local diner—anonymous, brightly lit, the light exposing every crevice in their faces.

"I've wanted the two of you to meet for some time. This is my son, Luke Reader. Yes, he's Groznyy's son. My family brought him up to keep Groznyy out of the picture. As I told you, he's taken an English form of a name from my mother's family."

As if on cue, Holly's brother, Boris Goodenough, came in and joined them. "We don't know one another, but I have a favor to ask you on behalf of Holly, who thinks she's asked too much already. And Luke is too shy. Will you stay friends with us?"

Hermione knew another change was coming.

"News of Holly's success has crossed the Atlantic. Everywhere she goes stateside the ghost of Groznyy casts a huge shadow. It's as if she's walking in leg irons dragging his terrible reputation and having to field press questions about BCU all the time, instead of being able to concentrate on what she can do like no one else: sing.

"A club in Paris has invited her over for a season. Parisians don't pry into the lives of celebrities like other Europeans do—like the British press. You can be a celebrity there and still have a private life."

"You would like me to keep in touch through Luke, to look after him?" Hermione asked.

"Will you? Is it too much to ask?"

"Well, I know what Oscar Wilde said in a play—something like, 'When good Americans die, they go to Paris.'"

As Holly mouthed, "Thank you," Luke took a tiny jewel case from his pocket and said, "Mother found this in a bedroom drawer. It belongs to you."

Hermione almost quivered as she tugged open the case. It was the ring: her father's ring, her ring, Modest's ring. She melted.

When Hermione went back to the Golden Cockerel, she was surprised that Holly came with her, left Luke downstairs to chat to Benny, and went upstairs to see the princess.

On the table in the upper room was Benny's miniature of the provost's old reception room with the tiny figure of Modest lying atop the dropped beam. In front of the princess were what looked like two bottles of contact lens solution and a wad of cotton wool.

"Yes, it is cotton wool, but it has been doused—impregnated"—here the princess darted a mean look at Holly as she savored the word—"with something. Dry, it's harmless; wet, it ain't."

"Something?"

"Better not ask. Stay innocent. Don't think Cleopatra had to use something as unpredictable as an asp to kill herself. When it comes to dealing death, the Rurik dynasty leaves the Ptolemies at the starting post."

"And the contact lens bottles?"

"Not. One is a bottle that usually contains contact lens solution. The other is a bottle that usually contains chloramphenicol. It's medication for eye infections like conjunctivitis. There's something else inside."

Holly said nothing.

"He killed Modest. He caused the death of your unborn child. He spreads misery like other people spread butter on bread. What do you want? Groznyy's clever lawyer to get him off on some technicality? Reduced sentence for manslaughter? For the state to have to support his worthless life in a long, expensive jail term?"

"You want Groznyy to drink death?"

"That's not practical. Yes, contact lens bottles are stock-in-trade of the new jackals—Afghan Arabs on the kill. I keep abreast of the situation."

"How can Groznyy taste death if he isn't going to drink it?"

"You tell me. He likes to play chess by himself against himself, doesn't he? He likes to suck on the domed heads of some pieces. You visit Darius Esen in jail. He's in the hospital wing, like Groznyy. You go to see Darius using your original name. Since Darius is not so sick, he has to work as an orderly, cleaning things. Somehow, you pass him the cotton wool and the bottle. You're skilled with makeup. You can fake conjunctivitis. Color one of your eyelids red to look as if it's inflamed so the bottle of medication and the cotton wool are legitimate.

"Darius hides the medication. Then, in his cleaning round, he polishes the chess pieces with the precious liquid. Sooner or later Groznyy will play chess and suck on the pieces. No one else will. Darius disposes of the evidence and washes his hands."

"How do I pass these things to Darius?"

"Hide them in your bra. Make sure you wear a low-cut top. Darius likes to fondle you. As I said, I keep abreast of the situation."

"And the cotton wool?"

"Backup."

"Darius will know I'm using him."

"Yes. But he loves you. He owes you big. Use your charm. Then you leave. And you don't just go back to Babel City. You see Darius in the afternoon as Esther Vashti. That evening, under your married name, you fly overnight to Paris and your new career.

"You don't tell Darius that you're going abroad. He didn't tell you he was leaving in 1993. You don't tell him anything now. Whatever happens, he knows enough not to confess. He can't point the finger at you without incriminating himself. And the medication is slow-acting. You will be well out of the way before it takes effect."

As Holly took her damnable little cargo, the princess collected the other tiny bottle labelled as contact lens solution.

When Holly emerged from the upper room, Hermione was in the lobby taking bookings. But she could tell Holly's upbeat mood had changed. Holly collected Luke, and left without saying anything.

Hermione was thinking ahead. When she took the princess her coffee upstairs, she was surprised to see Benny's miniature room there.

"You're asking Holly to do something difficult, something dangerous."

Before Hermione could finish, Benny came in and took over. "That's for us to know and for you never to find out."

When Hermione rose to go downstairs, Benny said simply, "Close the door behind you."

This abrupt order brought a sharp memory back to Hermione of when she had first visited the restaurant with Modest. She had overheard diners mention Benny's sporadic relationship with the Mafia. At the time it had unsettled her. Groznyy used people as pawns, but so did Benny and the princess. Hermione resolved to make a clean break with the restaurant for a modest suburban life and piano teaching. It would be safe.

But Hermione could not resist a parting shot, saying as she turned back at the door, casting one look at Benny's girth and a second at the princess, "I can't battle an elephant. But, then, you can't train your dragon."

So she left them: the spider woman with her yarn of kisses and her webs that she could go on regurgitating like some jaded TV soap villain, and also the overgrown man-boy with his dolls' houses peopled by "tinies" to be manipulated but never set free.

When she got back to her own Plumfield in New England, she threw off her coat and sat down to play Beethoven's "Hammerklavier" Sonata to cleanse herself of the Golden Cockerel.

Holly followed the princess's scenario. She had to keep a tight rein on her emotions. Getting herself ready for Paris and keeping track of the travel arrangements helped divert her, so she put her other mission at the back of her mind. The most difficult part would not be getting her contraband past the correction officers. It would be persuading Darius by leading him on.

They sat in the dreary prison meeting room of the medical wing. The walls were a lackluster pastel color that had gone muddy.

"I know you hate him, and why," said Darius. "Your friends are my friends. Your enemies are mine. He deserves damnation far more than these prisoners."

Darius was smarting with uneasy fear. He was used to hiding what he was thinking. Was Holly using him? Yes. Was she going to leave him? Like other inmates, he was already stir-crazy. Like the others, he depended on visitors to put cash in his prison account so that he could buy shampoo and get cold cuts from the concession counter. Holly was the only American he had ever trusted. And she had never betrayed him—unlike he her. If he did not do as she asked, he would lose her.

Sitting at the next table was a prisoner whose broad face Holly thought she half-remembered, perhaps from the audience at one of her gigs. Opposite this sturdy man with a bandaged forehead and such an unruly appearance must be his parents. His father was a dark African American with a face creased with worry and his mother was an assertive woman with a Muslim headscarf.

"Prison's the best place for you," the mother said. "It's a terrible thing to say. But here you get three meals a day. Your father and I know you are safe because everything is decided for you—when you get up, what you do and when you do it. What your being in prison does for us is to give us peace of mind. We sleep easier at night."

The burly son scowled.

Holly found this little unresolved spat a welcome diversion from her own tortured feelings. Somehow it set her emotions in a wider context. No one had it easy with a loved one inside.

Darius knew Holly was reading his mind. His mind was telling him, "You're taking a big risk—you, not her. You may never see her again. You think she still cares for you? Think again. You let her down before. You almost betrayed the cause. She's got you where she wants you."

His thoughts were cheerless. Had he done more wrong by inaction? Whose fault was it that he was in jail? Who had ruined his life?

"You're all I have," he said to Holly.

Holly smiled with a surface sweetness like a siren in an old movie.

"What an actress," he thought.

Holly moved slightly as if she were going to leave. The princess had told her how to play it. And Benny had told her that all prisoners in jail would do anything—certainly say anything—while they were inside. This was because they depended on their partners, families, and friends for the little necessaries of life and to have a link with the outside world. All Holly had to do, according to the bible of Benny and the princess, was make her request and imply—without saying—that fulfilling the little poison scenario was a precondition of future contact. Darius would fall in with their plans.

Then, instead of leaving, Holly simply undid two buttons of her blouse. He was hers. He fondled her lovely breasts. He did so openly with the correction officers standing silently by. He wanted to linger over the soft curves but he knew he had to press ahead, pinching her nipple slightly, and then getting the tiny phial from her bra.

Her breast gave him the bottle. Her hand gave him the Egyptian cotton. Then they were both back in their separate worlds—but not quite.

"Just a minute," a correction officer called out abruptly just after Holly had left the visiting room. "Just a minute, honey. Where's your ID tag?"

Holly colored. She felt her top. Her ID tag had gone. Had she dropped it inside during their love fumble?

"Just a minute, ma'am. We have to search you."

Holly froze. She was still behind bars. Her anxiety was doubled. They would search her but find nothing. Worse, they would search Darius and find the toxic contraband. Would he squeal?

Then it came to her: the prisoner at the next table with his parents was Mukhtar, Modest's friend. But she was back to the harsh reality of the present.

Each of the two ex-lovers thought of the anxiety of the other.

The prison officers looking for the missing ID tag now targeted Darius.

"Okay, boy. Face the wall. Spread your legs. Keep your arms up and on the wall," a male correction officer called out to Darius in the inner corridor.

For a moment the guard was distracted by a cry farther along the corridor. That brief moment was enough. Darius clenched his fist and thrust the bottle and the wad of cotton into the grip of the man next in line. It was Mukhtar, his old acquaintance from BCU. Like him, he was bandaged but across his forehead.

"Say nothing. I'll owe you," Darius whispered.

Now Darius concentrated on controlling his emotions as the correction officers strip-searched him. They pulled off his clothes, tugging at his top and practically tearing his bottoms. They spread his cheeks, peered up his hairy anus, yanked up his arms, grabbed his face, and, when they turned him round and prised open his mouth, they marveled at his perfectly even teeth. Darius stared ahead. The woman correction officer savored his toned biceps, firm pecs, and washboard abs, and said, "Nice ass, son."

He felt shamed by this black woman surveying his flesh as if he were there for her sexual delectation.

The guards' search of the self-designated Esther Vashti was more discreet. Halfway through, an officer called from a doorway, "Found it. The ID had got caught in the trouser cuff of a lawyer visiting another client. Crisis over. Proceed."

Holly left with only Fevronia's song for comfort.

"Don't take it badly," Darius's renewed friend, Mukhtar, said later. "They disrespected you, but so does your good friend with the honeycomb figure. I wonder whom she's dissing now."

It was easier to follow Holly's scenario than Darius had thought. He retrieved the little bottle and the wad of cotton from Mukhtar, who gave him a look that signaled, "Now you belong to us." On one of his daily cleaning routines, Darius smeared the mystery liquid over the chess pieces and wiped them with the cotton. He got rid of the evidence. And he waited.

Darius guessed he would never get news from Holly. But he heard on the grapevine that she was forging a singing career in Paris as the Scheherazade of song.

He felt he was walking on a promontory out to sea. Behind him lay the confused landscape of his mixed cultural background, part Muslim, part Christian. And under the jostling streets and the competitive educational expectations running through his mind there was a continuous thud of orthodox hatred: condemn America; annihilate Israel.

When he and Mukhtar heard they were to be released in a day's time, Mukhtar handed Darius a magazine with a photo of the World Trade Center.

Mukhtar said, "The Yanks wanted open skies in the 1950s when they were the only power with enough planes to spy on other countries. Do they still want open skies? We'll give them thunder. Will you take your stand with us?"

Darius knew there was a world of difference between academic posturing and the shambolic preparations of student chemists. His mind raced back to his lecture in Milhous College on Israel and Palestine years ago. He was fired up all over again. If he became one of the would-be terrorists now, there would be no turning back.

"I take my stand. I fight with you."

He said it like an automaton.

Mukhtar, pointing at the crests of the twin towers, said, "It's just two identical boxes above a desolate plaza. It's our duty to bring them down."

From a secret cache, Mukhtar showed Darius press cuttings with references to al-Qaeda.

When Groznyy was calmer, the prison governor let him mix with others on the hospital ward. The officers thought his solo chess games against himself curious but harmless. His sporadic ranting subsided. They hardly noticed him sucking some of the pieces.

Groznyy felt he was being eaten inwardly by something he did not understand. He felt hot and cold, sick and queasy all together, but he did not want to admit it in case some half-assed lawyer seized on this as some confession of guilt.

Inwardly Groznyy was in some miasma that seemed to be speaking to his mind as he began to decline. Was it offering advice or acting as a script writer for his day in court?

"All the best qualities and virtues of learning and thought—education, courtesy, facts, analysis, interpretation—all of them succumb to the contemporary plague of political correctness. Everyone is crippled by the cruel sciatica of social conformity."

Groznyy knew some woman was now speaking to him but he could not identify the voice.

"'You're not guilty of lust for gold. Yes, it's glittering and it has very special transmuting qualities. Use it cleverly and it can turn what is black into white, what is criminal into what is legal, what is wrong and cowardly into what is right and upright, and it can turn what is low and base into what is high and mighty.

"'Your gold, my gold, my grandmother's gold'—isn't that what you would say?"

One night Cesare Groznyy had a seizure. He woke and felt blood rising in his cheeks. Just as suddenly it drained away. He was trying to speak but the words got trapped in his mouth. At first no one could hear him.

"Conscience? You want a reckoning. We'll see about that!"

Groznyy shuddered. He tried to stop the reeling in his head. He heard the princess's voice with its croaky insistence: "Modest, dear bloodstained child, is fixed in your eyes. He's groaning still."

Groznyy felt his face must be red and blustery, his facial muscles twitching, and his eyes staring wildly. "What's over there? Modest? He's getting bigger. Don't come closer. I never meant to harm you. Keep away."

At first no one could hear him. The commotion was short, sharp, and decisive. He died before anyone could come to his aid.

When the correction officer on duty who had found Groznyy drove home after his shift he found Groznyy's voice and words still ringing round and round in his ear.

"You scullery academics, go on living loathed and detested! Live long! No—live forever in the pitiless trench of your inadequacy! You conveyors of the court: you've simply cleared the court of wiser counsel than you. Why don't you speak instead to the general gallery of accumulated newspaper filth upstairs? My filth, your filth, my grandmother's filth."

The news that she had so longed for left the princess stupefied by emptiness. For decades she had run on the fuel of indignation and hatred for this impossible man. Yet in her mind she had coiled herself like malign ivy around his craggy, tortured personality. Hate was more binding than love.

The princess moved restlessly in and out of rooms in the restaurant-townhouse. She had looked her age for years, with or without makeup. Now she felt it and her numb feeling drained away any residual energy. She could not eat. She hardly slept. Her every move, her every gesture suggested the emptiness of a faded movie star who has had the misfortune to live after her last role.

She took the second contact lens bottle with its mystery liquid into the ersatz garden with artificial flowers. She unscrewed the top. Benny waited. He knew she would never do it. She preferred misery to release.

As he gave the princess a glass of cognac, he said, "I wonder how she's doing in Paris—the Scheherazade of song. She's a survivor."

"You can say that again," said the princess as they clinked

glasses. "Whatever happens, Holly Wood will still be here in five years' time."

In Paris Holly crossed the Pont Alexandre III across the River Seine deep in thought. It was a single-deck ornately decorated bridge connecting the area around the Champs-Élysées with the area around the Eiffel Tower. With all its fancy ornamentation it exuded Belle Époque confidence. Holly needed that. She had been nervous on her opening night in Paris. She was without support from her new manager (her brother Boris, who knew little about music), without Hermione for guidance, without the wit of the earthy Carmine who was now working for the Norse Hoven police.

For a new look, in keeping with her promotion as the Scheherazade of song, Holly chose an emerald green shift dress. She had begun with her warhorse number that had so entranced Brad Gable years ago: "The Trolley Song." But she was nervous throughout and it showed. And when Holly had finished her encore number, "Cry Me a River," she felt a particular set of eyes boring into her and was sure they must be yet another pair of Arab eyes.

When the reviews came out they were what is politely termed mixed—far from the uniform paean of praise Holly was used to stateside. The assistant the club had hired to help her had read them out and translated them. This cumbersome process made the snooty verdicts seem even harsher. It was like an abusive torrent:

"Her interpretations lack the melodramatic flair to give proper thrust to her singing"; "A voice of purity and tenderness remarkable in itself. She has the power to carry over the jazz band but not the artistic will"; "Her overall package—voice, interpretation, looks, stage presence—cannot be classified as important."

Holly did not know what made her feel worse: the unconstructive criticisms or the high-falutin' way they sounded in French-into-English words. So her walk across the famous bridge, symbol of the late nineteenth-century alliance between Republican France and Tsarist Russia, was Holly's own Holly Golightly moment, seeking assurance from buildings that seemed the epitome of capital probity.

As soon as Holly was back in her rented apartment, the phone rang. It was Kelly Danson, the girlfriend of Holly's brother, Boris, and soon to be her sister-in-law.

"Don't be disappointed. You've had the best sort of reviews—mixed, yes, I know. But this is what box offices prefer: mixed. And then there's one from an English paper that puts you among the greats. Listen to this: 'A great artist; uneven certainly; a genius nonetheless.' All this means the public is going to make up its own mind. They will come in greater numbers than if you had received ecstatic praise that would have had Parisians coming to find fault."

This cheered Holly up. And it came just before a call from the club manager to say it was a long time since they had had so many enquiries about a new artist.

A third phone call overwhelmed Holly. The magazine *Paris Match* wanted to interview her for a feature: "Le Nouveau Debut d'Holly Wood." Holly was beside herself with joy.

When she arrived at the club that night she was not surprised that a large bouquet of bougainvillea from the south of France awaited her. To her fashion ensemble she added a long white feather held upright in her blonde hair by a costume-jewelry circlet. She strutted onto the stage, quite the Arab sultana, and a seasoned pro whose only concern was to give her considerable best to her fans. She began as she should have done on the first night with her version of Fevronia's aria.

As she sang her heart out she had the same sense as on the first night of being appraised by someone in particular.

Again this made her uneasy. Her rudimentary French was not up to making discreet enquiries, so she concentrated on her jazz interpretation of Despina's flirtatious aria in *Cosi fan tutte* about the right of women aged fifteen and over to enjoy themselves with men. This earned a storm of applause.

Someone in the stage crew swung light across the audience. Then Holly saw his face. There was no mistake. It was Darko grinning away and then blowing a kiss, fully expecting Holly to see him. What surprised her was Darko's mouth, now open but still. When the stage light swung back again Holly noted the outline of his lips as she had never noticed them before. His mouth was like a little dagger with a curved blade. What would Hermione call it? A scimitar— that was the word. And when Darko showed his teeth they looked—again Holly needed a word Hermione would have known: feral, that was it. Holly had never thought of Darko as in the least bit cruel. But her foreboding increased. Was this reappearance a turn of the screw or a twist of the knife? Was a "fate worse than death" really worse than death?

What would Holly Wood do next?

The end of *War in Pieces*

Hermione and Luke, and Detective Leo Guerra, return in
Luke Reader, Blind Detective

Afterword and Acknowledgements

War in Pieces 2 is a chase novel. Professors and journalists, police and family, hunt supreme narcissist Cesare Groznyy across college, cloister, and court in the 1990s, a time when both CIA and FBI are tracking down terrorist fanatic Ramzi Yousef, principal agent in the 1993 bomb against the World Trade Center.

Since the turn of the century the Age of Terror has become ever more horrible—almost beyond description. This is how atrocities committed by terrorist fanatics from the self-proclaimed Islamic State in the Middle East now seem to us in the 2010s. Terrorism started to become ever more degraded with al-Qaeda's airline demolition of the Twin Towers in Manhattan and its attack on the Pentagon in September 2001. Fanatics' emphasis on the rights of the Palestinian people has now morphed into obsessive determination to destroy western capitalist democracies from a new base: IS, Daesh or Islamic State.

Whether through bloody intervention as in Iraq or abstention as in Syria, western responses to the spreading crises of the Arab Spring in Egypt, Tunisia, Libya, and Syria have so far proved ill-considered, irresolute, and ineffective.

Meanwhile, terrorist attacks in London, Paris, Brussels, Istanbul, and Kabul have widened and deepened western fears so that sharp memories of the original bomb attack of 1993 have faded. Yet this, the central event of both *War in Pieces* novels, was the initial outrage on western soil that proclaimed an Age of Terror as the Cold War came to an end.

In New York and New England, as elsewhere in America, people were living out their everyday lives with their successes and failures, their joys and sorrows. In this novel the sorrows include those inflicted by the malign pursuits of

Cesare Groznyy, who casts himself as a modern Ivan the Terrible and tyrannizes loyal employees at two conjoined colleges in New England. With such a megalomanic boss there are no immense physical outrages to compare with the almost inconceivable losses of life caused by modern terrorists. But the smaller scale of psychological torture by a headstrong tyrant has its own insidious power of soul-boring destruction rippling across a workforce—especially when combined with the boss's own empty spirit and lack of positive achievements.

The life of the original Ivan the Terrible provided the idea for the central character and the plot of *War in Pieces*.

Purely American details in this modern reworking of the story for recent times come from the corrupt presidency of Warren Harding and the Ohio Gang as unfolded by Mark Sullivan in *Our Times: The Twenties,* especially the contributions of Harry Daugherty, attorney general, his two suicide stooges, and the shady Mrs. Phillips.

Another inspiration for this book was public revelations in the case in New York when the State Board of Regents investigated the trustees of Adelphi University and dismissed all but one of them in 1997—a case that was the climax of a bitter conflict simmering since the 1980s. The *New York Times* covered the 1990s case in firsthand observation, interviews, and court records in articles, principally by Bruce Lambert, whose stimulating account of the shenanigans has been a source for some of this book. What participants said in court or to reporters is a matter of public record.

Intertwined with the fictional Cesare Groznyy invented from several composites is the rise of the jazz singer who has taken on the showbiz name of Holly Wood, drawn from various singers on screen and disk.

Whereas the original Ivan the Terrible, first tsar of all Russia, faced up to challenges from the East in the sixteenth century, our antihero Cesare Groznyy does not face up to terrorist fanatics who burst on the scene with that first bomb on the World Trade Center in 1993.

Terrorist leader Ramzi Yousef was a misfit fanatic, vitriolic in his condemnation of Israel and support of the Palestinian people. Ramzi Yousef is a real historical character but he is also, as the lead song of a musical has it, his own special creation, taking on and discarding other names, even in the early twenty-first century (if rumor is correct) allegedly converting to Christianity.

While in custody awaiting trial, Yousef's only permitted interview was with Raghida Dergham, senior correspondent of a London-based Islamic newspaper. Her article was widely circulated across the Middle East. What leaked out of Yousef's attempt at self-justification was that he liked to present himself as a freedom fighter for the Palestinian people, claiming he was serving "terror for terror."

His public words and actions were most famously described from written and oral sources in journalist Simon Reeve's pioneer bestseller, *The New Jackals*. The tracking down and capture of terrorist Ramzi Yousef is undoubtedly a stirring story of derring-do by intrepid Feds. It has been told several times from the vantage point of a leading player in a particular adventure. Some stories have been dramatized for TV and their heroes and heroines glamorized. These are separate stories.

What I imagine might be Ramzi Yousef's' private thoughts are in my own words as distinct from his courtroom statements in the public domain.

The 1993 bomb attack on the World Trade Center was not immediately seen as a decisive turning point in world affairs. I was in New York the day of the attack. My words here come from what I knew at the time, learnt later, and read about in accounts that followed over the next twenty years, including Internet sources.

Apart from Ramzi Yousef and his terrorist chums (referred

to in passing), the characters here are fictions, based on impressions and observations of various people. These fictional composites are not intended to represent specific individuals alive or dead.

Full of cheeky quotations this novel certainly is. Many works of art, music, and literature are referenced in *War in Pieces* 2. Works referred to but not specifically acknowledged in the text include four Russian operas (Rimsky-Korsakov's *The Tsar's Bride*, Mussorgsky's *Boris Godunov*, Tchaikovsky's *Cherevichki* aka *The Tsarina's Slippers*, and the Verdi–Piave *La forza del destino*, premiered in St. Petersburg), as well as three more operas: Ravel's *L'enfant et les sortilèges*, the Strauss–Hofmannsthal *Die Frau ohne Schatten*, and Bartók's *Bluebeard's Castle*. Productions of Russian operas at the Royal Opera House, Covent Garden, in London over the last ten years have been accompanied by informative articles in the printed programs. Their summaries and ideas stimulated ideas for situations and themes in this book.

I have also drawn ideas and situations from classic literature, including Shakespeare's *Timon of Athens* and *The Merchant of Venice*, Chaucer's *The Merchant's Tale*, and *Tales of the Thousand and One Nights*, and in modern literature from Ken Follett's *The Man from St. Petersburg* and *The Key to Rebecca*. Drawing inspiration from these imaginative works has been a privilege.

The two parts of *War in Pieces* are the first two of three books on characters in the Reader family living in New England. The third book, *Luke Reader, Blind Detective* (the first to be written and published), moves from a macro into a micro subject: one man's experiences of coming to terms with sight loss and the intervention of social services in the late 1990s.

For *War in Pieces* 2 I thank my long-standing friend, Kenneth McArthur, who offered trenchant and constructive criticism of the manuscript at an early stage. I also thank

Miles Bailey, director of the Choir Press, his colleagues Rachel Woodman and Adrian Sysum, and the copyeditor Harriet Evans, who also wrote the blurb, for their care, diligence and courtesy preparing the book for publication.

Successive deaths of Donald and Basha Baerman at the beginning and end of the publishing process of both parts of *War in Pieces* bring the curtain down on fifty yeas of my life. I owe immense debts of gratitude to architect Don and his dear wife, Basha, whom I first lived with in a co-operative house in Connecticut and named "Rochdale" after a town of the co-operative movement in Lancashire, England.

Nobody could be more considerate than Don and Basha as we know from the little army of Yale architects who passed through their house in North Haven and who gained much more than technical grounding in Don's speciality—specifications. Their own family histories, one steeped in northeast American Protestant work ethic and the other in Russian-Jewish and New Yorker traditions led them both to approach work and people with understanding and humanity.

I would never have been able to write so much and endure all manner of setbacks without their love to sustain me. Don, Basha, and I shared an interest in politics wider than political parties—and about which their knowledge was encyclopaedic—as well as their love of classical composers of the first Viennese school.

Don and Basha's artistic legacy lives on in their four talented children and their trilingual grandchildren.

Sean Dennis Cashman,
Manchester 2016.

ABOUT THE AUTHOR

Sean Dennis Cashman studied history at Oxford and Yale and disability studies at Leeds. He combined careers as a professor of US history and as a writer, principally for New York University Press and the Ford Foundation, and as music and theater journalist in New Haven, Connecticut. His classic history for NYU Press, *America in the Gilded Age*, has remained a focal text for the period 1865–1901 since it was first published in 1984.

War in Pieces 2: The Holly Wood Years of Ivan the Terrible is the second in a series of novels set in New York and New England in the 1980s and 1990s at the dawn of the Age of Terror. The first is *War in Pieces 1: Ivan the Terrible—from Tulsa*. The third, moving to a micro view of society, is *Luke Reader, Blind Detective*.

Books by this author include:

**War in Pieces 1:
Ivan the Terrible—from Tulsa**, 2016

Luke Reader, Blind Detective, 2012

**America Ascendant:
From Theodore Roosevelt to FDR in the American Century, 1901–1945**, 1998

**America in the Age of the Titans:
The Progressive Era and World War I**, 1988

SEAN DENNIS CASHMAN

AMERICA

FROM THE DEATH OF LINCOLN TO

IN THE

THE RISE OF THEODORE ROOSEVELT

GILDED

THIRD EDITION

AGE

AMERICA
ASCENDANT

From Theodore Roosevelt to FDR
in the Century of American Power, 1901-1945

SEAN DENNIS CASHMAN

SEAN DENNIS
CASHMAN

Luke
Reader
blind detective

WAR IN PIECES 1
Ivan the Terrible
from Tulsa

SEAN DENNIS CASHMAN